Laura

Books by Larry Watson

In a Dark Time
Leaving Dakota
Montana 1948
Justice
White Crosses
Laura

LARRY WATSON

POCKET BOOKS

NEW YORK LONDON TORONTO SYDNEY SINGAPORE

POCKET BOOKS, a division of Simon & Schuster Inc.
1230 Avenue of the Americas, New York, NY 10020

Copyright © 2000 by Larry Watson

Library of Congress Cataloging-in-Publication Data

Watson, Larry, 1947–
  Laura / Larry Watson.
    p. cm.
  ISBN: 0-671-56774-8
  1. Men—Psychology—Fiction. 2. Man-woman relationships—Fiction. I. Title.

PS3573.A853 L38 2000
813'.54—dc21   99-089060

First Pocket Books hardcover printing June 2000

10 9 8 7 6 5 4 3 2 1

POCKET and colophon are registered trademarks
of Simon & Schuster Inc.

Designed by Joseph Rutt

Printed in the U.S.A.

To Susan

Acknowledgments

Thanks to Greer Kessel Hendricks, my gifted editor, for her perceptive and inspiring criticism; to Sharon Friedman, my agent without peer, for her invaluable friendship and unwavering encouragement; to the National Endowment for the Arts and the University of Wisconsin/Stevens Point for providing time and financial support; to Sandy Wanserski for technical support; to Cecelia Hunt, for her careful editorial eye; to Al Hart, Mark Miller, Ralph Vicinanza, and Eben Weiss for moral support and practical advice. A special thanks to Elly, Amy, and to Prissy. And my deepest gratitude to my wife, Susan, whose belief in this novel lasted longer and ran deeper than anyone's.

Does the imagination dwell the most
Upon a woman won or a woman lost?
—William Butler Yeats
"The Tower"

Le cœur a ses raisons, que la raison ne connaît point.
(The heart has its reasons which reason knows nothing of.)
—Blaise Pascal
Pensées

One

In the summer of 1955 New England lay shimmering under one of the worst heat waves of the century. But don't try to verify this in any of the weather annals. No, this heat was intolerable not because of record-setting temperatures but because of what seemed like an unending succession of sweltering days. Swimming pools that summer were so swarming with people you couldn't swim a stroke, and beaches were so littered with bodies you couldn't walk fast enough to let the air move around you. Movie theaters, because they advertised their air-conditioning in icy blue letters, did record business, and stores that sold Popsicles, electric fans, or cold beer were certain to sell out. If you lived in a city and could leave, you left.

In 1955 my family was one of the lucky ones who could escape. My father, Robert Finley, was an editor at Harrison House, and he was not often required to be in his office during the summer. He frequently brought his work home to read and edit anyway. My mother, Doreen, taught English at Westcott College for Women—as it was called then—and always had the summer off. So, after the middle of June, when my sister, Janie, and I finished our week of French camp, our family headed for the cool green hills of Vermont and left behind our fellow Bostonians, stuck to the city and each other with their own sweat. That summer Janie was eight and I was eleven.

In Vermont we rented a large old Victorian house with a huge front porch that tilted toward New Hampshire. The house was in the middle of an empty, sun-struck field, and less than fifty yards away a stagnant pond steamed and stunk in the heat, but my sister and I were forbidden to mention the smell. Trees were ringed all around us, but not one was within a hundred yards of the house. Standing stupidly by itself, the house looked as if everything had been warned away from it.

My parents' friends, however, certainly heard no warning, for they came visiting in droves. From New York or Boston or Philadelphia, they ran toward Vermont and us like animals that know the forest is burning behind them. When they arrived at our house, they put down their bags, sighed, smiled, and set themselves to days and nights of unrelieved, slightly hysterical, drunken recreation.

Most of my mother's and father's friends were writers, artists, and intellectuals, and many of them were younger than my parents. The few who were married were childless. That naturally made Janie and me curiosities, yet still figures to whom obeisance had to be paid. These were people who worshipped the spirit of youth, if not children themselves. So when the visitors arrived that summer, they brought toys, games, or sporting equipment for us. The problem, however, was that these gifts quickly found their way into the hands of the adults. Late into the night they sat around the kitchen table and played with Janie's Chinese checkers; they used my football in the early evening touch football games; in the heat of the afternoon women and men pulled lawn chairs up to the small blue inflatable wading pool Avis Holman brought for us and sat with their feet in the water and sweating gin-and-tonics in their hands; they played badminton with our rackets and croquet with our mallets; three of my baseballs were hit into the pond; and others put as many miles on our bicycles as we did.

In the midst of all those adults having so much fun, Janie and I were never exactly sure of what to do. We were not invited to join in, and it was clear our presence would be inhibiting. Nothing makes adults more self-conscious about playing children's games than children standing on the sidelines watching.

So how did Janie and I behave that summer? Both of us were, to begin with, inclined toward silence and seriousness, and to that part of our natures we drifted even further. Janie began to lower her gaze (my memory of her is always of her walking with her head down), looking away from the faces of people and down to the earth's surface, to the grasses, plants, weeds, and wildflowers growing there. I, on the other hand, developed and practiced a skill that I continued to sharpen in all the years after: I watched others while trying to remain unnoticed myself.

But all this is backdrop and stage-setting, my attempt to set the time and place of that season's essential occurrence: in the summer of 1955 I met Laura Coe Pettit, and the moment of that meeting was the one from which I began a measurement of time. Clocks and calendars can try to convince us that time always passes in equal measure, but we know better. Our thirty-fifth summer passes five times faster than our seventh, and for years my life speeded up or slowed down according to my meetings with or departures from Laura.

IN OUR RENTED HOUSE my bedroom was right over the kitchen, the room where my parents and their partying friends always ended up because it was the one room where air moved—the night breeze from the north blew in through the small window over the sink, fluttered the lace curtains, and fanned out through the big, brightly lit space before traveling out the screen door and past the porch where those people who couldn't fit in the kitchen sat. The scene was always noisy; a porch-sitter would tell a story loudly enough so a cupboard leaner could hear it. Laughter was constant, and ranged from one man's slow bass *"huh-huh-huh"* (a sound like heavy boots climbing the basement stairs) to a woman's staccato, soprano *"ih-ih-ih-ih"* (a giggle that reminded me of a birdcall). After the phonograph was moved into the kitchen, it never returned to the living room. Beer bottles clinked, glasses rattled, ice tinkled, the refrigerator door opened and closed, and I did my best to sleep through it all.

So why, if I could sleep through that commotion, would someone's silence wake me?

When I opened my eyes she was standing in front of my window, gazing out toward the pond. She was smoking a cigarette, and as she exhaled, the smoke billowed through the screen so it looked as though the night were steaming right outside my window.

Though I tried not to, I must have made a sound—a whisper of sheets as I jerked awake or perhaps my snoring stopped—and she turned to me quickly and said, "Please. Don't tell anyone I'm here." Her voice had that low, reedy sound of exhaustion in it.

Her request was so urgent I immediately told her I wouldn't say anything, though I didn't know whom I could tell even if I wanted to.

"The door wasn't locked," she said. "I just ducked in here to get away from the party awhile. I thought I could hide here without bothering anyone. I didn't mean to wake you."

I was afraid, but I knew I wasn't threatened, so my fear was the type that people—children, especially—feel in the presence of something that mystifies and confuses them. And, of course, I couldn't go back to sleep, so I lay quietly in bed and tried to study this person who had found her way into my bedroom. The moon shone on that warm, clear night, and my narrow, floor-to-ceiling window let in enough light for me to get a look at her.

It's difficult for children to judge someone's height (every adult is tall) without standing next to that person or seeing him or her in a group, but by the way she was framed in my window I could see she was not much more than five feet. I could also tell she was extraordinarily pale because she wore a white shirt and both the shirt and her face had the same bluish-white luminescence in the moonlight. The sleeves of the shirt were rolled to her elbows. Her dark hair was very short, and with the hand not holding the cigarette she ruffled her hair over and over again, a motion so agitated and methodical it seemed she was trying to work an unpleasant thought out of her mind. I couldn't see her features clearly, but I could tell they were small and fine. If it weren't for her voice, I might have thought another child was in the room with me.

She bent over and crushed out her cigarette in the space between the window ledge and the screen. Then, slowly and carefully, as if she were worried that in the dark she might step on a piece of glass, she walked over to my bed.

"Are you Paul?" she asked. "Have I stumbled into Paul's room?"

"Yes," I answered, concerned about how she knew my name when we hadn't met.

"You're going to let me hide in here for a while?"

"Yes."

"Yes, yes, oh, yes—is that all you can say? Are you going to do anything I ask?" She laughed, a low, soft sound almost like a cough.

I didn't want to say "yes" again. "I guess so."

"You guess so. Well, I guess so too. We all guess so." She sighed and sat down heavily on my bed.

Asleep, I had slid down toward the middle of the bed, but now I pushed my way back toward the top, pulling my pillow under my head.

"What's the matter?" she asked when I moved. "Are you afraid of me, Paul?"

"Not really."

"You're not? That's good. I don't want people to be afraid of me. But maybe you should be. Maybe you should be a little afraid. Just a little."

She was drunk. She wavered as she sat on the bed, as if, without something to support her back, her spine couldn't hold her head straight, and her head moved back and forth slightly, nodding in time to music only she could hear. I could smell the liquor on her breath, that heavy aroma like something sweet about to go sour. I had learned to identify the smell from my father. He often tucked me in at night, and as he bent over to kiss me, I would sniff his breath and ask, "What's that?" "A fine scotch," he would say. Or "Gin, clear as water," "Vodka, Russia's only current contribution to civilization," "Beer—and here's one of its kids," and he would belch. To this day I like the aroma of liquor on a man's or woman's breath. For some reason, it reminds me of death, but of a natural, welcome dying, like leaves decaying.

Her speech also told me how drunk she was. I had heard enough examples to know drunken talk when I heard it—the repetitions, riddles, and pointless revelations, the wide loops and short circles of conversation, the way drunks will grab on to your name and wave it around to show how strong their grip is. It was important, I knew, to be patient with them and polite, and soon they would lose interest and leave you alone.

However, I did not want her to leave me alone. As bewildered, apprehensive, and uncertain as I was about her presence, I still wanted her to
stay. At eleven, though baseball and the Boy Scout manual dominated my
life, another part of me escaped their rule. This was the part interested in,
among other things, romantic novels about errant knights and endan-
gered maidens. And I did more than read about the subject. More than
once I had climbed the stairs with an imaginary sword in my hand and a
cascade of bloodied foes behind me. When I reached the tower (my room)
I burst through the door, ready to rescue the diaphanously gowned woman
who was lashed to a chair just the way the woman was on the cover of
Montaldo's Revenge, a paperback lying around the house that summer.
(The ropes crossed her breasts in an X, and high on her bare arm was the
red mark of the lash.) No doubt this play was part of my awakening sexu-
ality, but I wasn't yet aware of it.And now a peculiar version of my fantasy
was coming true. A beautiful young woman was in my room, though I,
without sword or shield, was probably the one in need of rescue. I slept in
my underpants, and I tried to pin down the sheet that covered me by
unobtrusively pressing down on one of its folds with my forearm.

After peering around the room, she said, "Are we going to keep this
in the dark or can we have some light?"

"I don't care."

She reached over to my bedside table and groped around the lamp
until she found the little chain that turned on the light. At the sudden
brightness, she covered her eyes and turned her head. "Oooh," she said
painfully, "maybe that wasn't such a good idea."

Wanting to please, I asked her if she wanted me to turn it off.

"No," she said, lifting her head, "I'll learn to live with it."

When she uncovered her eyes, I noticed something I hadn't seen in
the dark. Under her right eye she had a thin red scar, a crescent that
followed perfectly the bone of the eye socket. On another face, one
not as unlined as hers, it might not have been as noticeable, since it
was right where circles form. But on her small, pale, unblemished face
it drew my attention and would not let it go. I liked the scar immediately; it was not disfiguring, and it gave her a look of danger and
worldly experience. Here was someone, no matter how young she may

have looked, to whom things happened, and she had a scar to prove it.

Does it go without saying I was already in love? Why wouldn't it have been so? Consider what elements worked together to move my heart. Here was an adult who had left the company of other adults to be with a child (that was my interpretation anyway). A pretty woman teetering on the ledge of who-knew-what drunken impulse. Moonlight. The sound of revelry below. My near nakedness. Sleep still in the corner of my eyes. How could I have resisted?

"Now that you've got me here," she said. "What are you going to do to entertain me?"

"I don't know." I had reached the point where my tongue-tiedness was the result, not of nervousness at saying the wrong thing, but of the fervent wish to say the right thing. The responses in either case might have been the same—timid monosyllables and phrases of uncertainty—but the motives were completely different, one rising from fear and the other from love. The truth was, I was shy, though that fact usually caused my parents more consternation than it did me. In fact, I had caught on to using it as an excuse to get me through uncomfortable situations. Rather than make the awkward attempt at conversation with people I had newly met, I held my tongue and waited for Mother or Father to say, "You'll have to forgive Paul, he's shy." But, oh, how I wanted now to be one of those unself-conscious, glib children who could yammer his way to endearment.

From the floor beside my bed she picked up my copy of *Boy's Life*. "Is this yours? Are you a Boy Scout?"

"Yes."

"And are you honest and trustworthy and loyal and true and always prepared, and do you help old ladies across the street?"

"Sometimes. If I'm around, I mean."

"But if you're not around, then they're on their own, right?" She began to page through the magazine.

"I guess."

She stopped when she came to the section in the magazine about a heroic deed a Scout had performed. The feature, printed like a comic strip, was my favorite in the magazine.

"Look at this," she said. "This boy rescued three of his friends when their boat tipped over. Wasn't that brave of him?" She closed the magazine but kept her finger inside on the page.

"Would you do that, Paul? What if I were drowning—would you rescue me?"

"I don't have my Lifesaving Badge." What a terrible answer! Once again, I had allowed my literal-mindedness to get in the way of the heroic gesture.

"So you'd let me drown?"

"No . . . I'd try."

"What if I pulled you down with me? What if we both drowned? What then?"

I hated the turn this talk had taken. It had become the kind of conversation designed to show children they were wrong to be certain of anything. My father was a master at this—the series of unanswerable questions that left you unsure of your own existence, which was exactly what he wanted.

"There are things you can do," I said, struggling to show her my authority, "if the person you're trying to save isn't . . . is fighting you—"

She interrupted, "The best thing you can do is let go. Just let go and save yourself." She opened the magazine again and tapped the page where the Boy Scout was saving his friends. "And you can tell them I said so."

She flipped through the magazine until she got to the back pages and the advertisements for official Scout products.

"I love these," she said, pointing to a picture of a canvas belt with a gold buckle that had the Boy Scout fleur-de-lis stamped on it. "Do you have one?"

"I don't have it here. It's at home with my uniform."

"Your uniform? Oh, I bet you look wonderful in it. Men always look wonderful in uniforms. Soldiers. Baseball players . . . Mailmen . . . Boy Scouts . . . Milkmen . . . Janitors . . ." She let the magazine fall to the floor. "You can tell I'm running out of things to talk about, can't you?" She rubbed her eyes with the heels of her hand, and then she smiled apologetically at me.

Another unanswerable question. "I guess."

"I want to talk to you. I want to be able to talk to children, but I can't, I just can't. I don't know what you care about. I never know." She pushed the sleeves of her shirt further up her arms. "You don't understand what I'm talking about, do you?"

At some point I realized I was, in a strange way, in charge of her and her emotions. With my new power I knew it was important for me to be careful about how I responded to her. "I think I understand," I said. Indeed, I believed I did. One of the ways I thought I was different from other children was in an ability to understand the problems of others, including grown-ups. It was not only a mistaken notion, but also an arrogant one.

"Do you?" she said. "I wish you did, but I don't believe you do. You can't."

Then, to show her I was capable of grasping adult difficulties, I said, "Our cleaning lady told me her husband's an alcoholic. She said he drinks every penny she earns." As I said that I imagined, as I always did, Ray, the cleaning woman's husband, emptying rolls of pennies down his throat.

Solemnly, she asked, "And did you advise her on how to handle this situation?"

"Sort of. I told her she should be patient with him."

"Oh, you did? Well, wasn't that wise. Maybe I should tell you one of my problems, and you can see what advice you have for me."

"Okay," I said.

She sat up primly, folded her hands on her lap, and looked straight ahead. "My problem is very simple. It's this: I came to Vermont to be alone with your father, and I can't seem to manage this arrangement."

She must have seen in my eyes what she had done, because immediately she said, "Oh, Jesus, did I say that? Oh, shit!" For myself, I wasn't sure what she had revealed, but from her alarmed reaction, I knew it must have been a revelation both imprudent and profound.

She slid off the bed—I held on to the sheet—and landed heavily on the floor. She thumped down so hard I thought they might hear her downstairs and someone might come. In spite of everything, I still did not want that to happen. She clapped her hand to her mouth so hard it seemed she was trying to stop her breath.

Then, quickly, she turned to me. "I didn't mean to say that, Paul. Believe me. I'm always opening my mouth and letting the worst, most outrageous things out. Do you know what I think of sometimes?"

I shook my head.

"Have you ever seen pictures of baby snakes? Of those crawling nests of newborn snakes?"

"Yes."

"Sometimes I think that's what lives in my mouth. A nest of snakes. Right under my tongue." She opened her mouth and lifted her tongue. I looked in, not expecting to see anything but wanting to take advantage of the opportunity to peek in where sight was usually not allowed. The talk of snakes and this furtive look into her pink mouth brought inexplicably to my mind blood and heat, the body's interior elements. She quickly popped her mouth shut and then went on talking. "See, I can't keep them from crawling out. Especially when I drink. When I drink I simply cannot keep them in. That's why I write. If I write I can keep them in, or I can let them out one at a time. But you shouldn't listen to me when I say certain things. You shouldn't."

"I won't," I lied.

"I did come here to see your father," she said in a blandly cheerful, unconvincing voice. "But I came because I work for him, in a way. He's my editor. Or he's going to be. He wanted me to come here so we could start working on the book I might do for him." She stopped abruptly and stared down at the floor for a long time. When she looked up again, it was with a different expression, very placid, almost blank. She put her elbows up on the bed like a child saying her bedtime prayers. "I think I'll stop now, Paul. I don't want to say any more, and I don't want to start lying either."

Downstairs someone whooped and shouted, "Azure! Triple word! Thirty-seven!" and I knew they were playing Scrabble, one of the few games I was good at.

But right now, my thoughts were hopelessly scattered, like the tiles on a Scrabble board that will not line up to form a single word. . . .

Even if I had the letters, I couldn't have made the word "extramarital" and perhaps not even the word "affair." They were not part of my child's vocabulary or comprehension. Yet for a while I had felt that something was not right in my parents' marriage. Now, with this woman's remark about wanting to be alone with my father and her subsequent consternation over letting that bit of information out, that "not rightness," like a photograph in the first stages of development, began dimly to define itself. I was not sure of the answers, but I thought I knew the questions: Did my father love someone other than my mother? Did he have girl-friends? Was this young woman one of them?

She pushed herself slowly up from the floor and sat again on my bed. She looked carefully around the room as if she had set something down and now couldn't find it. Finally, she looked back at me and let her gaze rest on me for so long I was almost forced into nervous speech.

"You can be quiet," she said softly. "That's good. So many people can't stand silence and they have to fill it any way they can. So we have all this talk, talk, talk." She sighed tiredly. "Don't ever be afraid to be quiet."

I wasn't sure if she was trying to make me feel better about my shyness, or if she was trying subtly to caution me not to tell anyone what she had said about her and my father. I remained quiet.

"Look at your hair," she said. "You must have slept on it funny. It's sticking straight up." She reached out and put her hand on the cowlick at my hairline. She didn't pat the hair or brush it down with her fin-gers; she simply held her hand there and exerted the slightest pressure. Her hand, like a child's, was small, damp, soft, and cool. I closed my eyes.

She took her hand away and stood up. "I better go downstairs before they start looking for me." She turned out the light. "And you better get back to sleep. Thank you for letting me hide in here."

Before she opened the door, I found my tongue in time to ask, "Are you staying here tonight?"

She didn't give me a satisfying answer; instead she issued an impossi-ble command. "Forget me," she said, her voice even rougher in its whis-per. "Forget everything."

*   *   *

NOT KNOWING THAT the greatest danger lay in darkness, not in light, I got up early the next morning to protect my family. I wet my hair down so it was stuck to my head, put on a pair of gym shorts and a white T-shirt, and went downstairs. It was Sunday, and everyone in the house was still asleep, everyone except Hal Davenport, who sat at the kitchen table drinking coffee, smoking, and working a crossword puzzle.

The house had that quiet, morning-after-a-party feel that I always loved, perhaps because it meant my sister and I would have the place to ourselves. In the kitchen someone had lined up all the empty beer bottles on the cupboard, and in the bright morning they glistened like brown jewels. On the other side of the sink were the house's ashtrays, all of them full. They were a sign not of slovenliness but of concern. My father would never let anyone dump an ashtray into the garbage before bed. A live ash might begin to smolder while everyone slept. The sink was heaped with dirty glasses, and the room smelled of spilled beer and cigarette smoke.

When Hal Davenport saw me, he said, "Hey, Judge. What's the good word?" "Judge" was my family nickname, awarded to me in infancy because I never smiled.

Hal Davenport and my father grew up together in Beckwith, a small town in upstate New York. Hal was starting forward and my father the center of their high school basketball team that took second place in the state their senior year. They were roommates at Dartmouth, and when the war broke out, my father was classified 4-F because of a perforated eardrum, and Hal Davenport was shipped to France, where he lost his right arm in a Jeep accident. After the war he moved to a small town in Maine, where he was sports editor for the local newspaper. "He's a damn good sportswriter," my father often said. "If he'd get out of there, he could do something."

Hal Davenport was one of the few of my parents' friends with whom I felt comfortable. He was talkative, sad, funny, and friendly, and since he didn't fit in particularly well with the rest of their group, he always had time for my sister and me. He wasn't married, and he loved to talk to children in ways that their parents wouldn't approve of, which of course endeared him to children. He had the ability to ask questions that encouraged you to talk about yourself, and he was interested in your answers. And he remembered what you said. If I told him I was playing third base for my Little League team, then the next time I saw him he would ask me how things were on the hot corner.

I sat down at the table across from him.

"What's the matter? Couldn't sleep?" he asked. "Was I making too much racket down here?"

Hal Davenport was freshly shaved, and among the room's stale, morning-after smells his aftershave was like perfume. He wore a long-sleeved white shirt, and he had the right sleeve neatly folded and pinned with a small gold safety pin to the front of his shirt. The left sleeve was buttoned at the wrist. On the table next to him were two horseshoes. Even after losing his arm, he continued to play what sports he could; he bowled, he pitched horseshoes, he ice-skated, he even played one-armed golf. When my father introduced Hal Davenport to people, my father called him the world's fastest one-handed typist.

I was tempted that morning to tell Hal Davenport what had happened in my room the night before and to see what advice he had to offer. I decided against it, not because I didn't think he would be sympathetic, but because I still wanted to hoard the experience. Walking about in the sunlight with the previous night's secret gave me a sense of romantic self-importance. I felt very adult that morning, and the scene—two men sitting at the kitchen table with the remnants of the previous night's party all around them—only heightened that feeling.

For a while we talked about baseball, inevitably coming around to our favorite topic: who was the better center fielder—Mantle or Mays? I argued in favor of Mantle; he played in the American League, and I was an American Leaguer through and through. Hal Davenport, a lifelong Giants fan, argued for Willie Mays. "Better arm and more speed on the bases," he said.

Gradually I left baseball in order to creep up on the subject in which I was more interested. (I must have passed, without knowing it, a threshold—something actually interested me more than baseball.) Pointing upstairs in the direction of the household's sleeping occupants, I casually asked, "Who's here?"

"I'm not sure. I arrived late last night. I had to cover an American Legion doubleheader. The party was already going pretty good when I got here. Some folks were planning to stay over in Hartley."

Hartley, a small resort town, was twelve miles away.

I said, "There were a lot of people I didn't know either."

"That bother you? Strangers in the house?"

"Not really."

"It would me. But maybe I don't adjust as easily as you do."

"There was one person I was wondering about. She was real short. . . ." I tried to say this as nonchalantly as possible, hoping Hal Davenport would answer without thinking there was anything unusual about my inquiry.

"Short, you say?" He was looking intently at his crossword puzzle, and I was afraid he wasn't paying attention to me at all.

"I bet she wasn't much over five feet."

"Uh-huh."

"I never saw her before. I was just wondering if you knew who she was."

"Oh, yeah." He was still staring at the paper.

"You do? You know who she is?"

He set his pencil down deliberately, picked up his pack of Chesterfields, and shook one up to his lips. He took a book of matches from his shirt pocket, bent a match in half, and scratched the match aflame without removing it from the book. It was a routine I had enjoyed watching him perform many times; now it seemed a delaying operation calculated to torment me.

"I think you are talking about Laura Coe Pettit."

He exhaled smoke through his nostrils, and I let her name run through my mind as many times as I could before he spoke again. Laura Coe Pettit, Laura Coe Pettit, Laura Coe Pettit, Laura.

"And," Hal Davenport said, "she will soon be famous across this land, known by everybody. Well, perhaps not everybody. Everybody who reads poetry. A hundred, two hundred people, maybe."

"She's a writer?"

"Not a writer, Judge. I'm a writer. I get paid for what I write. She's a poet. That's different. Much higher class. Poets don't get paid for what they write, and nobody reads their stuff. You can see what an exalted plain that puts them on."

I must have looked both pathetic and uncomprehending, because he changed his tone and said, "Okay, I was having a little joke. Don't pay any attention. Yeah, she's a poet. Very hot right now, I guess. Big write-up in *The New York Times* and even an article in *Time*, and *Time* never writes up poets unless they're the old, lovable kind. I can't remember the name of her book; *Dreams Women Have*, or something like that. I haven't read it, but a lot of folks are talking about it."

"She looks so young."

"Well, she is. Twenty-two, twenty-three, something like that. A real child prodigy. And that's what I thought when I first met her—a cute, quiet kid. Then she got into it last night with Leonard Shelter, and that changed my mind about her pronto."

I was eager to hear what happened, yet I was a little hurt, too. I wanted her only performance to have been for me. "What happened?"

"You know who Leonard Shelter is?"

I had a vague recollection of meeting a skinny man with a pencil mustache and a big Adam's apple, but mostly I knew him as a name in my parents' conversation. "He's a writer too, isn't he?"

"Judge, you know too much. Is your dad his editor? No, that wouldn't be right. Leonard's with Random House." Hal Davenport stubbed out his cigarette and got up to get himself more coffee.

I was always fascinated with the way Hal Davenport did things, how the simple, everyday actions that other people were able to perform simultaneously, he had to do serially: first, put the coffee cup down; pick up the coffeepot; pour the coffee in the cup; put down the pot; pick up the cup. Ordinary routines received a special emphasis when he did them, like someone speaking your native language with a foreign accent. Sometimes when no one was around, I would put one hand behind my back and do everything the way Hal Davenport would.

Back at the table he continued with his story. "Someone asked your friend Miss Pettit if she'd read Leonard's stories. She was standing right over there by the sink. Smoking a cigarette and drinking ice water or gin, who can tell? She said yes, she'd read them. I don't think she wanted to say any more, but someone kept pushing her, asking her what she thought, and Leonard was right there too, waiting with his tongue hanging out.

"Finally she said it was obvious that Leonard had talent—and Leonard beamed a little more—and then she let him have it, really lowered the boom on him."

"What did she do?"

"She didn't do much of anything. Kept leaning on the cupboard just the way she was before anyone noticed her. It was what she said. Right after she said he had talent, right after she complimented him, she took it all away: she said it was too bad he used that talent to advance the most ridiculous ideas. His ideas were so ridiculous, she said, they would be funny if they weren't contemptible. You know what 'contemptible' means, Judge?"

"Sort of," I said.

"Well, it means not just stupid or wrong, but worthless, maybe even bad. Jesus, it's hard to explain. See, Leonard's book is full of stories about men who find themselves during the war. They find out what they're made of, so to speak."

I remember how she had paged through my *Boy's Life* the night before and how unimpressed she was by the Scout who saved his friends from drowning.

"One of the things the men in Leonard's book find out," Hal Davenport continued, "is that they liked the war, or the excitement of it anyway. Remember now, I'm summing up very simply a whole collection of stories."

I didn't care how he represented or misrepresented Leonard Shelter's themes. I wanted to hear more of what she said. I said, "I kind of know what you mean."

"What I liked," Hal Davenport said, smiling, "was the look on Leonard's face when she was talking. He got all puckered-up, like maybe this was supposed to be a joke and he wanted to be ready to laugh. But he couldn't even if he wanted to. Maybe he could have cried. And she didn't slow down once she got started. Said she couldn't believe how someone could glorify anything that cost millions of lives. Or wasn't he aware of that? she asked. Maybe he thought World War Two was just an excuse for men to get together out of the house, like the Harvard-Yale football game or something. Then she said—well, I won't tell you what she said next. Your mother would boot me out of the house if I told you that."

"Please," I said. "I won't tell anyone you told me."

"You promise?" Hal Davenport held up the palm of his left hand, indicating I was to take a vow.

"I promise."

He leaned over the table and lowered his voice. "She told Leonard Shelter that if he thought war was so glorious, then why didn't he take one of his souvenir Japanese bayonets and"—his voice went down to a whisper—"and stick it up his ass. Then maybe he'd have some idea of the pain of war. So you see," Hal Davenport said, his voice coming back to its normal volume, "she ain't no kid."

"What did Mr. Shelter say?"

"Not much. Stammered a bit about how she hadn't understood what his book was about, how many critics had compared him to Hemingway. And she said, as cool as can be, that Hemingway could stick a bayonet up his ass too!"

I whistled softly between my teeth. My father had met Hemingway a few times, and my father loved to tell a story about a lunch he once had with the great writer. At the time, Hemingway was so angry with a particular literary critic that he wanted to buy a spiked dog collar and put it on the critic so everyone would know "what a vicious cur the man was." My father told the story in a way that mocked Hemingway.

Hal Davenport snapped his fingers and said, "That's right! I almost forgot the best part. Leonard had to find some way to save face, so he turned to your dad and said, 'I don't think I should have to take this, Robert.' And your dad said, 'You're right. Bye-bye, Leonard.' Oh, I tell you, Judge, it was something to see."

I approved of my father taking Laura's side, yet it was also more evidence of a connection between them. "What did my mom do?"

"Your mom? Now, where was your mom? I don't remember her being around when that was going on."

"Maybe she was sleeping."

"I don't know, Judge. Could be." Hal Davenport finished his coffee in a long swallow. He was serious now, as if he was suddenly aware that he had been taking too much pleasure in telling it all. "I guess adults can act pretty foolishly, can't they?" That summarizing remark was supposed to convey a moral to me; it was also a signal that we were not going to spend any more time on the subject.

I looked around the kitchen again, now seeing it as the scene of the confrontation between Leonard Shelter and Laura Pettit. Last night, I imagined, the overhead light would have been on, and mosquitoes, gnats, and moths would have clustered around the globe the way they did on evenings when someone was always opening the screen door. The room must have flashed with light, noise, and anger, and it contrasted in my mind with Laura's hushed presence in my dark room.

"What do you say, Judge?" Hal Davenport said. "This is too nice a day to spend indoors. Let's get out there and move around. What do you want to do—pitch horseshoes or play catch?"

Since I couldn't tell him that all I wanted to do was to sit in the house and wait for Laura Pettit's appearance, I told him we could play catch. We got gloves and a scuffed, gray baseball from the woodbox next to the back door.

Hal Davenport's light blue Nash was parked in the yard, and he rolled down its windows and positioned himself with his back to the car so that if he missed the ball or if I threw wildly, it would be blocked by the car. Of course, if the ball rolled under the car, I had to retrieve it.

Playing catch with Hal Davenport was awkward. He wore his glove on his left hand, and after catching the ball, he had to hold the ball between his legs, let the glove fall to the ground, grab the ball again, and then throw it. His throwing was ungainly and distorted, not only because he was not a natural left-hander but also because he didn't have the other arm available for balance and leverage. He refused to let the stump of his right arm come free of the pinned shirt. He threw weakly but accurately, almost as if he were aiming a dart at a bull's-eye.

After we played for a few minutes, Hal Davenport became frustrated with taking the glove off and putting it back on. He dropped the glove to the ground and left it there. "Go ahead, Judge," he called out across the fifteen yards between us, "fire them as hard as you like. I can handle them bare-handed."

And perhaps he could, but I didn't dare do anything more than lob the ball to him. If he had so much as jammed a finger, he would have been incapacitated, and I didn't want to be the one responsible. So, our activity in the Sunday morning sunshine was not spirited and invigorating, but tentative, restrained, and, I think for both of us, halfhearted.

Soon he was throwing high, head-tilting fly balls that shortened the distance between us but had me ranging back and forth across the yard. He said he wanted to give me practice catching pop-ups, but I believe the real reason was to allow him to toss the ball underhanded and not worry about accuracy.

I dropped one of his fly balls, and when it came down, it hit a stone and skittered off through the patchy, dry, unmowed grass. I chased the ball down, and when I turned back to Hal Davenport, I saw her standing on the porch.

Laura Coe Pettit was leaning on the porch balustrade. She was wearing an oversize white shirt and a dark blue skirt, and her hair was wet and combed back from her face. Her eyes were puffy, and she squinted in the morning light. Next to her stood my mother, one hand resting on Laura's shoulder, her other hand pointing toward the trees far beyond our yard. My mother was wearing a long, white, satiny robe, and the glasses she didn't really need hung around her neck from a thin gold chain. Both women were smoking, and my mother was laughing as she directed Laura Pettit's attention.

My heart quickened as I stared at them and tried to decide which woman was prettier.

My mother was thirty-five that summer, and she was, by anyone's standards, a lovely woman. Her hair, dark blond and threatening every year to become brown, was brushed and hung to her shoulders. Her laughter was, as usual, bright and easy, perfectly suited to Sunday summer mornings. She was graceful, tall, and slender, and though she had a fair complexion, her cheeks always had a streak of color that made her look slightly sun- or wind-burned. Although she was completely unathletic, she had a glowing, breathless quality that made it seem as though she had only moments before finished some physical exertion. As she smoked, she threw her head back to exhale.

Next to my mother, Laura Pettit's shortness was emphasized. In fact, as they stood side by side, they seemed a study in contrasts. Unlike my mother's cheerful expression, Laura Pettit's was solemn, almost frowning, and in Laura Pettit's pallor there was no hint of vitality or vigor; she looked tired, almost wasted, and though she was more than ten years younger than my mother, she was the one who carried age's weariness. She was as thin as my mother but more compact, and while my mother looked as though she got up every morning and stretched wide-eyed toward the sun, Laura Pettit looked as though she bent toward the earth and listened.

As the women competed unwittingly in the sunlight, I tried to make my choice. And how would I choose? There was my mother, with the hold on my heart that all mothers have, and there was Laura Coe Pettit, with that new grip on me that mothers never have. But the choice, of course, was not simply between new love and old, between a boy's mother and the first of many women who vie to replace her in his affections. This was more complicated. Laura Pettit could also have been my mother's competitor for my father. Perhaps I should have called out a warning at that moment; perhaps I should have told my mother that the woman upon whose shoulder her hand rested was a danger to her, to all of the family. But I kept silent, and at that moment began to learn the long lesson of how we can hate someone we love, love someone we hate, and how each feeling wraps around the other and becomes a new inseparable thing, stronger than either.

So, though I still had some of the small boy's bias that sees his mother as the most beautiful woman in the world, I had to admit that Laura Pettit was the more compellingly attractive of the two. Have you ever looked at a photograph of a crowd and noticed that one face out of the many demands your attention? Perhaps it is because he or she is the only one staring directly at the camera and so seems to be gazing right back at you. No matter what the reason, something keeps bringing you back to that face.

That was true of Laura Coe Pettit. As she stood alongside my mother, my mother's beauty seemed to fade in degrees from conventional to ordinary to uninteresting, while the mystery of Laura's looks deepened.

"Hey, Judge!" Hal Davenport's shout brought me out of my reverie. "Come on! Let's go, let's go. Throw the ball."

But playing catch became impossible. It was difficult enough to concentrate when my attention (and eye) kept wandering to the porch, but I couldn't even show off as we played. I couldn't throw the ball hard to Hal Davenport, and his tosses to me came lower and softer and were embarrassingly easy to catch.

Finally, my mother saved me by calling, "Paul! Could you come here a moment?"

I shrugged at Hal Davenport as if to say, what can I do—it's my mother.

My mother said, "Paul, I have someone I would like you to meet."

I wasn't sure how I should handle this introduction. Should I say we had already met and have my mother question me about the circumstances? Or should I say nothing and risk having Laura reveal our meeting and thereby make it seem as though I was concealing something? I kept quiet, and Laura did the same. The knot of our conspiracy tightened.

My mother told me why she had interrupted my ball playing. "Laura is going to borrow Jane's bike and go for a ride this morning, and I told her about that lovely lane over on the other side of the highway. You know which one I'm talking about? Where they're building those two new houses?"

I said I knew which one she meant.

"I hope you don't mind," my mother said, "but I told Laura you'd show her the way. Is that all right? Did you have something else planned this morning?"

The last question was part of the pretense my mother and father upheld about our summers in Vermont. They pretended that the vacations were not for them and their friends but for Janie and me—"the children"—and that our days were full of so many exciting activities there weren't enough hours to hold them all. The days, in fact, were often long, boring, and blank as sunlight.

"No," I told my mother. "I don't have any plans."

Laura said, "I'll be ready in a few minutes. I just need some coffee." That deep voice, well suited to my dark room, was startling in the light.

I excused myself to Hal Davenport and told him I had to do a favor for my mother. He looked relieved.

I brought both bikes up from the shed to the house, leaning them against the porch. My heart was pounding but not from exertion.

Janie's bike was an old, rattling, rusty-red Schwinn, and mine was a somewhat sleeker blue Raleigh with a missing front fender. My parents bought both bikes secondhand when we came to Vermont, and although Janie seldom rode hers, I often went for long excursions, pedaling up and down the blacktopped county highways, the gravel roads, and the dirt paths of the fields. I wiped the dust from Janie's bike with a rag, and then I sat on the porch steps and waited for Laura.

She took longer than the few minutes she promised, and I filled the time by concocting a fantasy about Laura and me on our bike ride.

I imagined us riding along a high stretch of rocky road that I knew, a road arched over by giant elms on each side. The road wound around a small swamp. Laura insisted we stop so she could gather scraggly, brilliant wildflowers that seemed to blossom right out of the summer air. As she edged her way down a slope to pick a purple violet, she lost her footing and began to slide down toward the scum-green water. "Paul! Help! I can't swim!" She clung desperately to the loose strand of a tree's exposed root.

Without worrying about my own safety, I jumped off the road and reached out to her. "Take my hand," I said. "I'll pull you up."

She hesitated, but I told her not to worry; I could hold her.

Just as the root she was holding gave way, I grabbed her wrist, and with one great pull, brought her to her feet and back up to the road.

In relief and gratitude, she threw her arms around me and sighed, as only someone in a fantasy would, "Paul, you saved me! How can I ever thank you?"

There my fantasy ended. Perhaps because it was enough for me simply to think of being in a grown woman's embrace, and perhaps not even my imagination dared go any further.

After about half an hour, Laura returned. She was smoking and carrying a small paper bag. The screen door slammed behind her, and she said, "Okay, I'm ready, Which one is mine?"

"The red one."

"Then you take this," she said, dropping the bag into my dented wire basket. "Lead the way."

"Where do you want to go?"

"You decide."

I pedaled off down our long unpaved driveway and out onto the county highway. Laura followed, how near or far I could tell by the clatter of the loose chain guard on Janie's bike. Now that I had what I wanted—to be alone again with Laura—I was too nervous to take advantage of it, and that was why I stayed ahead. It made conversation impossible.

After going less than a quarter of a mile down the highway, I turned off, ran down a ditch, and came back up again next to a large hayfield. I had to stand up to pedal through some weeds and tall grass, but soon I was at the field's edge and onto a smooth two-wheel path worn down to dirt by a farmer's truck. When I looked back at Laura, I expected to see her walking her bike through the hard-going grass, but she was also standing up on her pedals and moving steadily along. "This is a shortcut," I called back to her.

We rode silently up the length of the field until it ended in a row of field-cleared rocks and boulders. Then we turned west and followed the same path through a heavy stand of scrub oak and elms until it came out in the sunlight next to a cornfield. We were not far from the home of the farmer who owned this land nor even from my parents' house, but the configuration of alternating fields and forest made the area seem isolated and remote. Except for Janie, who occasionally rode here with me, I never saw another person in my wanderings along those trails. When my parents went walking along the country road that was Laura's and my destination, they always took the car, drove the long way around, and parked along the shoulder of the highway before their stroll.

Soon we were past the cornfield, and we pedaled to the top of a small treeless rise. To show her I knew where I was going, I shouted over my shoulder, "It's not much farther. The highway's just over there."

"Wait," she said.

I stopped quickly. "Is something wrong?"

She was straddling Janie's bike and pointing to a stand of tall pines on a ridge off to our left. The trees were on high ground too, but a steep downward slope and another hill separated us. "I want to go over there," said Laura.

"But the place my mom was talking about is the other way."

"Over there," she repeated.

I shrugged and turned my bike around so we could go back along the path we rode in on.

"Let's go straight over. Down the hill," Laura suggested.

I looked again down the steep, grassy, pathless hill. "It's not that far to go around."

"Oh, come on," said Laura. "Let's try going straight down the hill."

I wasn't only afraid we would rocket down the hill so fast that we wouldn't be able to control our bikes and would tumble down the hill in a tangle of handlebars, wheels, and bicycle chains, I was also concerned because I was supposed to be Laura's escort and to see that no harm came to her. "I don't think we should," I said. "These bikes are kind of old."

"Fine," she said. "You go around the other way. I'm going down the hill." She straddle-walked her bike over to the hill's crest, and just before she pushed off, she looked back over her shoulder at me and said, "Chicken."

It's strange, but in trying to decide my course of action, I asked myself what my father would do. I had an adult's duty in guiding Laura that morning, so I wanted to behave as an adult would, and since I also wanted her to love me, it figured I should be like the man I believed she loved. And there was no question, my father—whom everyone regarded as headstrong and fearless—would go right down the hill after her.

Laura leaned out over her handlebars and pushed hard down the hill. As she picked up speed, she let out an undulating, drawn-out shriek that was half fear and half exhilaration.

Just as I did the first time I jumped feet-first from the high diving board, I held my breath so hard my ears plugged; then I took off after her, keeping my foot pressed back lightly on the brake. I was in trouble already; you can't decide to rush headlong down a hill and at the same time put on the brakes.

Ahead of me, Laura was again standing up on her pedals, and her white shirt filled with wind and ballooned around her body, making her look ridiculously fat. The track her tires made in the high grass was perfectly straight, like the precise part in a fastidious man's hair.

I was not doing as well. I had swerved to avoid a rock, and that sideways motion slowed me down and gave me the idea of going back and forth down the hill like a skier slaloming down a mountain. I hoped that might give me more control.

But the wheels of a bicycle are not like skis, and as the hill steepened, my wheels began to slide out from under me, so I was rolling sideways across the hill but also skidding slowly down it. I wrenched the handlebars hard to try to get back on track, and that made matters worse. I fell, so hard and swift I couldn't even get a bracing leg under me.

I landed hard on my left side, my arm and shoulder slamming into the hill. But since I was still on my bicycle, the worst of my injuries were actually the result of my body banging against the bicycle's unyielding parts. The chain took a bite of my bare calf, the cross brace of the frame bruised its way hard into my thigh, and the spokes of the front wheel somehow twisted my foot between them. But none of these injuries was severe; in fact, I didn't even notice them at first. What I did notice was the way the end of the handlebars landed under me. The handlebars didn't have any rubber grips, so it was like landing on the open end of a length of pipe. Into my left side, just under my heart, the handlebar gouged, and when it did, my breath blew out of me.

As soon as I could breathe again, I rolled onto my back and lay very still, the way you do when you're afraid you might be hurt seriously and you don't want to take a chance of aggravating any injury—the slightest movement might cause that broken rib to puncture a lung, or the stray vertebra to sever the spinal cord, or the torn vein to start leaking blood so fast it won't stop. And that was exactly the way my thoughts ran. As a child I was so sensitive to any injury or illness that I worried a bump could break a bone and a fever signal the start of a fatal disease. A few years earlier, I had lain in bed night after night systematically moving my toes, feet, and legs, checking for any sign of the oncoming paralysis of polio. I knew it could happen. In school there were three or four children, victims of polio, who clumped up and down the halls in their heavy shoes and leg braces. Worse were the films we saw of people fated to spend their lives in iron lungs, those awful cylinders that looked like oversized water heaters. Until the vaccine, I was terrified I was going to contract the disease.

Lying on the ground still tangled in my bicycle, I took short breaths because I was afraid of the pain if I fully expanded my lungs. Then, while I lay believing I was seriously, perhaps critically injured, I heard laughter.

At first I thought the sound must have some source in nature—a bird with a deep, chuckling call, the wind shuttling its way through the pine boughs, a dog barking another hill away, but finally there was no doubt it was human laughter; it was as clear and joyful as the blue sky above me.

I turned in its direction and saw Laura halfway up the hill across from me. She was off her bike and laughing without restraint. When her laughter subsided, she turned and began to walk up the hill. With her back to me she shouted, "Hurry up, Paul. I want to go up there."

How dare she? I was hurt—who knew how badly?—and she was laughing! I was so angry that I resolved to get up, no matter what it cost in pain. And I hoped that once I got up I would immediately collapse, thereby demonstrating to her just how serious my injuries were. Let her kneel over my unconscious body and weep, "Oh, Paul. I'm sorry! I had no idea it was this bad!"

I did not collapse, however. I rose shakily to my feet and began to take small, hesitant steps down the hill. My side, where I landed on the handlebars, hurt, and I kept my left arm pressed against my ribs and maintained my shallow breathing. A strand of blood rolled down my leg from the cut on my calf.

When it became clear that I was not going to pass out from pain, loss of blood, or internal injuries, I decided on a different plan. I would play the stoic and hide my wounds from Laura. Later, that night perhaps, when I would have to be taken away by ambulance, she would be forced to say, "My God, I had no idea he was hurt so badly! He never let on!" One way or the other, I would get the sympathy I thought I had coming.

From the crest of the hill Laura called down to me, "Do you still have the bag?"

Miraculously, the bag was still in my basket. "I've got it!" I shouted angrily. At first, I was stunned that she was more concerned about what was in the basket than what had happened to me, and then another thought, even more stunning, pushed that one aside: She was having fun.

All of it, the changed route, the wild ride down the hill, had only been an attempt to have fun. She was not trying to sabotage me or humiliate me, or put me through any trial; she only wanted a little excitement out of a Sunday bike ride. She was the adult and I was the child, yet she was the one who tried to find some pleasure, some amusement, in the dull day. The ride down the hill was not a test of skill or courage; it was merely an experience, a grassy roller-coaster ride. I was learning something about Laura and what she wanted of life, and if I could have looked inward as easily as outward, I could have learned something about myself as well.

When I finally got to the top of the hill, I couldn't see Laura. She was not there waiting for me, as I hoped she would be.

I rested my bike on its kickstand and began to look around, wondering how she could have vanished so quickly. Could I have made some mistake—climbed the wrong hill? Failed to hear her say she was going on ahead? Now I was not afraid that I would be in trouble for failing as Laura's escort; I was afraid that I was going to be left alone, injured and far from home.

Then I heard her call, and at her voice my heart flooded with relief. "Paul! Over here!" Her voice came from the stand of pine trees that thickly grew twenty yards back from the hilltop. "And bring the bag!"

Once I stepped into the shade of the pines, it felt as though I had entered a cool, dim room. Underfoot was not the rocky clay of the hilltop but a cushioned carpet of pine needles. Sunlight had to struggle through layers of branches, and the heat remained outside as well. And then another season intruded. The clean Christmas smell of evergreen rose to my nostrils as each of my steps crushed more needles. In the center of this half-lit area sat Laura, waiting for me on the trunk of a long-ago fallen pine. She was smoking, and in that windless interior, the smoke rose straight up.

I held out the bag with my right hand, my left arm still pressed tightly to my side.

She took out a red and white can of Budweiser, the brand my father always bought. She also took out a can opener.

Just as she was about to lever open the can, I said, "It really got shook up. When I fell."

She acknowledged my warning by turning her head slightly to the side and holding the can farther out in front of her. It opened with a metallic gasp, and beer sprayed out explosively in the air between us before settling down to a bubbling foam in the can's open triangle. Laura made another, smaller opening in the top of the can before bringing it to her lips for a long swallow.

"God," she said, "I've been thirsty since I got up this morning. I must have had six glasses of water before we left the house."

I remembered something my father said to me one Saturday morning after a long, loud party the night before. He was standing in his bathrobe by the kitchen sink, drinking glass after glass of water. "Whiskey," he said to me, "the more you pour in, the more it dries you out. Crazy, huh, Judge?"

Laura held the can out to me. "Do you want a sip? It's not very cold, but it's wet."

"No thanks."

"Never touch the stuff?"

"I do sometimes." Which was true. My father always encouraged Janie and me to sample his drinks. "It takes a long time to learn to like the stuff," he would say. "You might as well get an early start." The only alcoholic beverages I liked were sweet, the cordials, liqueurs, or the occasional old-fashioned my father drank. "I don't like the taste of beer," I told Laura.

She shrugged. "You're better off."

I wanted to draw attention to the fact that I was hurt, but I couldn't simply announce it because that would have made it seem as if I were whining. I settled for limping in a small circle in front of the fallen pine, flexing my leg as if I were worried it would stiffen up.

Laura finally took her cue and said, "You went down pretty hard, huh?"

Now I had my opportunity to be brave. "I'll be okay."

"Your leg's bleeding."

I looked down as if I were surprised. I reached down and lightly touched my fingertips to the blood that was already drying and turning dark. "It doesn't hurt."

"Any other injuries?"

"My side."

She motioned for me to come closer. "Should I take a look?"

My bravery had limits, and as badly as I wanted to impress her with my courage, I wanted even more to know if I was seriously injured. I stepped meekly forward to let her diagnose me.

"Which side?" she asked.

In response, I wordlessly pulled up my T-shirt, exposing my pale, rib-skinny torso for her inspection. By now I felt like crying, not because of physical pain, but because I knew how diminished I must have become in her eyes. It was hopeless—I was a child, and after this behavior there was no pretending otherwise.

She winced slightly when she looked at me. "*Oooh.* Yeah, you got it all right."

Her expression made me look down. On my chest, just under my left nipple, was a dark purple ring, exactly the circumference of the bicycle's handlebar. The skin was slightly raised where the blood was welling up beneath. The contusion frightened me—it was an ugly little wound, more so for its perfect geometric shape—yet it also satisfied me. See, I really was hurt.

"Can you take a deep breath?" she asked.

I inhaled gingerly, letting my lungs gradually fill. It hurt, but the pain was not markedly worse. "It's okay," I said, my stoicism creeping back.

"I don't think anything's broken." She put her right hand, palm out and fingers pressed together, toward the injury on my chest. Less than two inches from my flesh, she stopped her hand. "Do you want me to heal you?" she asked.

Standing this close to her I smelled her beery breath and something else. It must have been her body, sweating from the heat and the bike ride, and it was the smell of sweat and a flowery fragrance mingled, as though someone had poured perfume on freshly dug dirt. "I don't know what you mean," I said.

"You know, should I heal you? Like Oral Roberts. Don't you ever watch that program?"

Was there anyone in 1955 who hadn't seen Oral Roberts lay his hand on the afflicted and make goiters disappear, arthritic fingers straighten, and blind eyes blink into sight?

At that moment, however, what tempted me was not any promise of a miraculous cure but simply the possibility of her touch. I could not move forward those scant inches to make the contact myself, no matter how I longed for it, yet all I had to do was give her my permission.

"Okay," I said. "Heal me."

I must have closed my eyes, for I have no recollection of what her hand looked like on my chest, yet I remember the feeling exactly.

She touched lightly, only the heel of her hand and the tips of her fingers making contact, and her touch was cool, as if her hand, like the grass, could not hold any of the summer's heat.

Her hand was perfectly still, while it seemed my skin was quivering, my muscles twitching, ribs vibrating, and heart lurching.

It was a moment of knowing and not knowing. I was having an erotic experience—the first my memory can reach—but since I didn't know what an erotic experience was, I was going through something without having any awareness of it, without having a name for it or a category to put it in. It was happening only on the level of feeling—my mind was not ahead of what was happening on the five-inch span of flesh on my left side, and although I have had physical experiences more intense than that moment, nothing has ever approached its purity.

"Do you believe?" she said. "You have to believe." On the last syllable of "believe" her voice rose like a television evangelist's.

"Yes," I said. "I believe."

"And what do you believe in?"

I searched for something to say and then blurted out, "Water."

I have no idea why I said that. Perhaps the green, swaying light in the pines made me feel as though I were underwater. Or the air, warm and humid, seemed to resist and slow our movements. Or my inability to breathe easily. . . . Or perhaps you can always find a reason to say "water."

"Water?" Laura said. "You believe in *water?*"

"I guess."

With the hand that was on my chest, she pushed me gently away and began to laugh. "I don't believe you," she said, shaking her head. "Water!" Now she was laughing so hard she began to cough.

I pulled my T-shirt down. "I didn't know what to say."

She stopped laughing long enough to take another swallow of beer. When she brought the can down, she had a foamy little mustache on her upper lip, and she wiped it away with the tip of her ring finger.

"We don't know each other very well, do we?" she asked, serious again.

"Not really."

"I mean, how could we? We just met last night. That's not very long."

"No, it isn't."

"But I like that, that we're new to each other. Do you know why?"

I shook my head, feeling myself being led someplace I hadn't been before.

"Because we can create ourselves for each other."

Once more I was unable to follow what she was talking about, and all I could do was stand there and stare dumbly at her.

She leaned forward. "See, Paul, since we don't know each other, we can do or say anything and that will be who we are." She paused and ran her hand through her hair. "Damn it, I'm not explaining it right."

She lit another cigarette with one of those heavy, brushed chrome Zippo lighters that it seemed every man in the 1950s carried. Her cigarettes were Pall Malls. "What I'm trying to say is, haven't you ever wanted to be brand-new, to have everyone see you for the first time, so no matter what you do or say, that will be who they think you are? Haven't you ever wanted that?"

It was another urgent question, so I politely answered, "I guess so."

She looked warily at me for a long time. Finally she said, "You haven't, have you?"

"I guess not."

She drank some more beer. "Forget it. It's too stupid anyway. None of it makes sense. I spend half my time writing things so people will know who I am, and the rest of my time I spend hoping that no one in the world will know who I am."

She jumped down off the log and brushed bits of bark and dried resin from her skirt. For the first time I noticed her shoes. They were brown canvas with darker brown laces and thick crepe soles. They were men's shoes—or I had only seen men wear them—but they were so small I couldn't imagine them available in any men's sizes. She wasn't wearing socks.

Laura walked a few steps from me and then turned quite suddenly. "So, Paul, how about you? Let's get back to you." She was talking very rapidly. "What's your favorite book? *Black Beauty? Treasure Island? My Gun Is Quick?*"

She didn't seem as though she was truly interested, but I wanted nevertheless to name a title that would impress her. I just couldn't think of one. Finally, since I had to say something, I blurted out a name that came to mind only because I had heard it earlier in the day.

"Hemingway," I answered.

"Hemingway? Hemingway's not a book. Do you mean a book by him? Which one?"

"I can't remember the name."

"What's it about?"

"War." My unthinking responses were leading me, I realized, toward the same bog that Leonard Shelter had walked into the night before. In an attempt to save myself I hastily added, "It was about war, but I didn't really like it that much."

"Your favorite book is one you don't like very much?"

I could feel my face heat into a fine, bright blush.

"Forget it," she said. She walked back to the log where she had been sitting. "Do you like coming up here?" she asked. "To Vermont?"

I nodded enthusiastically, glad to be moving on to a subject I thought I could handle.

"You do?" Laura said. "What do you like about it? What do you do all the time?"

"Ride my bike."

"What else?"

"I don't know. Different things."

"Like what kind of different things?—like playing baseball with a one-armed man?"

I had by then caught on to her cruelty, how she could not resist making certain comments, no matter how cutting, if they were clever. These remarks were not blunders—"the snakes crawling out," as she said the night before—but deliberate, and though they might have hurt, her intent was probably not malicious; I think she simply wanted to make you feel. Here, she was saying, feel this, experience this. I didn't mind; I was learning what it was like to be around her—and that it was never safe or easy.

"What about your friends?" asked Laura. "Don't you have friends in Boston?"

"I suppose."

"And don't you miss them?"

"I do things with my sister and my mom and dad."

"*Mm-hmh.* Like what?"

"Go for hikes. Bike rides."

"Is that what your father does? What does he like to do?"

"With me, you mean?"

"Whatever."

"He likes to play golf. And tennis."

"Does he ever leave you here and go back to Boston? Because he has to work?"

The conversation made me squirm, because I knew what Laura was doing—using me to gather information on my father—but neither did I want to stop because at last I had been put onto a subject I could handle.

"He went back once," I said, "for a couple days."

"Has he ever come here?" She looked at the ground, and with one foot she kicked away the thick layer of rust-colored pine needles and gouged a bare spot on the dirt. "Right here? Where we are now?"

"I don't think so." Her question—simply the asking of it—made me feel my father's presence in the pine trees. I looked at the trunks of the trees, at the height where all the branches grew. The pines were so old and high they had pulled the branches up over the years so no branch was closer than five feet from the ground. He wouldn't fit, I thought. My father was six foot four, and he just wouldn't fit in this evergreen room, not without stooping over. This was a place made for Laura and me.

"What about your mother? What does she do all summer?"

This question was difficult to answer, not only because I wasn't sure why Laura wanted to know—did she want to find out if there was a time when my mother was away from the house and my father?—but also because what my mother did was difficult to define. She did very little, especially during the summer. She didn't swim, play golf, or tennis; she didn't ride a bike, and she didn't often go for walks. She stayed close to the house. She didn't like to drive to any of the outlying towns to shop unless it was absolutely necessary. She usually slept late, and when she did get up, she spent the late morning or early afternoon hours listening to the radio, usually the classical music station from Montreal. Sometimes she would go out in the yard, spread a towel over one of the lawn chairs, and sit in the sun. My mother enjoyed having guests, and she came to life when they were around, laughing gaily and moving from one conversation to another, only stopping long enough to say something witty. Still, she never joined any of the games they played, and if asked, she would beg off by saying, "Oh, you only want me so I'll lose. I'm the world's worst." During the school year when my mother was teaching, she didn't do much more. She read a lot, but she did not take notes or make outlines for lectures. She had neither the ambition nor the desire to publish books or articles, and when she was asked about that by a writer friend, she said, "The world does not need more tedious, second-rate criticism, which is exactly what I would produce." Her efforts at keeping house and serving meals were family jokes, and my father often said, when he brought home sandwiches from the delicatessen, "I did not marry your mother for her domestic skills." I recognized when I was quite young that my mother was lazy, but since she made no attempt to hide it and was cheerfully unconcerned about it, I never loved her any less for it. Nor did anyone else, as far as I knew. People had a protective affection for my mother.

I told Laura quite honestly, "She doesn't do much."

"Doesn't she know how to be serious?"

"I guess not," I said, and immediately I felt a pang of guilt that I knew would hurt even worse later when I looked back at the moment I betrayed my mother.

Laura said, "I mean, she doesn't seem to be serious about *anything*. She's a teacher—isn't she even serious about her work?"

"She's just like that," I said, in weak defense of my mother.

"Well, I don't understand it."

Laura finished her beer and dropped the empty can on the ground. She stepped on it hard, and as it caved in, the ends of the steel can curled around her foot like the bars of a trap. "Help!" she cried in mock alarm. "It's got me!" She shook her foot, but the can stayed clamped to her shoe. "Paul—get it off me!"

I dropped to the ground and took hold of the can with one hand and with the other I instinctively grabbed the back of her leg below her right calf, where the bulge of muscle begins its stately taper down to the ankle.

I knew immediately that my hand on her leg was wrong, and that knowledge was not moral but physical. Her leg was so cold it felt like stone, and its clear, instant message was that this was flesh not meant to be touched.

I let go of her leg and grabbed the can with both hands. The can fell off easily.

"It's off," I said. I didn't raise my head for fear I might be looking up her skirt.

"Thank you, kind sir." She reached down and gently rubbed the back of my neck with her fingertips. "You may rise now."

I continued to look down at her feet and her curious brown shoes. A thin layer of dirt darkened her ankles down to the tops of her shoes, and then there was a sliver of perfectly white clean skin where her shoes kept the dirt away.

"Come on, Paul," she said, now gently tapping the back of my head. "Let's go. We should get back."

I remained on the ground, kneeling with my head bowed.

"Paul," she repeated, "let's go."

"I can't," I said. "I don't want to."

She crouched down in front of me, but I still did not look up. "Is something wrong?" she asked.

"I just don't want to."

A couple years earlier, when I was in fourth grade, a fat blond boy in my class named Douglas Falla took a dislike to me for reasons I never understood. One day, Douglas told me he was going to "pound on me" after school. I was no fighter, I had no friends big enough to protect me from Douglas, and when the school bell rang at three-thirty I didn't know what to do. I tried to solve the problem by remaining at my desk. Mrs. Taylor, my teacher, asked me if anything was wrong, and when I said no, she informed me that I would have to leave the classroom. I remained seated. I knew it wasn't going to do any good, that I would eventually have to leave the building and that I wouldn't be able to avoid Douglas forever, but I simply did not know what else to do. I tried to find a way out of my dilemma by one of the few avenues open to me or any child: obstinacy. When Mrs. Taylor finally harried me from the school, Douglas was gone, and he soon lost interest in me.

Kneeling on the pine-needle floor, I was trying something equally desperate. I did not want the time to come when Laura and I would have to go back, and I tried to delay it by a willful, stubborn gesture.

Laura cupped my chin in her hand and lifted my face so I had to look at her. "What's going on here?" she asked, concern and irritation in her voice.

I noticed again the scar under her eye and thought of how its size and shape matched the mark the handlebar made on my chest. "How did you get that?" I asked, reaching my finger out slowly until I was touching the scar.

Now, as I remember this moment, something strange happens. The camera that has been making this record in my memory has been looking out from my eyes, and all its images are of what my eyes fell upon.

Suddenly, the camera, as if it were on a crane, pulls back from its vantage point of my vision and rises, rises rapidly until it is looking down on this scene from high in the boughs, from the height of sunlight itself. Down below are two figures touching their hands to each other's faces.

I don't know which is cause and which is effect. Do I remember this moment from outside myself because I acted in such an uncharacteristic way—asking a brash question and putting my finger to someone's scar— or had I already stepped out of my character that day and that gives rise to my memory's sense of separateness?

It doesn't matter. A boy boldly puts his finger on a woman's cheek. Her hand on his chin seems, from that height, affectionate, perhaps even adoring.

I wish the camera were taking not movies but still photographs and I could bring out that picture whenever I wanted. Whenever I wanted to deceive myself about the circumstances of Laura's holding my face.

The camera dropped back down, and once again I was looking into her eyes.

Laura took her hand from my chin and slowly drew it back to my hand on her face. I tried to pull my hand away, but she held it, pinning my finger to her scar. Something in her green eyes flared, and it reminded me of how leaves on a tree caught in a sudden gust of wind will flip over and show a new shade of green.

"If I tell you," she said, "can we go back?"

I agreed, and she let go of my hand. We remained kneeling on the ground.

"I think I was five years old. Maybe six. I was playing with my brother, who's five years older than I am. We were in the upstairs bedroom that had been my grandmother's until she died a few months earlier. She died right in that room. Edward—that's my brother—was in there when she died, and he saw my mama put pennies on Grandmother's eyes. Do you know about that? Do you know why they do that?"

I shook my head.

"They do it so the eyes stay shut. You see, if you die with your eyes open, then they want to stay that way. Wide open and staring at nothing at all. So you put something on them, a coin, some kind of weight, and they'll stay closed. That's what my brother and I were doing that day in Grandmother's room. We were playing death."

I imagined Laura and her brother in a tiny attic room with windows boarded over.

Laura went on. "We were pretending that I had died, and Edward laid me out right on what had been my grandmother's bed. Since he didn't have any coins, Edward put bottle caps on my eyes. Hires root beer bottle caps. But the bottle caps wouldn't stay in place or I wouldn't keep my eyes closed. I'd blink and they'd pop right off. Well now, you can't have your dead person opening her eyes all the time—that will never do—so Edward got up on the bed and sat on my chest and took his thumb and pushed down on the bottle cap as hard as he could and said, 'Now stay, goddamnit!'" She put her own finger to the scar and lightly traced its shape back and forth. "I was lucky he didn't push down evenly, or it might have damaged my eye. If you look close, you can still see the ragged edge of the bottle cap."

She leaned her face right up to mine and closed her eyes, not squeezing them tightly shut, but letting the lids fall like a shade pulled down. I could see the unevenness of the scar and the small white dots where the doctor's needle stitched her up.

"Can you see it?" asked Laura.

"Yes," I said.

She opened her eyes and stood up quickly. "Okay. Now we can go back—right?"

"Were you mad at your brother?"

"Not right away. I was too scared. When the bottle cap cut me, there was so much blood it made a little pool all around my eye and I couldn't see. I still remember trying to see through that bright red smear. . . . Later I was so mad at Edward I tried to kill him."

She must have seen the look of disbelief on my face, because she said, "It's true. I tried to poison him. We used to keep some kind of nectar in the house. It was purple and sweet, and it came in a big brown bottle that looked like a medicine bottle. I took the nectar outside, and I added to it weeds and dirt and water from the gutter. Then I took it to Edward and said, 'Here, this is for you.' And Edward took the bottle right into the bathroom and poured it down the sink. 'I saw you put something in there,' he said. Edward, let me tell you, I could never get anything by that boy."

Laura motioned upward with her palms. "Now. Let's go, let's go."

I stood up slowly. "Do you think I'm going to have a scar?"

"Let me take another look."

I pulled up my T-shirt and stepped up to her again for inspection. I knew what I wanted her to say, that I was going to be scarred for life, and then I would have a scar to commemorate the day Laura and I were alone in the pinewoods.

"I don't think so," she said, looking closely at my chest. "The skin's not broken. That's more like a bruise. You'll be sore for a while, but it's going to heal all right."

Then she did something so sudden and unexpected that it was over before I had a chance to appreciate what was happening.

Laura hugged me in a quick, clumsy, one-armed embrace. She let go as quickly as she had grabbed me. Yet the second she held me was long enough for me to take away distinct impressions. I felt, for example, that she was a woman, for at the same time I noticed how childishly small she was—how she could not encircle me completely but only press my body to hers—I noticed also the distinct pressure of her breasts, hard and soft at the same time, and the upturned tilt of the hip she used as a lever for the hug.

When she let me go, she said, "We've gotten to be friends, haven't we?"

After her sudden show of affection my speechlessness returned, and I merely nodded.

"You know, I never told anyone that story about my brother and the bottle cap. I've tried to write about it, but I've never told it. Did you believe me? Did you think it was a true story?"

I was confused. Was she asking me if the story was hard to believe, or was she saying that it was untrue and she was checking to see if she had made it sufficiently convincing? "I believe you," I said, wanting to assert my faith in her.

"That's good," she said absently. She was looking around now, gazing up at the pines and turning in a slow circle as if she were looking for a particular tree. "Paul, do you think you could give someone directions on how to get here?"

I didn't have to look around. I knew, with that question, exactly where we were. "I guess." I stared down to where the sandy soil and the cover of pine needles prevented anything from growing.

She smiled. "Good. Now let's get back on the bikes."

I picked up my bicycle and looked it over carefully to see if I had bent a wheel, knocked the handlebars out of alignment, or pulled the chain off the sprocket. Everything seemed to be all right, but I was in no hurry to get back on. I was afraid, first of all, that it would hurt to ride, and I was also reluctant to return to the hot sunlight and leave behind the cool, piney shade.

"Maybe I'll walk back," I said.

Laura was already on Janie's bicycle, but she paused, straddling the bike, to light a cigarette. "Are you sure?"

"I'm sure. Do you know the way?" She was not aimed down the steep hill but along the ridge and the edge of the pines—the long way back.

"I'll figure it out." She put her cigarette between her lips and began to pedal away.

"Wait!" I called after her. "Wait! I want to ask you something."

I knew she heard me. On that clear, windless day our shouts traveled the air as easily as a bird's wing. But she pedaled another ten yards before she stopped. "What is it, Paul? I want to get back."

"Your leg," I said. "When I felt it. Why is it so cold?"

She laughed just as she had when I fell off my bike. "Poor circulation. It's from pretending I was dead when I was little."

I TOOK MY TIME getting back to the house, and when I arrived a few people were preparing to leave. A man was loading suitcases into the back of a station wagon, and everyone was laughing at a joke someone made about the chrome hood ornament on Hal Davenport's Nash. The ornament was of a woman's naked torso.

Laura stood by the back door of the station wagon, and she was not laughing. She was smoking and scowling, and somehow I knew she was one of those who was leaving.

Up on the porch, looking like a king surveying his departing armies, stood my father. When he saw me approaching, he waved and called out, "There he is! What say, Judge? We heard you took a tumble."

The presence of all those people, after so long a time alone in the woods with Laura, was dizzying, and I wanted to get away. "I'm okay," I said to my father.

"You sure?" he asked. "Should we have the doctor look at you?" That was a family joke. My mother's doctorate was from Columbia, and my father liked to call her "the doctor of the house."

"I'm okay," I repeated. I parked my bike next to the porch, walked up the steps and into the house. I wondered why Laura was leaving. Had she given up hope of meeting my father? Had they fought? Had my mother found out and intervened? Or had I misunderstood the nature of their relationship? For the first time I considered that what she had said the night before about being alone with my father may have been nothing more than a drunken, tasteless joke. Or—and this was more likely—a remark that my child's mind had completely misunderstood. With that thought came the foolish, immature hope that perhaps Laura might be mine.

Janie was in the living room, and when I saw her I thought I might tell her everything that had happened, but then she looked up at me and I changed my mind. She was sitting in front of the electric fan, and when she turned to me with her expressionless gaze, her long, thin, blond hair blew across her face in weightless strands, and she looked as though she were underwater, holding her breath and letting her hair float free, and I knew I would keep it all to myself.

I waved to her but said nothing; at the moment she seemed to have all she could handle in the air rushing across her face.

AROUND TEN O'CLOCK that night my father came into my room. He was wearing blue plaid Bermuda shorts, a white T-shirt, and torn laceless tennis shoes. He was drinking ginger ale from the bottle, and when my father drank ginger ale, it always meant he was trying to step back from having drunk too much alcohol. The next day he would prob-ably go for a long walk or play frantic, exhausting tennis in order to further cleanse his system. And for a few days he would drink nothing stronger than beer.

"How are you doing, Judge?" he said. He was so much heavier than Laura that when he sat down on the edge of my bed the other side of the mattress jumped up and the bed springs bounced.

"Is everyone gone?" I asked.

"Hal's still here. He's going back early tomorrow morning."

"Do you have to work this week?"

"I've got a meeting on Thursday, so I'll probably go in on Wednesday, and then I'll be back Thursday night or Friday. Why—was there something you wanted to do this week?"

"No. I was just wondering."

"Do you want to do some fishing?" That was another private joke. Earlier that summer my father and I had gone fishing in a small trout stream. My father was an accomplished fly fisherman, but for my benefit, we left the fly rods and his hand-tied flies at home and instead brought spin-cast rods and a can of worms. I was the only one who caught anything that day, and I hooked a spiny, four-inch, muddy-black, prehistoric-looking fish that looked like a cross between a shark and a horned toad. The wriggling fish was so ugly—its eyes bulged from its oversize head—that I could not bring myself to remove it from the hook. My father found the incident hilarious, and whenever I looked bored, he would ask me if I wanted to go fishing; when I said no, he always laughed heartily. The variation on his question on going fishing was, "Do you think the sculpin are biting today?"

I do not tell this story to demonstrate that my father could be cruel, because, though my feelings were hurt, that was not his intent. Instead, it could be taken as another example of my father's self-centeredness. He could not, first of all, understand that someone might be squeamish about taking a fish from a hook, since he would never feel that way. Second, he would never be able to comprehend that someone might not think funny anything that he found to be so.

To change the subject, I touched my father's cheek. "Did you just shave?"

He rubbed his other cheek. "Yep. It shows, huh?"

Right after shaving, his face took on a translucent look, as though his jawbone was lighted like a fluorescent bulb and shone through the layers of skin. Once, when our family was having dinner in a restaurant with Frances Dillon, a novelist whose work my father edited, she asked my mother, following another of my father's bad jokes, what my mother saw in him. My mother reached over to my father and stroked his cheek with the back of her fingers. "He's the cleanest shaven man in America," my mother said.

"Are you going out?" I asked my father.

"Not tonight. It's early to bed for me tonight. I'm pooped." With his index finger he tapped me on the forehead. "You'll probably still be reading long after I'm asleep."

"I'm kind of tired too."

"Big day, huh?" My father often intimated that my life was richer than it actually was.

"I guess."

"I heard you made a new friend today."

I knew he was referring to Laura, but I didn't want to talk with him about her. As it was, it bothered me that he knew about us; I didn't want to give any more over to him. "Sort of," I said.

"Sort of? She sure went for you. She thinks you're the greatest thing since zippers."

I wanted desperately to know what she had said about me, but I didn't want to hear it from him.

"She was pretty neat," I said.

"Did she tell you what she does?"

"She's a writer, isn't she?"

"A poet, Judge. A hell of a poet. Someday she's going to be very famous. And you can tell people you know her." My father's self-satisfied smile was exactly the look he gave Janie or me when we did or said something precocious, something that could give him that parental pride that is akin to the pride of ownership.

I had a strong impulse to blurt out everything I had learned about Laura—to punish my father with all I knew. Do you know her brother's name? I could say. Do you know how she got her scar? Do you know how she wants to make herself new for every person she meets? How she likes to ride a bicycle so fast the wind tears a scream right out of her? How her legs feel so cold it's as if they're made of stone? And then if he would believe those things, then perhaps I could convince him of something that wasn't true, that Laura said he was such a foolish man she couldn't stand to be around him.

Instead of saying any of those things, I asked my father, "Are you her editor?"

"No, Judge. I told you, she's a poet. We don't publish any poetry. You know that, don't you?"

"I forgot."

My father leaned his face right down to mine, so close our foreheads touched.

"I knew she'd like you, Judge." His voice was too loud for our nearness. "And I'm glad you liked her too." He moved his head back and forth, grinding our skulls together. I closed my eyes and waited for this demonstration to pass. How do we reach the point where we resent our parents' affections and prefer their inattention?

Soon he stood up and said, "Sleep the good sleep," his standard goodnight.

Two

As a child I spent hours in solitary play: arranging opposing armies of toy soldiers in battle across my bedroom's braided rug; lurking in our dark, musty cellar with a toy revolver, ready to arrest the bank robbers who had held up the First National of Boston, killed two guards, and kidnapped a female teller; keeping my sword sharp and my shield polished for any attack by foes of the Round Table. I invented my own baseball league. I used a spin-dial baseball game my father gave me, and I made up the names of my own players as substitutes for the real ones on the game's cards. I kept track of won-lost records, batting averages, and I wrote press releases.

However, in the five months that passed after I met Laura those imaginary realms gradually dissolved. We returned to Boston, and I began to live exclusively in the solid real world. I even spent less time in my room, where most of my pretending had gone on. Now I did my homework on the kitchen or dining room table and stayed the rest of the time in the parlor on the main floor, situating myself in an overstuffed chair next to a reading lamp. From there I could see the television, but best of all, through the room's glass doors I could see the stairs and the main entrance and monitor the comings and goings of the family.

And that was one of the reasons I gave up play—to watch over the family. I had to watch my father to be sure he was not sneaking out in the evening to meet Laura or any other woman. I had to watch my mother to make sure she did not find some bit of indicting evidence—a dropped note, a careless remark, an overheard telephone conversation—with which to convict my father. And I had to watch Janie to make sure she came across nothing that would cause her to suspect what I had come to know, that another world of complication and intrigue was waiting as soon as you stepped out of the simple child's world.

My play also stopped because I had a grown-up matter on my mind. I couldn't concoct imaginary baseball leagues because my mind was occupied with another fantasy: I thought day and night of making Laura mine. And what did "having Laura" mean to my eleven-year-old mind? It was quite simple. I dreamed of marrying her. Like all fantasies it had its blank spots and blurred edges, and it ignored most logical, realistic, and practical considerations—how an eleven-year-old could be issued a marriage license, how we would live, what it meant to be husband and wife (my fantasy was fairly chaste), what a child and an adult would say to each other. And like all fantasies it ignored a fundamental truth: fantasies are solitary and usually unshared by their object. In many ways it was like a son's plan to marry his mother. Nevertheless, I imagined Laura and me wedded, living in the Rocky Mountains. Our cabin was in a high meadow ringed by snowcapped peaks. This Alpine setting was inspired, I believe, by the movie *Shane*, which I saw with my father. In the film, Van Heflin and Jean Arthur lived in just such a place as I imagined for Laura and me. I didn't dwell on the fact that Brandon de Wilde, a child actor not much younger than I, also starred in the movie and played Heflin's and Arthur's son. There, in our cabin, Laura would write her poems all day, and I would ride a horse up and down the hills, as if either activity were enough to bring in a living.

With that fantasy occupying me, I put my toy soldiers away and took to sitting night after night in my chair, my watching chair.

And I was there on that cold evening in November, the Wednesday before Thanksgiving, when my father brought Laura home with him at six. All day the wind had torn loose gusts of fine-grained snow, and when my father came through the front door, he shouted, "My God, there's got to be a mistake!"

I looked up and saw Laura right behind my father, and I thought that she was the mistake, that she had followed him home when she wasn't supposed to, that they had gone to the wrong address, that he had forgotten his family would be there . . . Then my father completed his statement: "This is November, not January, for Christ's sake!"

Laura was wearing a long wool cape the same shade of gray the sky had been all day, and when she saw me, she pushed her arm free of the heavy fabric and put a black-gloved finger to her lips, signaling me to be silent before I could think of a thing to say. Immediately I was curious as to what I was supposed to be quiet about. Everything, I realized, everything.

"Doreen," my father called. "Look what the wind blew in!"

My mother, who had been reading in the small study off the kitchen, came out to see why my father was shouting. She was dressed as she had been the last time I saw her with Laura. She was wearing a robe again (this time it was wool tartan), her glasses were hanging around her neck, and she had a cigarette in one hand and a book in the other. As she came out, she started, stopped, started again, and craned her neck forward as though she was trying to peer around a corner. From her expression—a look bewildered yet aggressive, as though whatever was puzzling her could not possibly be her fault—I thought it likely that my mother had been drinking.

When she saw Laura, my mother sighed, as though the mere thought of a guest exhausted her.

Laura cautiously said, "Hello, Doreen."

My father opened the door to the parlor, leaned into the room, and said to me, "Look alive, Judge. We have company. Is your sister in there with you?"

"She's upstairs."

"Run up and get her, will you? I've got something for her."

As I passed Laura, I heard her make a soft, clucking sound with her tongue, and my heart lurched. The smell of whiskey came off both of them like steam.

As I climbed the stairs, I heard my mother say, "We haven't any food. Not a crumb."

I waited to hear my father's response. "We're going out. Get yourself bundled up."

"Tomorrow," my mother said. "For tomorrow. It's Thanksgiving, and we haven't a crumb. Not for the children and not for our guest." Yes, she was drunk.

"Doreen," said my father, his voice full of irritation, "I mean tonight. We'll go out and eat tonight. Tomorrow we're going to Allen's as we planned."

Then my mother said, "And, Laura. Can you join us?"

"I'm sorry," I heard Laura say, and crestfallen, I hurried up to Janie's room without waiting to hear more.

Sitting on the floor by her bed, Janie was counting pennies from her bank into paper rolls of fifty. She didn't look up when I came in.

"Dad's home," I said.

"I know."

"He wants you. He says he has something for you."

She continued her counting. I knew she would not come down until she finished that roll, and even then she would descend the stairs so slowly your own legs would ache with impatience. Being slow was how Janie drew attention to herself, and her sluggishness and tardiness had become so habitual the family had turned it into a joke. "As slow as molasses in January," my father often said.

Halfway down the steps I heard my father. "No, at Boston College. Isn't that what you said, Laura—that you were reading today at Boston College?"

"I read there last night. Today I visited a class. And met with some people from the English department."

"I know someone who teaches there," said my mother. "Sidney Garrett. Did you meet him?"

"I don't think so," said Laura. "I might have. I met so many people."

"I'm sure you'd remember him," my mother said. "He's a pinched little man who wears tweeds that smell like piss and pipe tobacco."

Laura laughed. "Yes, I'm sure I'd remember him."

All three of them were standing by the stairs. Laura and my mother were side by side, and my father stood off a ways, leaning against the wall. His hands were thrust into the pockets of his overcoat, and he was smiling drowsily at Laura and my mother as though he was contemplating a very pleasant dream.

Laura had her hands back inside her cape, so she looked like a gray stone statue carved by a sculptor who ran out of time before he could finish the arms. My mother, meanwhile, was fidgeting; she held her hands in front of her and kept rolling the fingers of her right hand around her left thumb as if she were trying to tighten her thumb to her hand. I stopped on the stairs for a moment, pretending to wait for Janie but secretly looking at the two women, trying to figure out why the sight of them pleased my father so. Since their being together only made me nervous, I couldn't understand his smile.

I backed up two steps and hissed at Janie, who was slowly descending the stairs, "Dad wants you right now."

She did not alter her pace. "I'm coming."

When my father saw her, he hurried toward her. "There she is! Come here, Penguin. Give me a wet one!" My father called Janie "Penguin" after a cartoon and comic book character, Chilly Willy the Penguin. Janie was such an undemonstrative child, unwilling even to return a kiss or a hug without being coaxed, that my father teased her about her cold heart.

When she got to the second step, my father hugged her and whirled her around the narrow hallway, bumping her feet against the wall and barely missing one of the glass panels in the parlor door. Janie's face was turned away from his. If she had smelled liquor on his breath, she would be disgusted.

Laura caught my eye and said, "Hello, Paul. Read any good books lately?"

"Hello," I answered, and quickly added, "No." In the few moments since I'd seen her, I had made a small vow: I was going to keep my wits about me and not let myself be dizzied by her questions or attentions. Let her see me alongside my father and notice how unpredictable and childish he was and how stolid and mature I could be.

My father put Janie down and ran his hands up and down her arms as if he were trying to straighten her out. "Are you ready for a present, Penguin?"

"I guess."

My father turned to Laura and nodded.

Laura groped around inside her cape for a moment before pulling out a handful of black cloth. She handed it to my father, and he swiftly put it behind his back before going on with his story.

"Laura and I were in the Alhambra—"

"When was this?" my mother interrupted.

"Right after work. I told you we stopped there. Now let me tell this."

As though she was suddenly very tired, my mother sat down heavily on the bench in the hallway.

"We're standing at the bar," my father went on, "and over in the corner playing the pinball machine is the screwiest character you've ever seen. He's playing pinball, and he's dancing around in front of the machine, bumping it and hopping up and down on one foot and then the other and gyrating from side to side. And every time the ball goes down the hole he sort of whimpers, like a dog crying. You should have seen his getup. Beat-up sneakers, high-water pants, an old gray overcoat, and on his head a little black beret. Everybody in the place was watching the guy and trying not to laugh. Well, Laura was wearing a beret just like his and after watching him for a few minutes, she took hers off and slammed it down on the bar. 'I'll never wear this again,' she said. Sammy behind the bar said to her, 'That's not the problem. Get him to take his off.'"

Then, with an elaborate flourish, my father brought the black cloth out from behind his back and placed the beret on Janie's head. "There you go, Penguin," he said. "This one was Laura's. I told her if she didn't want it, I'd bring it home for you."

Janie stood still under the beret. It was too large for her, and my father put it on crookedly, so it pulled her bangs back from her forehead and made it look as though her head were wrapped in a black bandage.

"You don't have to wear it, honey," my mother said to Janie.

Janie left us and went back upstairs. I watched her all the way, and she never touched the beret, never reached up to adjust it or, out of my father's sight, to take it off.

"I'm afraid," my mother said, "that the point of your barroom experience eludes me. Was it one of those occasions where one had to be there?"

My father started to say something in response, then seemed to think better of it. Instead, he rubbed his hands together enthusiastically and said, "All right. While we've still got our coats on, let's go out and get something to eat. The last decent meal we'll get before Valerie's god-awful turkey. If it's anything like last year's bird, it'll be so dry it'll suck the juices out of your mouth like a sponge."

My mother remained sitting. "I don't have my coat on. In case you haven't noticed. I'm in my bathrobe. And I don't feel like getting dressed."

"Oh, come on, Doreen—" said my father.

"Only you and Laura have coats on," my mother continued. "No one else. If you want to go out to eat, go ahead. I'm not hungry anyway. I had a hard-boiled egg after school."

My father did a quick half turn as if he was about to leave the room, but then he stopped. When he halted he was facing me, and he looked right at me. His expression was without recognition or acknowledgment; I could have been the newel post. That was why I was startled when he spoke to me. "How about you, Judge?" he asked. "Do you and your sister want to go?"

His look was so grim I didn't think he could possibly be sincere about wanting us to go along. Perhaps he was trying to convince my mother that dinner with Laura was so innocent even children could come along.

I looked quickly to my mother, and she waved her hand toward me as if she were shooing me away. "If you want to go, go."

My father went quickly to the stairs and ran halfway up. "Janie! Come on down here. We're going out to eat. And wear the beret Laura gave you!" As he came down past me, he snapped me hard between the shoulder blades with his finger. "Dress warm. It's cold out there too."

When we left, my mother was still sitting on the bench in the hall-way. She was reading in the dim light, and she nonchalantly waved good-bye without looking up.

* * *

WE WENT TO the Appian Way, an Italian restaurant on Connor Street that my father favored. The restaurant was in a building on the end of the street and right where an entire city block came sharply to a point. The entrance to the restaurant, on the corner, jutted out into an intersection where five busy streets met, and it was frightening to stand outside and watch the cars zooming in and out of the streets and shaving right by the sidewalk where you stood. Inside, the Appian Way widened out like a wedge of pie, and the owners had partitioned the pieces crazily. It was full of narrow halls and banquet rooms, of tables set haphazardly across a room and long lines of high-backed booths, of stairs that led up to balconies large enough for only one table or down to the long, copper bar.

We were seated in a hallway, and my father and Laura sat at one small table, and Janie and I at another right across from them. The only light shined from candles in red glass jars on the tables. Waiters or customers walking past had to turn their bodies to the side because the passageway was narrow, and it reminded me of the way people steered down the aisle of a moving train. The red candlelight lit up people's faces from below, making them look both frightening and sorrowful.

Laura and my father talked all during dinner, but I had difficulty hearing what they were saying because they kept their voices low and because the people at the table next to Janie and me, separated from us by only a latticed wall, were very loud.

But I overheard part of one conversation. They began to talk about writers, and my father said that someone's work "stunk." Soon they were talking about all the writers they disliked, and for every name they mentioned they had a specific foul odor to characterize that writer's work. I no longer remember the writers they discussed, but I still recall the litany of smells they recited: Someone's novel smelled of boiled cabbage, another of burning tires; one woman's poems had the reek of urine-soaked diapers and someone else's was full of fresh dog turds. Gasoline-soaked rags, sour milk, limburger cheese—they had so much fun making up their list that they began to giggle, and I was embarrassed for both of them. If Janie heard any of their talk, she gave no sign; she had brought a book along, and she propped it up on the table and read by the candle's flickering light.

Before the food arrived, my father excused himself to go to the rest room, and as soon as he was gone, Laura leaned over to me and said, "Paul, can I ask you something?"

I leaned over to her so our heads blocked the aisle.

"What was the matter with your mother tonight?"

Although I was where I wanted to be that night—in the restaurant with Laura—I felt guilty enough about my mother staying behind that I said something heedless in response to Laura's question. "Maybe she knows something."

Laura quickly drew back. "What's that supposed to mean?"

I sat back as well. "You know. . . ."

"No," said Laura. "I don't know. I don't know what the hell you're talking about. Why don't you tell me?"

Laura had become angry so quickly that it unnerved me, and I wanted to find something to say that would undo what I had done. "Maybe she knows about my dad is what I meant."

"What about him?"

I looked at Janie first and then around the restaurant in an attempt to signal Laura that this was a subject we shouldn't discuss publicly.

She wouldn't be put off. "What does she know about him, Paul?"

"That he's sick." I put my head down as I said this, but I could see, from the corner of my eye, Janie's head turn quickly toward me. I was not a child who lied easily or often, so that lie surprised and frightened me, yet I liked it too. It immediately seemed useful, and it slid into place like a door's bolt.

Laura slid off her chair and came over to our table. Kneeling beside me, she whispered, "How is your father sick? What do you mean?"

"I don't know."

Out of Janie's sight Laura grabbed my knee hard. "Don't say you don't know. Don't. How is he sick?"

Tentatively I said, "Does he have cancer?"

"Does he?"

"I think."

You must remember, this was November of 1955, and the two short syllables of "cancer"—a word that can be clearly pronounced without moving the lips and through clenched teeth in perfect expression of pain—fell into any conversation like the mention of death itself.

Laura looked up and down the hallway. "How do you know?"

"I heard my dad and Mr. Harrison talking."

"What did they say? How sick is he?"

I looked over at Janie, but she had lowered her head.

Laura squeezed my leg again. "What did they say, Paul?"

I knew, of course, what a lie was, that it was a fiction, yet something happened in uttering it that made me think the impossible—that maybe my lie was truth. The lie made me feel so powerful I began to fear that I had another power—the power to make something be simply by giving voice to it. What if he did have cancer? What if I was not lying but prophesying?

"He's not too sick," I said, trying to soften the sentence I had given my father. "But maybe he has to have an operation."

Just then my father returned from the rest room. At his approach Laura returned to her seat. I prayed silently that neither Laura nor Janie would say anything to my father and that my lie would hold.

Shortly after my father sat down, the waiter brought our food. "Wait till you taste this," my father said to Laura loud enough for the waiter to hear. "The food's lousy, but they give you so goddamn much you have to love it."

I turned to my food, and as I did Janie reached across the table to me. She didn't say anything, but she urgently patted the table next to my water glass until I looked up. Of what I had said to Laura, Janie had heard enough to be frightened. I couldn't tell her I had lied—not then—but I wanted to reassure her in some way. I shook my head once, a motion so swift and short I might have been clearing a strand of candle smoke from my vision. It was enough. Janie drew her hand away and directed her attention back to her meal. In all our years as brother and sister that moment was the only instance I can recall in which she and I experienced that wordless, transcendent understanding reputed to be possible between siblings.

The rest of the meal passed without incident. My father ate heartily, as he always did. Laura ate almost nothing, and she smoked all through the meal, so there were times when she had her fork in one hand and a cigarette in the other. When the first few minutes passed without her telling my father about the illness I had given him, I began to relax and to think I might get away with it.

When we were through, Laura said she had to go back to Cambridge, to the apartment where she was staying with friends. My father tried to talk her into coming back to our house, but she was adamant. Further, she insisted on taking a cab from the restaurant and would not accept the ride that my father so fervently offered.

We stood in the cold outside the Appian Way and wished each other happy Thanksgiving. When Laura was finally in her cab, my father leaned in the back door and asked her something that I could not hear. In response to his question Laura shook her head vigorously and said, "You. I'll call you." As the cab sped away, snow began to fall again, heavy, wet flakes that flew thicker with each breath of wind.

IN OUR KITCHEN the cupboards and the table were stacked with food. There were pies; loaves of bread; rolls and cakes; jars of pickles, olives, and herring; canned and fresh vegetables; bags of apples and oranges; a ten-pound burlap sack of potatoes; a bag of cranberries; bottles of milk and cream; a case of soda; two large boxes of chocolates; a bag of mixed nuts; and resting across the sink—unable to fit wholly in it—was a huge, pastey-white turkey, trussed and ready to be roasted if an oven large enough could be found.

We had just come in from the snowy dark, and the room and all its bounty gleamed with light and warmth. In the midst of it all was my mother, turning slowly in a small circle and looking as confused as if she were in a room she had never been in before. She was no longer wearing her robe but had on the dress she had worn earlier in the day.

I thought at first there had been some kind of mix-up, that the groceries meant for someone else had mistakenly been delivered to us. But there was too much food for that—this quantity could never be for only a single family. I wondered then if we had won a sweepstakes, one of those "win enough groceries for a year" contests.

My father was not interested in speculating about the source of the food. Across the room he shouted, "Doreen, what the hell *is* all this?"

Mother made one more turn before she faced my father. "I bought groceries," she said, her voice still spinning in slow circles. "If we're going to have a guest for dinner tomorrow, I want to be able to provide a decent meal."

"A guest?" said my father. "What guest are we going to have?"

"Why, won't Laura be staying over?"

My father walked wearily to the kitchen table, pulled out a chair, and sat down. He picked up a bag of sugar-covered, jellied orange slices. He bounced the bag in his hand as if he were testing its weight. No one in our family liked that kind of candy.

Quietly my father asked, "Where did all this come from?"

"Baker's." Baker's was a small, family-owned neighborhood market not far from us, and it was where my parents shopped when they only needed a few items. Their major grocery shopping was conducted at the A&P.

"Did they deliver it?" my father asked.

"Sam did." Sam worked at Baker's stocking shelves, working the register, bagging groceries, and making deliveries. He was frail and stooped, and he must have been at least seventy years old.

My father muttered, "You probably broke his back with all this."

My mother backed up slowly until she was stopped in the corner where the cupboards converged.

"How much did it cost, Doreen?"

"If we're going to have company for Thanksgiving—"

My father interrupted. "Just tell me how much it cost. Over a hundred dollars? A hundred fifty?"

Though they were not wealthy, my parents made respectable salaries, and furthermore they both came from well-off families. My father's father had once owned a chain of hardware stores in upstate New York, and after his death my grandmother was left with a generous estate. My mother's father was a dean at a private college in Minnesota. I never remember my parents discussing whether they could afford something; they seemed to know instinctively how to live comfortably within their means. Yet sometimes they still quarreled over money—though never *before* it was spent, always *after*. Did you have to pick up the check at dinner? my mother would say to my father. Is that set of books something you needed? my father would ask. What was wrong with your other coat? Do we need two of these? Couldn't you have found a cheaper one? What is the bill for this going to look like? Yet the money was always there. What, I wondered, were they really fighting about when they pretended to fight over money?

As if they were playing a guessing game, my mother answered, "More than a hundred. Less than a hundred fifty."

"Over a hundred dollars' worth of food," said my father, shaking his head. "And we're going to Allen's for dinner."

"If we're going to have a guest—"

My father slammed his open palm on the table. "Goddamnit! God *damn* it, Doreen! Will you stop? Will you stop that!"

My mother pressed her hand over her mouth as if that would stop my father's shouting. Then she tried once more, more meekly than ever. "If I'm supposed to feed Laura, I need to have food in the house."

My father got up from his chair and approached my mother. I knew he would never hit her, yet his expression was so menacing I was frightened. Janie had been close at my side, but when my father stood up, I felt her slide silently away.

My father walked up to my mother, leaned over, and put a hand on the cupboard on each side of her, trapping her in the corner. "I want you to understand this." He said "this" so cruelly, it might have accompanied a slap across the face. "Laura is not having dinner with us. She never was. She's staying with friends tonight, and she's going back to New York in the morning. I don't know where you got the idea she was having dinner with us, but she will not. She never was."

My mother's eyes narrowed, and her lips tightened as if she were walking into a cold wind. "I only thought—"

Before she could finish, my father brought his large hands up to hold the sides of her head. "Can you make your mind right?" he asked. His hands were positioned to squeeze the proper thoughts into her brain. "Can you?"

Now, I thought, now, now he will hurt her if I don't do something. Out of the same helplessness, the same desperation as that day in the pines with Laura when I wouldn't get up, I sat down, letting all my weight come loudly down on the linoleum. "I'm here!" I shouted, making my witness known. "I'm here!"

When I spoke, my father moved suddenly, as though he had forgotten I was there, but what he did was not what I expected. His hands went from the side of my mother's head around to her back, and he pulled her to his chest as if he were protecting her. He performed this maneuver so quickly it must have been instinctive.

They were turned halfway to me when my father brusquely said, "We know you're here, Judge."

Now my mother had her arms around my father. Her stunned, innocent expression was like an infant's who has been scolded but cannot comprehend the reason why. She could have been sucking her thumb.

"I was wondering when we're going tomorrow," I asked.

"Around noon," my father said. "Now go to bed. Your mother and I are going to be putting groceries away for a while." He released my mother, but she remained close at his side. "And, Judge? You and your sister eat all you want the next few days. Eat a lot."

As a CHILD I was accustomed to getting what I wanted, and this fact was, I always believed, less a matter of my parents' indulgence and more a matter of my own will. I may have been in some ways a meek child, but when it came to acquiring something I desired, I could be relentlessly single-minded, firm, and even, after a fashion, industrious. If, for example, I decided on a particular baseball glove, I took advantage of every opportunity to lead my father to the exact aisle in the sporting goods store where the glove lay; I pointed out to him the athlete's signature (Harvey Kuenn's) on the glove so there could be no mistake. If for Christmas I needed a specific car for my electric train, I marked the page in the catalogue and circled the item so my mother would not have to guess what to buy me. When it looked as though I would be assigned to Mrs. Frisch's room for third grade (and not Miss Bedford's, where my best friend Bobby Rice would be), I let my parents know not only how miserable I would be in the class of the strict, short-tempered Mrs. Frisch but how intellectually stunted I would be as a result—exactly the appeal that prompted my mother to make a trip to the school to make certain I was in the class of the progressive Miss Bedford.

I was not always sure how I got what I wanted—that football, that pair of tennis shoes, inclusion into that group—but I was always sure my desire helped make it so. When I looked at others, it seemed their yearning was passive, a matter of lying back, staring at the sky, and wishing helplessly. Not for me; I cast my desires out into the world and kept casting until I netted what I wished for.

The earliest recurring dream I can remember—I must have first had it when I was less than four years old—was of a toy I wanted badly. In the dream I had the toy in my hands; I owned it; it was *mine*. Then, still dreaming, I could feel myself start to wake. Morning light began to erase the dark outlines of my sleep until, in the instant before waking, all that was left in the dream was the toy I wanted so badly. At this point I concentrated hard, held on to the object as tightly as I could, and tried to carry it with me from dream world to waking. And when I fully woke, empty-handed as I had to be, morning light was never harsher.

That dream has always seemed the perfect paradigm to explain longing. What can be as intimately close yet as hopelessly distant as what we dream of?

The next day, when we would be at the country home of Allen Harrison, the owner of the publishing company where my father worked, there would be a small ritual that occurred every Thanksgiving. Right before we ate, when the food was already brought from the kitchen and set upon the long trestle table where the twenty or more guests were seated (adults only, children at card tables off to the side), Mr. Harrison would tap his water glass until he got everyone's attention. Then he would make the small speech he made every year: "Perhaps it has become unfashionable—corny, some would call it—to give thanks, but I'm of the mind that all of us have something to be thankful for, and I'd like to take a few minutes to go around the room and give everyone the opportunity to make a public expression of gratitude."

Children were not exempt from this ceremony, so I always planned the night before what I would be thankful for. Of course it would not do for me to say selfishly that I was grateful for a new Boy Scout hatchet or a transistor radio, so I usually offered my thanks for good health, loving parents, or dedicated teachers.

But that night I had watched Laura ride away in a taxi, and as the snow tried to fill in the growing distance between us, I felt as I did on those mornings when I woke empty-handed from my dreams. If I could not have Laura, how could I pretend I was grateful for anything?

THREE WEEKS AFTER Thanksgiving, when the stores of Boston were flocked with red velvet and white cotton and strung with colored lights, when my friends and I were carrying on two simultaneous count-downs—one for the end of school before Christmas vacation and one for Christmas itself—I was caught in the lie I had told Laura about my father having cancer.

During the 1950s my parents went to and gave a great number of par-ties—dinner parties, cocktail parties, costume parties, lawn parties, birthday parties and wedding parties, before-the-concert parties and after-theater parties, quick parties on the way home from work, and long parties that lasted from Friday evening to Sunday afternoon. During the holiday season the number of parties increased. My parents were always dressing to go out, and it seemed that more evenings than not Janie and I ate dinner by ourselves and were sent to bed by our housekeeper or a baby-sitter.

On one of those December party evenings my father called me into the bathroom while he was shaving. The room was warm and moist from my mother's bath and my father's shower, and the steamy air held the smell of soap and shaving lather and the faintly medicinal smell of my mother's makeup, hairspray, and perfume. As soon as I entered the room, my father called down the hall to their bedroom, "Doreen! He's here. Are you going to get in on this? And bring my cigarettes."

My mother brought a drink in with her, and after putting my father's cigarettes on the back of the toilet, she sat on the edge of the tub. I stood in the narrow space between the toilet and the tub.

My father finished shaving, rinsed the last scraps of lather from his face and neck, and briskly toweled himself dry. Then he lit a cigarette and began: "Paul, your mother and I want to talk to you about your crazy idea that I have a disease of some kind. Now, we don't know where or how you got such a notion, but it's most emphatically not true. Do you understand that, first of all? Can we get that taken care of straightaway?"

I knew I was in trouble, but I didn't care; there was something I had to know. "When did you talk to her?" I asked. "When did she tell you?"

"What?" my father said. "What are you saying? When did who tell me what?"

"When did you talk to Laura? To Miss Pettit, I mean."

"What are you asking?" my father repeated.

"When did you talk to her?"

My mother interjected, "Bob, he wants to know when you found out about what he said."

"Just a minute." My father put his hand to his head. "Wait. Let's deal with the issue at hand."

"Is she coming here?" I asked. "Is she in Boston? Is she?"

"I thought you talked to her on the phone?" said my mother to my father. "Isn't that what you told me? About a book proposal?"

"Goddamnit!" My father took a step toward me. "Do you want to hear that I'm not going to die of cancer or are you more interested in who's coming to visit?"

My mother said, "Is she? Is she coming here?"

My father had started to bend down toward me, but when my mother spoke, he stood straight up, his hands on his hips. "Doreen, could we do this the way we agreed?"

"All right." I heard the glassy scrape of her picking up her drink. "You go ahead."

"Tell me, Judge," my father continued, trying to be calm, "how did you come by this idea that I'm sick?"

I answered my father with the rote, all-purpose response children use so often. "I don't know. I just thought that."

"No!" he said loudly. "No, no, no, that's not going to do it! You're not going to stand there and tell us you don't know how you know. Not this time. You do know and you're going to tell us." He reached out and took hold of my forearm and pulled me away from the wall. "And come out here while we're talking. You'd think we beat you or something."

I couldn't confess that it had been a lie for Laura because that would only raise more questions. I needed a new lie to cover the old one. I remembered what I had told Laura. "I heard you talking to Mom."

"When?"

"I don't remember. A long time ago."

"How long ago? Try to remember."

"Robert," my mother said. "Is that important?"

"I want to know, all right? I want to know when this happened."

"It was late," I said. "You and Mom were in the kitchen, and I started to come in, but when I heard you talking, I stopped and listened for a minute."

"You were eavesdropping," my father calmly said. He stressed each syllable as if it were important that the proper term be applied to what I had done.

"I just listened for a second. Then I went back upstairs."

"That doesn't change what you were doing, does it? How long you were doing it?"

"Don't you want to hear," my mother said, "what he heard?" My father was blocking my view of her, but I heard the tinkle of ice as she raised her glass again to drink.

He looked around at her. "Are we together on this?"

"I'm losing interest."

My father turned back to me. "All right. So what did you hear that made you think I had cancer? And when was this? Don't say it was late at night. You know what I mean."

"I thought you said you talked to the doctor. . . ."

"That's it? You heard me say I talked to a doctor, so you jump to the conclusion that I'm dying?"

"I bet it was last fall," suggested my mother. "When we found out about Howard going into the hospital." "Howard" was Howard Gell, a literary agent my father knew who had been seriously ill since the previous October.

At that moment my father wore an expression that was completely unfamiliar to me. His lips, which were usually relaxed into a small smile, now curled back from his teeth as if he were having trouble finding the words of a new language. His eyes, which usually had a heavy-lidded look that caused more than one person to compare him to Robert Mitchum, bulged as though he had had a coughing fit.

"Why are you so mad?" I asked him. The question was not a ploy. He was still my father, and I was still his son.

"I'm angry, Paul, because you've told something about me that wasn't true, and you have no idea what the consequences of that could be. You simply have no idea."

"Did you tell your sister?" asked my mother.

I shook my head.

"Who did you tell?" asked my father.

"Nobody."

"Nobody but Laura Pettit, you mean?"

My mother leaned to the side to peer around my father. "Why did you tell her, Paul?"

I shrugged.

"Did she ask you something about me?" my father said.

"For God's sake, Robert," my mother said, but my father's suggestion opened the door a crack, and I thought I could see a way out.

Hopefully I said, "She wanted to know if you were all right. She said she was kind of worried."

"And this was at Thanksgiving? When we were at the restaurant?"

I nodded.

"Why was she worried? What did she say?"

"I don't remember. She said you looked tired or something." At this point I could feel my throat begin to close and the tears well up, though less from emotion than from strain. The release felt good, as though I had been holding my eyes open a long time and could finally blink.

My mother saw the tears immediately. "For God's sake, Robert!"

"I'm trying to find something out here."

"He thought you were going to die!" shouted my mother. "For weeks he's been thinking his father is going to die! Have some compassion."

At that moment I thought one of them would come forward and

embrace me, but neither did. They stood stock-still for a long time while the room's cold white surfaces waited to echo the next person's speech.

Finally my father said softly to me, "Well, you can see I'm not going to die, can't you, Judge?"

"Yes," I said.

"You were just mistaken, weren't you?"

"Yes," I sniffed.

"In fact, look at me." He forced a smile and flexed his biceps in a mock muscleman pose. "The picture of health."

My mother sat down again. "Oh, yes," she said. "He's fine. Daddy's perfectly fine."

Without saying another word, my father stepped over to where my mother sat, lifted his leg like a dog about to urinate on a bush, and kicked her drink into the bathtub.

Against the echoing porcelain the ice cubes rang like rocks, the bourbon sprayed up and over the sides, and shards of glass slid up and down the tub's surface like deadly soap slivers.

As I watched my father walk away, I noticed how his shoulders rolled slightly from front to back, and I wondered if I would walk that way when I was an adult. My mother remained sitting on the tub but hung her head in her hands like a woman deep in grief.

Three

On the rare occasions when I had our house to myself, I prowled everywhere, looking into closets and drawers, under beds, behind furniture, under towels and sheets, on high shelves—anywhere something could be hidden. I was not looking for anything specific, only for secrets in general, for those furtive peeks into the lives of my parents or my sister. I wanted to know them, especially the parts they were not willing to offer openly, and these private sorties were the best way to gain that knowledge.

The knowledge I was seeking was no doubt sexual. I have a distinct memory of visiting Dwight Bartlett's home and having him show me two secret caches: his father's collection of yellowed, grainy French postcards, hidden under the mattress on his father's side of the bed; and his older sister's black lace bra and panties tucked under some sweaters in her dresser drawer. It was Dwight who urged me to find where my father kept his condoms. When I told Dwight I didn't believe my father had any, Dwight, an ignorant kid who was nonetheless able to reason certain things out for himself, said, "Sure, he's got some. They only got you and your sister, ain't they?"

On one of those days when I was alone in the house, a Saturday in March, I found Laura's book of poems.

I had not been looking for it, and it was not hidden, yet when I found it, I felt as though I had come across something forbidden and, more, as though I had found something alive in a place where everything was usually dead, the one breathing, eye-blinking animal in the museum of stuffed animals.

The book was in a knee-high pile on the floor of my parents' bedroom right next to my mother's vanity. The house's bookshelves could never contain my parents' books, and there were always little spillover stacks gathering on tables or cupboards or on the floor in out-of-the-way corners.

The book was small and thin and had a black dust jacket. Its only adornment was a curved, gray-white shape like a quarter moon resting on its horns, and like a quarter moon, it looked like the one thing in darkness on which light fell. When I looked closer, it seemed as though it might be skin, for it was dimpled and dimensional, like a bare shoulder, hip, or buttock, the only body part not in shadow. I looked carefully all over the rest of the cover for another faint line that might allow me to imagine the rest of the anatomy, but there was nothing. Above the white shape was the book's title, *Dreams a Woman Has,* and below, "Poems by Laura Coe Pettit."

On the book's back cover were the standard paragraphs of praise for Laura's poems. I didn't know any of the writers quoted, but they obviously held her work in high esteem and the jacket was lined with such phrases as, "an original voice," "not a poet of promise but one who has arrived," "a poet equally capable of shouting or whispering, singing or weeping." And the phrase that most intrigued me, "a fierce, almost frightening need to embrace the world and all that's in it."

Before I opened the book to look at the poems (the delay was a self-teasing attempt to heighten the pleasure I thought would be mine when I finally read the poems), I read the brief biographical note inside the back cover: "Laura Coe Pettit was born and raised in Pomona, California, and educated in its public schools. She attended the University of Southern California. She currently lives in New York City. This is her first book-length publication." In the note's stubborn reliance on impersonal, unrevealing facts, I thought I caught a glimpse of the woman who wanted to make herself over anew for every person she met. There was no photograph.

Preliminaries finally over, I sat on the floor at the foot of my parents' bed and opened the book.

I'm not sure what I expected to find. With the exception of an annual memorized poem in the classroom ("Trees" one year, "The Village Blacksmith" another), I had no experience with poetry. Perhaps I thought I would be stricken instantly, heart and head, as the words of the woman I loved leaped from the page at me. I knew she had written the book before we met, yet I half believed I would find myself on those pages, or at least a secret message only I could decode.

But the first poem right through to the last remained incomprehensible to me. Poem after poem I stared at as if it were one of those blownup photographs of everyday objects shot in such extreme close-up that the familiar—a flower's petal, a kitchen match, a thimble—seems as though it has dropped to earth from another planet. Finally, I stopped examining individual words of the poems and looked instead at their shape on the page, hoping to find some meaning in the way they quivered quick and snakelike down the page or squatted like blocks of stone. One poem had the same shape on the page as Minnesota's outline on a map, and for a moment I thought that might be a clue to its meaning.

Since they were often nothing more than numbers or dates, the titles were no help—"Poem #37," "August 14"—or abstractions—"Politics," "A Study in Economics," "Moral Philosophy."

I paged again through the book, going faster and faster, flipping back and forth, wondering if the single word that occasionally flashed to my eye might find some sense that my straining mind could not. I tried to circumvent thought and instead take meaning in through my senses.

The only words, however, that my eye caught were the ones that the sexually omnivorous preadolescent is always alert to—"breast," "flesh," "body," "hip," "belly," "mouth"—and an entire phrase almost impossible for my eye to leave, "moon-licked and thrice fallen, cock cannot find its new day." And once I stopped on these words, I searched their surroundings just as I had searched the front cover for the lines that revealed the rest of the body, the context that revealed meaning.

When I was finished, I did not put the book back in the pile. I took it to my bedroom and put it in my drawer under my socks, and the following Monday I brought *Dreams a Woman Has* to school with me.

HAD LAURA NOT already captured my heart, I might very well have succumbed that year to the charms of another older woman: Mrs. Schultz, my sixth-grade teacher.

Mrs. Schultz was a plump, big-bosomed young woman not much taller than the tallest boys and girls in the classroom. She spoke English with a German accent, and though she was pretty, she was especially well liked because she had an unfailingly cheerful disposition and because she was openly affectionate with her students. She hugged us, put her arms around our shoulders, and kissed us on the top of the head, on the cheek, or on the forehead. We knew she had been warned about these displays because after rewarding Morris Belter with a hug for one of his rare academic successes, she said, "Oh, and they said I shouldn't!" Morris was a tough, sullen, dirty, dull-witted boy on whom every other teacher had given up.

I waited until class was dismissed before showing Laura's book to Mrs. Schultz.

I walked up to her desk, lay the book in front of her, and said, "The person who wrote this is sort of a friend of mine."

"Oh, yes?" She picked up Laura's book and read the title and the author. "I didn't know you liked poems." The word "poems," as pronounced by Mrs. Schultz, had two distinct syllables.

Mrs. Schultz opened the book. "I haven't heard of this writer. Does she write good poems?"

"I guess so. I know her though, so it's kind of different."

"May I read?"

"Sure." I wasn't certain if she meant she wanted to borrow the book and I was to leave it with her, or if she simply wanted to read the poem on the page in front of her. Since it meant the book would stay in my sight, I decided to remain beside Mrs. Schultz's desk.

As she read, Mrs. Schultz swiveled a quarter turn so she faced the window instead of me. Meanwhile, I looked around the room, at the rows of desks, at the week's spelling words on the blackboard, and at the busy surface of Mrs. Schultz's desk. On top of one pile of papers was a drawing on manila paper of two World War II fighter planes. The planes were drawn to scale, carefully colored, and in a box in the upper left-hand corner it said, "To Mrs. Schultz from Gary Seagrave." Gary was a quiet, shy classmate. I was not the only one who sought to impress Mrs. Schultz.

When she had been reading so long I thought she was totally engrossed and had forgotten about me, Mrs. Schultz abruptly turned to me and asked, "How do you know this person?" She closed the book and held it upright, so I wasn't sure if I was supposed to take it back or not.

"I met her last summer in Vermont. When we were on vacation."

"She is a friend of your parents?"

Her expression was stern. I no longer felt I should insist on that relationship with Laura that moments ago I boasted about. "Yes."

"Do they know you have this book?"

"Yes."

Mrs. Schultz tapped the spine of Laura's book against her open palm. "I will tell you something, Paul. If you were my son, this is not a book I would want you to have. This is a wicked book. You're not my boy, but this is my classroom, and I have to insist that you don't bring it to school and show it to other boys and girls. Will you promise that you'll leave it at home?"

She held the book out for me to take it from her. I reached out slowly, trying to control my trembling hand. As I took the book from Mrs. Schultz, she repeated, "Do you promise?"

"I promise." I whispered my response because when I went to find my voice, it was not in my throat.

Mrs. Schultz's expression lightened. "You're a good boy, Paul. I know that."

As I walked from the room, my humiliation threatened to stagger me. Darkness edged all around my vision, caused, it seemed, by the blood that rushed to my head in an unceasing blush. I focused on the window in the classroom door, for I knew that once I got out into the hallway, I would be all right—the wire that bound my chest would snap, the weights attached to my legs would fall away, and I would run from the school so fast my breath would still be in the corridors after I was out the door.

I ran home that afternoon feeling as though I held in my hand some-thing powerful. It had to be to have caused Mrs. Schultz to react as she did. I vowed I would read the book again and again, read until I found both the greatness in the poems and the wickedness Mrs. Schultz spoke of.

And that evening I stayed in my room and struggled with Laura's poems. But again it was no use. Just as it is impossible to understand a foreign language without instruction, so it was beyond my power, beyond my intelligence and experience, to understand Laura's poems.

Nevertheless, as I put Laura's book back in my drawer, I felt not defeated but victorious, for throughout my ordeal with Mrs. Schultz I believed I had, in a way I couldn't explain, remained faithful to Laura.

Four

The following summer, for the first time in many years, we didn't go to Vermont. We didn't go because that summer my parents divorced. But that is stating it dramatically; more accurately, they separated in preparation for their divorce.

When the breakup came, many of my parents' friends were surprised, but these must have been the same people who, oblivious of the signs all around them, are astonished every year to find that winter has passed and spring arrived. And before my parents divorced, there were many signs. My father traveled on more and longer business trips, while my mother spent less and less time at school. Both of them drank more, and they did it deliberately, grimly, joylessly. Their glasses, empty but for the water left from the melted ice cubes, were abandoned everywhere around the house and always alongside an ashtray filled with the butts of only one brand of cigarette. They were always tired, without the energy to look beyond their own circumstances.

And, paradoxically, they quarreled less. They had always been a volatile pair, both of them prideful and quick to anger, and all too accurate in hurling insults in the other's direction. Yet these frequent fights indicated passion in their relationship, and when they

71

stopped quarreling, it was a sure sign that something was over for them.

In place of their quarrels, my father and mother filled the house with silences so long and deep they changed the way the dwelling itself felt. Hallways seemed longer and the distances between rooms greater. There seemed to be fewer pieces of furniture. The effect of all this, when a heavy footstep or a handclap threatened to send a violating echo through the house, was to make everyone quieter still.

I saw all these signs, though I wished I hadn't, and beyond that I also had access to private information. The night that my parents settled the question of their separation I overheard their conversation.

It was a night in late May, and I had gotten up at about two A.M. to use the bathroom. On the way back to my room, I noticed the door to my parents' room was partially open, and I heard them talking. Their voices were tired and low, as though they barely had the energy to speak, yet I still heard everything they said. My father once made clear to me the low regard he had for eavesdroppers, but I could not resist the temptation to listen in on this conversation.

My father asked, "Have you told Anne?"

From nothing more than those four words resignedly spoken—those words, the months of tension in the house, the temperaments of my mother and father inevitably suited not to complement but to clash, and the unasked-for but finally accepted awareness that even love can have a lifespan—I knew exactly what my parents were talking about:

My parents were going to be divorced, and my father wanted to know if my mother had yet notified her sister, Anne.

I was so certain I was right I could have walked away at that moment and not been troubled by doubt. But I did not. I wished more than anything that I had never heard what I did (and, by a child's illogic, therefore that the fact would not be so), yet, wounded by my own curiosity, I could not move away.

"I haven't told anyone," my mother answered. "How about you?"

"Allen. But he had a pretty good idea already. You know, he's a hell of a lot more perceptive than people give him credit for being."

"Since no one gives him any credit at all . . ." said my mother, and they both laughed softly.

At that moment I wanted to burst into the room, to scream at my parents, "Listen to yourselves! Listen to how you're getting along! You can be together! You can!"

Of course, that was my child's naivete. I didn't know that at that point my parents were no longer measuring their marriage by the moments when they enjoyed each other's company, but by the moments when they did not.

A match scratched, and then my mother sighed as she did when she exhaled cigarette smoke. "God, I'm not looking forward to that. Notifying the family."

"Sounds like an accident report, doesn't it? 'Notifying the next of kin.'"

"I just want to be done with it."

"That'll be the last hard thing," my father said. "The last."

"Promise?"

"After that, smooth sailing. Smooth sailing, baby."

My father, trying to console and reassure her, called my mother "baby." Neither before nor since that moment have I heard a sadder word.

Baby. On that word I slid away and back to my room. I closed my door silently, got back into bed, and pulled my pillow over my head until I was deaf to the world.

WHEN I GOT up the next morning, a Saturday, my father was in the kitchen making orange juice.

He looked as if he had not been to bed. He still wore the dark gray suit pants he had worn the day before, and though he wasn't wearing a tie, his white shirt was buttoned to the throat as if he were using that means to pull himself together. He was barefoot.

On the cupboard around him he must have had a dozen oranges, all sliced in half, and one at a time he placed the oranges on the dome of the squeezer, a heavy, foot-high steel-and-enamel affair with a lever that lowered weight onto the orange half and which, if you leaned hard enough and long enough, squeezed all the juice from the orange. The pulpy juice then trickled and dripped down into a glass trough at the base of the squeezer. On the cupboard on one side of the squeezer were the wrung-out orange rinds; on the other were the halves waiting to be squeezed.

"Good morning, Judge," he said heartily. "You want to be the first one at this juice?"

"I sort of have a sore throat, and orange juice might make it hurt worse."

"What? I'm doing all this for nothing? Fresh squeezed and every-thing?"

"I'll go ask Janie. She always wants orange juice." I turned to leave the room.

"Whoa! Just a minute, Judge."

I waited in the doorway.

"I don't think it would be a very good idea for you to go up there right now. Your mother and your sister are going to be having a little discussion this morning. You know, girl talk."

I didn't have to ask what they were going to talk about. My mother was going to tell Janie about the divorce. And who was going to tell me? I wanted to hurry from the room.

"Where are you going, Judge?"

"I was going to watch cartoons."

"Come on." My father leaned his weight down on another orange half. "Since when do you watch those things?"

"I still do sometimes."

"Why don't you come on in here. Keep me company while I fix break-fast. You want me to wreck some eggs for you?"

"I'm not really hungry." I took another step back. The room smelled so strongly of oranges I had a sharp, acidic taste in my mouth, and though I hadn't eaten or drunk anything, I felt my stomach puckering.

"Hold on, Judge." His voice changed from suggestion to command. "Come in here and sit down. There's something I want to talk to you about."

For an instant I thought of telling him not to bother, that I knew everything already. That would have freed both of us from something we each devoutly wished to get out of. I also considered racing from the room, running through the house until I found a corner to hide in. Yet I did neither because I knew, in the same way I knew at the onset of a childhood illness, that I was in the presence of something that could not be avoided but only endured.

Dutifully I sat down at the kitchen table, and as soon as I did, my father stopped mashing oranges. He went to the sink, washed the sticky juice from his hands, dried them, and poured himself a cup of coffee. "Throw me my cigarettes, would you, Judge?"

I tossed him his crumpled pack of Camels. While he probed for a cigarette, I thought, over and over, if you're going to tell me, do it, do it, do it now.

He finally began. "Do you want to go to that camp again this summer?"

"Not especially." Neither Janie nor I had ever made any secret of our dislike for French camp. It was really an ordinary summer camp but for the daily hourlong language lesson, and the French words we used for the food. *Pommes de terre frites*. Every night, *pommes de terres frites*. . . .

"All right. You don't want to go, you don't have to go."

"Thanks."

He waved his hand. "You don't have to thank me. In fact, the reason you don't have to go to French camp is"—he paused to inhale deeply—"is that a number of things will be different around here this summer."

"Is Janie going?"

"Not if she doesn't want to. That'll be up to her too."

"Are we still going to Vermont?" Since he was obviously having difficulty, I wanted to lead my father as quickly as possible down the trail to the point of our discussion.

"Kind of doubt it, Judge." He took a long swallow of coffee, holding his cup not by the handle but like a water glass. Then he rubbed his jaw, testing how badly he needed a shave. "Shit. . . . I've got to say this right out. Then you can ask questions if you like. All right?"

"Okay," I answered. I was still in my pajamas, and I hung my head and stared at the pattern of small blue biplanes across my lap.

"The thing is, Judge. This marriage, your mom's and my marriage, isn't working. Not the way it's supposed to. It's just out of whack or something." In 1956, the year this conversation took place, everything—

automobiles, washing machines, baseball players' contracts, marriages—was supposed to function properly and to last.

My father went on: "I guess I'm not telling you anything you don't know. We've tried to keep our problems to ourselves, but we haven't done a very good job of it. So, now we're going to try living apart for a while. We're going to have what they call a separation. Jesus, I'm talking to you like you're a baby. You know what a separation is. We're not saying right now we're getting a divorce. . . . But, hell, let's face it. Everybody says they're going to try separating for a while, but they always end up getting a divorce sooner or later. I don't want to kid you about this. This is probably it for your mom and me."

He was so tired he was honest. He didn't have the energy to wrap his message in tact.

Perhaps he was direct for another reason. I had the feeling, as he spoke, that my father was giving up on us, on him and me, on any remaining possibility that he and I might still have one of those traditional, playing-catch-in-the-yard, going-to-the-Harvard-Yale-game, teaching-me-how-to-drive-to-hunt-to-fish-to-drink-whiskey-pick-out-women-vote-Republican father-and-son relationships. Whatever our relationship was at that moment, it would never be more. And I don't believe my father was gladdened or saddened by this prospect; he simply saw what the future held and, for that reason, saw no need to soften or sweeten his words. Strangely, I was flattered.

"One of the things your mom and I agreed on," he continued, "is that if you don't want to tell anybody about this, you don't have to. I mean, your mom and I have tried not to advertise our problems, so if you want to keep it quiet, you won't get any trouble from us. You know what I'm saying?"

"You don't want me to tell anyone?"

He rubbed his eyes. "No, no. If you want to tell people, go ahead. Shout it from the rooftops if you like. I'm just saying that if you don't want to talk about it, you don't have to. That's all."

I didn't know anyone whose parents were divorced, and I wondered where I would find a model to help me with my new role. Should I be ashamed? Angry? Melancholy?

"You're pretty quiet, Judge. I know I'm throwing an awful lot your way all at once. Maybe I better slow down and give you a chance to ask questions."

Before I even knew I had decided to ask, the question was out. "Is Miss Pettit going to be our new mother?"

The sudden clatter on the back porch meant the milkman had arrived with the glass bottles rattling in his steel rack. He was always late on Saturday, and now he would open the milkbox, see that my mother had left no dairy slip, and then he would knock on the back door to ask if we were sure we didn't want anything, and my father would turn away to talk to the milkman and never answer my question.

The lid of the milkbox fell, the milkman turned and went back down the steps, and my father said, "Jesus Christ, Judge. Where did you get an idea like that?"

"I thought you liked her."

"Liked her? Well, yeah . . . I do like her, but Christ! That doesn't mean I'm going to marry her. She's half my age. You know that, don't you?"

"Yes." Closer to my age I might have said.

"I mean, she and I have a drink when she's in town. We have some laughs, gossip a little, argue about politics. . . . But hell, she's your mother's friend too."

"Who is?" I looked up as my mother came through the kitchen door, her pale blue peignoir moving about her as though she were the only one the wind could find.

"How's it going upstairs?" asked my father.

"We haven't gotten to it yet. Who's my friend?"

"What's taking so long?"

"Let me do this my way, all right?" My mother poured a cup of coffee.

"Do you want me to come up?"

She ignored his offer. "Who were you talking about when I came in, Paul?"

I glanced at my father. "Miss Pettit."

"And how did her name happen to come up?" she asked my father.

"Janie's got to be told," he said. "If you can't tell her—"

My mother tossed her head impatiently from side to side, a gesture I imagined her using in the classroom when she was exasperated with her students. "I want to fill her in on some background, all right? There's some history here, and I'd like her to know about it, all right? Who knows, it might be useful to her someday."

I said, "Dad said Miss Pettit was your friend too."

My mother looked directly at my father. "Yes, that's so. I believe however that at this point it would be fair to say she's more your father's friend." Then she turned and walked out of the room.

For a long time after she left, my father said nothing, but I knew he was trying to hold on to his temper. Finally he said, "Judge, have you heard me speak against your mother to you or your sister?"

"No."

"That's right. I've made it a point not to, and now she's probably up there poisoning the well as far as your sister's concerned." He shook his head sadly. "So now I'm going to tell you something, and then that's going to be it. You'll never hear anything like this from me again."

I tried to look very serious.

"Yes, I've been out with Laura Pettit a few times, and if I have anything to say about it, we'll go out some more. But that's all that will happen; it's not going to get serious." He pointed his finger at me for emphasis. "And that's not my idea either. If I had my way . . . Well, I'll tell you, Judge. She's a very interesting woman. I've never known anyone quite like her."

"What's interesting about her?" I asked eagerly.

"Oh, I don't know," he answered distractedly, his mind drifting away from the woman with whom he was angry—my mother—and floating to the woman whom he wished, I could tell, to be with. "For one thing, she's a very independent, self-reliant person. She's used to making it on her own. She's an orphan, did you know that, Judge? Her parents were killed in a car accident when she was a baby, and she grew up living with relatives and in foster homes. And that's a tough way to grow up in this world, isn't it?"

I nodded in agreement. "Independence," "self-reliance," "toughness"—when he used those words my father was talking about qualities he prized above all others. In fact, he liked to pretend that he grew up with those traits ingrained in his own character, but my father always seemed to be a man of privilege, someone to whom everything had come easily.

"But there's something else about her," he went on. "Something hard to describe. One minute she acts as if you're the only person in the world she cares about, and the next minute she doesn't give a damn. And when she cools off like that, why, that's when you start falling all over yourself to get back in her good graces. It's hard to explain. . . . She can be a very moody person, Judge."

"Does she have a lot of boyfriends?"

"No. She says her work, her writing, is the most important thing in her life, and I believe her. But if she wanted boyfriends, believe me, she wouldn't have any trouble in that regard." He stopped talking and abruptly crushed out his cigarette. When he spoke again, his voice was louder, edgier. "But I was going to tell you something about your mother. I don't want all this talk about Laura Coe Pettit to give you the impression that she or anyone else is the reason your mother and I are separating. The reason, plain and simple, is that we can't get along.

"I know you don't understand," he said. "Maybe you will." He got up from the table and started cleaning up the mess from the orange juice, dumping all the oranges, sliced and unsliced, into the garbage. "And maybe you won't."

He carried the freshly squeezed juice itself, a tall glass three-quarters full, to the sink and stopped, the glass held poised above the drain. "You sure you don't want any of this?"

I shook my head. "Where are you going to live?" I asked him. I had a vision of my father staying permanently at one of the downtown hotels, perhaps the one where visiting baseball teams stayed when they came to play the Red Sox. I'd visit my father and in the hotel lobby I'd see Mickey Mantle, Jim Lemon, Roy Sievers, Bobby Shantz, Nellie Fox . . .

My father poured the orange juice down the drain. "Oh, Christ, I knew I wasn't doing this right." I thought he was talking about the orange juice until he turned around to face me. "Judge, I'm sorry. I should have told you this right away. I'm going to stay here, in the house.

At least for a while. Later we might try to sell it. But you and your mother and your sister are going to stay with Grandpa and Grandma Madden in Minnesota. I'm sorry I didn't tell you that right away."

His apology didn't help. Immediately I began to cry, and the salty tears that ran down my cheeks mixed with the room's bitter smell of oranges, so that my tears seemed to turn to acid. I had known, I thought, everything, and now this, this surprise, this trick that showed me how quickly the world could cave in and how I could not prevent it. I cried because I would be leaving my friends, my school, my house, because I would never see them again, because I would never see Laura again. I was a child, and any adult of any size could pick me up and carry me out of my own life.

My father dropped to his knees beside my chair. He put his hands on my ribs and shook me gently, lovingly, back and forth as if I were a baby that needed to be jollied from his tears. "Don't, Judge, please don't. Oh, Jesus, don't. This is hard enough."

And then he started crying too, his own tears brimming over and streaking his cheeks like raindrops running down a windowpane. And just as the rain distorts the view through the window glass, so was my father's face contorted by his crying. He put his arms around me, bumping his hand hard against the back of the chair. He let his head fall forward into my lap, so I could no longer see his misshapen face; but from the way his back bounced, as though he had hiccups, I could tell his sobs continued. I patted the back of his head, right where his thinning hair let the skin show through. It was the first and last time I saw my father cry.

There we sat, weeping over our separation to come, but for now closer than we had ever been. Finally, exhaustion and embarrassment caught up with both of us, and we sniffled to a stop at the same time.

My father looked up at me, his eyes glistening and his eyelashes stuck together in little spikes. "But this isn't going to happen right away, Judge. We'll still have most of the summer together. We're going to see the Red Sox. In fact, we'll keep going to ball games until Teddy hits one out. What do you say to that? Even if it takes all season. Even if he doesn't hit one until September."

* * *

AS IT HAPPENED, we didn't get to a ball game until a Sunday in mid-July, an overcast day so oppressively humid Fenway Park seemed to have a lid on it. Even though my father had long since forgotten his promise that we would attend games until Ted Williams hit a home run, on that day Williams ironically hit a three-run homer off White Sox pitcher Billy Pierce in the bottom of the first. That was the start of a rout so complete that by the seventh inning the Red Sox were up by eleven runs, and we left early, with thunder rumbling around Boston like a train that couldn't stop circling the city.

It stood to reason that you wouldn't have to attend many Red Sox games before seeing Ted Williams hit a home run, and it was just as well we didn't have to wait until season's end because by mid-August I was living in Fairmont, Minnesota, a town of fewer than ten thousand people. Fairmont was the home of Afton College, a small, private school where my grandfather, Philip Madden, was dean of men.

But I am getting ahead of myself. Before we moved, something happened that thrilled me but also perplexed me: I received a letter from Laura.

I have saved that letter for all these years. The pale blue paper has faded to a grayish-white, the only remaining blue along the paper's creases and faintly around the typewritten letters themselves, as though their black ink has bled to blue. The letter was single-spaced, and though it was typed, it still had a crammed, messy look, full of strikeovers and inked-in insertions.

Dear Paul,

I hear in a letter from your dad that your family is having some difficulties. I'm very sorry. I can sympathize because that happened in my family. My parents were divorced when I wasn't any older than you.

I remember how tough that period of my life was. But things gradually got better. I was also insufferably somber much of the time. Don't forget to laugh. And don't forget that both your mom and dad love you, even if they don't live under the same roof. The big news in my life is that I no longer live alone. I'm now sharing my little apartment with Evan. Evan is part German shepherd and part husky, and he loves potato chips. He'll eat anything, but potato chips are his favorites. He's very gentle (even with strangers—he'd make a terrible watchdog). If you ever come to New York, call me and we'll go out for hamburgers (my treat), and we'll take Evan for a long walk.

Yours,
Laura

I read the letter so many times it was no longer accurate to say I was reading it; I studied it, the way a scholar studies a text, turning each word over and over until it gives up all its meaning. In her closing sentence, for example, Laura had said "long walk" and not merely "walk." Was that because only a long walk would do for all we had to talk over? And had she known that my heart would stop when she said she was sharing her apartment with Evan—only to start beating again in the next sentence when she revealed he was a dog? Was she serious in her invitation for me to call her if I ever visited New York, or was she only being polite? No matter that the letter was innocuous, mundane, an adult's awkward effort to communicate with a child on a child's level, I pored over it ceaselessly.

Oddly enough, I passed quickly over the lie. In her letter to me she said her parents were divorced; to my father she said she was an orphan. Certainly both were possible; her parents may have divorced first then died. That, however, was not how I accounted for it. I simply assumed she lied to both of us, but lied *for* us rather than for herself. My father wanted to believe she was self-sufficient, so she made herself an orphan. I needed to believe that she and I shared some experience, so she concocted a different story for me.

I began that afternoon to write back to Laura, but since I had trouble filling the page, three days passed before I finished the letter. It went through so many drafts I think I knew it by heart when I finally finished it. I tried very hard to sound stoic and worldly in the letter, and the final effect was ludicrous.

Dear Laura,

Thank you for your letter. You don't have to worry about me. I'm no stranger to rough times. I've gone through them before, and I guess I've learned something about how to get by. I'm glad you have a dog, especially a big dog. They can be a comfort when you live alone in a big city. I hardly ever get to New York. If I do, I'll call you. Thank you again for writing.

Yours truly,
Paul Finley

Unsurprisingly, considering the B-movie language and pose I struck, Laura didn't write back.

WHEN IT WAS TIME for us to leave for Minnesota, my grandfather came to pick us up with his station wagon and a borrowed trailer. My father, grandfather, and I did the packing, and before we were finished, when some of our possessions were still sitting on the sidewalk in the bright August sunlight, it became obvious that we would not have room for everything. Either we could get all our belongings into the station wagon and trailer and have no room left for mother, Janie, and me, or we could leave some things behind.

My mother stood next to the curb shaking her head. "No," she said, "no. I'm not leaving anything. I want these things with me." Though her father was present, my mother had been drinking, and the alcohol had washed away any trace of flexibility or good sense.

"Jesus, Doreen," said my father. "I can ship some of this to you. Books. I can ship those cheaply enough."

"It all goes," repeated my mother. "Nothing stays here, not for one more day."

My father, who had been especially tolerant and careful around my mother since they decided to separate, merely shrugged. "Okay, we'll try rearranging some of this stuff to see if we can't get it all in."

My grandfather, a mild, taciturn man who doted on my mother and also liked my father, silently set to helping my father unpack the trailer so they could try a new arrangement.

It was no use. The boxes and trunks full of books and clothes, the dishes and bric-a-brac, the newspaper-wrapped antiques and prints, and the few pieces of furniture—Mother's antique desk and her high-backed rocking chair—could not be made to fit, yet my mother's insistence that nothing be left behind was as unyielding as the trailer's limited space.

Finally, a solution was reached, though it was neither practical nor inexpensive. All our belongings would be loaded into the station wagon and trailer, and since doing that wouldn't leave room in the car for anyone but Grandfather, it was decided that Janie, Mother, and I would take the train to Minnesota. Actually, my mother decided that, and my father could not reason her out of it. Grandfather didn't even try; he stood off to the side and watched my parents argue. It may have been my imagination, but I thought that just as the argument was ending he gave my father a sad, knowing look that said, see, if you'd learned as I did long ago to let her have her way, none of this would have happened, and I'd be in my garden in Minnesota and all these possessions would be in your house where they belong. There was some discussion about us flying to Minnesota, but Mother ruled that out. That would be too expensive, even though my father was going to pay transportation costs; besides, if we flew, we would arrive before our belongings, and for some reason Mother did not want that.

WE WERE TWO full nights and one day on the train, and on the second night, since I couldn't sleep, I sat up alone in the Vista-Dome. I looked out at the farmlands of Illinois and Indiana and thought how boring the landscape seemed with its tireless repetition of bare hills and flat fields. Occasionally I would turn away or close my eyes for a few moments, and when I looked out again, the scene would seem unchanged, and I began to feel that no matter how long we rode, no matter how hard the train steamed and clattered through the night, we would get nowhere. Towns passed by so quickly they seemed nothing more than a flashlight shone in the train's window. Outside the towns, the only illumination came from an occasional farm's yard light, burning through the night's distance and darkness like a torch. Why were they on? I wondered. Why would a farm family leave a bright, exterior light on all night? Eventually I reached a conclusion that matched my desolate, uprooted mood. They were waiting for someone to come home, someone who had been gone a long time and who might never return, and this light was to guide him home.

Oh, I was full of self-pity as only a twelve-year-old could be. I felt I was the only child who had ever been forced to move, to leave behind his house, his neighborhood, his city, his friends. In an outpouring of romantic remorse, I even pretended I would miss the ocean. Never again would I stand on the beach, the sand fleeing beneath my feet, and look out over the limitless waves. In truth, we had seldom visited the seaside, and the only time I had actually been on the ocean was three years earlier, when we had visited the Randalls who were summering at Martha's Vineyard and David Randall took my father and me sailing. Nevertheless, the ocean was there, and with Boston bumped up against it my world was enclosed. Now, however, I was headed for the Midwest and its plains, where, as if I were lost at sea, I would be exposed to nothingness on every side.

The truth was, I knew, and would have admitted if pressed, that I would see my father again, that I had no friends who were irreplaceable, and that I would someday stand on another ocean's strand. But I had no idea how I would see Laura again, and there my sorrow was genuine and inconsolable. I pressed my hand against the observation car's window—the glass cooled by the cooling night—and whispered to the night that I would keep Laura's memory, keep it burning like the yard lights at those lonely farms. Then my mother found me and insisted I return to our compartment.

Five

ven if I had been willing to forget Laura, it would have been impossible, and strangely, paradoxically, it was my mother who repeatedly spoke the name of Laura Coe Pettit. If Laura published an article or a book, if she made a public appearance, if someone prominent mentioned her name, my mother somehow knew of it and notified the rest of us. She made these announcements as calmly, as nonchalantly, as she might comment on any minor item in the news. She would note that Laura had a poem in *The Atlantic Monthly* with no more emotion than she would mention that a city street was going to be widened. Only once did my mother rise to anger at Laura's name and then not for the reason you might expect. When my mother, Janie, and I were out for a Sunday drive with Grandfather, my mother remarked that "a friend of ours has a review in *The New York Times Book Review*." Janie said, "You mean Daddy's friend," and Mother snapped back, "She's my friend too!"

How did it happen that my mother could bear to contemplate—much less to speak about—a woman who had contributed to the dissolution of her marriage without being overcome by sorrow, jealousy, or rage? I have puzzled over this for years. Could Laura's powers have somehow worked on my mother as they worked on others, enchanting her and stanching her anger before it could flow through her being? That was doubtful. My mother had too much of the realist's self-knowledge to fall under anyone's spell.

Did she talk about Laura simply to demonstrate that she could? That was improbable, since there was no one around to whom my mother had anything to prove.

Was she simply so proud to know someone of Laura's stature that she was willing to set jealousy aside so she could continue to claim a relationship with a well-known poet? This explanation didn't play well. My parents had always known famous people, and fame alone did not impress them.

Was my mother perhaps forcing herself to utter Laura's name, thereby trying to demonstrate that she was above bitterness, that Doreen Finley could not be undone by another woman? No, my mother was not that good an actor; I saw no evidence of a clenched jaw as she made these announcements about Laura and her career.

My best explanation for Mother's ability to speak Laura's name without rancor grew out of the change that I observed in my mother after we moved to Minnesota.

Once she took up residence again in the home she had lived in as a child, she seemed to find a long-lost ease and comfort in her own life. She allowed her mother and father to do things for her just as she must have when she was a girl. Grandmother handled all the major domestic duties, while mother helped in a child's way—making her bed, setting and clearing the table, sweeping the kitchen. My grandfather was able to get her a job at the college teaching one or two classes a semester. He bought her a used car, a white Studebaker, and kept up its maintenance. And he saw to it that all the bills were paid. Yet all this pampering only brought out the best in my mother. She stopped drinking and no longer seemed tense, confused, or unsure of herself. Perhaps strangest of all, my mother, who had always been social, who needed to have others around, was able to enjoy her own company. If you found her sitting on the front porch steps staring into the distance, it was not in spiteful brooding or drunken reverie but in peaceful contemplation.

It was unlikely that place alone could have wrought such a transfor-
mation. So the conclusion was inescapable: my mother's disposition
improved not because she lived in a different house but because she no
longer lived with my father.

She certainly never expressed gratitude at being out of the marriage.
Even if she felt that way, she owed some loyalty to the years she and my
father had spent in each other's company.

So perhaps it made a certain kind of sense that my mother's anger
toward Laura would dissolve in the wash of relief she felt at being out of
her marriage. And perhaps she saw no reason to single out Laura for
resentment. There had been other women in my father's life. Laura had
only been the most recent.

Whatever the reason, Mother found it possible to speak of Laura and
her accomplishments, and when she did, Grandmother and Grandfather
were politely interested. Janie was indifferent, and I, though I tried to
pretend indifference, had a ravenous desire to know more. As it was,
there was much to know, for in the two years following our move to
Minnesota, Laura no longer owed her fame only to those who read (or
read about) poetry. She approached the status of true celebrity, known
more for being known than for any deeds or accomplishments.

She published another volume of poetry, *Looking into Black Water*. Its
title came from the image that opens the book: a woman driving across
a bridge stops her car and gets out to stare down at the river. *Looking* was
a book-length narrative poem about a woman who has a nervous break-
down, recovers with the help of her husband and family, but finally
chooses madness again. Though the book didn't have the sensational
impact of *Dreams a Woman Has*, it was critically well-received and further enhanced Laura's reputation.

The publication, however, that did the most to spread the name of
Laura Pettit was her best-selling collection of essays *Walking the Night to
Dawn*, a book that prefigured the feminist movement of the 1960s.
These pieces, some as long as twenty pages, some no longer than a para-
graph, were inspired by the walks Laura took every night through the
streets of New York or any other city, town, or countryside she happened
to be in. She walked late, often in that hour when night melted into

dawn, and her writing was full of early morning imagery—which birds sang earliest, how fog began in the vacant lots and spread out over the city, which corners the paperboys waited on for the trucks with the stacked, bundled newspapers, how cops handled drunks and derelicts, the way shopkeepers arrived early to shovel their sidewalks on snowy mornings—and though the shortest pieces were pure imagery, the longest ones began with a particular sight but went on to reflect on social, political, philosophical matters. She was mugged once, sexually threatened more than once, and almost arrested. These incidents led to essays, one about street crime and one that discussed a woman's lack of freedom on America's streets.

As she walked, she thought, and the pieces in this collection were often as random as her travels. She was as likely to turn down a street leading her to a series of speculations on modern literature—Hemingway came under attack again—as she was to enter a park and meditate on religious experiences. In another essay, a conversation with a prostitute inspired a look at modern relationships, especially at the wife's role in marriage.

It was this collection that caused her to be regarded, as one critic said, "as a voice we can rely on to tell us the truth about ourselves," and she was often sought out for her views on a number of subjects, from political candidates to movie stars, from civil rights issues to the ban-the-bomb movement. She was always willing to offer an opinion, and journalists found her good copy.

This book was the first of Laura's I was able to read and understand. Unlike her poetry, which was spare, intense, cryptic, and full of references and allusions to a symbolic system to which I had no access, her essays were plainspoken and straightforward, as clear as Minnesota springwater. I was thirteen years old when this book came out, and though I probably wasn't able to understand everything the author intended, I nevertheless felt these essays spoke directly to me. I read *Walking* over and over and continued to search for some reference to me or my family. But I looked in vain. Finally, I decided that if I couldn't find any place where Laura had put me in her book, I would try to take the book inside me.

It was simple enough to let her opinions (for the most part liberal, with a few crankily conservative views on art and education) be mine, but I wanted to do more. I tried to imitate the actions that inspired the book. If I walked the streets at the same hours she did, if I contemplated the same sights, perhaps, I clumsily reasoned, perhaps something that breathed in Laura would breathe in me.

Laura often walked at dawn, but she had usually been awake all night before going out. That was impossible for me, so I set my alarm and came at dawn from the other end. For ten months I rose early, usually before anyone else in the house, and walked. In the summer I awoke so early the previous day's heat sometimes still hadn't broken, and the air had a heavy, yeasty smell like an open oven that has been baking bread. I was out early on fall mornings when every blade of grass bristled with frost. I walked on dark winter mornings before the plows were out or the wind picked up, and snow left the town as pathless as the woods. I stopped going out in the spring but not before being out on a morning when, even in the predawn chill, you felt that on that day the sun would finally warm earth and everyone on it.

Predictably, I remained uninspired. I was, after all, an adolescent who walked the streets at dawn searching for something I wasn't capable of recognizing, and while I may have been looking outward all the time, I always kept watch on myself, trying to see if I was becoming worthy of Laura. And that motive guaranteed that I would never see any of what she saw.

Of the many things written and said about Laura after the publication of *Walking*, my favorite was an article that appeared in *Life* magazine. This was the same issue in which the famous Thorpe photograph of her first appeared. In the black-and-white photograph she is sitting backward on a wooden chair, her legs straddling it, her bare feet up on the rungs, one arm along the chair's high back, the other hand holding a cigarette between thumb and forefinger. The camera is to the side, and Laura has turned to face the photographer. She looks tired, her dark eyes sunken and shadowed, and she is not smiling. In fact, she looks angry; her mouth is open and the words frozen on her lips could be "stop," "don't," "go away." Her hair is cut bluntly short, and in the next instant she'll brush it back from her face and tuck it behind her ears. The photograph must have been taken in summer because she's tanned. Right after she pulls back her hair, she'll lick her pale, dry lips. She is wearing a dark T-shirt and faded jeans. The thin arm projecting from the shirt-sleeve looks lightly muscled, and if she were not holding a cigarette, showing off that shadow of muscle might be the reason for her pose. Her T-shirt—hers? it looks like a man's—is tucked into her jeans, and her posture on the chair makes her waist look narrow and her breasts full. The photograph's full, magical effect is of a young, strong, intelligent, sensual, slightly dissolute, self-assured, and totally free woman. I'm sure I was not the only male in America in love with that picture. And I'm sure I was not the only male in America intimidated by it.

The *Life* article gave me more than an image. It helped me add details to my own portrait of Laura.

The article said, for example, that her parents were killed in a car accident in northern Nevada when Laura was seven years old. She and her brother had been in the car at the time of the accident, and she distinctly remembered being lifted from the overturned wreck and being carried away by a man in a green-and-black-plaid wool shirt. She said that if she closed her eyes, she could still recall perfectly the texture of his rough wool shirt on her cheek. Laura was not seriously hurt in the accident, but her brother's leg was broken so badly he limped forever after. She and her brother were subsequently raised in Los Angeles by their grandmother.

Laura also revealed why she took such a keen interest in the problems of America's criminal justice system. Her brother was imprisoned—where and for what crime she refused to say, and though she would not discuss any of the circumstances of his crime, she insisted that his continued incarceration was unjust. She spent a significant amount of time, she said, writing letters on his behalf. (I remembered his name: Edward, who put the scar under Laura's eye.)

Laura's famously misquoted remark—"Writing is like drowning"—came from this article. What she actually said was that writing reminded her of something that happened when she was a girl. She was at a lake with friends, and they were all swimming out to a raft. Laura felt herself tiring, and for an instant, she feared she might drown. She knew she would not—the raft wasn't far, the lake wasn't deep, her friends were near—yet the fear still struck her. That, she said, was what writing was like: knowing rationally you won't drown but feeling the fear anyway. And continuing to go in the water knowing what you will inevitably feel.

All the information, all the material I collected about Laura I hid. The oak dresser I used in my grandparents' house had four deep drawers, and the top drawer had a shallow tray that fit over the rest of the interior. In the tray I kept the handkerchiefs that my grandmother and mother insisted that I have, but which I never carried. Under the tray, however, was my secret storage bin. There I kept a pack of rum-soaked Crooks cigars that a friend stole from Land's Rexall; the neat little square of blue foil that held a condom; a stag-handled, rusty-bladed hunting knife I found in the woods; a copy of *Argosy* magazine with a lurid article about a San Francisco vice cop; and a baseball autographed by the Red Sox. And copies of Laura's books, the article from *Life* magazine, her letter, and any other clippings that held her name. There was no reason for me to hide everything that pertained to Laura, no reason but my own guilt.

I DON'T WISH to give the wrong impression. I was not as heartsick and miserable in Minnesota as I wanted and pretended to be, and outwardly I wasn't much different from other boys. Their interests were generally my interests, and those that weren't, I tried to embrace. We were busy, in season, with baseball, football, basketball, and hockey, with hiking the woods and fishing the lakes, streams, and rivers. Few of the boys I hung around with cared about schoolwork, and I tried to adopt their academic nonchalance, but in truth, I did my homework, handed my assignments in on time, studied for exams, and remained a good student, traitor to the adolescent cause. My friends and I were interested in cars, and when we could, we gathered at the garage of Lannie Bishop, a high school boy who was rebuilding a 1938 Ford. (Forever rebuilding; I don't recall that he ever drove his car out of the garage.) And certainly we were interested in girls. Together we talked of girls, of women, in the leering, boastful, anatomically inaccurate way that boys have. (In my defense, I listened more than I talked.) Collectively we talked about "pieces of ass." Yet singly we often dreamed of nothing more than holding hands. Our mouths were vulgar, but our souls were romantic.

Yet in one fundamental way I was different. At that age boys have one love attachment after another, picking up and dropping infatuations like fistfuls of candy too large for their hands to hold. But I had none. I remained Laura's constant lover. And how ludicrous that term is to apply to a boy in love with a grown woman he barely knows and whom he has not seen for over two years! It was not natural, and anyone, boy or man, who holds on to a love that hopeless is sooner or later going to be in emotional difficulty. Even then I knew it, but could do nothing. As a result, I was losing something during this period of my life, some capacity for feeling. I don't know any other way to explain it. What else can it be when a boy can't feel for those near enough to touch—the soft, pink, crisp, clean young girls wrapped in their soft, pink sweaters or tucked into their crisp, clean blouses—because he is saving himself for someone impossibly distant, out of reach in every way? I couldn't help it; the girls my age, despite being frequently wrapped in pastel, seemed hopelessly drab compared to Laura.

Then one day when I was fourteen years old, two-and-a-half years after our move to Minnesota, the news arrived. In early January my father was coming for one of his visits. And Laura was the reason why.

As the letter explained to my mother, who explained it to Janie and me, Laura had an interview for a teaching job at the University of Minnesota, and my father planned to fly out with her, rent a car, and drive down to Fairmont to see us. I decided God would not let Laura come so near to me without allowing me to see her.

JANUARY WAS UNSEASONABLY warm that year. Chinook winds blew their warm breath down the eastern slopes of the Rockies and melted their way across Montana and the Dakotas until they found us. The pre-Christmas drifts shrunk rapidly, and soon the only snow was in the shelter of the woods, the ditches, or in the sun-forsaken shade of houses and barns. I watched daily for my father (he gave us three possible days when he might arrive), and when the mounds of snow I had made when I shoveled the sidewalks and the driveway had melted down to what looked like small piles of dirty rags, my father appeared.

He drove up on a bright, glittering Saturday afternoon when water ran through the gutters and the day sang a song of early spring. Janie was the first to see him, and from the upstairs window where she must have been keeping watch, she called out, "Dad's here!"

I ran to the porch and then went no farther. From there I watched as my father stood in the street in front of his car. He bent over stiffly as if he were trying to pull a knot out of his lower back. Then he straightened up quickly, rolled his shoulders inside his sport coat until it hung properly, shot his cuffs, and came toward the house with those long strides that seemed to match each block in the sidewalk.

When he saw me, he dropped his arms to his sides, palms turned out, and said, "Judge. For Christ's sake. What are they feeding you?"

My father had last seen me the summer before, but in that six-month interim I had grown almost five inches and gained thirty pounds. (In our first three years in Minnesota I grew eleven inches and reached, before I was fifteen, my adult height of six feet two inches.)

I couldn't do anything but shrug my shoulders and grin.

Janie ran down the stairs, and when my father saw her, he said, "Ah, there she is—there's my Penguin! Come over here and let me give you a hug. And be quick about it!"

Janie, as she never did when we all lived in the same house, went directly to him, threw her arms around him, and my father lifted her in an embrace. Over her shoulder he said to me, "I don't want you trying this on me, Judge. You might crush me." When he put her down, he said, "But you can shake my hand."

For the first time I noticed how large my father's hands were. They were wide, square, and cold, and it felt as though I had my hand on a slab of beef right from the butcher's freezer.

My mother joined our conclave by the front door. She was wearing a pair of old, baggy brown wool slacks and a mottled, pale blue, stretched-out shetland cardigan that once belonged to my grandfather. Even as Saturday attire the outfit was uncharacteristically sloppy for my mother, and I thought she must have been sending my father a message: Look at my clothes; see how little your coming means to me? In contrast, my father was wearing a black-and-white-houndstooth-check jacket, a white shirt open at the throat, a red sweater vest, and dark gray slacks.

"Doreen," my father said, "what's going on with this weather? I come out to Minnesota expecting to freeze my ass, and it feels like spring."

"It's crazy, I know," she replied. "It's been like this for days. It's all anybody can talk about."

"And who's complaining? If I know the Norwegians around here, they're still finding something to complain about."

My mother laughed. "The ice fishermen!"

"I knew it!" He snapped his fingers. "I knew somebody wouldn't be satisfied."

"Where are your glasses?" my mother asked. I thought the question was odd, since my father didn't wear glasses.

"I left them in the car," he answered.

"But you wore them while you were driving?"

My father raised his right hand as if he were taking an oath. "I wore them while I was driving."

I didn't know which revelation I found more significant—that my father wore glasses or that my mother and father had been communicating often enough for her to know that he now wore glasses.

"How about these two?" My father hung an arm on Janie and me. "They're getting so big they're making me feel like an old man." By now my initial excitement had diminished. Other people talked about the weather and how much we had grown; from my father I expected something more original and interesting.

My father continued, "No wonder their clothes cost me a fortune."

"They're not doing this on purpose, Robert."

"Did I say they were?"

My mother took a quick sideways step as if she were getting out of the way. "We have fresh coffee—"

"Now, that sounds like just the thing. Where are Phil and Glenna?"

"They went to the grocery store."

"So—it's just the four of us."

"Just the four of us," repeated my mother. Though each of them spoke precisely the same words I heard in their voices the opposing sounds of anticipation and regret, of hope and resignation, of sorrow and relief. The trouble was, in that complexity of tones, I didn't know to whom those feelings should be assigned.

LATER THAT AFTERNOON my grandparents returned, and at first, just as they did every time my father visited, they stayed away from him like little animals frightened by his size and the volume of his voice. Grandfather had some work in the garage he had to attend to; Grandmother insisted on baking an apple pie—without anyone's help. Gradually, however, they settled down and by that evening all four of them were sitting at the dining room table playing bridge and drinking Grandmother's coffee, which was, my father said, the best in the world. It was at that table, over cards, coffee, and apple pie, that they discussed my father's proposal. How would it be, he wondered, if he took Janie and me up to Minneapolis for a couple days and then brought us back? He made no attempt to hide the fact that Laura would be there, but said she would be busy at the university. My mother pointed out the obvious, that Janie and I would miss school. No matter, my father replied, the trip itself would be educational; he'd see to it we went to a museum, and he'd buy us each a book. Grandfather, Grandmother, and my mother agreed readily to his suggestion once mother mused that it would be good for us to have some time with our father. That done, they called Janie and me into the room to see how we felt about it. I had already heard everything; I had been in the kitchen pretending to be doing my homework, but I was actually listening.

Of course we wanted to go, and the plans were set. The next morning, Sunday, we would leave on the 180-mile trip to Minneapolis, and we would return on Tuesday.

That night, however, something happened that put the trip in jeopardy.

During the night I woke up because I heard what I thought at first was Grandmother's cat Buster, hurt outside in a fight and now meowing to be let in. But the sound was more like a kitten's, mewing over and over for its mother. I listened carefully and finally determined where it was coming from. In the room next to mine Janie was crying. I got out of bed and walked down the hall to my mother's room.

At the door I called softly, "Mom? Janie's crying." There was no response, so I tried again, this time a little louder. "Mom, something's wrong with Janie."

Still no answer. I pushed the door open and peered in. The blankets were thrown back, and her bed was empty. I was about to go down to the other end of the hall to wake my grandmother, when I noticed a light on downstairs. I went down.

My mother and father were in the living room sitting on opposite ends of the sofa. Each was in robe and pajamas, and my father was smoking and holding a jelly glass with a couple inches of, I assumed, whiskey. Resting on the table next to my father was a pair of black, horn-rimmed glasses I had never seen before.

When I came into the room, both of them looked up so furtively I almost backed out and tried another entrance. "Mom, Janie's crying."

Without saying a word she ran quickly up the stairs. My father stood but did not leave the room. For a long time we faced each other in uncomfortable silence, neither of us with the training or emotion to help us through the moment.

Then the furnace kicked in, the house lurched, and the warm breath coming from the hot air register melted some of the silence's sharpest edges.

"Did she sound as though she was in pain?" my father asked.

"I couldn't really tell. I think so."

"Probably just a stomachache. Too much of your grandmother's pie." He sat back down and motioned to the chair across from him. "Sit down, Judge. Nothing we can do but wait and see, so we might as well be comfortable."

I hesitated, and he quickly added, "Unless you want to go back to bed? There's no reason for you to wait up."

"No, that's okay." I sat down.

"Are you playing basketball this year? It looks like you've got the size for it."

"A few guys are taller than me."

"But you are playing?"

"Yeah."

"What position?"

"Forward."

"Tough position. You have to be able to do it all—rebound, pass, shoot, play good defense. I was always glad they stuck me in the pivot. You ever have a chance to use that hook shot I showed you?"

"Just in practice. I haven't been in games that much."

"You've got to make a place for yourself, Judge. Make them need you—" My father leaned forward urgently on the sofa and waved away the cigarette smoke drifting between us. Suddenly he slumped back. "*Ahhh*, what am I telling you? I blow in here for a few days and tell you how to live your life. . . . You just get by the best you can, Paul. Get by however you can."

Mother came back down the stairs, and as she did my father stood up again.

"She's got a fever," my mother said. "And a sore throat."

"Another one," my father said resignedly. Throughout her childhood Janie was often stricken by tonsillitis. Back in Boston one doctor strongly advised that she have her tonsils removed; another doctor said the condition would probably improve as she grew older.

Defensively, my mother replied, "It's been over a year since she's been sick. I was hoping . . . But that's not why she's crying. She's crying because she's afraid she won't be able to go tomorrow."

"Who's your doctor? Are you going to call him?"

"Dad's calling him now. Dr. Macmillan. They're old golfing buddies."

My father picked up his glass and stared at it a long time, as if he were suspicious of its contents. Then he drained what was left. "No sense you staying up too, Judge. Go to bed, and we'll see how Janie feels in the morning."

As I walked past her, my mother gently squeezed my arm. "Good night, honey. And don't worry; she's going to be all right."

I couldn't tell her it was not my sister's health that worried me but the possibility that I would not be able to see Laura.

*   *   *

THE NEXT DAY Janie was no better, and after church Dr. Macmillan came to the house. He gave Janie a penicillin shot and scolded my mother. "Why make the child go through this time and time again?" he said. "Let's get her into the hospital next summer, yank them out, and be done with it once and for all." After the doctor's visit Janie improved slightly, but there was no question of her being able to go to Minneapolis.

Yet no one said whether the trip would be canceled or postponed, and I spent the morning in the worst kind of waiting. Janie's sickness, the doctor's appearance, the hushed voices, the smell of simmering chicken soup, the hopeless sunshine outside the drawn curtains—all these gave the house the feel of quarantine.

Finally, shortly after noon, my father called me into the dining room. His face was solemn, and I was sure he would tell me that he would have to return to Minneapolis alone and that we would postpone the trip until a time when Janie felt better.

Instead, he asked, "Judge, would you still want to go even if your sister can't?"

The answer was so obvious I didn't know why he asked. Was it a test of loyalty? A test to determine the extent of my selfishness? I didn't care if I passed or failed. "Yes, sure," I said.

"Okay, go upstairs and pack your things. And bring some decent clothes. Something dressy."

We didn't get started until four, when the winter afternoon's light was already draining into evening. Before we left, my father made me go to Janie's room to ask her if there was something we could bring her.

She was propped up on pillows, and blankets and quilts were mounded so high on the bed you couldn't see the outline of her legs. She looked as if she were all torso. The room smelled of Mentholatum.

"Dad wants to know," I said, "if we can bring you back anything."

She shook her head no. I knew it hurt her to speak.

"Are you sure? You know he'll get you anything you want."

"I'm sure," she softly rasped.

"Okay, I'll see you in a couple days."

"Wait—"

I stopped at the door, and she motioned me back to the bedside.

"What if he marries her?"

"What? What if who—"

She swallowed painfully. "What if she gets a job in Minneapolis? What if Dad marries her? I bet he'd live there too."

"That's not going to happen."

"If he lived there, we'd see him all the time."

"It's not going to happen."

"I miss him."

"I miss him too, Penguin. But you know he'd never leave Boston. Besides, they're just friends. They wouldn't ever get married."

"They might."

"They won't. I know."

"You don't know everything."

"I know more about this than you do."

Janie turned her head and looked for a long time in the direction of her dresser, where the microscope my father had given her two Christmases ago sat, right next to its varnished box and the small draw-ers full of the slides she loved to make. She had specimens of a bird's feather, human and rabbit hair, dried blood, grains of sand, dirt, a leaf, saliva, an eyelash, skin . . . examples of those fragments and particles that most of us step on, over, or around but which Janie noticed and studied for hours.

When she looked at me again, her eyes were brimming with tears. "You could make him."

"No, I can't. How could I?"

"Tell him you don't care. Tell him you don't care if he marries Laura Pettit."

I shook my head.

"It would be okay," Janie pleaded. "She's famous."

"It doesn't matter what I say. They don't want to get married. Neither one. It's not that kind of, of a—"

"Dad said you don't want them to."

"When?"

"I don't know. A long time ago. I asked him if they were going to, and he said, 'I don't think your brother would like that.' So tell him."

To warm up the room, Grandmother had put an electric space heater in the corner, and as it came on, it hummed and ticked with heat, its coils turning bright orange. I felt I had to leave the room before I developed my own fever.

"So you don't want us to bring you anything?"

Janie shook her head vigorously three times and then stopped when once again she turned away from me. But I did not accept that as our good-bye. I walked around the bed and kissed her. Her cheeks were wet with tears.

MY FATHER KEPT the car's heater turned up high all the way to Minneapolis. The interior was uncomfortably warm, but my father still complained of a chill. Twice he had me reach into the glove compartment for a thin silver flask.

"Brandy, Judge," he told me after his first drink. "Don't worry. Strictly therapeutic, something to melt the frost that must be gathering in me. My circulation is out of whack or something. I just can't seem to warm up. Here, feel this."

He reached his bare hand out to me. His fingers were so cold they felt damp, as if he had been making snowballs. I remembered how cool Laura's hands could be, and when I thought of the two of them touching, I imagined them sticking to each other, the way your tongue will adhere to any outside metal on a winter day.

WE CHECKED INTO the hotel around eight. Laura also had a room in the hotel, but she was having dinner that evening with people from the university, and we wouldn't see her until the next morning, and even then only briefly. She was scheduled to be on campus all day, visiting classes and meeting with faculty and students. Tomorrow evening, my father said, she would meet us for dinner. After settling into our room, my father and I went down to the coffee shop and had ham sandwiches and blueberry pie for our late supper. Then my father took me back upstairs, while he went down to the lounge for a "nightcap." He gave me no instructions about going to bed, but I wanted to get to sleep, knowing it would help hurry along the hours until I saw Laura.

THE NEXT MORNING the coffee shop was bright and busy, full of the clatter of cups and plates and business conversations and smelling of coffee and first cigarettes. And Laura was already there, waiting at a table in front of the window.

My father and I walked across the room toward her, carefully avoiding the waitresses balancing their trays. When we arrived at the table, Laura stood up, and when she did, I saw something that shocked me so much I almost lost my breath.

She was shorter than I was!

I hadn't forgotten her height or that I had grown, but somehow I had lost the sense that those two facts would lead to another—now she looked up at me. In my imagination the relationship between our sizes had remained constant: I had always thought of myself gazing upward to where her green eyes looked down on me.

But she had changed. She had gained weight—ten pounds perhaps? It was difficult to tell because of the clothes she wore: a gray wool skirt and a bulky black turtleneck. Her face was fuller, and the weight made her look older and more serious, as if the years had crawled under her flesh and made another layer between skin and bone. We shook hands, and her hand felt small and cool.

I didn't, however, notice these changes with disapproval. She looked as beautiful to me as ever, and the weight—or the sweater—made her breasts look fuller.

What else? I could still see no signs of vanity. She was not wearing any makeup or jewelry, and her hair was, as before, short and bluntly cut. On the table in front of her were a pair of horn-rimmed glasses that looked like a man's (like my father's, actually) but which must have been hers.

The first words she spoke to me were: "Paul, I'll bet you're sick of people telling you how much you've grown, aren't you?"

All I could do was dumbly nod.

To my father, she said, "Haven't I always said he was going to be tall like you?"

My father managed a silly smile to accompany *his* nodding.

Through breakfast, while she talked to my father about her day's schedule, I watched her closely but surreptitiously.

She still smoked heavily, lighting one Pall Mall after another, and while she held her cigarette in her left hand, with her right she picked up a slice of toast and nibbled its corners. Smoking and eating simultaneously, just as she had during that meal on Thanksgiving eve.

When she listened, she leaned forward intently and held her lips slightly parted as if she were ready to say your words for you if you began to stammer.

She still pulled her hand back through her hair, making her hair rise and fall as high grass rises and falls in the wind.

She still held her tongue pressed against the bottoms of her top front teeth.

Her voice was still husky and deep as a man's.

She still made a circle of her thumb and forefinger and ran it around her wrist as though she were feeling for a bracelet that wasn't there.

Her full lower lip still seemed ready to ripen into a pout or a passion if she did not hold it firm.

Every one of these characteristics was dear to me, and I knew I could close my eyes at that moment, that night, any night, and call them all back. I had memorized them that well.

At the end of breakfast we made our plans to meet again: my father and I were going to wander the day away through Minneapolis's stores and museums while Laura spent the day at the university. That evening we would meet for dinner at the hotel's restaurant. When we said goodbye, I felt a pang. Twelve hours! I had to wait another twelve hours!

THE REST OF the day, however, my father kept me so busy that I seldom missed Laura. In fact, I never enjoyed a day with my father as much as that January day.

First, he wanted to buy me a suit, not just a sport coat but a suit, my first from the men's rather than the boys' department. We tried the large stores first—Dayton's, Donaldson's, Powers—but he found nothing satisfactory in any of them. We finally settled in a small shop that had the air of a men's club. In the back portion of the store amid a fireplace, coffee table, and overstuffed leather chairs, the suits hung on long, facing racks built into the walls.

The suit my father insisted on buying for me was a heavy, gray flannel. I had been partial to the dark green whipcord with a tan doeskin vest on a mannequin, but my father said, "Not green. The second time you wear it everyone will say, 'There's that damn green suit again.'" The suit cost over eighty dollars, and my father also bought me a tie (thin red stripes on a navy background, and when he caught me looking at the tie tacks, he said, "This is a silk tie—why would you want to poke holes in it?") and a light blue shirt ("white will go with anything, but someone will always give you a white shirt for Christmas."). Then he took me slowly through the store and pointed out the other ties, shirts, belts, sweaters, and vests I could wear with my suit. He took me down a rack of sport coats and showed me the blazers and tweeds I could wear with the trousers of my suit, and on a table of shoes he quizzed me about which styles and shades would go with my suit. (Black, yes, but I failed to pick out the cordovans.)

After my father paid for my new clothes—and put down a few extra dollars so the alterations would be done later that day—we went back out on the streets of Minneapolis. As we walked, we watched women.

That activity began when my father asked me which women I thought were pretty. His question embarrassed me, and at first I was reluctant to play, but when he convinced me it was a game and not a test, I joined in. Soon we were nudging each other and pointing up and down the sidewalks, across streets, through store windows, and whispering, "There's one! How about her? Her! The one with the red coat! With the black hair!"

No one escaped our examination or evaluation—not the tired-eyed women who worked the floor at Woolworth's or walked back and forth behind the counter at the coffee shop, not the overdressed women in from the suburbs, not the bohemian college students or the hooky-playing high school girls, not the trim, efficient secretaries or the bored perfume sellers in the department stores—every figure, every face, whether it was wind-scrubbed and plain or a model's smooth mask, got the once-over from my father and me.

Later, when we stopped for lunch at a café with a window on the street so we could continue looking at women walking by, my father said, "You know, Judge, you can tell a lot about a fellow by the kinds of women he finds attractive. You, for instance. You've got a good eye, a discerning eye. A lot of men just go for the flash—big tits, long legs, the bleached blonde. But I could tell by some of the women you picked that you can see the subtler qualities."

"Like what? Which one did I notice?" My father's energy and interest in the game was waning, but I, like the infant who can roll the ball back and forth across the room longer than any adult, wanted to continue.

"Oh, I don't remember now." My father still stared out the window, but his eyes were no longer searching.

"And could I tell about you?" I asked.

My question barely brought him back. "Judge, all you could tell about me is that I love to look at women. All of them." He paused to light a cigarette. "Jesus, do I love to look at them."

"But which ones do you like best?"

"Oh, I don't know. . . ."

"But if you had to pick."

He looked around the restaurant as if the answer were in the room. "Okay. You want to know? I like the mysteries. The kind you look at and look at, and you never come to the bottom of them. They're like roses; they keep opening, unfolding . . ."

Had I been willing to listen and ask more questions, I might have learned something about my father, but I wasn't interested in hearing about women like roses. I thought we were two men out on the town, and I wanted the conversation to turn toward women who, as my friends liked to say, "wanted it," and how they could be identified. Would they look at you in a certain way? Did they reveal it physically? With a walk? By throwing back their shoulders and pushing forward their breasts? Arching their backs? By licking their lips? Twisting strands of hair? I had long known that my father was a "womanizer," a "skirt chaser"—the labels that in that era were most frequently pasted on men like my father. I had also previously realized that Laura was not the only woman my father had pursued, in or out of his marriage. No single revelation brought this knowledge to me; I simply grew into it the way one grows into an article that has been too large through one's childhood. One day the accumulation of details—the hushed phone calls, the raised eyebrows when a certain woman's name was spoken, the hotel matchbooks, the absences that couldn't be explained away—suddenly make a pattern of sense. I also believed, in a similar intuitive way, that of all the women who entered and exited my father's life, only Laura and my mother staked a claim on his heart that could have been other than temporary. I didn't like or approve of my father's philandering, but since I knew I couldn't change him, why couldn't I at least get the benefit of his special expertise? But my father was through, both with playing our women-watching game and with talking about it, and we finished lunch in silence while the waitresses scurried around us in their flat, comfortable shoes.

Before we picked up my suit and went back to the hotel to dress for dinner, my father and I went to a bookstore to buy a book for Janie. (He had already bought her a sweater, a skirt, and a doll.) In the store my father showed me some of the books published by his company, and he made special note of the books he edited.

"Working with writers, Judge," he said to me with a sigh, "is a real education. An ongoing education."

My father and mother had never avoided discussing their work in front of Janie and me, but neither had they gone out of their way to talk about it with us.

"It's hard, you mean?" I asked.

As we strolled up and down the aisles of books, he answered, "Hard? Not exactly. Well, in a way it's hard. Their personalities make it difficult. See, Judge, all writers are babies. Big babies. Old babies. And what do babies want? They want their parents to love them, but they cry and whine and shit their pants, so they think they're not worthy. That's the way it is with writers; they all think they're not good enough. And you have to spend all your energy convincing them they are, that their book is great, that they're great, and that everyone loves them."

"Are they all like that?" I held out hope for Laura.

"Without exception, Judge. Every goddamn one of them." He pulled from the shelf an edition of *The Adventures of Robin Hood*, the one with the N. C. Wyeth illustrations. "In fact," he said as he riffled the pages, "I sometimes think that was part of the problem between your mother and me. She needed some of that same reassurance, and after working with writers all day, I simply didn't have any more to give." He put the book back. "That's why it's good she's living with your grandma and grandpa. They give her what she needs."

I decided to sneak one more question in. "And is that why you wouldn't marry Miss Pettit?"

He continued to concentrate on the rows of book. "That's one of the reasons, kiddo. Just one of the reasons."

When we left the bookstore, it was late afternoon and getting dark, and the day's unseasonable warmth left a light fog behind when the temperature fell with the sun. The sidewalks glistened wetly, and every streetlamp glowed with its own nimbus. Minneapolis still wore its Christmas decorations, and over the street the tin-foil bells that were hung with strands of garland swung weightlessly and silently in the faint breeze. It was quitting time, and in this first hour of darkness the streets were busier than they had been all day. It was exactly the kind of rushing, pushing city scene my father loved, but that day the street's quickening pulse brought him no pleasure. He was tired and said so; he wanted to take a nap before meeting Laura for dinner.

"I'm not as young as I used to be, Judge," he said. "If I'm going to keep up with you young racehorses, I have to make preparations in advance."

THAT EVENING WHEN my father and I walked into the hotel's chandeliered dining room—I, chafing and nervous in my new suit, and he, rested, freshly shaved and perfectly at ease in his gray glen-plaid suit—Laura was already there. And she was not alone.

Seated next to her at the table was a heavy-set man who looked to be in his sixties. He wore a salt-and-pepper tweed suit with a red vest, a black knit tie and tattersall shirt, and though he was nattily dressed, his stylish clothing did not match his head or body. He was red-faced, large-headed, and thick-featured. The top of his head bristled with a pure white crew cut, and in the center of his face was a wide sprawl of a nose, humped and flattened from what looked like multiple breaks. He had a fussy, perfectly clipped mustache that looked silly below his misshapen nose and above his thick lips.

He stood when he saw my father, and my father, his face erupting in a grin, rushed across the room to greet him.

"Stanley!" my father said. "Stanley!" And to Laura: "My God, where did you find *him?*"

Then Stanley and my father embraced, and Laura stood to the side, beaming like a mother who has given her child an expensive toy.

"Stanley," I gradually learned, was Stanley Fowler, an old friend of my parents' who now taught economics at the University of Minnesota. ("Imagine," he said later in the evening, "they let an old socialist teach dollars and cents to their babies.") He had heard through a friend in the English department that Laura was on campus, and since he knew that Laura was an "acquaintance" of my father's, he decided to introduce himself. When he learned that my father was in Minneapolis, he invited himself along for dinner.

"And I'm glad you did," said my father. Then, when he remembered me, my father said, "Judge, you remember Mr. Fowler, don't you? He used to come over to the house, and he even visited us in Vermont."

I didn't remember him, but I lied and said I did. Mr. Fowler and I exchanged a perfunctory handshake, we all sat down, and he and my father concentrated on each other to the exclusion of Laura and me. Mr. Fowler spoke with an accent I guessed was British, yet I never heard him say anything that indicated he was from a foreign country.

Throughout dinner Laura looked bored. She smoked, ran her fingertips up and down the stem of her wineglass, and arranged her knife and spoon at various angles. Once, when she caught me staring at her, she smiled politely and asked if I was enjoying school this year. "Not especially," I replied, determined to give honest answers to even casual questions. "I can't say I blame you," she said and went back to surveying the room.

Meanwhile my father and Stanley Fowler continued to reminisce about people whose names meant nothing to me. I was as bored as Laura was.

One of the few claims on my interest was watching Stanley Fowler drink. He drank shots of V.O., and he must have had seven or eight before dinner was over. As soon as the waitress set the shot glass in front of him, he picked it up carefully; with his large hand all he could manage was to pinch it between his thumb and thick index finger. He held the glass steady for a long time; then, rather than bring it to his lips, he brought his mouth to it. When he drained the glass, he seemed to do it without tilting it up. Rather, he wrapped his lips around the glass and seemed to suck the whiskey out of it.

And, finally, he became perceptibly drunk. For a long time I marveled at how he seemed to be able to put away so much liquor and not be affected. At meal's end, however, Stanley Fowler pushed himself back from the table, puffed out his barrel chest, and began to speak in a voice too loud for that space. He punctuated his sentences with frightening punches to the air.

"I tell you, Robert," Stanley Fowler said to my father, "I see these faces in this country, these smiling faces, these stupid smiling faces, and I think, don't they know, don't these people know how bad it will get."

My father, who seldom shared anyone's sense of gravity or doom, simply smiled at him. "Stanley, ever since I've known you you've been making dire predictions. These are pleasant times. Why not enjoy them?"

Stanley Fowler pointed a threatening finger at my father. "You listen. It's coming. And it will be bad, very bad."

My father looked mock-frantically around the room. "Here? Surely it's not coming here."

Stanley Fowler disgustedly waved his hand at my father. "Yes, make a joke. I had forgotten that about you, Robert. Your jokes."

"We don't have armed insurrections in this country, Stanley. We have too many ways for people to make themselves happy."

"It will come from the Negroes." He nodded his massive head at a black busboy clearing a table next to us. "There it has started already. And once your consciences—if you still have them—are awakened, you will see how corrupt your society is. And how it must be dismantled completely if it is to be made right."

"Okay, Stanley," my father said cheerfully, "if you say the revolution's coming, I guess it's coming. What advice do you have? What should I do to get ready?"

Stanley Fowler leaned out over the table. He opened and closed his fists a few times like a boxer testing the wrap on his hands. Then, nodding vigorously, he began: "Very well. Tonight I will not be the theorist but the practical man. What should you do, you ask? What should you do? First, I would take this boy and hide him away. I would hide him before the generals find him and then find some mud where he can die. And don't think they're not looking. They're looking all the time."

He paused and looked around for a waiter, no doubt so he could order another drink. He looked tired now, as though the weight of both the evening and his own head had become too much for him. He was having difficulty focusing, but he stopped for a moment and looked as directly as he could at Laura.

"And this. Your young poetess here. Your beautiful young poetess. I would lock her up too. Lock her up where no one—not even toothless old bears like me—can come near her. Yes. Lock her up with short chains."

The word "poetess" as spoken by Stanley Fowler sounded both lewd and disdainful. My father must have thought so too, because his smile vanished. At that moment I wished my father would stand up and knock that old drunk to the floor.

As it was, Stanley Fowler now slumped in his chair. Mouth open, he worked his tongue obscenely back and forth in his cheek as if he were trying to dislodge something stubborn and foul tasting.

Suddenly, before my father could speak, if he was going to, Laura threw her head back and let loose a rich, full-throated laugh.

When Laura's laughter subsided, she leaned across the table to Stanley Fowler, who now looked as though he had been slapped out of sleep, and whispered, "Do you think you can touch me? Do you? You can't. You can't come within a million miles of me."

My father fumbled nervously with his napkin. "Well, the wine's been flowing tonight, hasn't it? That's what happens when you drink your dinner . . ."

Laura turned angrily to him. "Don't. You didn't say anything before; don't say anything now." Then she turned to me. "Paul, I'm going out for some fresh air. Do you want to join me? Or would you prefer to stay with the men?" Before saying "men," she paused as though her mouth were reluctant to make the word's shape.

I stood up immediately, then hesitated, looking at my father. He closed his eyes and nodded his permission.

Laura was already walking to the door, and I had to hurry to catch up to her. As she reached the maître d's post, a woman in a red dress stepped into Laura's path. "Pardon me," the woman said timidly to Laura. "I shouldn't, I know, but I've been watching you, and you look so familiar to me. Are you—"

Laura didn't stop but pushed past the woman, and as she went by said brusquely, "You have no idea who I am."

Laura swiftly crossed the lobby and headed toward the hotel's front doors. Close behind, I entered the revolving door right behind her, but a partition of glass remained between us. The metaphor was not lost on me; no matter how hard I pressed, I was going to come no closer to her, no matter how long we stayed within that small circle.

Outside, the evening was still surprisingly mild. Up and down the avenue small groups of people stood talking and laughing in the gift of a night January had generously given them.

Laura leaned against the hotel's brick wall and crossed her arms against the evening's chill.

"Are you cold?" I asked. "Would you like my jacket?"

She looked at me, I'm sorry to say, as though she had forgotten I was there. "We'll go back," she said.

"I'm fine," I insisted. "I don't need my jacket."

"We'll go back," she said again.

We did not return to the dining room, however. At the far end of the lobby, out of view of the front desk, was a row of four overstuffed chairs facing an equal number of phone booths. When we sat down, a man using one of the phones eased shut the door of his booth.

Laura slouched in her chair as though she were hiding. We were quiet for a long time, and finally I was the one who spoke.

"Do you think this means you won't get the job?"

"What do you mean, Paul?"

"Since you had the"—I wasn't sure what to call it—"the situation with Mr. Fowler. Do you think that means you won't get the job here?"

She shrugged off the question. "I probably won't get the job. But not because of him. He doesn't have anything to say about it."

"Why won't you get it?"

"I'm not their type. They're looking for someone with a scholarly background. You know, someone who writes poems occasionally but most of the time writes about poems—something I am not interested in doing." She leaned forward to look at me. "But, Paul, what makes you so sure I want the job? I came here to look them over too."

"*Do* you want it?"

"I'm not sure. I'm not sure I want to teach anyplace. I visited a class today. I can't even remember what it was—American Literature something. Anyway, the teacher brought me into the classroom, and then he had to leave for a minute. So he left me there, standing right in front of the class where they could all stare at me. The room was tiny. It seemed as if I could reach out and touch the back wall. But even in that small room the students still crowded toward the back row—as if they were afraid to get too close! I thought, do I want to try to teach these people? People who are afraid to sit near me? I went to the window and looked outside, and I couldn't see a single person moving out there. Then I heard the sniffling. I had my back to the class, and it sounded as though every one of them had a runny nose and every few seconds someone would sniff. And it struck me: I was in a room full of babies! A small, hot room full of big, shy, blond, runny-nosed babies!

"Soon the teacher came back, and the class got started. The teacher talked a bit, said some flattering things about my work, and then he asked me a few questions. I talked for a while but didn't say much. Some very standard, predictable things about poetry that I wished I hadn't said because I don't know if I believe them. Then the students had a chance to ask me questions. And they in turn asked some very standard, very predictable things about poetry. My God, Paul, if I had ever had a chance to ask a poet anything I wanted! I would have asked, 'Aren't you afraid when you write? What is it like to know you can't have secrets if you're going to write? When you're shining light where it's always been dark—is there any power in the world like that?' I sure as hell wouldn't have wasted it by asking, 'Who's your favorite writer?' 'How much money did you make with your first book?' Only one person, a skinny girl with big brown eyes, asked an interesting question. She said, 'If you knew you were going to die tomorrow, would you try to write a poem first?' And then most of the class snickered."

Just then, the man came out of the phone booth and Laura stopped talking. He stared at us, and we looked back at him. He wore a brown double-breasted suit that seemed to belong to an earlier decade. He had a narrow, sharp-featured face, but his nose was bulbous, red, pitted, and looked as though it had been grafted from someone else's face onto his. We looked at each other for so long I wondered if we were supposed to know one another. Or perhaps he recognized Laura too?

He finally said, "Are you waiting to use the phone? The others out of order or something?"

"We're hiding out," Laura said, her finger to her lips.

The man glanced to the right and the left. "Oh, yeah? Someone after you?"

Laura pointed at me. "His father."

The man grinned at me. "Yeah, kid? What did you do?"

I didn't know what to say and looked to Laura for help. She said, "He wants to take the boy back to Hungary. His father wants him to help in the fight for freedom over there. But the boy wants to stay in this country. He wants to stay here and watch baseball and eat hamburgers."

The man took a step closer to us. "That right, kid? You want to stay here with us?"

Again I looked at Laura. "He speaks no English," said Laura solemnly.

"What are you?" he asked her. "His sister? His interpreter?"

"He came to me for help. I feel it's my duty to do whatever I can."

"You're not even related? You just speak Hungarian or something?"

"I'm not related to him by blood, if that's what you mean."

Wanting to play my part as well as I could, I put on a blank, bewildered expression, the look I imagined a foreigner would have.

The man came closer until he was standing right in front of Laura's chair. "And you say the kid's father is looking for him?" he said conspiratorially. "Right here in the hotel?"

"I'm certain he's nearby," Laura whispered.

The man bent down toward Laura but kept his eye on me as if he still thought I could understand him. At that distance I could see the pores in his nose, so many of them and so large the skin's surface resembled a sponge. When he spoke, I could smell the liquor on his breath. "This doesn't sound like something that's too good to get mixed up in. You could leave him here, and I could take you someplace where you could call the cops or the FBI or whoever."

I wasn't supposed to understand, much less speak, but at his suggestion a choked sound escaped from my throat.

Laura either didn't hear me or pretended not to. "Do you have a room here?" she asked him eagerly. "Could I call from there?"

"Yeah, sure . . . *Absolutely.*"

"And your phone would work better than that one?" She pointed to the phone booths. "Or that one?"

"Hey, I thought you'd want to get away from the kid."

"Him? I want to get away from *you.*"

"Look, lady, I was just—"

"You were trying to pick me up. That's what you were 'just' trying to do." Now Laura was straining so far forward in her chair it seemed only an invisible hand was holding her back and preventing her from flying at the man. "And you wouldn't give a damn if the Hungarian army were about to put him before a firing squad. Now, why don't you get out of here before I call the FBI to take *you* away."

The man backed up a step. He stared incredulously at Laura for a moment before regaining his confidence. Then he straightened his tie and gave Laura a crooked smile. "Okay, okay. But you know something, lady? You're crazy."

He looked directly at me and said, as if he were quite certain I understood him, "She's crazy. You know?"

He walked briskly away from us, his heels ringing against the marble floor and echoing up to the lobby's high ceiling.

When we no longer heard his footsteps, Laura shuddered and said, "What a creep!"

"Did you see his nose?" I asked. "It made me sick!"

Laura asked, "What about his personality? That's what made me sick. Booze will give you a nose like that. Booze and maybe a venereal disease. But I don't know where you get that kind of personality."

"Maybe you shouldn't have teased him," I suggested cautiously. Being a part of Laura's little diversion had been fun, but something about it made me uneasy. The trap she set had caught a snake, but couldn't she as easily have snared a rabbit?

She shrugged noncommittally. "I had a good idea what he was interested in." As an afterthought, she added, "He makes two tonight."

"Two what?"

"Two—two men. Two men who pretended to one thing but wanted another."

"I don't get you." I had long since stopped trying to impress Laura with my knowledge and sophistication. Besides, by admitting my ignorance, I had a chance to learn from her.

She reached over the chair's arm and touched me lightly on the wrist. "I don't have to worry about shocking you, do I?"

I emphatically shook my head no.

"No, I didn't think so. Not old unshockable Paul. Well. You knew that man with the hideous nose was trying to pick me up, didn't you? I mean, right from the start? That's what he had in mind. And his offer to help us—help you—that was merely a gimmick. Like a salesman giving away a free sample so you'll buy something more expensive. But maybe you didn't know that's what Mr. Fowler was after too. Not when he was reminiscing with your dad, but when he was showing off with all his social and economic theories. Oh, hell, probably when he was reminiscing too. Especially with that story about taking off his trousers to push someone's car out of the mud."

My regard for Laura was so armor-clad almost nothing she could say or do would pierce it, but here—in her view of the situation with Stanley Fowler—I believed she was simply wrong, and felt I had to tell her.

"Mr. Fowler? Are you sure?"

"*Mm-hmh.*"

"Maybe I shouldn't say this, but I don't think he even liked you."

"He didn't."

"And with my dad right there . . ."

"That's right."

"I never saw anything."

"You weren't supposed to."

"How about my dad?"

"What about him? He knew what was going on. If he wanted to know, he knew."

Behind me I heard the laughter and loud voices of a group of men and women crossing the lobby. I was having trouble with what Laura was telling me, and I had a momentary impulse to turn around and tell them to shut up because I was trying to concentrate. "So are you saying Mr. Fowler was making a pass at you?"

"In a manner of speaking." Laura leaned forward and spoke softly but forcefully. "Look, Paul, what's so hard to understand. You find yourself attracted to a lot of girls—women—don't you? Of course you do. And you only want to have sex with them, don't you? I mean, you don't have to like them to feel this way, do you? Or love them. I know you don't—you don't have to pretend. And that was the case with our Mr. Fowler. He may not have liked me, but he wasn't about to let that interfere with his desires. He wouldn't let his hatred for women stand in the way of his desire for them."

I had nothing to say, so I laughed uneasily. It seemed the safest course to follow; that way I could appear to be saying, ah, yes, well, certainly I know how these things are. I didn't.

But Laura was not joking, and when she began again, her seriousness was clear. "What makes me angry are the ways men cannot be direct. How devious they are! How they have to pretend that they're talking about economics or poetry or politics or about how hard they worked loading hay bales when they were boys. And they never stop competing. 'Look how handsome I am, how wealthy, how kind, how strong, how bright, how humble, how proud'—and through it all they never take their eyes off the women they're trying to win. They never stop saying, 'Look at me, love me.' Because though it doesn't matter to them if they love *you* or not, they always expect *you* to love them."

Laura stopped abruptly, her lips frozen on her next word, her hand in midair. For seconds she waited motionlessly, as if she were waiting for a chill to pass through her. Then a corner of her mouth turned up in that half-grin that seemed as if she were trying to smile and to withhold her smile at the same time. Everything about her, even this simplest expression, had its tension. "But listen to me lecturing you, Paul. I don't know why I always pick on you like this. Maybe because you're so polite and you keep listening and anyone else would tell me to shut up and go away."

"I wouldn't—"

"No, I know. *Ssshh*. You don't have to say anything. But before I get off this subject, I want to do one more thing. I want you to promise me that when you want something from a girl, or maybe I should say if you want something *with* her, then you'll come right out and say so. You won't try to trick her or deceive her; you won't say one thing and mean another. You won't try to show off and get what you want that way. You won't bully her, and you won't try to get her to feel sorry for you. Will you promise me?"

"Yes."

"Promise—say you promise." The lobby's light was yellow, warm, smoky, like a fading color photograph, yet in that muted light, Laura's green eyes glowed.

"I promise," I said.

She smiled comfortingly. "Thank you. Thank you for promising me." She sat up straight and smoothed her dress across her. "Of course it's too late, isn't it? It's already too late. Now let's see if we can find your father. Before *he* starts to worry. Although after that little nonperformance of his at dinner, he deserves to worry."

Laura stood and extended the crook of her elbow. I rose and gingerly put my arm through hers, and we proceeded through the lobby. With my new suit and my height advantage over her, I felt, perhaps for the first time in my life, that I could pretend to some adult maturity, but the small part of me that has always stood apart and analyzed the acting self reminded me that I was only pretending.

We found my father by the entrance to the coffee shop, and as soon as he saw us, he said, "I was beginning to wonder if you two caught a bus out of town."

Laura and I disengaged. I don't know who initiated the separation. Perhaps we both did, simultaneously.

"Where's your friend?" asked Laura.

"Stanley? Ha-ha-ha!" My father's laughter rang no more sincerely than the foil bells hanging over the streets of Minneapolis. "I put him in a cab and sent him home. I guess he got away from himself, didn't he? I'm afraid that when I talked about him before, I left out a crucial point: the old bastard is brilliant, but he's a first-class drunk." My father's stance—leaning against the wall, his hands in his pockets, one leg crossed, the toe of one shoe balanced on the floor—was too studied, too purposely nonchalant. He was drunk too.

"You never talked about Mr. Fowler before," she said. "Not to me."

"You sure? I never mentioned Stanley? That's hard to believe." He shook his head at a private memory. "Stanley and his shots of V.O."

"I've heard of him," Laura said impatiently, "but not from you."

"Okay. If you say so."

"I say so."

My father turned to me. "What did you think, Judge? Stanley seem the way you remember him? You remember him lushing it up like that?"

"I don't know if I remember him. There used to be so many people around."

"'Used to be.'" He repeated my phrase slowly, thoughtfully, as if the separation between past and present had never occurred to him before. "'Used to be.' Yeah. There was quite a crowd in those days. A helluva crowd."

To my father Laura said coolly, "You weren't much help in there."

"With Stanley?" my father asked. "I didn't know it was help you were looking for. You seemed to be holding your own."

"And you remained at ringside."

"Jesus. What did you expect?" my father replied sharply. "The man's a friend, an old friend."

"And his friendship's important to you . . ."

My father reached into his coat pocket and pulled out our room key. Extending it to me, he said, "You go on up, Judge. I'll be there in a little bit. We're going to try to get an early start tomorrow, so you get some sleep." He rubbed the sides of his nose right where his glasses had made small indentations.

Before I left, Laura smiled at me and said, "Thank you for keeping me company, Paul."

"That's okay," I said.

I walked away gripping the key so tightly it made an impression in my palm, as though I planned to forge a duplicate from my own flesh. The situation made no sense. The two of them stood silently seething at each other while I—the one who loved them both so ardently that anger at either seemed unimaginable—was sent away.

I GOT INTO BED right away and realized when I did how tired I was, both from the tension of the quarrels and simply from watching Laura and the disturbances—like electric currents—that she set off about her.

I woke an hour or two later when my father came back into the room, but since he was trying not to disturb me, I said nothing. He didn't turn on any lights except in the bathroom. Then, when he was sitting on the edge of the bed in his pajamas and smoking his last cigarette of the day, I finally spoke. "Dad?"

"What is it, Judge?" he answered quietly.

"Could I ask you something?" I had awakened with a question stuck in my mind: asking it would be hard; leaving it unasked would be harder.

"As long as it isn't too complicated. I'm awfully tired."

"It's about something Miss Pettit said."

"Then it's going to be complicated. But go ahead."

"She said that at dinner tonight when, uh, when Mr. Fowler was talking all the time that what he was really saying was . . . what he meant . . ." My question had vaguely to do with sex, for me the most difficult subject to bring up. "He sort of had his eye on her."

My father stabbed out his cigarette, and the glass ashtray rattled against the glass top of the bedside table. Then he pulled the covers back and got into bed before he answered. "She said that, did she?" I couldn't tell if he was angry.

"I'm pretty sure that's what she was saying."

"Well, hell," he said with a sigh. "If that's the way she said it was, then that's probably the way it was. Some things escape me. I'd be the first to admit that. Yeah, I guess she's right again. Stanley always was a hound. No reason to think he's any different now."

For a long time my father and I lay in silence while the night sounds of Minneapolis—the horn honking, the car gunning its engine, the door slamming, the man yelling the woman's name—climbed up from the street only to fall feebly back down when they reached our window. I could tell by the pattern of his breathing he was still awake, so I ventured another question. "Dad?"

"Uh-huh."

"Why is she always so mad?"

He stirred beneath the blankets. "I don't know, Judge. I do know it wears me down sometimes. She said once that she has one great fear. She's afraid of being a 'good girl.' 'Now what the hell does that mean?' I asked her. I supposed it was something about being dull and bourgeois and all that. 'Never mind,' she told me. But if she ever became that—a good girl—she'd be as good as dead. We might as well bury her. 'But if I don't even know what it means, how can I tell if you turn into one?' I said. 'You'll know,' she said. What can I tell you, Judge? I can't figure her most of the time."

Soon my father fell asleep, but I couldn't. I knew what I must have been in Laura's eyes, and the realization left me lost, condemned, beyond hope. I was, I knew—and certainly Laura knew it too—a good boy, irredeemably and forever, a good boy.

THE NEXT MORNING the weather turned sharply colder, and it was snowing lightly when we left Minneapolis for Fairmont. Laura was with us, and the plan was that my father and she would drop me off at my grandparents' and then turn around and come back the same day. We were less than an hour on the road, however, when it looked as though those plans might have to change. The snow began to slant down heavier and harder, the wind began to blow, and soon fingers of snow reached across the highway. When my father drove through these drifts, the car gave a little bump.

When we first left the city, Laura and my father had chatted steadily and cheerfully (obviously the difficulties of the night before had been resolved), but with the heavier snow they turned grimly silent. My father no longer smoked but kept both hands on the steering wheel. Laura smoked but kept quiet so she would not disturb my father's concentration. From the backseat I watched out the rear window, trying to judge the storm's worsening effects by counting how many telephone poles I could see behind us. Four, then three, then two . . . and when the wind gusted again, the telephone pole we just passed was erased from sight like a chalk mark on a blackboard.

Out the front window, the highway ahead of us stretched, in one instant, almost a hundred yards, and in the next instant it vanished. My father slowed the car down from sixty-five, to sixty, to fifty, to forty-five. Once, as we rounded a curve, he seemed to lose sight of the road, and the tires on the right side crunched on the snow and gravel on the shoulder.

My father quickly got the car back, but he said, "Maybe I should stay over there. The traction's better." By now the highway's entire surface was snow-packed and glazed.

Several minutes passed, then Laura asked, "Do you think this will let up soon?"

"Are you kidding?" my father replied. "Blizzards out here can last for days."

Laura leaned forward and peered out the windshield as though all it took to see through the blinding snow was concentration. "Of course it blows like this. My God, isn't there anything between here and Canada to stop the wind? Have we seen a single tree since we left Minneapolis?"

"There was a billboard about ten miles back," said my father.

Laura turned to me in the backseat. "This is another reason I wouldn't want to live in Minnesota."

In what must have sounded like a sudden burst of state pride, I said, "It's not always like this!"

With a long, mordant chuckle, my father added, "He's right. You should see the summers. They get so hot they'll shrivel you up like a raisin. And the mosquitoes are big enough to carry you away. I could never figure out which was the worst time of year to visit Doreen's parents."

"Maybe Paul's saying," Laura graciously offered, "that it snows in the east too."

"Sure," said my father, "we can count on Boston getting hit with at least one blizzard every year." He kept on talking as if he were trying to distract us from the storm. "No, Minnesota's got no monopoly on snow. Where I grew up in upstate New York, we'd get—I don't know—a hundred inches a year. Or better. I remember one winter—" He stopped talking and slowed as a truck going by in the other lane threw up so much snow my father was temporarily blinded. "One winter it came down for three days, and blowing like hell the whole time. When it was over, I visited a friend out in the country, and he had a drift up to the top of the barn. Must have been thirty feet. We had a new hill to sled down."

Laura said, "I remember when I first saw snow. I don't know how old I was. Four or five maybe. I'm sure I could look up the year—I mean, how many times has it snowed in southern California in the last hundred years? Anyway, I remember my grandmother Pettit waking me up and saying, 'You better look outside, Laurie.' I ran to the window, and everything was covered with snow, although I'm sure there wasn't more than an inch. And do you know what I remember thinking? It looked good enough to eat. The whole world—the grass and the trees and the bushes and the cars and the rooftops—looked edible. I thought the snow looked like frosting." She turned to the side and looked out at what little she could see of the Minnesota landscape. "I don't see anything out there I'd want to eat."

For a time the storm lessened, and some distance was given back to us. My father speeded up, trying to travel as many miles as he could while the weather allowed.

Then, on a straightaway and without warning or visible cause, I felt the car's rear end sliding across the middle line. Suddenly the car was spinning around completely, sliding and turning helplessly down the highway as if a huge hand had grabbed the car and spun it like a coin on a tabletop.

It happened almost too quickly for me to be frightened, and it was over as suddenly as it began. And then there we were, sitting on the opposite shoulder of the road and facing in the opposite direction, back toward Minneapolis.

After a long silence, my father said what must have been on all our minds: "It's a good thing no cars were coming."

Laura's head was bowed and she had her hands to her face. I wondered for a second if she had been hurt in the car's violent spin. Then, sitting up straighter and turning to look out the car's back window—in the direction we were supposed to be traveling—she said flatly but emphatically, "I don't want to go any farther." Her face looked as pale and cold as the snowfields we were parked next to.

The car had stalled, and my father turned the key in the ignition and started it again. "The first town we come to," he said. "We'll stop."

"No," said Laura. "Let's just stay here. Until the storm lets up."

"It's not going to let up," my father said in a low voice. "It's only going to get worse. We've got to get someplace while we can."

Though her expression didn't change, Laura began to cry, the tears running down her cheeks like hot water poured over a cold stone. "Not here. Not this. Please, Robert." Her voice cracked like ice, and when she went on, it was in chips and pieces of sentences. "My parents died on the highway. I can't. *I can't* . . . In a car . . . No!"

My father patted her shoulder. "*Ssshh*. It's all right. We're not going to die. But we can't stay here. It's dangerous."

Laura tried to speak but only another sob broke loose.

"Listen," said my father, "if we stay here, another car could plow right into us. They might not see us. Or we could freeze. We could get drifted in here and not get out. Sooner or later we'd run out of gas, and we wouldn't be able to run the heater. We *have to* keep going. There'll be a town soon. Someplace we can stop."

Laura made an effort to pull herself together.

"Do you want to lie down in the backseat?" my father asked her. "Judge can come up here, and you can lie down back there, and you don't even have to look at the storm."

Laura wiped her eyes. "I'm okay. Give me a cigarette."

My father offered her one from his pack. Her fingers trembled as she lit it, but once she had inhaled deeply, she repeated, "I'm okay. We can go. Go ahead. *Go*."

Carefully my father turned the car around, and once again we were going in the right direction, though even slower than before.

Brightly, gaily, Laura said, "I already decided this morning I don't want to live in Minnesota. So I sure as hell don't want to die here."

I reached forward and, just as my father had, put my hand on Laura's shoulder. Laura put her hand over mine and pressed down so hard I was sure I could feel all the way through the fearfully tense muscle right down to bone.

WITHIN AN HOUR we had checked into adjoining rooms—one for Laura and one for my father and me—in the Blue Ribbon Motor Inn, a motel in the small town of Burns Lake, Minnesota.

We put our luggage in our rooms, and then Laura and my father went down to the lounge for a drink. "Don't you think I deserve one," my father asked me, "for bringing us safely through the storm?" I stayed in the room and tried to watch television, but it received only one channel clearly and that showed soap operas and then a farm-price program. It was a pay TV with a coin-operated box, and though I had no interest in watching, I kept plugging in the quarters my father left me.

Hours passed, and finally Laura and my father returned. They were both drunk. While my father talked to me, Laura stood unsteadily before the television and regarded the screen curiously.

"You should've seen the bar, Judge," said my father. "It was full of people coming in out of the storm. Truckers and traveling salesmen and one old couple from Arizona. Hey, hey, Laurie—"

She turned around.

"—Did that old couple ever say what they were doing so far from home?"

"Don't think so."

"Anyway. Judge, I've never seen a happier bar in all my life. You couldn't buy your own drink even if you wanted to. Everybody was standing a round. Even the owner. Hell, why wouldn't he? He's got a full house."

I felt as though I were the stern, disapproving parent, and Laura and my father were the wayward children trying to pacify me.

"And, Judge. I called your mother. Told her you were safe and sound. Told her we'd call her again if we couldn't get you home tomorrow."

Laura finally moved away from the TV. "I'm going to take a bath. A nice, hot bath."

My father said, "And I'm going to take a nap. A nice, hot nap." At that they both started laughing again.

When they were finally under control, they decided we would meet in the motel's café for dinner at seven. My father fell asleep right away, and while he slept, I sat by the window and watched the blizzard. Across the parking lot from our room a semi with the words "FIXX WINDOWS" stenciled in white on the dark trailer was parked, and I judged whether the storm was lessening or worsening by how well those white letters burned through the driving snow. When it seemed as though the storm might abate, I was saddened. I wanted us to stay in those two rooms for as long as possible.

WE ATE THICK hamburgers and drank malteds that evening in the motel café. The motel owner, a burly, blond-bearded man, came to our booth and told my father that the weather forecast was for the storm to end during the night and for the skies to clear. "I talked to my brother-in-law back in North Dakota," the owner said, "and it's all over back there. Saw a little blue sky at sunset. You won't have any trouble traveling tomorrow."

"That's good news, Frank," said my father. "But Laura and I agreed that if we had to be snowed in somewhere, we couldn't think of a better place for it to happen. And I'm going to spread the word around Boston about the great treatment we got at the Blue Ribbon."

"Well, don't be in too big a hurry to leave. It's going to take the county boys a while to get the roads plowed."

I wasn't surprised by the goodwill between my father and the motel owner. Everywhere my father went he made friends. In fact, when I was younger, I sometimes resented him because he spent so much of his goodwill on strangers.

We stayed for a long time in the café while my father and Laura drank coffee and talked about how it was best that Laura not take the teaching job.

"It would take time from writing," she said, "and I'd end up hating my students for this."

"And you'd let them intrude," said my father. "You couldn't help yourself. If you're going to teach, you need to know how to protect yourself." Then my father told about how one of his writers was so ruthless with his time he refused to speak to students outside the classroom.

Neither of them said a word about how Laura's living in Minneapolis would put too many miles between them, but I knew it was foremost in their minds. For myself, I had been thinking of the short distance between Fairmont and Minneapolis, and I even imagined myself hitchhiking to see Laura. Though my realistic self knew it was something I would never do, my romantic self insisted it was at least possible, whereas getting to New York was not.

After eating we walked Laura back to her room, and my father told her we'd give her a call around eight, have breakfast, and then drive on to Fairmont. As we said good night to Laura in the dim, echoing hallway, I noticed again how lovely she looked. All the tension, anger, and fear that had been crowding out her beauty in Minneapolis and in the car had now receded, and in their absence she seemed to possess again that radiance that one has after lying in the sun. Though she was as pale as winter, some light still seemed to fall on her that fell on no one else. When the door closed, I couldn't stop my sigh.

My father and I had to share a bed, but before my father got into bed he plugged enough quarters into the television to carry us through Jack Paar and well beyond. "I hope you don't mind, Judge," he said as he settled back on the pillow. "I've had so much coffee I don't think I'll be able to get to sleep." The television didn't keep either of us awake. I was asleep before the end of the program, and my father was snoring before that.

During the night I woke with a throat so sore it felt as though a sliver of glass were caught in it. The TV was still on, though the screen displayed nothing but gray-white electric snow. My father was not in the bed.

In our family we made too much of illness. If Janie or I looked flushed or behaved listlessly or complained of the mildest discomfort, my mother became immediately concerned and began feeling our foreheads or checking our throats. Over the years my mother's excessive concern and frequent alarm over illness communicated itself to Janie and me, and as a result we eventually became fearful and panicky at our first symptom, real or imagined.

I make this point to try to explain why that night in the Blue Ribbon Motor Inn I thought it necessary to get out of bed, find my father, and tell him that I didn't feel well.

Though the bathroom was dark, I nevertheless checked there for my father. The room was empty.

I looked at our motel room door, and the chain lock was still attached, so, I falsely reasoned, he could not have left the room.

Soon I saw the answer to the puzzle: the door leading to Laura's adjoining room was ajar. I went to the door and opened it, only to be faced with the blank of another door. I was still sleepy, and I felt ill; these facts and the strange configuration of the two doors made me feel as though I were dreaming. Then I noticed that Laura's door was not tightly shut either, and I pushed it inches open and said softly—as much to warn of my approach as to call to my father—"Dad? Are you there?"

He was in Laura's room, but he did not hear me. The television was on, tuned, I remember distinctly, to an old movie starring Franchot Tone. My father was sitting on a straight-backed wooden chair facing the desk and mirror, and Laura, facing my father, was sitting on his lap. She had her arms extended straight forward on the chair back as if she were bracing herself. Her head was thrown back, her robe was open and off her shoulders. . . .

It took me a moment, a second, an instant, all my years of existence and knowledge, before I realized they were having intercourse, and after that realization—after, I swear and not before—I saw more evidence to confirm that it was so: My father's pajama bottoms were lying on the floor around his ankles as if he had his feet in a puddle. His hands, pushing, stroking upward as if he were sculpting her, were on Laura's breasts. Though my father's hands were moving, the rest of his body remained still, tense, poised, as if he had been warned not to move. Laura however lifted herself rhythmically, forcefully, up and down and forth and back, as though she were trying to set the chair, my father, and herself all rocking to the same motion.

I stepped back from the door, and my vision darkened, just as it does when you jump up quickly and feel faint, as though you have been caught in a blizzard of black snow. I was reeling not only from what my eyes saw but also from what I was learning. Some of this new knowing was intellectual, some emotional.

I learned that the expression on the faces of men and women making love was not rapture but concentration.

I learned that though Laura was pale, her nipples were dark and not the faint pink or rose of the naked women my friends and I saw in magazines.

I learned that in lovemaking a woman did not passively receive her pleasure but actively sought it, despite what I had been led to believe by my ignorant friends and cheap novels.

Then there were things I knew immediately upon seeing Laura and my father, though it would not be fair to say I learned these things *from* seeing them. This was simply knowledge I grew into at that moment, just as we come to know other things as a natural consequence of aging, without having to contemplate them or reason through them. One morning years later we simply wake with the knowledge of why grandfather spent so much time in the basement, why Jimmy Driscoll's mother insisted we play outside when Mr. Driscoll was home, why Mary Towne's father never attended school programs. . . .

Similarly I knew at that moment that on the night Janie fell ill, my mother and father made love. And I knew that women were attracted to my father not, as I had always thought, solely because of his smooth manners, his quick intelligence, and his good humor (qualities I could conceivably emulate) but because they found him sexy (and I had no idea how to acquire that trait).

Through the barely opened door I could hear Laura's rapid, heavy breaths as they hissed through her clenched teeth. I tried to match my breathing to hers so I would know exactly the panting pace of a woman in passion, but I couldn't do it. I was still having too much trouble catching up to my own shocked breath.

I wanted to peek through the door again to see more of Laura's exposed body, but I couldn't make myself look. I was not afraid of being discovered; their angle to the adjoining door, the room's faint, flickering gray light, and their all-other-obliterating closed-eye study made that unlikely. No, I could not look because I would not be able to see Laura without seeing my father as well.

Finally I gave up, gently pushed the door shut, and stood again in our darkened room.

Then I did something that to this day surprises me. From the moment I saw Laura and my father on that chair I had been shivering with betrayal, though I knew I had no right to that emotion. My father and Laura were lovers, and that night they were doing what lovers naturally did. But I was not going to calm down by reasoning with myself. And I couldn't simply climb back into bed and forget what I had seen. I had to do *something*. I considered again calling for my father, this time so loudly they would both hear and have to stop what they were doing.

I saw my father's wallet on the desk. The once-brown leather was almost black, its edges were cracked and peeling, and along the fold it was worn paper-thin and beginning to tear. Janie and I had given my father that wallet for Christmas years before. Sitting on the desk, the wallet was at least two inches thick, stuffed as it was with photographs, business and credit cards, newspaper clippings, receipts, personal lists, and currency. To me, this wallet had always represented adulthood. No child could ever have a wallet like that. How did it get that way? I wondered. And the answer always came back, the years, all those living years, found their way into this leather envelope, so that a man couldn't even sit down without feeling his age bulge at his buttocks and hip.

My father had over three hundred dollars, and before I had time to ask myself why or what I expected to accomplish, I took fifty out for myself.

I had never stolen anything before nor have I since, but that night I took fifty dollars from that sacred place, my father's wallet, and rolled it up inside a sock and stuffed the sock inside a dirty T-shirt and put the T-shirt back in my suitcase.

From this distance of years I can explain the act—my father, through his affair with Laura, took something from me, and I in turn took something from him—but that too-pat, tepid psychological interpretation only considers what I did and does not explain where within me I found the resoluteness or the malevolence to do it.

Did my father ever notice the money was missing? He never said anything to me, although, as closely as he watched a dollar, it is hard to believe he wouldn't notice that sum absent. I saved the money for at least a year (to show it was not the money I wanted) before I spent any of it. During that time I kept my father's fifty dollars hidden in my dresser drawer with my articles and clippings about Laura.

The next morning I was sick (with strep throat I caught from Janie, I learned once I saw the doctor back in Fairmont), so during the ride home I sat feverish and miserable in the backseat and squinted or closed my eyes to shut out the blinding light that reflected off the drifts and dunes of new snow stretching out for miles on every side of us. Laura and my father didn't say much either, yet their silence was not strained but comfortable and affectionate. Whenever my father wanted a cigarette, Laura lit one for him and one for herself.

After they brought me home, they only stayed for coffee, then turned around and went back to Minneapolis. Without being ordered, I went directly to bed, where I lay and languished in my illness, a fitting state, I believed, for someone who had endured what I had the night before.

To NO ONE'S surprise, the University of Minnesota did not hire Laura, yet within the year she was in a classroom. In the fall of 1959 she took a job teaching at Dorson College, a small, private school in southern Vermont. Dorson, coincidentally, was not far from the place where our family used to spend part of every summer, the place where I first met Laura.

And by the fall of that year I was finally able to close my eyes and see—with all the clarity of an acid-etched photographic plate—the image of Laura that I wanted: her astride the motel room chair, her head thrown back and her shoulders and breasts bared. It took those many months before I could call back that picture of her without automatically seeing my father as well, but once I was able to block him out or relegate him to shadow, I was free to enter that darkness myself, so in my imagination it was my lap she sat on, it was she and I who made love in a motel room.

Or in my bedroom. Or in her bedroom. Or in the bedroom of the house in Vermont where I first saw her standing before the window— and now she was naked, moonlight casting her body in white marble. Or in the bathroom in the shower. Or in a wooded field near my grandparents' house. Or in the backseat of my grandfather's station wagon, the car I was learning to drive.

For now I was in the period of my life when sexual desire was on me like a hunger that could not be satisfied, and it was always Laura I fantasized beneath me or beside me or above me. Like my friends, I was sometimes able to get my hands on magazines full of pictures of impossibly large-breasted women, but though I might have taken those magazines into the bathroom with me, though I might have been first aroused by thoughts of Doris Bishop, who sat across from me in Latin class, as soon as my hand was on my cock and my eyes were closed, it was only Laura I saw, only Laura I wanted to see.

Six

My father's funeral took place on a day as lovely as June is capable of producing. The sunlight was undiluted by cloud or haze. Grass, leaves, and flowers still wore the bright colors of spring, and the inevitable heat and dust of August that would darken and dull all those shades seemed impossibly far away. The day's beauty didn't cancel out sorrow, yet that beauty could not be ignored either, and all day people felt their attention pulled in opposite directions: down toward my father and his death and up toward sunlight and blue sky. When we came out of the church, for example, ready to walk that short distance to where the open grave waited, I believe that for one brief moment we were all stunned out of our grief. Inside, in the stained-glass light, with everyone sinking lower under the weight of the eulogy, it was easy to forget that any day could be beautiful. And then, that sunlight, that green fragrance . . . Finally, I believe, over the years in everyone's recollection, death and the day's magnificence knotted and could not be separated. My father's death reminded everyone of how few and precious are such days, and the day in turn put an additional gloss on memories of my father.

My father died outside his office building in downtown Boston. He had hailed a cab and opened its back door when the car for some reason suddenly lurched forward, leaving my father with a choice of either letting go of the door or trying to jump into the moving vehicle. He jumped, and his heart took that opportunity to explode, so it is quite possible my father died in midair. This happened on June 24, 1961, when my father was forty-nine years old. I had graduated from high school just a few weeks before.

My father's body was brought to Beckwith, New York, the town where he was born and raised, to be buried. He hadn't lived there for decades, but somehow, long before, arrangements had been made for him to return after his death, and there, with all earth's patience in such matters, a plot waited for him beside his father and mother.

It had also been years since I was in Beckwith. In fact, as we drove there from Albany, the closest city with an airport, my mother, Janie, and I tried to figure how long it had been since we had all visited that small town. We finally settled on March of 1952, when I was eight and Janie was five, and we all drove up from Boston to spend Easter with Grandmother Finley.

And then there we were in that church again, sitting quietly while a minister who never knew my father offered the consolations of a religion my father had probably no longer believed in.

Many of my father's friends showed up for the funeral. Allen Harrison and his wife were present, though Mr. Harrison himself looked close to death. He had grown so thin his face showed all the features of his skull, liver spots covered his bald head, and beneath his wispy mustache, his mouth, perhaps from poorly fitting false teeth, had twisted into a cramped, humorless smile. With Mr. Harrison was Barbara, his fourth wife, a tanned, raven-haired woman in her thirties who towered over him as if he were her young son. Hal Davenport was there, his empty sleeve neatly pinned to his black suit coat. I recognized Leon Field, the author of a series of best-selling novels about a handsome, dashing psychiatrist who, without his patients' knowledge and in a manner that always involved out-of-office adventures, solved his patients' problems. My father once said, "Leon couldn't write a graceful sentence to save his life, but when it comes to knowing what the reading public wants, he's got the magic touch." Leon Field was accompanied by an actress from a popular television series. She looked to be in her twenties, though in her series she played a teenager, the oldest child in a farm family of seven.

But most of the people I *almost* knew, the way upon waking we almost remember a dream. These were, after all, men and women I hadn't seen in years, but more than that, theirs were faces that belonged to another era. Not that many years had passed since my parents' divorce, but Boston and our lives there had come to seem as far away as . . . well, as childhood. I felt now as though I stood on the promontory of adulthood and far below were the small, growing-smaller figures from my earlier years.

Perhaps I recognized so few people because I scanned their faces quickly, pausing only long enough to determine that no, it was not Laura's, not Laura's, not Laura's . . .

Not that I had any real hope she would be there. She and my father had stopped seeing each other, another fact I learned by looking where I was not supposed to.

One morning my mother left open on the kitchen table a letter from my father, and walking past, I glanced at it. Laura's name jumped out at me as though its letters were printed in neon. "I am no longer to be found in the company of Miss Pettit," my father wrote. "She seems to prefer living hermitlike in Vermont to any human company in the city, and during my recent visits she has been something less than delighted with my presence." When I read the letter, written in the mock-formal language that my father often adopted for the sake of both humor and emotional detachment, I felt both pleased—since my father and Laura were no longer attached, perhaps that meant an empty space was available at her side—and discouraged—my father had been my only means for getting near Laura.

So when my father died, I had already stopped thinking that he and I could be in competition for Laura. In fact, my father's death seemed so sadly lonely that I found myself wishing that Laura—that anyone—had been waiting for him in the back of that taxi. I would have preferred that my father died with his head on Laura's lap, her tears falling on his face, than with his last breath pressed into the cab's upholstery.

Once I heard her name. In no hurry to leave the sunshine for the church's interior gloom, people stood around outside before the service. As I walked past a group of men, none of whom I knew, I heard one man say, "Laura Pettit." Quickly, I circled back so I could hear what they were saying. A red-haired, sunburnt man said to the others, "Young pussy. That's what did him in. He couldn't leave it alone, and it finished him off." For the sake of my father's memory I should have taken offense, but I couldn't.

First of all, I knew he was right. Oh, not that a sexual relationship with a younger woman could be fatal, but that my father had an obsession that drew him not only to Laura but to other women as well. That was one more realization that I had previously grown to fit as I left childhood. What the man said also reminded me of another sad truth: my father wished to be younger so he might be a better match for younger women—Laura especially—while I wished to be older only for Laura. Now that my father was dead, I could safely grieve over the fact that he and I would never talk over our paradoxically similar misery. The truth was, we would probably never have talked about it, no matter how long either of us lived.

After the red-haired man's remark, another man in the group coughed conspicuously and jerked his head in my direction. When they all turned to me, the cougher waved and said, "Paul! Good to see you again. God, you're getting to be tall. . . ." I didn't recognize the man, but after he greeted me, the other men in the group stood silently and stared at their shoes.

The Lutheran service was agreeably brief, and though the young Pastor Lindahl's eulogy had that tentative tone of hearsay, he was still able to speak truthfully and kindly of my father. Those in attendance who needed to hear about redemption and eternal life were reassured.

Not until we walked the short distance from the church to the graveyard, not until we stood beside the coffin and the covered grave, not until we were out again in the day's golden sunlight, not until then did anything happen to disturb the quiet series of rituals that we had all been placidly observing.

We were beside the green-draped platform that concealed the

grave, and I had my arm linked in my mother's. Janie was on her other side. As the minister began to speak, I felt Mother give a slight tremor, like someone who had caught a sudden chill. Soon that tremor was followed by another, then quickly another and another, and then she was shaking hard and rattling with sobs. She bent over, and I didn't know if she was going to faint or if she was crying so hard that she no longer had the strength to stand up. She leaned harder on my arm, and then I had to put my other arm around her to try to hold her up.

I looked around for help, but the minister was staring into his Bible and going on with the ceremony and the other mourners had their heads bowed.

Mother's crying worsened to the point where I feared it would consume her completely. Not knowing what else to do, I turned her from the grave and led her away. As we stepped back, the minister stopped, but then Mrs. Montgomery, my father's cousin and the one who had made all the arrangements in Beckwith, said quietly, "That's all right. You can go ahead."

I walked my mother back toward the rows of cars parked on the grass in front of the church. When we got to our dark blue rental Buick, I opened the back door and helped her in. As soon as she sat down, she moaned and fell back across the seat. She brought her hands up to cover her face, as though she had been struck and was trying to protect herself from further blows. The hem of her navy blue dress rode up until the tops of her nylons and garter belt showed. I didn't want anyone to come by and see her like that, so I tried to get her to sit up.

"Mom?" I raised my voice as if she were hard of hearing. "Are you all right? Are you going to be okay?"

Her only response was an even louder wailing, so I simply decided to let her tears run their course. I stood in front of her, turned my back, and leaned on the open car door.

Back at the cemetery, the knot of people at the grave had loosened, and in twos and threes they were walking back toward the church or toward their parked cars. The minister, his white robes flashing like polished silver in the sunlight, walked alone behind the last mourner.

I turned around, kneeled in the gravel and dust beside the car, and said, "Mom, it's over. The funeral's over."

I don't know if those words worked some magic or if it was a coincidence of timing, but right after I spoke, her weeping subsided, and soon she was able to sit up. She kept her handkerchief pressed to her mouth as if she were trying to filter out some bad air.

Finally she said, "Oh, Paul! Oh, God! What have I done? I'm sorry! I'm so sorry! I've made you miss your father's funeral!"

"That's okay," I said. "I heard enough."

"And who am I? I'm *nobody*! I'm just the ex-wife. And you're his son. You're *supposed* to be here. You have a *right* to be here."

I was sure more tears would follow this outburst, so I quickly said, "It's okay. Really. I was glad to have an excuse to get away from there."

"Are you sure?"

"Positive. I didn't want to stand there any more. None of that had anything to do with Dad anyway."

She looked through her purse, pulled out her crumpled cigarette pack, and with her fingernails picked out a slightly bent cigarette. "One of the things that always gets me about funerals is how alone the dead seem. Isn't that silly? I mean, I know they're dead and can't feel a thing, but still . . . There are all the friends and relatives gathered in one place, and then just to emphasize how separate, how far from us the dead are, they're put in the ground."

She put her head down as another sob briefly shook her. "But I never even got that far in thinking about your father. What did me in was what I discovered last night. I couldn't sleep, and I was going back over our marriage, trying to figure out why it didn't last. And the problem was not, as our so-very-wise friends thought, that your father chased around and drank too much. That I could live with. Always. I made that peace before our wedding day. I think the problem was that I never took care of him or babied him. I don't mean to compete with other women. Not like that. Just, you know, to watch over him. See that he was eating right. That he took it easy when he was coming down with a cold. That he didn't drive too fast and smoke so much. And maybe if I would have done that for him . . ."

This line of talk led her back to the well of tears, and I stood up again and waited for this bout of weeping to end.

Still, her words, her *maybes* hung in the air like insects. *Maybe, maybe. Maybe, maybe.* She could not stop thinking about what might have been: *if only this had been different . . . if only that condition could have been altered . . . if only what happened hadn't happened . . . if only this instead of that. . . .* That futile, wishful line of thinking was mine too, and there was no better example of it in my life than Laura. If only I were older, if only she were younger, if only we didn't live so far apart, if only we had met under other circumstances, if only my father were not my rival. . . . Well. There you had it. In that small churchyard cemetery less than two hundred yards away was, in my father's mahogany casket, an early wish of mine belatedly come true, come true when I no longer wished for it, and with this realization, all the grief and guilt I had been dodging found me. The weight of it settled over my heart and made it difficult to breathe, and I tried to take in great gulps of sweet summer air. When that failed, I knelt down before my weeping mother, the stones of the gravel road biting into my knees, and at last let loose my own tears.

My mother's crying subsided before mine, and she slipped a crumpled Kleenex into my hand. "We should get back. We've deserted your sister. She's probably with everyone else back at the church." The Women's Lutheran League was holding a reception in the church basement.

She waited another moment, then asked, "Okay?"

"Okay," I said, and stood up slowly.

My mother rose and put her arm around my waist, and we walked back toward the church. "Funerals," she said. "What they put us through."

When we got back to the flagstone walk connecting the church and the cemetery, my mother gestured toward my father's grave.

"But maybe you want to—?" she asked and stopped short.

I knew what she meant: did I wish to go back to the grave and make my own farewell?

"I guess I do."

"I'm going inside," said my mother. "I've had enough for today."

I started toward my father's grave but never arrived.

As I stepped off the stones and onto the soft cemetery grass, I saw Laura, standing at the graveyard's edge in the darkness of a grove of trees. Immediately I changed my course and started in her direction. I fought off the impulse to run.

She watched me approach but made no move to come forward to greet me. When I was close enough for her to hear me, when both of us stood in the same shadow, I said, "I didn't think you were coming."

She wore a white blouse, a pinstriped vest that looked as though it belonged with a man's suit, a dark skirt, and sandals. Her hair was longer than it had been when I saw her last in Minnesota. She was smoking, and she exhaled before she answered me. "How's your mother?"

"She's okay."

"They always think they're holding on. Until they get to the grave. The grave gets them every time."

"You too?"

The circles under her eyes were so dark I wanted to take her out into the light and let the sun melt those shadowy rings.

"Why do you think I'm standing back here?" she said.

I looked back over my shoulder, gauging the distance to my father's grave. Yes, we seemed to be far enough away.

"How about you?" she asked. "How are you doing?" In the shelter of the trees the air was still, and the liquor on her breath traveled to my nostrils.

"I wish I knew what to say to all the people who keep coming up to me and saying, 'I'm sorry.'"

"Just say, 'Thank you.' You don't mean it, but say it anyway. The secret of good manners."

"That's what I've been doing."

"Sure. You've been brought up right."

"I didn't think you and my dad were—"

"—We weren't. Not since last fall. You wouldn't believe how I heard about it. Jesus." She dropped her cigarette in the dirt, ground it out with her heel, and immediately began to hunt through her purse for another. "I was in New York for the first time in a long time. A conference at NYU. Less than a week ago. At a party after a lecture, a young man—his name is Dennis Kaplan, an absolute asshole but apparently a very gifted writer—was complaining about his editor. Dennis had just signed a contract for his first book, and his editor had up and died on him. Now I wasn't even talking to the young gentleman—I was standing nearby when he made this pronouncement—but as soon as I heard this, I knew he was talking about your father. I *knew* it. And this was the strange part; I knew it from the way I felt, as if someone had grabbed my heart with an ice-cold hand—but how could I feel that without knowing?

"I could have walked out of the room at that moment, and there wouldn't have been a doubt in my mind. Maybe I should have. But I didn't. Instead I worked my way over to Mr. Kaplan and asked him the name of his publisher. He said Harrison House, just as I knew he would. Then I asked him the name of his editor. He said Robert Finley, just as I knew he would. Then I surely should have walked out. But I didn't. No. No, instead I called our young Mr. Kaplan a very vulgar name, and I . . . I meant to throw the drink I was holding, but it didn't work quite the way it does in the movies. The glass . . . I misjudged the distance or the motion of the wrist one is apparently supposed to make when one is splashing whiskey in a young man's face, and I hit him in the face with the glass. I managed to get the whiskey in his face, but I hadn't meant to bloody his lip. Not that the little bastard didn't deserve it. It's just that I don't think your father would have approved of me bashing his writers in the face, now would he?"

"Probably not."

"Absolutely not. Absolutely he would not. Your father loved writers. In the abstract anyway. He had his problems with a few individuals."

Laura had been looking so persistently over my shoulder and beyond me while she spoke that I finally had to turn to see what she was looking at. Nothing. Mounds of grass. A few robins hunting worms. Rows of tilting gravestones, the oldest of them bone-white with age. When I turned back to Laura, tears were running down her cheeks, and she made no attempt to wipe them away. I started to reach out to her but stopped myself.

"So," she said, "if you ever read or hear anything about this incident with Mr. Kaplan, and if they say how uncivilized I am, or if they mark it down to my being drunk, remember that I told you the truth. I did it defending your father's name." Now she wiped her cheeks with the heel of her hand. "Are you done out here?"

I looked once more toward my father's grave; I had come close enough. "I'm ready."

As we walked toward the church, Laura said, "I heard you graduated. How come I didn't get an announcement?"

"I didn't send any."

"What was behind that decision?"

"It didn't seem like that big a deal. Not something to shout to the world."

"How about college?"

"I'm only going to Afton."

"And living at home?"

I shrugged.

"There are worse things," she said. "I stayed at home too when I started college. It wasn't ideal, but it certainly had to be better than living in one of those goddamn dormitories—or fraternity or sorority houses, worse yet."

Until that moment I had planned on pledging a specific fraternity at Afton, and then I hoped my sophomore year I'd be able to move into their fraternity house, a three-story ivy-covered brick building on a creek at the edge of campus. But once Laura disparaged fraternal life that fraternity and its big brick house abruptly left my mind.

"How did you know I graduated this spring?" I asked.

"Your father told me."

"I thought you and he weren't . . . You know."

"We weren't. But we were still friends. We talked on the phone occasionally."

"He couldn't make it for graduation," I said.

"And that bothered you? You said it wasn't such a big deal."

"It wasn't."

Laura bumped me with her shoulder. "Come on, Paul. You can't have it both ways."

We were at the doors of the church. "Just a second," I said. "I've got something for you." I took a pack of gum from my jacket pocket and offered her a stick.

She took the gum but didn't unwrap it. "Are you trying to tell me something?"

"I thought you could use it, that's all."

"Paul. You're trying to look out for me, aren't you?"

"I just think I know what kind of people these are. You know, from Beckwith. From small towns."

"I think I do too," she said, reaching up to pat my cheek. She dropped the unopened stick of gum into her purse.

TWO LONG FOLDING tables were set up in the church basement, and the tables were covered with food—platters of sliced ham, bowls of potato salad, molds of Jell-O, mounds of rolls and buns, crocks of baked beans, cakes, pies, and cookies. And to drink, cold milk, Kool-Aid, or coffee. All that food prepared by women who didn't know my father but who knew that after grieving we come back to the body, the body that doesn't know how to stop its hunger.

At the bottom of the stairs Laura and I stopped, blocked by all the people, most of them balancing plates of food. Almost everyone seemed to have stayed for the reception, taking the opportunity to have a meal before leaving town.

"Stay close, Paul," Laura whispered. "If this crowd turns hostile, I don't want to be left alone."

"You know a lot of these people."

"And they know me. The mistress of the deceased." I saw my mother on the other side of the room, and at that same instant she saw us. I wondered if Laura were right about being unwelcome, because immediately Mother came toward us.

"Here comes my mother," I said to Laura, in case she wanted a warning.

"Doreen? Oh, I want to see her!"

The people in front of us moved gracefully aside like dancers performing an elaborate step, and Laura and my mother were facing each other.

My mother said, "When I didn't see you all day, I almost gave up."

At that they fell into an embrace. Hate each other? How could they? In their special love for my father they shared something that no one else in that room could feel. I was going to excuse myself and leave them alone, but they would not have heard me anyway, so I simply walked away.

Hal Davenport sat alone in a folding chair. He was drinking coffee and smoking a cigarette, alternately resting his cup or his cigarette on a saucer balanced on his knee. He looked like the saddest man in the world.

I sat down next to him. "Hello, Mr. Davenport. What do you think of all these people invading Beckwith?"

He turned his gaunt, intense gaze on me. His eyes were red-rimmed. "Paul, this is God's own truth: I wish it were me being buried out there instead of your father."

"You and Dad were pretty close," I offered weakly.

"I'll never have another friend like him. Never. I drove around town last night. Over by the high school. The football field. Hagen's Dairy where your father and I worked summers. The old neighborhoods. The country roads. I tell you, there wasn't anywhere I could look that didn't bring back a memory of your dad. It felt as though I wasn't all there, like I was the ghost."

Helplessly, I said, "I'm sorry. . . ."

"Oh, Christ Jesus, Paul. He was your father, and here I am . . ."

"That's okay."

"Nobody understands this. Nobody. Your father was special. You see, Paul, he let me, he let me love him. That's the only way to say it. He . . . I know it doesn't sound like so much. But a lot of men would have turned away. Not your dad. He knew what it meant. What it meant to me. He couldn't . . . He wasn't interested, but he didn't turn away either. You know we stayed friends? Always?" Finally I understood what he was halt-ingly trying to confess. Hal Davenport was homosexual, and though my father was not, he never spurned Hal Davenport or removed himself from Hal Davenport's affection. Of course, yes of course, that was exactly my father's gift: he knew how to be loved even if he did not always know how to love in return.

"You don't have to explain," I said.

"I don't want to give you this, Paul." With his thumb he wiped a tear from his eye before it spilled over his lashes. "Not if you don't want to hear."

"I understand," I said.

"I hope you do," Hal Davenport said. "Understand, I'm not telling you something about your dad, something you never knew. I'm talking about me. What he meant to me."

"I understand," I repeated.

"Sure?"

"I'm sure."

"Okay." He clapped his hand on my shoulder, squeezed, then removed his hand quickly. "What do you say we get something to eat?"

"You go ahead. I don't have much of an appetite."

He set aside his cup and saucer, stood and started toward the food table, then stopped and turned back to me. "Take care of yourself, Judge."

I knew he was saying good-bye to me. "You too."

I wandered off by myself but didn't get very far before Janie found me, grabbed my arm, and said gleefully, "Come over here! We found something you have to see!"

She led me to a corner of the room where, on a pine-paneled wall, framed photographs of boys and girls hung, as few as two or three young people in some pictures, as many as twenty in others. Below each photograph was an index card with a year boldly printed and then in typescript the names, presumably, of the children in the picture. Laura and my mother were peering intently at the photographs.

"Okay," Janie said. "See if you can find Dad."

"You're kidding! There must be fifty pictures here!"

An old woman standing next to my mother said, "Oh, not that many. They didn't start putting up the confirmation class pictures until 1915, and there were classes before that."

My mother introduced me to the old woman. She was Enid Harris, and she had been a friend of my grandmother's.

"Go ahead," Janie urged again. "Find Dad. And no fair looking at names."

I wasn't sure where to begin looking. Finally, I concentrated on the years 1922 to 1927, when my father was ten to fifteen years old.

No matter how carefully I looked, however, I saw no face that resembled my father's. Meanwhile, Mrs. Harris told Janie and my mother how Grandmother Finley saw to it that my father attended church regularly and received religious instruction; that was something she had to do, since Grandfather Finley was, in her word, "godless." Of course, the Irish Catholics in town were appalled that a Finley was brought up Lutheran.

"I give up," I told my mother. "Which one is Dad?"

Simultaneously Janie and my mother pointed to the picture above the card that said 1926. In the picture were five children: three girls and two boys, and in neither of the boys' faces could I see my father. I glanced down at the typed names, and there it was: "second row, R. Finley and J. Persson." My father was a pale, somber, blank-eyed face above a white shirt and a bow tie. His arms were stiffly at his sides. The seated girls all had dark hair and white dresses with high collars.

My mother said to Janie, "What do you think? He's about your age in that picture. Is he better-looking than any of the boys in your class?"

"With that hair?" Janie asked. In the photograph my father's hair was parted in the middle and pasted wetly to his skull.

Mrs. Harris said, "He certainly doesn't look like someone who raised as much Cain as your father did, does he?"

While I continued to look at the photograph, Laura put her hand on my shoulder and asked, "Who does he look like, Paul?"

"I don't know. I can't even see him. I can't see him in there anywhere."

"He looks like *you*."

I looked to my mother for confirmation. She smiled and nodded.

I got up close to the photograph one more time, trying to imagine that I was gazing not into my father's eyes but into a mirror. I stared and stared, but the picture gave nothing back.

My mother asked Mrs. Harris, "What's your opinion? Does Paul resemble his father?"

"Oh, my. Let me tell you. When I saw this young man outside the church this afternoon, I had to catch myself before I called out 'Robert!'"

"Is this what you wanted to show me?" I asked Janie.

"Isn't it great? I can't get over how serious he looks. Like a judge." She laughed again.

"I'm going outside for a while." I turned my back on the four women and left the confusion of the dim basement for the sunlight.

Perhaps I could not see a resemblance in that old photograph because I had for so many years insistently denied any similarity between my father and me. I had too many reasons to see us as opposites—his heartiness and vigor, my shyness and quietude, his extroversion, my introversion—and in the years when I imagined us both vying for Laura, I always thought any chance I had for her lay in my being unlike my father.

I had not pondered these matters for long when Laura came out to join me.

"Want to go for a ride?" She jangled her keys in my face.

"Where?"

"Mrs. Harris told me how to get to an old country school that your dad attended. About five miles outside of town."

"I better check with my mother. She might want to go back to the hotel."

"I already told her you were going with me."

Expecting me to follow, she walked past me.

And follow I did, jogging a few steps until I caught up. "How did you know I wanted to go?"

She stopped suddenly. "Don't tell me you'd say no to me?"

Before I could answer, she laughed and walked on.

Laura led me to a black MG parked at the end of the line of cars.

"Well, what do you think of my transportation?" asked Laura.

"Nice."

"Nice? Is that it? 'Nice'?"

"Okay, great. It's great. How long have you had it?"

"It's not mine. I borrowed it from a teacher at the college. He told me to keep it as long as I need it. So while I'm driving around in this, he's pedaling around on my bicycle."

I wondered if he was her boyfriend.

"I hope it doesn't rain before I get it back to him. The top won't go up. Or I don't know how to put it up."

"Do you want me to try?"

"Forget it. We might not get it down again, and it's too nice a day." She held up the keys again. "Would you like to drive?"

The only cars I ever drove were my mother's Studebaker and my grandfather's station wagon. Both had automatic transmissions, and I knew I wouldn't be able to handle the MG's stick shift.

"No, that's okay," I said. "You go ahead."

Laura drove fast, as I somehow knew she would. She downshifted into curves and accelerated coming out of them. The wind and her speed blew her hair into her face from every direction, and she impatiently brushed it back.

As she drove, she talked, changing subjects rapidly, as if the wind tore the words from her mouth. "God, I love to drive. Maybe it's from growing up in California. You have to drive everywhere out there. Although neither of my grandmothers had a car. They walked or took the bus. Or sent my brother or me. I remember having a crush on an older boy who lived across the street. I liked him because of his car. He had a white convertible, and I thought that car was the most beautiful object I had ever seen. When I went to a museum or looked in art books, I never saw a painting or a sculpture that seemed as beautiful as that car. What was his name? Lester? Lester Cook? When he worked on his car, he wore tight black trousers and a white shirt. They looked like good clothes to me, but I supposed that anyone who could afford a white convertible could afford to get his good clothes dirty. Lester—that name still doesn't sound right. Chester? Anyway, he taught me how to drive. I'm sure it wasn't out of any affection for me. He simply wanted to show off what he knew about cars and driving, and since I was always around, hanging on his every word . . . I'll have to ask Edward what that boy's name was. Edward remembers every name, every street."

The ride was exciting, intimate in its way—the car's small interior kept our shoulders only inches apart, Laura reached out almost to my knee as she shifted gears—but that excitement was glazed with sadness. In spite of how physically close we were, I knew we could come no closer.

This was something I always logically knew, yet in all my solitary hours of fantasizing I managed to suppress that logic and to replace it with wild, erotic imagining. Now, however, with Laura actually beside me on the day of my father's funeral, reason had its way.

Laura continued to talk. "So if I like to drive so much, why don't I have a car? I always think of getting one. Or think I should. I mean, how can you live in America and not own a goddamn car? It's simply not right. Maybe I don't have one because then I don't have to make up an excuse about not driving in the winter. God, the idea of driving in ice and snow scares the hell out of me. Do you remember the blizzard we drove through a couple years ago?"

"Three years ago," I snapped. I had begun to grow impatient with her casual banter. We hadn't seen each other in years, it was my father's funeral, and all she could talk about was driving.

"Was it three years? Now, *that* trip scared me. I mean, I was absolutely petrified. Not many things frighten me, but traveling in the winter does. Let's see, we were supposed to turn at the end of a low stone wall. Have you seen a stone wall?"

My irritation prompted a question edged with cruelty. "What about your parents?"

"What about them?" she said, serious in return.

"It just seems strange that you'd love driving so much considering what happened to them."

"Yes, I suppose it might seem strange"—Laura paused—"to someone who is interested in making judgments about what is strange in other people's lives."

After that remark I shut up and so did she. She did not speak again until she turned off at the stone wall.

"Now," she said, driving slower on the narrow gravel road, "it's supposed to be about a half mile down this road. It's on your side, so keep watching."

"I don't get it," I said. "How come my dad went to a country school when he lived in town?"

"Mrs. Harris said there were three small towns right around here, all in the same county, all about the same size, and instead of having three different schools they just put one right in the middle. Didn't your dad ever tell you about going to a country school? All those corny stories about trudging wintry miles with his lunch in a pail?"

"No."

"There it is!"

Laura turned off in front of the school, an old, weathered two-story wood-frame building that looked as square as a box. Not a pane of glass was left in the building, and the small windows looked like dark expressionless eyes watching us. The paint was fading and peeling, especially around the windows, where the rocks kids had thrown had chipped and pocked the wood. Around the grounds were piles of fire-blackened logs and rusting beer cans.

"Want to go inside?" asked Laura.

"I don't suppose we'll find much."

"Now, there's an adventurous attitude." Laura opened her door. "Stay here if you'd like."

She was halfway to the building before I decided to follow.

"If you're coming," she called back to me, "reach under my coat and bring the bottle that's there."

Under her raincoat on the small ledge that passed for the car's backseat I found a half-full bottle of bourbon. I held it up by its neck. "Is this what you want?"

"That's it. Now hurry up!" Laura was already on her way inside, pushing aside the heavy door that had no knob and barely hung on its hinges.

Inside, the smell of mildew and wood rot was overwhelming. In spite of the day's warmth, the building was cool, as though a remnant of last winter's chill were still trapped inside. Shafts of sunlight made bright squares on the floor.

I was wrong about finding nothing inside: crumbling, bulging cardboard boxes of papers were stacked in the corners, and strewn all over the floors were old yellowing report cards and faded school records, attendance sheets and seating charts, examinations and worksheets and compositions. Where there weren't papers, there were dried leaves, dust balls larger than your fist, and dried rat and mouse turds. Only one room had any furniture, a heavy old teacher's desk, its wood warped, splintered, and gouged. It probably hadn't been carried away because it was in such bad shape and because it was bolted to the floor. Everywhere the dust lay so thick it looked as though it had turned to grease.

As she walked slowly through the rooms, Laura stopped now and then to look at a page. I guessed she was looking for something that might have my father's name on it. In a tuneless voice, she sang, "School days, school days, dear old golden rule days." She kept singing those words over and over. She carried the bottle of bourbon by the neck and from time-to-time brought it to her lips. She stopped singing long enough to announce that she was going upstairs.

She had only been gone a few moments when I heard her urgent call. "Paul! Paul! Come up here!"

I pounded up the stairs two and three at a time, and the wood groaned and sagged underfoot, and dust leaped up in small explosions.

When I breathlessly found her, Laura was sitting on the ledge of an open window.

"Look." She pointed outside. "The playground."

From the back door a path trailed about twenty-five yards downhill to an open space, a natural bowl the size of a football field.

"I remember your dad telling me about how he and the other boys used to chase up and down out there before school and at recess. They'd simply run back and forth, tackling and knocking each other over. No ball, no goal, no teams, no purpose. Just boys bashing into each other. And the girls along the sides watching." Laura walked to another window. "See this tree? Your dad said he used to sit right by a window and watch a tree lose its leaves in the fall and then watch the buds and the new leaves in the spring. That must be the tree, and he must have sat right here."

Laura took a long stride back from the window to where a desk might have been. I stepped over to the window and looked out at an oak tree whose branches reached to the building.

"He never told me any of those stories," I said.

Laura took another drink. "Jealous?"

"No. I don't know. Maybe."

"Did you ever ask him?"

"No."

"Why not?"

"I'm not sure. It was hard. And then we moved."

"Paul, Paul. Your father loved to tell stories. Ask the right question and he'd be off for an hour, talking nonstop."

"Yeah. . . ."

She held the bottle out. "Here. Have a drink. Maybe it'll loosen your tongue."

Years before, in Vermont, Laura had offered me a drink. Then it had been merely a sip of beer, but I was a child and I declined. This time I accepted. I took the bottle and brought it to my lips for a small, tentative swallow. The whiskey burned its way down my throat, and I handed the bottle back.

"Go ahead," she said. "Have another. Then I'm not drinking alone. Which I do entirely too often as it is."

I took another sip and handed it back to her, and the ritual was established: I drank, then she drank; she drank, then I drank. . . .

"Now," said Laura. "Where were we?"

"I don't know. Where?"

"Oh, no. It's not going to be that easy. I asked you why you never asked your dad about his childhood. But I bet you never asked him about anything. Hell, you never ask me anything. Why is that, Paul? Why don't you ask questions?"

"Maybe I'm not interested in the answers."

"Oh, bullshit," said Laura. "Don't try that tough guy pose. You want to know. I remember when you were younger how you'd stand back, but all the time you had your eyes wide open and your ears cocked like a puppy's."

I was accustomed, as any child is, to hearing others relate their memories of me, how Aunt Anne remembered the cute little sailor hat I wore when I was four, how Grandmother recalled how I mispronounced "tricycle," but I had hoped with Laura I was on different footing.

"You want to know what I think?" Laura went on. "I think you don't ask questions because you're afraid of the answers you'll get. And if you don't ask them, you can pretend that something else is true."

When I did hear others discuss my childhood, I often felt they were talking about someone like me but not me. How else to explain that I seldom shared their memories? No, they were talking about another boy, the boy whose life was on the pages of the family photo album, someone I could stand apart from and gaze at exactly as they did. But when Laura summed me up, I felt as though I had been caught and held before a mirror. And my first impulse was to wriggle free any way I could.

"How am I doing?" asked Laura.

"Not bad."

"I don't want to think I'm losing my aim."

"No, you're right on target."

"So how about it? Do you want to change?"

"Just tell me what to do."

"Ask me a question," she said. "Look right at me and ask me anything. And I'll answer you. I'll give you the absolute truth."

I had my question ready. It was perfect, I believed. Later, I might regret my manipulation of the moment, and I might regret the missed opportunity, but for now I was concerned only with scrambling out of the way.

I looked right at Laura. "Did you love my father?"

Laura opened her mouth to speak, but then she quickly turned her head as if the wind had gusted in her eyes. A sob so sudden and sharp it seemed a cry of pain escaped from her lips, and she ran from the room.

For a moment I stood motionless, marveling, barely believing in my own power. Then, as I heard Laura's footsteps echoing away from me, I called out, "Wait! Wait a minute!" and I ran after her.

I found her sitting on the desk in the first room we were in. She had her hand before her eyes as if she were hiding.

She wiped her tears and left behind a smudge of dirt on her cheek. "Maybe it's my fault. If someone asks that, maybe I didn't make something plain. . . ." She smiled weakly. "And I did say you could ask me anything."

"That's right."

"And I said I'd answer you. All right. Yes. Sure, I loved your father. You'd like more though, wouldn't you?"

I nodded.

"I've always attracted my share of—what shall we call them? Thrill-seekers? You know, men or boys who like the idea of being around someone who seems unconventional or wild or dangerous. But with your father . . . Your dad didn't want to hide me, he didn't want to show me off, he didn't want to change me, he . . . he simply treated me the way I knew he would treat any woman. That sounds so ordinary. But that was the wonderful part, the ordinariness. With your father I didn't feel like someone quivering with anger and neurosis, which is probably what I am. I felt like . . . I felt as though I wasn't so different from everyone I passed on the street. And *that* changed me. I stopped judging people so harshly; I became more forgiving, more tolerant—I'm still not very good at these things, but if you think I'm bad now, you should have seen me before. My writing changed too. I began to write poems that weren't about standing apart but about being a part. And then when your father and I stopped seeing each other, I felt myself gradually losing those qualities I had gained from being with him. Like helium leaking out of a balloon—you know? At night it's up on the ceiling, but in the morning it's on the floor. Yet it looks as if it's as full as ever. But what the hell could I do? I couldn't keep going out with your dad because it was good for me and my writing, could I? You tell me, Paul: what could I do?"

Brought so abruptly into her soliloquy, I said, "I'm not sure."

"And did I say he was charming? I didn't even believe in that until I met your father. Then I thought, why of course—it's magic, a goddamn magic charm. When you met Robert Finley, he enchanted you. And he made me laugh. Didn't he make you laugh, Paul?"

I thought for a moment. Laughter always surrounded my father and his friends, yet I didn't remember laughing. No, I remained sober. Sober as a judge.

"How's your sister doing?" Laura asked.

"All right. She wasn't that old when they were divorced, so she doesn't remember Dad being around that much."

Laura shook her head. "Be careful. Daughters have a special relationship with their fathers. Something you can't understand."

"I guess you're speaking from experience."

"Damn right." Laura reached into her pocket for her lighter and a package of Pall Malls.

By this time, all those swallows of whiskey were adding up. I felt as though the rope that usually tethered me was suddenly extended, as though I could roam farther and farther from whatever stake of morality or inhibition that I was usually staked to.

"Can I ask you another question?" I said. "Something I wanted to ask you for a long time."

"Another question. My, my. Aren't we becoming brave? Has my training paid off? What the hell, go ahead."

"After my parents split up, you wrote me a letter."

"I remember."

"You said you knew how I felt because your parents were divorced too."

"Yes."

"But I thought your parents were killed in a car accident. And you were with them."

"What's your point?"

"Which was it? Were your parents divorced or killed in a car accident?"

"How long have you been puzzling over this, Paul?"

"I don't know. A while."

"When you got my letter, did you already know about my parents?"

"Yes."

"So what did you think? That I lied?"

"I thought I might have gotten the stories screwed up."

"You took the blame yourself? Well, I'll tell you how it was, Paul. I'll tell you, then you won't have to live with this terrible burden of thinking that I'm untruthful. Or that you were confused. Both stories are true. My parents were divorced. And then they remarried a few years later. They drove from California to Nevada so they wouldn't have to wait to be married. They took my brother and me along, so it was both a wedding trip and a family vacation. When we were on our way home, we had the accident. There. Now you know how it could be that my parents were divorced and married. And you can believe this story or not."

Emboldened by whiskey, I did what I never thought I'd be able to do: I turned and walked away from Laura. I'd had enough of being scolded, lectured, or simply made foolish by her. I wanted to think of myself as a man—how could I do that if I was continually made small by Laura?

I got as far as the stairs.

When I returned, she was sitting on the floor. She had taken off her vest and rolled it up to use as a makeshift pillow against the wall. With both hands she held the bottle between her outstretched legs.

The sun had dropped behind the tall trees that circled the school, and as the building grew dimmer, its dirt and cobwebs seemed to come to life, rising off the floor or falling from the ceilings into the vacant space that light left behind. When I looked at Laura, it seemed to be through a dusty screen.

I took a few steps toward her, careful not to kick up more dust.

She looked up at me then let her head drop. Her vest slid to the floor. "I'm too drunk . . ." she said.

"Too drunk for what?"

"That's right. You hit it. Too drunk for what."

"I'm sorry."

"Don't be."

"I mean for the questions I asked. For doubting you."

She weakly raised a hand. "Please. You're right to doubt me. You should always doubt me. Always."

I sat down on the floor beside her.

"You're getting your suit dirty," she said.

"That's okay. I'm not going to any funerals for a while."

"I'm not going to any goddamn funerals *ever*. Positively my last."

"You didn't go to this one—remember?"

"You know what I mean." She handed the bottle to me. "Here. I'm done."

I should have been too, but I took the bottle, uncapped it, and drank. The liquor no longer burned.

"Do you still have your dog?" I asked Laura.

"Evan? Absolutely. I'll never be without Evan. He's my faithful companion. Woman's best goddamn friend."

"Did you bring him with you?"

"Couldn't. The occasion is too mournful. Evan can't cope with mournful occasions." Laura slumped over against my shoulder. "I miss my do-o-o-og."

I tried to keep her leaning against me with a joke. "Do you want me to bark?"

"Howl. Evan doesn't bark. He howls."

Obligingly, I dropped my head back and did a pitiful imitation of a wolf's howl. "How's that?"

"Terrible. Don't even try." Laura's voice was deep and slow. "I have to sleep," she said. "Just for a few minutes. Then we can go."

She slid down until her head was resting on my thigh. For a long time I stared at her face, especially her eyes, restless beneath their lids. The quiet, the stillness made me realize how drunk I was. If I stood, I would have trouble walking; if I spoke, I couldn't be sure what words would tumble out.

Just when Laura had been silent long enough for me to be convinced she was sleeping, she suddenly spoke, her words coming out in such fits and starts it was as if she were reading them from a TelePrompTer that was running too slowly. "Your dad. He knew how to be happy. Without reason. He could *will* himself to be happy. He could be up to his knees in shit. But he'd decide to be happy. I envied that so much. Then I hated him for it at other times."

"Yeah," I said. "He was a pretty happy guy."

"*Mm-mh,*" Laura said sleepily. "Pretty happy."

Then she was sleeping, breathing deeply and looking, as sleeping people sometimes do, as if she had gone away and left her body behind.

So I wouldn't disturb her, I sat still. I sat very still and I gazed at her.

I asked myself why I was so completely in her thrall. Her moods were mercurial; she was stubbornly independent, singularly unreliable, and possibly alcoholic. She neglected her beauty. She was as capable of cruelty as kindness; she could be as easily angry as affectionate. Yet after what began as a childhood infatuation, I was still pinned down by her, as my leg was under the weight of her head.

The top two buttons of Laura's shirt were undone, and the material had gapped open. I could see the lacy rim of her brassiere, the pale fleshy swell of her breast, and her cleavage, a darker shadow in a room now full of shadows.

Blame it on drunkenness. Blame it on desire. And if I can't remember which, it is because memory, traveling as it does by logic, has trouble reaching those irrational states. Then later, sober and without desire, it is almost impossible to remember what it was like to be lost in those kingdoms.

No matter what the motive, I did something then that was so out of character I later felt one part of me had betrayed another.

With all the stealth of a pickpocket, I slipped my hand inside that gap in her blouse. I moved slowly, so slowly my motion could hardly seem deliberate. Then my hand was there, above her breast, and then, even slower, I lowered my hand, lowered it until it was difficult to tell the precise instant that divided not-touching from touching.

But touching I was. I didn't do more than rest my hand, half on her rough-textured brassiere and half on that flesh that was soft and firm at the same time.

In my excitement, my exhilaration, I felt as though my body changed, as though I could fly to all the cobwebbed corners of that dusky classroom—but why would I fly when it would mean leaving the one spot on earth I most wanted to be on?

I had my hand on Laura's breast for no more than a minute—too short a time to do anything more than be amazed that it was there—when I came out of my reverie and looked down again at her.

Her eyes were open.

I didn't know what to do. The hand that only seconds before gave me more pleasure than I had ever known I now wished wasn't a part of me at all.

Then Laura said quite clearly, "I want to get up, Paul. Please move your hand." She waited motionlessly as if my hand were an explosive that had to be disconnected before she could safely move. After I slid my hand out, she stood, straightened her skirt and brushed herself off. She started to button her blouse but stopped. "Or maybe you want me to leave this undone?"

I couldn't tell if she was joking or serious. I dumbly shook my head no.

"I didn't know that's what you wanted, Paul. You should have come right out and said so. Didn't I once lecture you on that?"

I stood up unsteadily.

Laura hopped up on the desk and pulled her skirt high on her thighs. In the darkening room the flesh of her legs was as brightly pale as her shirt.

"Why didn't you say what you wanted, Paul? Why didn't you simply say that on the day of your father's funeral you wanted to fuck a woman he fucked?" She put her hands behind her and leaned back. She spread her legs and moved closer to the desk's edge.

"But I'm not going to do anything on this filthy floor," Laura said, "so you'll have to step up to the desk and work it out from this angle."

I stood in stunned silence, unable to comprehend, to speak, to act.

"Let's get on with it," she said impatiently. "I want to get this over with and take you back to town. I'm driving back to Vermont tonight."

When I still didn't move, she urged, "Come on. Just step right in there. But take it easy. I'm dry. And get it out before you come, will you. I'm not interested in having your kid."

By that time I couldn't have done anything if I had wanted to. And I had long since stopped wanting to. Ashamed and humiliated, I did the one thing that I thought would allow me to grab a last scrap of pride before it all blew away. Without saying a word, I turned and walked out of the room and out of the building. This time I didn't turn back. Once outside I quickened my pace until soon I was running, past Laura's car and down to the road.

I tried to stay close to the side of the road, but my stumbling drunkenness, my tears of mortification and anger, and the deepening darkness made it hard to see, much less negotiate, the road's narrow shoulder.

I wasn't far down the highway when I heard Laura's car, and soon her headlights threw my shadow out in front of me. She stayed close behind me for a long time, the sports car growling along in second gear.

Finally she pulled alongside me. "Come on, Paul," she said. "I'll take you back to town."

"I'd rather walk."

"Oh, get in, for Christ's sake. You're not even headed in the right direction. Where are you going—Buffalo?"

Because I couldn't even stalk off correctly, I decided to get in the car. I was also feeling too wobbly to walk much farther.

As soon as I shut the door, Laura threw the car into gear and took off. For a long time she drove silently, pushing the car hard through the road's hills and curves.

Finally, shouting above the rushing air and the car's engine, she asked, "What the hell was that all about back there?"

I didn't reply. I was afraid if I spoke I'd burst into tears.

"All right. Don't talk. Fuck it. Fuck *you*."

She drove faster still. We were on a road I didn't recognize. I was sure the road we came out on was flat, but this one was full of rises and dips, and each time the car flew over one my stomach lurched. When I couldn't take it any longer, I asked Laura, "Could you stop for a minute? I don't think . . . I don't feel that well."

She pulled off the road immediately, and as soon as the car stopped, I fumbled my way out the door. I hoped to get off in the woods, out of Laura's sight and hearing, but I didn't make it. I had just stepped off the dirt shoulder and into the ditch when the vomit boiled out of me. For the next few minutes I stood doubled over, retching again and again into the weeds.

When I finished, I stayed in the ditch and called back to Laura, "Maybe you should go on back. I really think I'll walk." My trousers were soaked to the knees from standing in the tall dew-wet grass.

Laura only laughed. "Get the hell up here and get in. Your face is as white as your shirt. You wouldn't get a hundred yards. Besides, you still don't know the way."

I slid into the car carefully. My head felt clearer but light, almost weightless, as though it could float away from my body at any time.

Laura reached down to the floor and brought up a box of Kleenex. "Here. Blow your nose. And if you're going to be sick again, for God's sake, tell me. I don't want to return a car that smells like puke."

"The guy who owns this car," I said. "Is he your boyfriend?"

"Not yet," she said, and sped off again.

When the lights of Beckwith were visible ahead, Laura suddenly said, "Blame it on the whiskey."

"What?"

"What you did at the schoolhouse. You can blame it on the whiskey. That's one of the wonderful features of alcohol. You can do outrageous things and then say it was because you were drunk. It's a terrific excuse. And the next day you can say you don't remember a goddamn thing."

I remained silent.

The hotel where my mother, Janie, and I were staying was on a public square in the middle of town, and Laura drove the sports car once around the square before stopping in front of the hotel.

"Here you are," Laura said. She stared straight ahead.

I opened the door then stopped. "Can I ask you one more thing?"

"If it's 'Am I angry?' the answer is no. But I am tired. I am very tired at this moment."

"That's not what I was going to ask."

"Am I going to tell your mother? Is that what you want to know?"

I took a deep breath. "Are you going to write a poem about my father?"

She turned to look at me. "Do you know what de Maupassant said about writers? 'A writer,' he said, 'is someone who, when he hears the dirt hitting his friend's coffin, thinks, now, how can I use that?'" She paused and tilted her head back as if she were searching for stars in the spring sky. "No, I'm not going to write a poem about your father. I'll never write another poem again before I write one about him. Even if that's the only poem I have left to write, I won't write about him."

Her answer surprised and disappointed me, but I couldn't say that. So there I was, stuck with one leg out of the car and one in and nothing to say but good-bye and I didn't want to say it because it would be forever.

But the engine was running, Laura was impatient to go on, and in the hotel my mother and Janie were waiting for me so we could return to Minnesota the next day.

"I guess I better go," I said as if it were my idea. "I'm sorry about tonight. Drive carefully. Good night. Good-bye. . . ." I tried closing the door gently, but it wouldn't catch and I had to slam it a second time.

"Take some aspirin before you go to bed," Laura said. "And don't be worried when you see how thirsty you are in the morning."

I walked toward the hotel. I was almost to the door when Laura called after me, "Paul! Wait!"

I turned around, and she was out of the car and coming quickly toward me. The car's engine was still running.

Laura walked directly up to me, stood on her tiptoes, reached her arms around my neck, and said, "I know this isn't what you had in mind. . . ." She kissed me on the mouth, a kiss that surprised, even frightened me with its fullness and intensity.

I had kissed a few girls before, but I never realized until Laura's kiss that with the others there was something withheld, something provisional, something tentative. Laura's mouth was open startlingly wide, and her lips felt as though they would yield forever, yet she pressed them against me with such force she could have moved me backward.

Then she let me go and ran back to the waiting car, and before I could think to speak, she was driving away and I was left watching her hair waving behind her in the wind, and then I couldn't tell where her hair's darkness quit and where the night's began.

AS FAR AS I know, Laura never wrote a poem about my father. Years later, however, when she was publishing more fiction than poetry, she had a story in *Esquire* called "Too Tired." The story is about a man's mistress who, on the day after the man's funeral, makes love to his son. The lovemaking takes place in a barn, and the son is sixteen, very thin, and recovering from pneumonia. The woman makes love to him because she knows how lonely her life is going to be, and she is unsure if she can afford to let any opportunity for intimacy pass.

I have read the story so many times it no longer seems in any way about Laura, my father, or me. Instead, it happens now in that impersonal world of art, that world where even our tears can give us pleasure because we shed them for lives not our own.

Seven

In January 1964, during my junior year at Afton, some friends and I, after a night of semidrunken wandering, ended up at an off-campus party. I didn't know whose party it was or even why we stayed, because we were plainly out of place. The people at the party were the art, literature, music, and drama majors, the self-styled bohemians, the artistes, the activists who passed out leaflets or circulated petitions in the student union. My friends and I, on the other hand, were the science, math, and engineering majors, the grinds, the colorless, unimaginative, apolitical students who paid attention to little in the world that couldn't be proven with an experiment or solved with an equation.

Uncomfortable, beer in hand, I walked around the party and eavesdropped. I listened to some blue-workshirt types discuss whether it was better to volunteer for the Peace Corps or to work in a poor region in this country. (I liked noticing that they hadn't volunteered for either.) Two young women tried to convince a friend of mine that Afton should not participate in intercollegiate athletics. Somewhere a stereo was playing a Bob Dylan album, and I heard an older woman say to a group of students that she had seen Dylan perform in Dinkytown in Minneapolis.

Then I saw Martha, though I didn't yet know her name. In the living room a few people were sitting on the floor around a hassock on which sat a ruddy-cheeked young woman in a plaid skirt and bulky, fisherman's-knit sweater. Though she was sitting, I could tell she was tall. She was also plump and heavy-breasted and pretty in a square-jawed, fresh-faced sort of way—what I often thought of as a typical farm girl.

She was holding a book at arm's length—probably to catch what little light was in the flickering, candlelit room—and reading aloud. She read with great feeling, and with her free hand she flipped back the long, straight blond hair that kept falling in her face. On the floor next to her was a glass of red wine from which she occasionally drank. I decided to get closer.

It didn't take long. I heard a word, a phrase, and I knew. She was reading from *Dreams a Woman Has*, Laura's first book of poems.

I circled quietly behind her and sat down a few feet away. She finished reading, closed the book, and reverently held it for a moment on her lap. After a moment of respectful silence, I said, "I know her."

It took a moment before she realized I was talking to her. "What did you say?"

I pointed to the copy of Laura's book, a well-worn paperback. "I know her."

She looked down at the book and then back up at me. She didn't understand what I was saying, but she kept smiling politely.

"I said, I know her, Laura Pettit. Isn't that *Dreams a Woman Has?*"

Once more she looked down at the book, this time curiously, as though now she wasn't quite sure what she held. "You know Laura Pettit?"

"She was a friend of my parents," I said.

At that she launched herself from the hassock and in one quick step landed next to me on the couch.

"Really?" she asked.

The room was uncomfortably warm, though it was below zero outside, and above Martha's upper lip and, in the not-quite-hairless space between her eyebrows tiny droplets of sweat glistened.

"My father was an editor for Harrison House. My parents knew a lot of writers."

"But do *you* know her?"

"I know her too."

"Okay. You have to tell me everything about her. Laura Coe Pettit is my absolute hero."

"What do you want to know?"

"I told you. Everything. *Everything.*"

"Well, she's short—should I start there?"

She waved her hands back and forth as if she were trying to erase something written in the air. "Not what she looks like. What she's *like.*"

I began then to tell her about Laura, but what I conveyed was, for the most part, a public persona—and not an entirely pleasant one. I said she was candid, impatient, short-tempered, not always understanding of others' failures or shortcomings, but of course I added intelligent, sensitive, without vanity, and courageous. To raise my account above the level of book jacket bio I tossed in a few details to verify my personal knowledge: I mentioned her skewering another writer on the subject of Hemingway and war in my parents' kitchen, her breathless bicycle ride up and down the Vermont hills, her chain-smoking, her habit of sometimes finishing your sentences for you. . . . Of course there was much that I withheld: my father's relationship with Laura and the tension she once caused our household, and naturally I said nothing about my love for her or about the pathetic pass I made on the day of my father's funeral.

AFTER THE PARTY I walked Martha back to her dormitory. Kessler Hall had two doors, an outer door that led into a small foyer and then a foyer door that led into the dorm's lobby. The outer doors were locked, on weekends, at twelve-thirty A.M., and residents had to be through the doors by that time. The inner door, however, remained open until 1:00 A.M., so it was possible to remain in the tiny foyer for half an hour. It was not uncommon for five, six, or seven couples to be jammed into that area that wasn't much larger than a closet for thirty minutes of making out. Inside the entryway you heard the sounds of heavy breathing and the rubbing and rustling of fabric and cloth, but no words. Once you stepped inside, it was all business. On winter nights the heat and steam of bodies and breath frosted the windows and glass doors, and the small space felt like a greenhouse, and smelled like one, perfume providing the floral scent and stored-up sex giving off some odor of earth. At five minutes to one, a buzzer sounded, but no embrace broke at that signal, not for four and a half more minutes.

There would be plenty of nights when Martha and I jostled for space in there, but that first night we stayed out and stepped off to the side into a sheltered, snowless space between a few fir trees and the front door.

Two things startled me that night when I kissed Martha. First, though I had been looking at her all night, I wasn't prepared for what her size felt like. When I held her—her bulk made all the greater by the woolen layers of sweater and toggle coat—it seemed my arms couldn't begin to go around her far enough to make any impression at all.

The second thing that surprised me was the kiss she gave me. The icy rims of our glasses clicked, our freezing cheeks brushed numbly against each other, our cold, chapped lips pressed together . . . Then out of all this chill into my mouth suddenly came Martha's warm tongue, and it was so unexpected I involuntarily broke our kiss. "What's the matter?" she asked.

Embarrassed, I said, "Nothing. I just . . . My foot slipped." As if feet had anything to do with it.

She laughed and kindly continued what she had started.

Despite the cold, I walked home that night heated by my own euphoria. Overhead the stars glittered like chips of ice, the packed snow creaked underfoot, my breath bloomed before me like a white flower, and the taste of Martha Lundegaard was still warm on my tongue. Then it occurred to me that I had Laura Pettit to thank for Martha's kisses, and immediately on the heels of that thought another rushed in to add, to conjecture how much better it would be to hold Laura herself in my arms. A chill ran through me, and the taste on my tongue turned to ash.

MARTHA LUNDEGAARD AND I had been going together for a few weeks when she asked if she could meet my mother. At least that was the way Martha worded her request, but when she showed up at my grandparents' on the appointed Saturday morning, it was plain, from the pen, notebook, and list of questions that Martha brought with her, that she did not wish merely to meet my mother but to interview her. The subject of the interview? Who else—Laura Coe Pettit, who was also the subject of a research paper Martha was writing.

My mother found the situation amusing ("Does this mean I'll be a bibliography entry?"), and she agreed to answer Martha's questions, most of them obvious and innocuous. One of my mother's responses, however, surprised both Martha and me. Martha asked my mother if Laura would be remembered as one of the greatest poets of the century. "Oh, no," my mother answered. "I really don't believe Laura is a very good *poet*. I'm fond of her, and I would certainly defend her against her detractors—isn't that a friend's job?—but just among us: No, I certainly don't think she will be remembered as one of our finer poets."

Martha's pen stopped scribbling. Slack-jawed and wide-eyed, Martha asked, "Really? Do you *really* think that?"

My mother smiled knowingly. Suddenly she was talking not to a guest in her living room but to a classroom of students. "I believe that absolutely. Laura Pettit's poetry certainly has an intensity about it, but as for craft . . . well, no matter how often I read her poems, I am unable to see that the words have arrived there by any but the most arbitrary means. Now, I am not about to insist that she work in fixed forms—I know that for better or worse we live in the age of free verse and to rail against that is to be nothing but a literary reactionary—but if Laura were to demonstrate in some way that she was the master of her words, that she bent and shaped them to *her* purposes rather than the other way around . . . But of course I am asking for her to be someone other than who she is. And then we wouldn't have any poems at all, would we? And flawed poems are better than no poems, aren't they?"

My mother's judgment startled me, but for the moment Martha's reaction commanded my attention. When my mother made her pronouncement, Martha's breathing seemed to stop. Her cheeks puffed up with the force of her held breath, and her florid complexion darkened to a deeper red. Then she let her breath go with an explosion of air. "You really don't think Laura Pettit is a *great* poet?"

My mother replied, "I don't even believe she's in the top twenty, if we were rating writers like records. And we're not. But I will agree that often Laura catches something, some dissatisfaction or anger or frustration or longing, that's floating around in the air today and she is able to bring this, this *zeitgeist* into her poems. But that only counts for popularity, not greatness. And we certainly know that those aren't the same thing, don't we?"

My mother offered Martha a cigarette, and Martha accepted. It looked as though Martha smoked without inhaling.

Into the silence made by the lighting of cigarettes, I spoke up. "I disagree."

Martha and my mother looked at me as though they had forgotten I was in the room. "Excuse me?" my mother said.

"I said I disagree. With what you said about Laura. I think she's a great poet."

Once, on one of our earliest summer trips to Vermont, I brought back to the house what was, I was sure, the world's largest frog, and when I showed it to my mother, it was with considerable pride. My mother hated frogs, lizards, turtles, and snakes, but she smiled pleasantly at me and then advised me to take the frog back to the pond so it could be with its family. She smiled the same smile when I made my statement about Laura and her poetry: my mother may have been proud of me for having an opinion, but she would just as soon I took it back to the pond.

"I didn't know," she said, "that you paid such attention to contemporary literature."

"I know Laura," I said. "I've read her poetry."

"Usually we need more than a single experience to make judgments. After all, if we had nothing to compare it to, we might think tapioca was the most delicious pudding in the world. And just because we like something doesn't necessarily make it good, does it? I mean, I once enjoyed—I was positively addicted to—the novels of Erle Stanley Gardner. I *liked* them, but I knew they were dreadful. You see the difference, don't you?"

"I think Laura's a great poet," I repeated. "The greatest."

My mother's smile widened but didn't become any warmer. "Of course you're not exactly free of prejudice, are you?"

My mother may only have been stating an obvious fact: that Laura was a family friend, my father's ex-mistress, and I couldn't possibly be impartial or disinterested where she was concerned. But perhaps my mother knew something of the life Laura lived in my fantasies and that was what she was alluding to. Either way, her tactic worked. I shut up.

And there the interview, such as it was, ended. Martha, perhaps sens-
ing that here were waters whose depths she did not want to test, excused
herself, saying that she had an exam she had to study for. I offered to give
her a ride back to the dorm, but she refused.

"Ever since I read that book of Pettit's," she said, "you know, the one
where she walks all the time? Ever since then I walk almost everywhere."

"I'll walk you then," I said. "I want to go to the library anyway."

In the hall, as the thank-yous, good-byes, and do-come-again pleas-
antries were being made, Martha turned quite suddenly and asked my
mother, "So if you don't think Laura Pettit is the greatest poet, who is?"

My mother laughed, shuddered in the chill from the open door, and
said, "In my opinion that would be Robert Lowell. And Paul once met
him too, but obviously Cal did not make the impression that Laura did."

While we walked through the snow to the campus, Martha told me
how pleased she was that I had defended Laura and her reputation. "I
wanted to say something, but you know. It's not just that she's your
mother; she's a teacher. Probably I could argue with her in class. You
know, I'm always starting arguments in my British Lit class. But in her
living room. I just couldn't think how to say anything. That's why I was
glad you said something."

Back at the house, my mother made only one comment to me about
Martha's visit and the disagreement that came out of the "interview." "If
you're going to question my literary judgments in front of others," she
said, "I suggest you try to gain some knowledge of the subject. That way
I'll feel free to argue with you and not worry about making you look
utterly foolish."

THOUGH I DIDN'T denounce my chemistry major or my group of sci-
ence-minded friends, Martha managed frequently to pull me loose from
them. She invited me to concerts, plays, lectures, and exhibits. I can't
say I particularly enjoyed all of them, but I dutifully tagged along wher-
ever Martha wanted to go. My attendance at these cultural events I
thought of as payment, and small payment indeed for what I was receiv-
ing in return.

By this time Martha and I had begun to sleep together, and though for that alone I felt grateful, there was even more I felt I should repay. Martha not only gave herself to me, but—and this was as important to me at the time—she gave herself totally, willingly, freely, ungrudgingly. I used to wonder why in spite of the anatomical fact of the sex act people always spoke of women giving and men getting. I wondered about this until I realized it had nothing to do with anatomy but everything to do with who had the greater gift and who the greater need. Martha saw that sex was what I wanted and, like a nurse bringing the cool cloth to the fevered forehead of her patient, took her pleasure less from satisfying her own needs and more from ministering to the needs of another. Martha would turn to me and earnestly ask, after we had been to the movie or the party or while we walked in the woods or watched television, "You want to, don't you?" And I would not even have to humble myself so far as to nod in assent but simply had to stare wishfully, needfully back at her, and Martha would instantly begin pulling off her sweater, unbuttoning her blouse, unfastening her bra and letting her large breasts tumble free, hiking up her skirt, and stepping out of her panties—which she always tucked into the sleeve of her blouse or sweater so she would not lose track of them.

Therefore if it meant that in return for these favors I went with Martha to listen to an evening of Bach or to see another production of a Beckett play or to hear another poet read poems I didn't understand, I was willing. And on one occasion, I was more than willing. . . .

ON A FEBRUARY morning in 1965, Martha burst into my grandparents' house and, waving a newspaper, shouted, "Guess who's coming!"

My mother and grandparents were shopping for groceries, a Saturday morning ritual for them, and as soon as Martha entered the house, Janie left too. Although she didn't dislike Martha, Janie was mildly disapproving of her and of our relationship. It was nothing personal. Unlike most teenagers, my sister was completely focused on a life of the mind. She was the top student at Fairmont High School, and she had chosen not only her college but also her career. She would study entomology at U.C. Berkeley, go on for her doctorate, and devote the rest of her years to insect research. When my father gave Janie that microscope so many years ago, he couldn't have known she would soon be lost to the rest of the world.

Martha rushed in without hat, mittens, or scarf and with her coat unbuttoned. Her wind-chapped cheeks and her breathlessness told me she must have run all the way from the college. Under her coat she wore an oversized Afton College T-shirt that came down to mid-thigh, plaid wool culottes, and tennis shoes. She was not wearing any makeup, her hair was loose, and if I was able to judge accurately, she wasn't wearing anything under her T-shirt.

"I can't believe it!" Martha said to me. "She's coming. . . ."

"Take it easy," I said. "Who's coming?"

"Laura Pettit!"

"She's coming *here*? When?"

Martha opened the newspaper and began excitedly to flip through the pages of the *Minneapolis Tribune*. "I know it's in here," she said.

I stepped back and let Martha look. I knew what my reaction to Laura's visit was supposed to be—my excitement should have surpassed Martha's—yet I felt a curious hesitancy, as if something I had always wanted was held out to me and now I was reluctant to accept it.

But I hadn't seen Laura since my father's funeral, the day I made the drunken, stupid, clumsy pass at her, and I didn't know how she felt about me or how she would react. I had seen a demonstration of her anger, and I had heard stories about her excoriating people in public or throwing drinks in their faces, and I didn't want to be another "Did you hear what Laura Pettit did this time?" anecdote. The Laura Pettit I possessed privately, in fantasy, was easier to control and predict than the volatile public one.

"Here it is!" said Martha. "Right here!" She thrust the newspaper at me.

At the bottom of the page was a black-bordered advertisement. The Lantern, a Minneapolis arts center, was announcing its schedule for the upcoming months. And there, amid the list of productions, concerts, and exhibits, was Laura's name. As part of a series of writers' lectures and readings, Laura Coe Pettit would read from her own work and discuss "The Poet As the World's Captive." On March 10, 1965, at seven-thirty P.M., Laura would be in Minneapolis again.

"She's going to be in Minneapolis," I said. "I thought you meant she was going to be *here.*"

"So what! It's close enough!"

"What day of the week is that?"

"You can introduce me to her. I can meet her."

"We might have to miss classes. . . ."

Martha grabbed my shoulders and looked intently at me. "We're going," she said. "Say it. We're going."

"Sure," I said jauntily. "We're going."

She let go of my shoulders and threw her arms around me in an embrace that knocked the wind out of me. I put my arms up inside her coat and T-shirt and ran my hands up her back. I had guessed right: she wasn't wearing a bra.

"Of course we're going," I said again. "Why wouldn't we?"

ON AN OVERCAST, misty day in March, Martha and I caught a ride to Minneapolis with three of Martha's female friends who were on their way to a Kinks concert. They would drop us at The Lantern, and after Laura's reading, Martha and I would spend the night at her parents' house in St. Paul. Early the next morning we would catch the bus back to Fairmont in time for afternoon classes. That was the stated plan, but I dreamed of ways that I might depart from it. I assumed Laura would be staying overnight in Minneapolis, and after the reading, I planned to attach myself to her and stay with her as long as I could. And if I had to leave Martha behind in my rush to follow Laura, so be it. As if to empha-size my willingness to betray, Martha and I did not sit together in her friend's black Volkswagen. I sat in the front seat, while Martha was wedged between her friends in the back. The car threw out so little heat we all kept our coats on.

As we were all college seniors, the conversation naturally turned to our lives after graduation. My future in particular was of concern, since, for males, leaving school meant losing one's 2-S, the student military defer-ment. Americans were killing and being killed already in Vietnam but quietly and in numbers small enough that being drafted was not yet the ticket to almost certain horror it would soon become. Still, my friends and

I constantly discussed ways of staying out of the army, and talk of medical and married deferments, of 4-Fs and 1-Ys, of joining the National Guard or Reserves, was as common as talk of exams, women, or beer.

Patty, the girl driving, asked me, "How about you, Paul? Are they going to get you when you graduate?"

"You could get married," Marcia said from the backseat and then giggled.

"I'm going to med school."

"If you get in," Martha reminded me.

"If I get in."

"God, I'm glad I'm not a guy," said Patty.

"Unless you get knocked up," Marcia said and giggled again.

"Unless I get knocked up," Patty said, and twisted the steering wheel of the Volkswagen, weaving back and forth across the deserted highway.

At that everyone laughed, even Martha and I. We could afford to; a married cousin supplied Martha with still rare but already legendary birth control pills, and I was reasonably confident that one of the schools I had applied to would accept me. No surprises in our futures.

IN THE LECTURE HALL where Laura was to appear, we sat, at Martha's insistence, in the front row, less than twenty feet from the stage and the lectern where Laura would stand. We would have a perfect view of her. And she of us. I hoped the rest of the seats in the hall would fill in quickly so when Laura came out and saw me in the audience she wouldn't automatically assume Martha and I were together.

Along with her battered copy of *Dreams a Woman Has* Martha held a loose-leaf notebook on her lap.

"What's that?" I pointed to the notebook. "Planning to take notes?"

Martha blushed. "Poems."

"Oh, yeah? Whose?"

Her blush deepened. "Mine."

In our months together I never knew that Martha wrote poetry, yet the revelation didn't surprise me. "Really? Let me see."

Martha pressed her hands tighter against her notebook. "I don't think so."

"Come on. We've got plenty of time. It's not supposed to start for half an hour. And she'll probably be late anyway. She's always late."

"No." Martha shifted the notebook farther from me.

"Why did you bring them if you won't let me read them?"

Sheepishly Martha said, "I thought maybe I could get Laura Pettit to look at them."

"You'll let a stranger see them but not me?"

"It's different. . . ."

"Different? How is it different?"

"She's a poet," Martha said impatiently. "I trust her opinion. She *knows*."

I laughed. "I don't want to judge them. I just want to read them. Besides, when is she going to read your poems?"

Martha grabbed my arm. "She will if you ask her to."

"Wait a minute. I don't know . . ."

"Please. She doesn't have to read them now. She can take them with her. I just have to know if they're any good."

I didn't say no immediately. I decided simply to trust that circumstances would solve the problem for me.

By seven-thirty the hall was full; people were standing at the back and sides of the room, and in the small open space between our row and the stage students were sitting on the floor. "They should have gotten a bigger room," Martha whispered to me. "They should have known everybody would want to hear Laura Pettit." I didn't say anything, but I wondered how this crowd compared to the one at the Kinks concert.

By seven-fifty Laura had not appeared, and the audience was restless. People fidgeted in their chairs, sighed, and asked those near them the time. A woman behind us said, "I heard this happens all the time. And sometimes she doesn't show up at all." Martha turned around angrily, but I said, "Take it easy. It's probably true."

At eight, Jeffrey Duncan, the young professor who would introduce Laura and would preside over the occasion, came out onto the stage, bent down to the microphone, and cautiously, as if he were afraid of electrical shock, tapped the mike twice to get our attention. He told us he had called Laura's hotel and though she would be delayed—appar-

ently there was some mix-up about the time her lecture was to begin—
she would be there. He asked for our patience.

Drunk, I thought. Laura was drunk and had forgotten about her
appearance or had passed out and slept through it. I looked at Martha
and said, as if I were responsible, "Sorry."

She smiled. "I can wait."

At eight-fifteen Duncan came out on stage again. This time he raised
his arms in the air like a referee signaling a touchdown. "She's here!" In
anticipation, Martha drew in her breath.

Even if the evening had been starting on time, his introduction would
have been too long. He mentioned all of Laura's publications and awards
and quoted critics in praise of her work. He then went into an even longer
discourse on the sacred role the poet plays in all societies. This part of the
introduction was designed to impress us not with Laura but with him. He
closed by saying that Miss Pettit had a train to catch that night and wouldn't
be able to answer questions from the audience following her talk. He even
had the temerity to say, "And now, without further ado, Laura Coe Pettit!"

The applause began, and I bowed my head and closed my eyes so I
wouldn't see her right away. I calculated how long it had been since I saw
her. Not quite four years. And if I kept my head down and my eyes shut,
if I didn't *have* to look at her, perhaps it would mean, perhaps I could pretend, that after four years the spell was broken.

Less than ten seconds later, when the applause was still at its peak,
when I could stand it no longer, I looked up to see her again.

Laura was walking swiftly across the stage. She held a cigarette and
her glasses in one hand and in the other a manila folder and her pack of
Pall Malls. She wore what it seemed she always wore, a black turtleneck
and a gray flannel skirt, though this skirt was shorter and tighter than
the ones she wore in the past. In place of her usual walking shoes were
high heels that emphasized her thin, shapely legs. The only jewelry I saw
was a thin silver strand around her right wrist. But in none of this was
there any surprise. That came when I saw her hair. It was short, boyishly
short, a length and style worn by Audrey Hepburn and other actresses
and models who were popularizing a waifish look. And her black hair
was generously flecked and streaked with gray.

Gray hair or not, she looked wonderful, and she had made conces-
sions to appearance she hadn't made before. She was wearing makeup,
mascara that made her eyes look exotically large and emphasized their
almond shape. Her lipstick was not the pale pink popular at the time but
a decisive deep red.

"She's beautiful!" Martha gasped.

Laura reached the lectern and put down her folder and cigarettes and
adjusted the microphone. She hadn't looked up or spoken to the audience when she motioned to someone offstage. She put her hand over the
microphone, but those of us in the front rows could hear her say, "I'm
going to need an ashtray." She held her cigarette upright to keep the
lengthening ash from falling to the floor.

I wondered if she would even notice me. The darkness we sat in was
not total, but the hall was dimly lit and the lights above the stage might
have brought down a curtain of shadows she couldn't see beyond.

Duncan appeared again, now carrying a Folgers coffee can. He
handed it to Laura and apologized. "This is the best I can do." Laura took
it, examined it curiously as if she had never seen a coffee can before,
then elaborately dumped the ashes from her cigarette into it. "It works!"
she cried. The audience laughed and applauded.

Laura was still not quite ready. She carefully arranged her notes,
crushed out her cigarette in the coffee can, immediately lit another, and
said into the microphone, "Hello, Paul. Is your mother here tonight?"

Amplified to the entire audience, her question didn't seem as though
it could possibly be for me, and for a moment I didn't say or do anything.
Martha nudged me. "She's talking to *you!*"

Then it sunk in and I responded automatically, "She couldn't make
it."

Still without looking up, Laura said, "Pity. Tell her I said hello."
Then, as explanation, she added, "Old friends of mine," and I felt myself
blush.

Laura thanked her introducer, The Lantern and its sponsors, and the
audience. Then she apologized, for being late, for being unable to stay
to answer questions, and for her voice—she was recovering from a cold
and hoped everyone would be able to hear her. Laura also said she had

a special affection for Minneapolis; she had fond memories of the city and its people. Laura confessed she had once considered moving to Minneapolis but a blizzard scared her away.

The audience's irritation and impatience vanished with Laura's first words of flattery, and now they applauded her remarks about their city, laughed at her references to blizzards, and moaned at her years-old decision not to move to Minneapolis.

Of all these admirers of Laura Pettit, however, I seemed to be the one to offer the briefest applause, and I wondered why, in the face of all her charm and beauty, I resisted.

Then the answer came to me: I was jealous. I *had* been devoted to Laura for years, yet now she spent her allure on strangers. I *had* fallen at her feet, but now I was simply one more occupied seat among these rows of fans. Martha leaned forward in her chair, eager for every word, every gesture, every nuance. Meanwhile, I sat formally upright, resolved that Laura was going to have to win me all over again.

"This evening was billed as a lecture," Laura began. "I don't know about you, but I hate lectures. I hate to give them, and I hate to sit through them." She was interrupted by applause. "So if it's all right with you, I'm simply going to read some of the poems I've been working on lately"—here the applause was even more enthusiastic—"and perhaps I can make a few remarks about them that will have something to do with the announced topic. That way no one can accuse us of false advertising." This time there was not only applause but also whistles and shouts of approval.

"Let's see. What was the topic? Ah yes. 'The Poet As the World's Captive.' Now, what the hell was I thinking when I proposed that? Maybe nothing more than this: Poets are always held captive by what they witness. Others might be able to walk away from what they see and hear as they schlepp through the world, but poets—poets can't get rid of the sound of that woman crying or that sight of the dead bird lying next to the fire hydrant. They can't get rid of these until they pay the ransom. And of course the poem is that ransom." Laura paused and looked at her watch. "There, that wasn't so bad, was it? Five minutes, and that concludes the lecture. Now let's get to some poems."

I had by this time realized another source of my annoyance with Laura: She was performing. It was not only that the audience loved her but that she played to them and played from a script she had rehearsed. And the Laura I had built up in my mind over the years would not do that. That Laura would have read her poems coolly; if the audience liked them, fine; if they didn't, they could go to hell. Yet the Laura before me obviously cared how her poems were received. She chanted them and whispered them; she was bent low by their weight and lifted high by their lyricism; she came out from behind the lectern and walked to the edge of the stage as if she were carrying them as close to us as she could— if we could only reach the rest of the way. She knew the poems by heart and seldom looked at the pages she had brought out with her.

Laura read for almost an hour and then (too obviously, I felt) looked at her watch. "I'm sorry, but I have a train to catch. This will have to be the last poem. And once again, I wish I had time to stay and answer questions, but I have to run. . . ." She clutched her throat. "Besides, I'm afraid I've run out of voice." She proceeded to read "The Old Complaint," her best known and most often reprinted poem.

Then she was done and backing off the stage and waving to us as if she were already on the train and it was pulling slowly from the station, and the love she had courted the audience for followed her in wave after wave of wild applause.

The lights in the auditorium came on, and reluctantly people stood and put on their coats. After the ovation, the hall was strangely hushed, as if no one dared put his or her voice into the silence. Wordlessly people shuffled toward the doors.

When we stood, Martha threw her arms around me and whispered in my ear, "Thank you!"

"What for?"

"This was the most . . . maybe the most important night of my life."

I pulled myself out of her embrace.

"What's the matter?" asked Martha.

"Nothing."

"Something is."

"Forget it. Get your coat."

"Aren't you going to try to find her?"

"You heard her. She's got a train to catch."

Martha pointed over my shoulder and at the same time someone spoke my name.

I turned and Laura was standing at the edge of the stage. "Don't tell me you were going to leave without saying good-bye."

She was smiling, not widely or openly, but slyly, elusively. Her hands were on her hips and her feet were wide set as if she were straddling a small stream. Like a cube of ice that cannot exercise its will in the hand's heat, the annoyance I had felt toward Laura over her performance began to melt. Like the heart that cannot hold its chill in the presence of love's heat.

I was aware of Martha beside me, and I wanted to show her how easy and self-possessed I could be with Laura. That was what I wanted; what I got was a stammering, "I just . . . I thought, you know, the train . . ."

"Don't worry about the train. I'll make it. Come here; let me see you."

I stepped to the stage. As I stood there, looking up at her, I knew, sadly, ironically, self-pityingly, that our positions at that moment perfectly illustrated our relationship.

"My," she said, in a tone that both mocked and complimented me, "you certainly look collegiate."

At her remark I looked down at my clothing to see if something might be wrong with what I wore. I had on what was then—and has been ever since—my uniform: loafers, khakis, a button-down shirt, and a crew-neck sweater. In honor of the occasion, I had worn a tweed sport coat (my grandfather's). I would never be the stylish dresser my father was.

Laura laughed gently. "You look fine. How are things going?"

"Good. Everything's going good. Well. Going well."

She laughed harder. "I'm not here to correct your grammar, Paul. Relax." Nodding toward Martha, Laura asked, "Who's with you?"

Instantly Martha bounded to my side. "This is Martha Lundegaard," I said. "She's . . . She goes to Afton too."

Martha reached up to shake Laura's hand. "I thought your reading was the best one I've ever gone to. It was great. *You're great!* Really."

Laura clasped her hands to her chest. "Please! No more!"

Jeffrey Duncan came out from backstage. He was wearing an over-coat, and with him was a slender, well-dressed woman with buckteeth that she displayed with an unwavering smile. "Miss Pettit?" Duncan said. "If we're going to get to the station . . ."

"All right, all right!" snapped Laura. "Maybe I'll say the hell with it instead. Stay over tonight." She paused, and my hopes rose. Then fell, as Laura said, "Okay. I'll be right with you."

She turned back to us. "Now. How about you two? Are you a pair? Or pinned or steadies or whatever term they're using now? At the school where I teach they say, 'They're a unit.'"

I didn't know where Laura learned this role—the old family friend, the kindly maiden aunt—or why she had adopted it, but I didn't care for it. Nor did I care for the fact that she had treated me more like an adult when I was eleven than she did now.

"Martha and I," I answered solemnly, "came up from Afton together for the reading. She's a big fan of yours."

Martha playfully punched my arm. "God! Thanks a lot! You make it sound like I'm your sister or something!"

Laura laughed and crouched down on the stage so that our heads were very nearly equal height. "What about this, Paul?" she asked in a low-ered, confidential voice.

When she squatted down, her skirt rode up high. Her bent knees were only inches from my chest, and into that blank space where the thoughts that do us no good always insert themselves, this came: it would not even have required the full length of my arm to slip my hand along the inside of her thigh and to reach . . . I concentrated on looking into her eyes.

"I didn't think that was what you were asking about," I said peevishly.

Martha said, "He's just like that. Shy or something." Furious, I felt like pushing her away and telling her she had no business explaining me to Laura.

Laura must have seen my anger. She stopped teasing me, stood up, and said, "Yes, he is. Shy or something."

Again, Duncan stepped forward to say, "If we're going to go—"

"I know," said Laura. "I'm coming." She asked Martha and me, "Do you have someplace you have to be? You could ride along to the station and at least catch me up on your mother."

I wanted nothing more ardently than that. Why, then, did I answer as I did? "We better not," I said and nodded toward the Duncans. "You're with them." Beside me, Martha gasped.

"Oh, don't worry about that," said Laura. She turned to the waiting couple. "It's all right, isn't it, if my friends ride along with us to the station?"

Duncan said, "Well, uh, we have some other people with us. . . . And my car's not large."

Laura simply stared at him.

Duncan looked helplessly at his wife. She said nothing but continued her expressionless smile. "We could, I suppose," he said, "have them take a cab. . . . If they wouldn't mind."

"Good. Do that," Laura said. She motioned to Martha and me. "Let's get going."

ON THE WAY to the station, Laura, Martha, and I sat in the backseat, and as soon as we left the parking lot, Laura reached into her purse and took out a small thin silver flask that looked exactly like the one that my father used to carry. Without comment, she uncapped it, took three quick swallows, and then put it back. None of us said anything. From the smell, I guessed it was gin.

While he drove, Duncan continually turned around to talk to Laura, and every time he did, his wife automatically reached toward the steering wheel.

"I'm sorry you can't stay," he said to Laura. "We had quite a reception planned for you after your lecture."

"My plans changed at the last minute. I want to be in Chicago early tomorrow, and if I stay over, I'd have to fly, which I avoid if I possibly can."

"Well, you're going to be leaving behind quite a few disappointed admirers who hoped to meet you." He laughed good-naturedly, but it wasn't enough to cover the faintly scolding tone of his remark.

Laura leaned forward in her seat. "Am I really? Tell me, would there be refreshment at this reception?"

Uncertainly he replied, "Yes, I think so. I mean, I'm sure. Yes."

"Of course there will be," said Laura. "Of course. Yes. There will be wine—something for everyone, a red, a white, perhaps a rosé—and definitely a bottle of vodka and a bottle of scotch. Perhaps a bourbon. And there will be cheese and crackers and canapés, but nothing so large it could have anything to do with an actual human appetite. And we will stand in small groups and make even smaller talk. Then when someone gets drunk enough, he will say to me, with just a small begrudging edge to his voice, 'And how is our famous poet tonight?' And then someone else will get drunker still and begin to tell me exactly what is wrong with my work—only meaning to help, of course. And in the midst of all this civility everyone will have an eye on someone they would like to take upstairs and fuck, but of course no one will speak of this. So, thank you very much, but I will pass on your reception. Thank you, but I've been there before."

Her tirade finished, Laura slumped wearily back in her seat.

No one said anything after that. Duncan no longer turned around to talk to her, and I suspected that even his wife's smile had ceased. Finally, Martha broke the silence by asking Laura, "Do you still go for walks every day?"

Laura brusquely answered, "The cartilage in my knee is bad."

As we rode silently through the streets, I tried to imagine what the others were thinking. Did they wonder how Laura could charm an auditorium full of people only a short time earlier and now be so unpleasant? If that was what was on their minds, I felt sorry for them. That meant they were trying to understand Laura by using the same standards that applied to everyone else in the world. And that was useless.

We arrived at the station about fifteen minutes before Laura's train was scheduled to leave. Duncan and his wife—both of them hurt, indignant, and pouting—wanted to know if it would be all right if they dropped Laura off but didn't stay, since they had guests waiting at their house. Laura assured them she didn't mind and then coolly thanked them for the ride, the introduction, and their hospitality. And, Laura added, she would "wait to find out if he could resolve the other matter." Martha and I said we would wait with Laura.

As Duncan and his wife drove away, Laura said, "And good riddance, asshole!"

I had Laura's suitcase in my hand. "What's the matter?" I asked.

"I was running late tonight anyway, and when I got to the theater, he told me there'd been a mistake about the honorarium—it was a hundred dollars short. But he'd make it right, he said, even if he had to pay the rest himself. Christ! That'll be the day. When he dips into his goddamn pocket. And then before I could go out on stage he had a stack of books—my books—that he wanted me to sign. The books looked new; he probably bought them this week. And I'm supposed to go to the son-ofabitch's party! I'm supposed to make *him* look good. Jesus!"

We started into the station, Laura leading the way. Martha hurried behind her and asked, "How much were they supposed to pay you?"

Laura stopped. Martha's question was tactless but perfectly in keeping with her curiosity. Considering Laura's dour mood, I was afraid she might flay Martha on the spot.

For a few moments Laura didn't say anything; she simply stared up at Martha's height. Sizing up her opponent, I thought. I put the suitcase down and positioned myself beside them, just where the referee stands when he gives the fighters instructions. Overhead the depot's bright fluorescent lights ticked and hummed and did their best to eliminate the night's shadows.

Laura reached up and gently touched Martha's cheek. "My God, what color. Are they always so red?"

"They're even worse in summer," Martha answered.

"They glow. It's incredible. I don't suppose you put anything on them?"

"A little powder sometimes. So they don't shine so much."

"Don't do a thing. I envy you. I'm so pale I always look ill."

"I think you're beautiful."

"Well, thank you. That's not necessary. And not true, but thank you." Laura reached for her suitcase, but I picked it up first. "Now what was your question?"

"I wondered how much they were supposed to pay you," Martha asked again.

"Five hundred dollars. They gave me four hundred. But that's not bad for an evening's work, is it?"

"They should give you even more. They're *so* lucky you came."

Laura laughed for the first time since the theater. "We think so, don't we? But we can't expect others to. Now, why don't you two wait here, and I'll find out where I'm supposed to be."

Martha and I sat on a wooden bench. The station was not crowded, and the people there were not hurrying but moving slowly, as though they had all been awakened from sleep and sent out into the night to catch their trains. The entire scene seemed so dreamlike that I considered doing something I would only do in a dream. I thought of buying a ticket on Laura's train. The car would be dark and quiet, the other travelers would be sleeping, and Laura and I would be hurtled off together into the night. But instead I sat still, and soon Laura returned.

"The train's late," she said disappointedly. "I won't be leaving for at least half an hour."

"Do you want to get something to eat?" I asked. "A sandwich or coffee or something?"

"No. I'm going to the rest room though. Look, you two don't have to wait. You must have something better to do."

Martha quickly said, "We want to stay!"

"Suit yourselves."

As Laura walked away, Martha sighed and said, "I still can't believe it! God! I'm with Laura Pettit. Not just sitting with a bunch of people in a theater looking at her but actually with her."

I wished more and more that Martha weren't there, not only because her presence kept me from having Laura entirely to myself, but also because her gushing and constant, starstruck prattling was embarrassing.

"Maybe to you it isn't a big deal," said Martha. "You've been around famous people since you were little."

"I suppose."

Martha suddenly put her arm through mine, squeezed mine tightly, and rested her head on my shoulder. "I'm *so* excited!" she said. "I can't wait to get you home later."

"What do you mean?"

"I want to suck you off," she whispered.

I looked at her but said nothing. Martha and I were sexually incompatible in one way: before we did anything, she liked to talk about what we were going to do, and afterward she wanted to talk about what we had done. I, on the other hand, preferred to proceed without discussion and to pretend that whatever happened happened spontaneously out of mutual passion and desire.

"Do you want that?" Martha asked again.

To understate matters greatly, her offer had its appeal. Oral sex was exactly what I had for months been hoping for, almost to the point of suggesting it outright. But I resented her offer now because it distracted me and caused me to hesitate slightly, to turn away momentarily from my goal, which was Laura.

So instead of thanking Martha for her splendid offer and thereby spending the rest of the evening eagerly awaiting pleasures to come—I replied cruelly, "Why would you do that? To thank me for introducing you to someone famous?"

As I had intended, my answer hurt her. "That wasn't the way I meant it," she said. "I'm happy tonight, and I thought we should do something special. You know, to celebrate. Yeah, I'm happy you introduced me to her. But I love you, and I feel especially close to you tonight."

"You don't owe me anything."

"I know."

"All right. Just so you have that straight."

I heard Laura coming back before I saw her. Her high heels tapped out the rhythm of her approach. And when I did look up, I saw a woman so vivid, so completely in possession of herself that other people in the station must have known she was somebody. Even in her fatigue she looked magnificent, and I looked at Martha—who was watching Laura too—and I became angry with Martha all over again. How could you, I thought of Martha, how could you presume to compete with her for my attention? Don't you see that even confronted with the certainty of sex with you, I would still have to choose the uncertainty of Laura, even Laura for a few public moments in this echoing, high-ceilinged, diesel-smelling station with its drunks and sleepwalkers standing by?

Laura stood above us and said, "You two look glum. Jesus, are you sure you don't have any place you'd rather be?"

"We're sure," I replied.

"Hard to believe," Laura muttered as she sat down on the bench next to Martha.

Immediately Martha turned to Laura and said, "Miss Pettit, while you're waiting for your train, would you do me a favor?"

Like a parent hesitant to blindly grant a child's wish, Laura answered warily, "That depends."

Martha reached into her purse and brought out her notebook. "Would you read some of my poems and tell me what you think?"

I cringed, sorry for Laura because of Martha's imposition and sorry for Martha because of what I was sure would be Laura's response.

Laura pretended to search her purse for her lighter. I thought—I couldn't be sure—but I thought she glanced at me. Whether she did or not, I knew what she wanted: would I get her out of the situation. All I could think of was to ask, "What time did you say your train was leaving?"

Martha answered for Laura. "It's still not for a while."

Laura lit her cigarette, deliberately not reaching for the notebook. "This really isn't the place for it," she said. "So hard to concentrate."

"You wouldn't have to read all of them," said Martha. "You could sort of skim them. . . ."

Laura smiled kindly. "I take poems too seriously to skim them. I prefer to take my time."

"Do you want to take these with you?" Martha asked eagerly. "You could send them back to me with your comments."

Laura let out a lungful of smoke. "You know, I teach poetry writing. I think you want me to do in a few minutes what I spend an entire semester on."

Martha shook her head. "Oh, you don't have to criticize them or anything. That's not what I meant. I just want you to tell me if they're any good. Like, do I have talent."

Laura still made no move to take the notebook, though Martha pushed it forward another inch and said, "Please?"—a plea so plaintive it was like a kitten's mew.

And that did it.

Laura took the notebook, put on her glasses, and turned to the first page. She read rapidly, never spending more than seconds on a page. From where I sat I had difficulty reading the poems—Martha's handwriting was cramped, tiny, and had an odd backhand slant. I got up and walked to the water fountain while Laura read and prepared her verdict.

On my way back I saw two young marines, thin, baby-faced, and looking, in their razor-creased red-white-and-blue uniforms, like boys playing soldiers. They were standing not far from Martha and Laura and were earnestly conferring about something. When one of them nodded toward the two women, I knew what was on the soldiers' minds. They had come upon two unescorted women and were planning a strategy for picking the women up. *The* women? My women. So help me, that was the way I thought that night.

Before the marines could make their move, I rushed back to Martha and Laura. Laura was still reading, scowling, smoking, and flipping pages. Martha sat stiffly beside her, looking off into what distance the station allowed.

"Don't look now," I said as I sat down, "but the marines have landed."

They both looked up. Laura took off her glasses and fixed her gaze on the marines. Then she turned to Martha. "What do you say? Shall we get rid of Paul and see what these young gentlemen have to offer?"

Martha laughed. "They are kind of cute."

Laura looked back at me. "And Paul's being such a shit tonight anyway."

"Are they brothers, do you think?" asked Martha. "They look so much alike. And they're so young."

Laura said, "We'd eat them alive." She put her glasses on again and directed her attention back to Martha's poems.

One of the soldiers came over to us. He took off his white cap and said to Laura, "Pardon me, ma'am." His southern drawl was as out of place in Minnesota as Georgia's red clay would be.

Laura glanced up. "Yes?"

"My companion and I wondered if you would consent to sign a scrap of paper for us. We are both great admirers of your writing. We would be honored."

"Certainly," Laura said. She turned to the blank pages at the back of Martha's notebook. "Do you mind?" she asked Martha before tearing out two sheets.

"Go ahead," said Martha.

"And to whom should I address these?" Laura held her empty hand in the air as if she were waiting for someone to slip a pen into it. I reached quickly to my jacket pocket, but it was empty.

The soldier handed Laura a pen. "My name is K. C. Oldham. Those are initials, ma'am. K period, C period. And Oldham is just what it sounds like: 'old ham.' My friend who is too shy to come over is Mr. Robert Bliss. You know, as in 'Ignorance is . . .' "

As she signed, Laura asked, "Where are you stationed, Mr. Oldham?"

"Camp Pendleton, ma'am. My friend Robert Bliss is from Minnesota, and I consented to accompany him home when we both got a furlough. But, damn, I didn't know it would be this cold up here. Not in March. Next time we visit my hometown."

"And where would that be?"

"Haddington, South Carolina, ma'am."

Laura handed the sheets of paper and the pen back to the soldier. "If we're on the same train, I'll be pleased if you'll let me buy you a drink. And you can tell me what other poets you read."

Oldham gave Laura a small quick bow. "Robert Bliss doesn't drink, ma'am. But I would be honored. Greatly honored."

Laura laughed. "But you have to stop calling me 'ma'am.' "

"Yes, ma'am, I will."

They both laughed, and the soldier returned to his friend.

Laura stared off at the departing marines. "Well, why not?" she said. "If soldiers are reading poetry, perhaps there's hope for the world after all."

Then Laura closed Martha's notebook and said to her, "But I'm afraid there's no hope at all for these poems. Without exception they're simply awful. I don't see any evidence of verbal skill or sense of craft or original vision or any of those traits I look for in young poets."

I felt rather than saw Martha's reaction. Her posture didn't change, but something went out of her. Not breath. Nothing so simple as that. What left her—and left behind Martha's bulk with nothing to move it, no strength of bone or muscle, no will of the blood—was her energy, her life's verve and push. I felt this though we were only touching lightly along the line of shoulder and arm, hip and thigh; I felt it as surely as if the solid bench I sat on had suddenly changed from wood to leaf.

"What field are you planning to go into?" Laura asked Martha.

In a thin, pale voice, Martha answered, "I'm not sure. Teaching maybe."

"Teaching would be a good idea. We certainly need good teachers." Laura peered into Martha's face. "Do you understand why I'm asking you that? I wouldn't want you to waste your time trying to write. And it *would be* a waste of time. Do you understand what I'm saying to you?"

"I understand," was Martha's mechanical reply.

The public address system crackled and screaked, and a voice tonelessly announced that the train for Chicago—with stops in Eau Claire, Wisconsin Dells, Portage, and Columbus—was now boarding on Track Nine.

"That's me," said Laura. Before she stood up, she patted Martha on the knee. "You be a teacher. They'll love you. You'll be a wonderful teacher." Martha remained seated, but I stood up. "I'll walk over with you."

Martha looked up at Laura and said numbly, "Thanks for coming. Thanks for . . . I'm glad I got to meet you. Thank you."

"I can find my way," Laura said to me.

"That's okay," I said, as we began to move in the direction that other people were moving. Martha seemed to be the only person in the building who wasn't rising and heavily, somnolently walking off to find a train.

"Don't you think you should stay with her?" asked Laura.

"She'll be okay."

"Are you sure? I hit her pretty hard."

"She's a big girl. She can take it."

The platform where Laura's train waited was dark and cold. A fine mist was falling, and the air smelled of diesel fumes. The train ticked, clanked, dripped, and hummed as if it were impatient to get moving. The wheels and the black oily machinery under the train were coated with a layer of snow so fine it looked like talcum powder.

At the small metal step stool that led up into the train, Laura stuck out her hand. "Good to see you again, Paul. Be sure to say hello to your mother for me."

I was panic-stricken, desperate. I couldn't simply say good-bye. "I'll help you find a seat."

"It's really not necessary, Paul."

"No, it's okay. They give you a chance to get off."

Laura shook her head in exasperation, but she didn't stop me from stepping up into the train behind her.

The lights in the car were off, and a few of the passengers were already asleep, their bodies contorted in their narrow seats, pillows awkwardly jammed under their heads. Those still awake stared openly at us, as if, having invaded their darkened world in this way, we were owed no courtesy. I didn't see the marines.

The only vacant seat was behind a tired-looking woman and her pajama-clad infant son, who stood backward in his seat, gripped the seat back, and bounced frantically up and down. Laura went into the next car.

This one was almost empty, and Laura chose a seat at the front of the car. She sat next to the window, spread her coat out on the seat next to her, and from her purse took her cigarettes and lighter, a book, and— quick flash of silver—her flask. She was ready to travel.

I stepped out of the aisle and into the narrow space opposing the seat where Laura's coat lay. I'm not leaving, I thought. This train is going to pull out and leave Martha and Minneapolis behind, but it's going to take Laura, so I'm staying put. Where it takes her, it will take me, and that will be my life. To hell with school. To hell with my grandparents' house and my room and the narrow bed where I lay in anguish over Laura anyway. To hell with my mother and sister. To hell with Martha. To hell with any obligation that wasn't to Laura.

The train lurched and I with it, but I made no move of my own power.

"Okay, Paul," said Laura. "You better go."

"It's all right. They'll tell me when I have to get off."

She lit a cigarette. "I'm telling you. You should be back there with, with—"

"—Martha."

"Martha. She probably wants you with her right now."

"What about what I want?"

She flipped up the small metal ashtray in the arm of her chair. "What about it? Fuck what you want. You can't always have what you want."

The window Laura sat by looked onto the empty train yard, and I could see rows of tracks, their burnished steel gleaming dully amid the black, oily gravel of the roadbed. "I was thinking I'd stay. You know, buy a ticket and go along for the ride."

Laura simply stared at me. In all its hissing and grumbling the train seemed to be gathering energy, getting stronger for the journey ahead. But the train didn't move, and neither did I. The ash on Laura's cigarette grew longer, and her glare deepened, but I didn't move.

Finally she said, "Why don't you give it up, Paul? Why don't you realize who the hell you are and who I am and give it up? Go back to that big apple-cheeked girl and put your arms around her and tell her you're sorry I spoke so harshly to her. And then the two of you go get a beer or go fuck or go throw a Frisbee or something that you're supposed to do. Do you understand what I'm saying to you? That's where you belong. That's *who you are*."

Behind me the door slid open, and the conductor, an older man bent over with arthritis, walked over to Laura and me and put out his gnarled hand. "Tickets. Let's see the tickets please."

Without saying anything, I brushed past him and walked off the train. If emotion were incarnate, I would have left a trail of blood that anyone could follow.

I stood on the platform for a few moments, hoping Laura would come after me, apologize, and say she hadn't meant a word of what she said. Yet I knew she wouldn't.

The train lurched again, this time remaining in motion, and slowly, slowly began to move down the tracks. I walked along with it, keeping my eyes on the train's windows, hoping to see Laura's pale face brightening one of those dark rectangles, Laura waving, smiling, and forgiving me again. She did not appear, and when the train picked up enough speed that it required me to run to keep up, I stopped and watched it pull away.

MARTHA WAS RIGHT where I left her. She was sitting primly upright, her hands folded on her lap, smiling dimly and looking around the station. Her posture reminded me of an old woman's, that of someone who has been battered by the tragedies of a long life yet remained cheerful and strong.

When I approached, her smile widened, yet her eyes didn't seem to recognize me. "Did Miss Pettit find a seat?" she asked politely.

"There was plenty of room." I put my hand out to Martha. "Come on. We'd better get to your parents'."

She rose and followed me out of the depot. She did not take my hand.

BY THE TIME the cab dropped us off at the Lundegaard home, it was after midnight, but as soon as we arrived, Dr. Lundegaard came to the door and greeted us warmly. "At last, the sojourners!"

Dr. Lundegaard was a tall, broad-shouldered man in his fifties who had a long jaw and a horsey smile. He was ruddy and blond and wore his hair in a bristling crew cut. It was obvious that Martha inherited from him not only her height, complexion, and hair color but her ebullience as well. Seconds after shaking my hand, Dr. Lundegaard began to bombard me with question after question. Efficiency more than friendliness seemed to be the force behind this interrogation. Dr. Lundegaard had likely determined that this was the method best suited for gaining the maximum amount of information about his daughter's suitor in the shortest period of time.

Did I know where I was going to medical school? Probably the University of Wisconsin or the University of Minnesota—both first-rate schools he said. Did I plan on a specialty? Not yet—and he assured me I needn't be in a hurry. Was I a Minnesota Twins fan? Red Sox. Had I ever played hockey? No. Did I enjoy camping, hiking, or canoeing? I lied and said yes to camping and hiking, both of which I had done as a Boy Scout. What did I think of Lyndon Johnson and his Great Society programs? They sounded okay to me, and he approved.

Dr. Lundegaard apologized for his wife; she had a headache and had to retire early. When he went to the kitchen to get us something to eat, Martha told me that her mother frequently had headaches. She rolled her eyes when she said it.

We talked for a while in the parlor as we ate the store-bought cookies and potato chips and drank the soda that Martha's father brought out for us. He sat in his easy chair while Martha and I sat on the floor, she at his feet and I across a coffee table from them. "So," Dr. Lundegaard said, "tell me all about it. What was it like to see your famous poet?"

Martha recounted the entire evening for him, including so many details he must have been bored by her narrative, yet he never stopped listening attentively or smiling sweetly at her.

Toward the end of her story, Martha said, "And then, Daddy, she said she'd read some of my poems and tell me what she thought of them. But she didn't like them. Not any of them. She thought they were awful." Martha stopped talking, and I could tell by her determinedly brave smile and the bright blushing splotches that spread downward from her cheeks to her throat that if she said another word she'd cry.

Dr. Lundegaard reached out and lightly stroked Martha's hair. "I'm sorry to hear that, honey," he said softly. "You know your mother and I love those poems of yours. I've saved every one you've sent us. I don't always understand them, but I love getting them."

I kept waiting for Dr. Lundegaard to look accusingly at me and say, how could you? How could you introduce my baby to someone who would hurt her so? Why didn't you protect her? But he didn't. He kept his attention on Martha, Martha whose eyes closed and who seemed to be falling asleep, safe at her father's feet.

I was given Martha's younger brother's bedroom for the night (he slept in the basement rec room), but I couldn't fall asleep. Martha's brother assembled model cars, and they and their faint but distinct glue smell were everywhere—on the dresser, bookcase, nightstand, and hanging from the ceiling.

But it was not the cars that kept me awake. I couldn't sleep because the questions that always wait until the lights are out and the house is dark, the questions that wait until we ache most for rest, those questions finally came out, and they raced around my head as if it were a stock-car track. Would Martha sneak into my room that night? I doubted it. Why had she never shown me any of her poems, especially since she had been mailing copies to her parents? And the largest question of all: What had Laura meant when she said I should give up and face who I was and where I belonged? Didn't she understand that after a decade of loving her, no matter how helplessly, no matter how futilely, that was who I was? That I had little identity or purpose beyond loving her?

Toward morning I finally dozed off, and when I woke in the early morning, I felt disoriented. I lay in bed until I heard the other people in the house get up and begin to move around.

Mrs. Lundegaard, a shy, quick little wren of a woman who seldom spoke because she was embarrassed about her thick Norwegian accent, made us a huge breakfast, pancakes and sausages and strong black coffee. Martha's brother, Douglas, joined us at the table, but after "How do you do" when we were introduced, he never said another word. He wore glasses with thick lenses—his eyes gone bad, I imagined, from all those hours of trying to piece together his model cars' miniature parts.

After we ate, Mrs. Lundegaard took us to the bus depot so we could get back to Afton in time for our afternoon classes.

There were only a few other riders on the bus, but Martha and I didn't talk much. Each of us took out a book and pretended to use the trip as an opportunity to catch up on our studies.

Did both of us know it was all over between us? I believe we did, though we may not have been able to articulate that knowledge. It was simply something sensed, the way we know a house we have entered is empty without having to look in every room.

And it was over, though we never declared it so. We continued to go out together and sleep together and to be in all the outward ways the couple we had always been. What was the difference? We began to talk of separate futures. Martha spoke occasionally about joining the Peace Corps, and her worry was no longer about being apart from me but about the tropical or equatorial sun and how hard it would be on her fair skin. Or she would talk about finding a teaching position, and it no longer mattered where, near me or far. When I discussed my concerns about medical school, it was only in terms of being able to handle the work, not about being apart from her. This change occurred without animosity. We understood that what we had was not meant to last. It was, I think now, like snow; when its season was over, it was gone.

Martha stopped talking about Laura too, though on the bus that day her name came up one more time.

I had closed my eyes and was trying to let the bus's bounce and sway put me to sleep when Martha nudged me.

Maybe I had dozed off, because when I next looked at her, I saw she had been crying—her mascara left muddy trails down her cheeks.

Without preface she said, "Why didn't you tell me you loved her?"

"*Sshh,*" I said, and put my hand on her thigh to quiet her.

It didn't work. She asked again. "Why didn't you tell me you loved her like that?"

I had choices. I could have feigned ignorance. Whom are you talking about? Laura Pettit? She's an old family friend; I've known her since I was a child. What are you talking about? Or I might have dismissed the subject with a simple, brisk denial. Love Laura Pettit? Don't be silly. I do not. Or I could have risked just enough truth telling to put her in her place. You think I love her? I'll tell you who loved her—my father, that's who. She was his mistress. She destroyed his marriage. I once saw them make love on a chair in a motel room.

Or I could have admitted what she said was true. I could have said, yes it's true. I do love Laura—and like that and like this and every way in between that someone can be a fool and love hopelessly. And I could have asked Martha, sweet, generous, good-hearted Martha, for her help. Yes, I could have said, I do love Laura and I know that nothing can come from it but my own senseless degradation. Help me. Talk me out of it. Convince me that you'll be good for me and that with you is where I belong.

Yes. Choices. There were a good many things I might have said.

But I said nothing.

Instead I turned to the bus window and looked out at the sodden, frost-heaved fields that we were speeding by. I looked outside and waited for Martha's weeping to stop and for the subject to change like a jukebox's record. A-2: LAURA PETTIT. C-6: THE UPCOMING EXAM IN BIOLOGY 412.

THE FOLLOWING JUNE after Martha and I had graduated, my grandfather secured me a summer job working on the college grounds crew while I waited to start medical school in the fall. Martha went back to St. Paul to prepare for a trip to Norway that she would take with her mother and her aunt. Martha had come back to Fairmont to say goodbye to friends; if she could get in, she was going to take classes at the University of Oslo in the fall. She had discarded her plans for the Peace Corps.

I was positioning sprinkler heads on the football field when she stopped by to say good-bye. We had been out the night before, so there was no need for this parting to be anything but brief. We promised to write, and then she was gone, and as a joke my friend turned on the sprinklers while I was still out on the field, and I ran off in the opposite direction from Martha. That was the last time I saw her.

We wrote for a while, but the letters soon gave way to cards—Christmas and birthday—and before long they stopped too, as if stores no longer sold cards that properly applied to our relationship or what it had been.

Yet I often wonder what would have happened if I had done something other than let Martha cry that day on the bus. Just as I wonder if rather than merely wish for her future happiness, I could have been part of it.

Eight

*I*n 1967, during my second year
of medical school at the University of Wisconsin, I shared an apartment
with Philip Reed, another second-year student, who looked, with his
long hair, beard, and serene blue eyes, exactly like those kitschy pictures
of an Aryan Jesus that so many grandmothers used to have hanging on
their walls. Philip came from a small town in upper Michigan, and he
had, coincidentally, started out as a divinity student. I used to tease him,
telling him he never should have given it up. Imagine the effect on the
congregation, I said, when they saw at the altar the embodiment of the
God they addressed in their prayers. Philip's original plan had been to
serve God and humanity, but when he lost his faith in God, he decided
to concentrate on humanity. That was why he was in medical school,
and no one who knew him questioned the sincerity of his motives. And
that was why I often felt chastened by Phil, though by his example and
not his words.

During this era, virtually every major national or international antiwar or radical organization had a chapter, cell, or cadre in Madison,
Wisconsin, and many of them had started there. The city burned constantly—always figuratively and sometimes literally—with the fires of

196

political, social, and civil unrest. Days seldom passed when I didn't see students somewhere on campus marching with their hand-lettered plac- ards. Sitting in a classroom or lab, you often faintly heard from outside the squawk and drone of someone shouting a speech into a bullhorn and then the mingled shouts of approval or disagreement from the gathered crowd. After a while this was simply background noise, and it no longer became necessary to run to the windows to see what was taking place. The sound of protest, of argument and harangue, became so common you stopped hearing it, like music in a waiting room. Just as you ignored the sheets of plywood that substituted for glass in the windows of stores and offices up and down State Street, the street leading from the capitol to the campus.

I have mentioned Madison's political climate and Philip Reed in such close conjunction because he was very much part of the Movement, that assortment of groups that focused on opposition to the war in Vietnam but which ranged wide enough to take in socialism, feminism, pacifism, black power, total revolution, or any combination thereof. I don't mean to sound cynical about these causes, for I was in sympathy with most of them. However, beyond believing in the right things and standing on the fringes of a few rallies, my involvement was minimal. And that was how Phil shamed me. He not only believed; he *acted*.

He marched, carried signs, passed out leaflets, stuffed envelopes, and made telephone calls. He made speeches before crowds or individuals. He read his Marx and Fanon and Gandhi. He littered the apartment with copies of the *Berkeley Barb* and *Ramparts* and issues of the under- ground newspapers that seemed to be born weekly in Madison. He fasted. He held a candle at silent vigils. He signed petitions and dis- tributed them. And since he did all these things and still managed to survive in medical school, I didn't have that excuse for my own inactiv- ity. No, Philip Reed was a daily reminder of how little I did to back up what I professed to believe. I couldn't even lessen my guilt by telling myself that at least I wasn't part of the opposition, because, as we were so often reminded back then, if you weren't part of the solution, you were part of the problem.

Phil never gave up on me, however. He continued to let me know about upcoming rallies or teach-ins and always invited me to come. And after I turned him down, he would simply shrug and say, "Maybe next time." And I would answer, "Sure, maybe next time."

In November of 1967 Phil brought home news about a "Peace on Earth" rally that was planned for Chicago in late December. The flyer announcing the day's activities said they would begin with an afternoon rally in Grant Park and wind up with a candlelight march down Michigan Avenue that night. There would be music—folksingers Phil Ochs and Roger Dale, the legendary Chicago bluesman Bobby "Little Fingers" Baylor, the Jump River Jug Band, Ded Ahed, and the Paul Butterfield Blues Band. Among the speakers they planned to have were Dr. Benjamin Spock, University of Chicago chaplain Daniel Lloyd, Illinois senatorial candidate Robert Rice, the chairman of Students United for Peace, and poets Allen Ginsberg and Laura Coe Pettit.

I wasn't surprised to learn that Laura would be appearing. Her credentials were in order. Earlier in the decade she had been part of the Ban-the-Bomb movement, she had worked with the Freedom Riders to register voters in Alabama, she had spoken on behalf of the Free Speech Movement at Berkeley, and recently she had become a vocal opponent of the war in Vietnam. She had been arrested twice, at the March on the Pentagon and at an induction center in New Jersey. She had been maced by police in San Francisco (and wrote an article about it for *The New Republic*) and spat upon by a soldier's mother at a demonstration in New York.

I stared so long and hard at her name on the flyer that I began to feel a slight dizziness, or at least its earliest anticipatory stage, as though I had just gotten onto a carnival ride and strapped myself in and though it hadn't yet picked up speed, I knew, as I knew every time I saw or heard Laura's name, that it was time to hang on again.

"What do you think?" Phil asked me. "Look like something you'd like to be a part of?"

"What?"

He pointed to the paper I was holding tightly. "The rally. You're welcome to come along. I've got a friend at the University of Chicago I can stay with. And he said bring as many people as I want."

"Did I ever tell you," I tapped the flyer next to Laura's name, "that I know her?"

"You told me."

"What did I say?"

Phil sighed. "I don't remember exactly." He pulled his hands back through his long hair. "I think you said she was almost your stepmother or something like that."

"I said what?"

"Didn't you say your father almost married her?"

I looked again at Laura's name to make sure her identity wasn't shifting on me. "It wasn't exactly like that. They went out a few times. That's all."

"Okay, I got it wrong," Phil said cheerfully. "So, do you want to see her again and at the same time strike a blow against the war machine?"

I never doubted that I would go. What I wondered was why. What could come of it? I had no answer, so I settled for this: For me something had started with Laura, and I had to stay with it until it was finished. If it ever could be.

"All right," I told Phil. "Sure, I'll go."

"Fantastic! You'll see. This is going to change you. You're stepping over the line."

"I guess so."

WE LEFT FOR CHICAGO on the morning of December 29 in Phil's rusting 1956 Chevrolet. Bill Hazen and Terry McGill, graduate students who belonged to one of Phil's coalitions, rode along. Just outside Madison we picked up a young man and woman, Lance and Donna, who were hitchhiking to the rally. He was heavyset, swarthy, and had a wispy mustache and a chipped front tooth. She was small and thin and looked about fourteen.

Lance was much more enthusiastic about the demonstration than Donna. When we were passed by yet another VW bus crammed with longhairs flashing us the peace sign, Lance said, "Goddamn! How many are going to be there anyway?"

Phil said, "No one knows for sure. Ten thousand. Twenty. Depends on the weather, I guess." The day was clear and cold, but snow was predicted for Chicago.

"Twenty thousand freaks!" said Lance. "We're going to raise some hell!"

Donna said, "I don't know if it's going to be like that."

"Oh, baby, it's going to be like that and then some!" Lance laughed.

Phil asked them, "Do you have a place to stay?"

"Nah," Lance said. "We're not worried. There ought to be plenty of places to crash."

"You want to watch yourselves," Phil said. "It's a big city."

"Fuck, man. I'm from Newark. I can take care of myself."

Phil ignored Lance's cockiness. "Let me give you an address. Then, if you can't find any place to stay . . ."

Donna asked, "Do you think there'll be arrests?"

"This is a nonviolent demonstration," answered Phil. "And the organizers want to keep it that way. They've got permits to assemble and to march. But there's going to be an opportunity for people to burn their draft cards if they want to, and that's a federal offense. And we're going to counsel young men to resist the draft. That's a crime too. So, yeah, there could be arrests."

From the backseat Bill Hazen said, "And don't forget, man. Chicago cops."

"What about them?" asked Donna.

"Nothing," Phil said quickly. "They can be a hassle, that's all."

Bill said, "If you call busting heads being a hassle."

"Fuck," said Lance, "all cops like to bust heads. That's why they're cops."

Phil's last words on the subject were, "If you get arrested, go easy. And tell them you'll go easy. Cops can be like dogs. You get excited; they get excited. So stay calm."

PHIL'S FRIEND, ALEX HOOVER, was a short, somber man of improbable parts. His black hair frizzed out into a white man's Afro, yet he wore a white shirt and a tie. He was slight yet muscular and tough, like a wrestler at one of the lower weights. Alex lived in Hyde Park, within walking distance of the University of Chicago, in an apartment that was surprisingly large and well furnished for a graduate student. I assumed Alex came from a wealthy family, and perhaps he did, but later that evening I found out more about his income.

Around ten o'clock, as we were drinking beer and waiting for the weather report that would tell us what was predicted for the following day, a young man in a sheepskin jacket dropped by.

Alex led him into the kitchen, and from where I sat I could only hear a fragment of their conversation, but it was enough. Alex asked him how much he wanted, and the young man said, "Just two tabs." Alex quoted him a price, and the deal was done. Alex, who was a graduate research assistant in chemistry and who worked in a lab in the Searle Chemistry Building and had access to its facilities and supplies, sold LSD out of his apartment.

Before the young man in the sheepskin jacket left, Alex gave him a sheet of paper. "Read this first." Later, I saw one of those sheets. It was a mimeographed, numbered set of directions and suggestions for anyone dropping acid, the advice ranging from where to take it ("a quiet, familiar atmosphere is probably best, especially for first-time trippers") to the addresses and phone numbers of area hospitals in case the trip went bad. Alex told us that since people were going to do drugs no matter what, someone might as well make sure they got quality stuff and took it safely and responsibly. "Let's be practical," said Alex. "This isn't about seeing God or making beautiful people. You want satisfied customers."

While Alex and Phil talked politics, I stared out the window. Laura was out there somewhere, and I would probably see her the following day, yet the thought brought me no solace. Once again she would be on a stage, and I would be down below, one more face swelling the crowd. . . .

Around midnight snow began to fall, flakes so fine they looked as though they had been sifted before falling to the earth. I watched them float through the light of a streetlamp for a while; then I told Alex and Phil that the snow had started.

"Shit," was Phil's reply.

THE NEXT MORNING conditions were even worse than the weather reports had predicted. The snow had fallen through the night, but the temperature had actually gone up—it was thirty-three degrees at eight o'clock—and the warm air coupled with a breeze off the lake brought the fat heavy flakes down at the rate of an inch an hour.

Phil was on the phone from early morning; all the organizers agreed that the rally had to go on—but plans and arrangements were changing from minute to minute. One of the bands canceled; two featured speakers—a SNCC leader and a woman from Mothers Against the War were stuck in a Toledo airport, and worst of all, the city rescinded its agreement and would no longer allow Grant Park to be used as the rally site.

City officials said the park could not be used because of the snow. It was piling up too rapidly, and by rally time people would have drifts to negotiate. Besides, if the temperature rose a few more degrees, the snow would turn to rain and the park would be a muddy field. Instead, the rally would be held in the parking lot of Soldier Field. The city snowplows could keep the lot cleared right up to rally time, and a temporary stage could be set up for speakers and musicians. Rally organizers were suspicious of the city's offer, but there seemed to be no choice but to agree. Besides, Soldier Field was near enough to Grant Park that people who came to the original site could easily be redirected.

THE SCENE AT the parking lot was not what I expected. The crowd was not the hoped-for ten or twenty thousand. Any estimate that exceeded two thousand would have been unrealistic. The participants seemed to be mostly students, but there were also a few older men and women in raincoats and young women with babies in covered strollers. The stage was nothing more than a two-foot-high platform with a canvas awning stretched over it. A man at the lectern had already begun shouting passionately into the microphone, but people behind him on the stage talked, laughed, and paid no attention to his speech. A few signs waved in the air—"Peace Now," "Stop the War," "U. of Illinois Against the Draft"—but what most people held aloft were umbrellas, and their thorny circles looked like black flowers blooming in the snow and deepening the gloom. People shifted back and forth on cold, wet feet, and if they didn't have a hat, hood, or umbrella, their hair was plastered wetly to their head and melted snow trickled down their face like tears. The righteous energy and enthusiasm that I had seen so often on the streets of Madison or in televised demonstrations was nowhere in evidence. But worse than the rally's dismal mood was the ominous presence of the police. They must have been at least two hundred strong, and they had set up their loosely strung-out perimeter about twenty to thirty yards back from the protesters.

Near the stage, but sufficiently off to the side so there couldn't be any question but that they were merely watching, was the press, a few photographers, reporters, and a truck from WGBI television. Everyone in that group seemed to have a steaming cup of coffee.

I left Phil and Alex to explore the crowd on my own.

I wandered into a small contingent of students toward the back who looked as though they expected trouble and had prepared for it. Some of them wore or carried football helmets. A few had their glasses taped to their faces. Others had bandannas or gas masks around their necks, ready for the first whiff of tear gas. Some of their faces had a strange sheen that I couldn't quite figure out; moisture beaded on their cheeks like rain on a freshly waxed car. Then I saw two young women in that group smearing their skin with Vaseline.

The taller one, a flat-faced woman who had a stocking cap pulled down over her dark blond hair, offered me the jar. "You want some?"

"No, that's okay," I said. "Uh, what's it for anyway?"

"Mace, man. You get it in the face, this'll keep it from burning your skin so bad."

"Think you're going to need it?"

"Are you kidding? Look at those fucking cops."

The other woman, who was wearing a ski jacket and wool muffler tied around the top of her head, said, "I heard they're going to burn cards pretty soon. When the first one hits the fire, the pigs will make a move."

"That's why they want us out here," the tall one added. "No trees or anything for cover. They can run us down so easy it's not even fucking funny."

"Maybe," I said hopefully, "it's too cold today."

The tall one laughed and held out the jar again. "You sure you don't want some?"

I shook my head and walked away.

Getting close to the stage was easy. Ropes and stanchions were set up, but you could simply walk around them to climb the stage or mingle with the musicians and speakers waiting their turn at the microphone. I was looking for Laura but didn't see her anywhere. I went back out with the crowd and listened to the folksinger Holly Rundell. I was beginning to wonder if Laura was stuck in a snowy airport somewhere. An announcement had already been made that Allen Ginsberg wouldn't be there because of the weather.

After only two songs, Holly Rundell was replaced on stage by an Illinois congressman who told us how important it was to support anti-war candidates in every election, local, state, and national. Like the rest of the crowd, I liked being entertained more than being lectured, and I wandered off again.

I didn't hear her introduced, but the next thing I knew I was hearing Laura's voice, its huskiness made even scratchier by the sound system's static. I ran back toward the stage, my boots slipping in the slushy snow. I stopped when I was less than twenty feet from her, close enough to see the steam of her breath as she spoke.

She had let her hair grow to shoulder length. She was wearing faded jeans, boots, and what looked to be the same gray wool cape she wore that Thanksgiving eve so many years before. The microphone was too high for her, and she had to strain upward to speak.

Laura told the crowd that she would not be reading any poems today. She no longer wrote poems, she said, and she would not as long as Americans were killing and being killed in Southeast Asia. She could not concentrate on trying to make beautiful things when that ugliness was going on.

When Laura made her announcement about writing no more poems, the crowd gave her an approving round of applause. An old man standing near me, however, reacted quite differently. He was stocky and stooped, and he had a white paper cutout in the shape of a dove pinned to the lapel of his overcoat. He took his gloveless hands from his pockets and waved toward Laura as though he were shooing her away. Then, shaking his head sadly, he turned to walk away.

"What's the matter?" I asked him.

"She don't even know her art," he said angrily. "Someday the war's over and then we don't have no art. Art don't stop for nothin'. It's more bullshit. I shouldn't've expected better from her."

I let him go his grumbling way.

Up on the stage, Laura was gesturing to someone in the crowd. "Duane, would you come up here, please?"

A thin young man—he looked no older than seventeen—with a blond crew cut and ruddy cheeks and a perfectly blank expression stepped onto the stage and stood next to Laura. He wore a tan raincoat like mine, but his looked brand-new. His coat was unbuttoned, so you could see he was wearing a suit and tie.

Laura put her hand on the young man's shoulder and brought him to her side at the lectern. "Duane recently completed a tour of duty in Vietnam," she said, "and since he came home, he has not been able to sleep well. He is haunted by memories of the things he and his fellow soldiers did over there. Duane is especially troubled over the death of a Vietnamese farmer, a simple man who wanted what all men want: to feed his family, to make love to his wife, to drink some wine, and smoke some tobacco. To watch his children grow up happy and healthy. He was no different from the farmers, the fathers, and the husbands of this country. Except he didn't live in this country. He lived in a village in South Vietnam, and because he did, American soldiers came into his community and burned his home and shot him dead. They shot him down the same way they shot his cow. And how do I know this is so? I know because the soldier who killed the Vietnamese farmer . . . that soldier is here." Once again she touched his shoulder.

Laura continued, "Duane came to me a few months ago because he was so ashamed of what he had done that he had to tell someone. He told me he had never done anything intentionally cruel in his life before he was sent to Vietnam. He grew up on a farm in Iowa, and when Duane killed that Vietnamese farmer, he killed a man like his own father. This is what the war is doing to us! Not only is it killing innocent men, women, and children in Southeast Asia, it is making killers out of innocent American boys! This government, men like Johnson and Rusk and

McNamara, get to keep their hands clean because they have a machine
that makes savages out of American young men, and then these young
men do Lyndon Johnson's killing!"

The crowd was stirred now and sure of its position—hating and con-
demning Lyndon Johnson and his administration was something all of us
did with absolute conviction—and cries of "Down with LBJ!" echoed
through the lot.

"Please!" Laura shouted. "There's something else I want to say! I want
to send Duane out among you, and as he walks around, I want you to
look closely at him. Talk to him if you like. I want you to see up close
someone who's been caught up in the American war machine! The special obscenity of this war is that it destroys innocence everywhere! And
that's why it must stop! Why we must do *everything* we can to stop this
war, to stop it now before there is no innocence left in the world!"

She released Duane, and he jumped down from the stage and began
to walk a slow zigzag path through the crowd. Meanwhile, Laura had
slipped off quietly, and in her place at the microphone, appearing without introduction, was Roger Dale. I didn't recognize him at first, and I
don't think many people did, because he was without his beard, his hair
hung down to his shoulders, and he wore a battered cowboy hat pulled
down low. He was wearing a bulky woolly parka with fur trim, jeans, and
cowboy boots, but he had his guitar, and as soon as he began to sing,
there was no question who he was.

In the fifties Roger Dale had been a vocalist and guitarist with the
Silvertones, a group that had one huge hit ("Toss Him Out"). In 1961,
Dale went solo and acoustic. He became part of the folk music scene,
and his first album, *Sailing at First Light,* with its black-and-white jacket
photo of a smiling, bearded Dale hugging two pale-eyed huskies, was
especially popular. Dale's special cause—and the subject of a few of his
songs—was the plight of prisoners, the lost souls in America's jails and
prisons, and it was rumored that one of the reasons he had such empa-
thy for these people was that he himself had served time. Rumors had
also suggested a romantic connection between him and Laura Coe
Pettit.

By now Duane was coming my way, his feet shuffling through the snow. At first his passage through the crowd was unobstructed; everyone stepped aside to let him pass.

When Duane was only a few yards from me, a young woman stopped him. Then she put her arms around him, while the man with her patted Duane on the back and said, "It's okay, man. It's okay." When she finally let Duane go and he began his walk again, he had not gone more than a few steps when another girl stopped him. She put a wilted flower through the top buttonhole of his coat. Duane did nothing to acknowledge this attention.

And then he was in front of me. I couldn't turn away, but I didn't have anything to say to him. I thought I would at least venture a look into his eyes to see if there was something there for me to learn.

No. The snow had streaked his glasses, so I couldn't see anything but a pale blue blur. It was like trying to look through two rectangles of wrinkled cellophane. Then he was past me, and a man behind me asked him, "Why, son? Do you know why?"

In a high-pitched toneless voice, Duane said, "I don't really know."

I decided to try to find Laura. No one prevented me from walking behind the stage to the area where the rally organizers, the guest musicians and speakers were clustered, so I was able to walk right over to where she stood next to the open side doors of a white Ford Econoline.

Laura's back was to me, but I could see she was smoking and listening to an angry man who wore an army surplus parka over his suit. "Now they say we can't march, goddamnit," he said. "Some bullshit about emergency snow removal. I tell you, they're just using this snow to jerk us around."

"What's the problem," Laura responded. "If we want to march, we march. And if they want to try to stop us, let them. It will be the city who looks bad."

"There'll be arrests. . . ."

"That's all right too," Laura reassured him. "We'll have an opportunity to issue statements that we might not have otherwise."

The man in the parka shook his head. "Jesus, I don't know."

Laura patted him on the shoulder. "Remember what we're trying to do. It has to get worse before it gets better."

The man in the parka noticed me and asked testily, "What do *you* want?"

I pointed to Laura's back and stammered, "I know Laura. . . ."

Laura spun around at the sound of my voice. "Is that Paul?" Without hesitation she came toward me and hugged me long and hard.

As we broke our embrace, I said, "I heard you speak. I thought you were great."

She ignored my compliment. "Do you live in Chicago?"

"Madison. I'm going to med school there."

"Medical school! Really! That's wonderful, Paul. Did I know about this?"

I shrugged.

"The last time I saw you," Laura continued cautiously, as if she were running a test on her memory, "was in Minneapolis, right? At a reading?"

"That's right."

"And you were with a tall blond girl, weren't you?"

"Right again," I said, flattered that she remembered.

"And is she here with you today?"

"No, that's over."

"I'm sorry to hear that. She seemed very nice."

"That's okay. It was just sort of a college thing. Nothing serious," I said, betraying once more the relationship between Martha and me.

"And now it's going to be Dr. Finley."

I laughed. "I'm only second year. I've got a ways to go."

By now Roger Dale had finished his set and was loping across the lot toward Laura. "Hey, babe!" he shouted to her. "What did you think?"

She kissed him and said, "You sounded wonderful!"

"Was it a mistake doing the Dylan song, do you think?"

Laura shook her head. "It's a good song. It was right for today."

"I wasn't going to, but what the fuck. He hardly does it himself anymore. Besides"—Roger Dale laughed loudly—"I do it better."

"Yes, you do." Laura kissed him again. "Rog, here's someone I want you to meet. Paul Finley. You've heard me mention him. Paul's father and I went out together for a while."

"Sure, I remember." Roger Dale shook my hand. "What do you say, man?"

Roger Dale was my height but much broader. Without his beard, his jaw looked massive. He was handsome but not quite as chiseled as in photographs; in fact his face was puffy. But it was the eyes especially that seemed wrong. I was used to seeing them on an album cover photograph behind the lenses of his wire-rimmed glasses, and those eyes glistened with a hard, pure, benevolent energy. Now they looked rheumy and tired. I also realized that Roger Dale was older than I thought; in his mid forties I guessed and perhaps a decade older than Laura.

"Paul is studying to be a doctor," Laura said.

"Yeah?" Roger Dale said. "Hey, Doc, when I do this"—he flapped his arms up and down—"it hurts."

"Don't do that," I said, supplying the punch line.

Roger Dale broke into a giggle that was in excess of the old joke's humor. "All *right.*" Then to Laura he said, "Babe, I heard Butterfield's here. I got to find him. See if we can work something out to do some shit together."

"You look cold, Paul. Have some of this." She held out a Thermos. "Cognac and coffee."

I unscrewed the cap and drank. The coffee was no longer hot but the cognac provided plenty of heat.

"How's your mother, Paul'?" Laura asked. "She isn't here today, is she?"

"She's okay. I saw her at Christmas," I said. "She was fighting off a virus but happy the semester was over."

"Be sure to give her my love," Laura said. "It's funny, but lately—the last year or two—I've seen so many of your parents' old friends. People I haven't seen for years. Old lefties mostly and the antiwar movement has brought them out. And when I see them, the connections aren't just political, they're personal. It makes me a little nostalgic for those times. And it gives me hope. There *are* good people around."

Our conversation was interrupted when the man in the parka came back. "Hey, Laura. There's a guy over there from *Chicago's Next Fire* and he says you said you'd talk to him." *Chicago's Next Fire* was an underground newspaper; I'd seen a copy in Alex's apartment.

"Shit!" Laura said. "Why do I say yes to these things? Look, Paul, I've got to run, but I'd like to talk some more. Are you going to stay overnight? Are you going to march tonight?"

"I'm staying over." I was still undecided about the march.

"Okay. We're at the Pick-Congress Hotel. It's right on Michigan Avenue; you can't miss it. I'm in room eight-ten. If you have time, stop by after the march and we can talk about old times."

"Room eight-ten. I've got it."

Laura began to walk away, then turned and came back. She hugged me again, harder this time. Snowflakes had collected on the top of her head, and I gently brushed them away. "You should wear a hat," I said. "You're going to catch cold."

She looked up at me and smiled. "Yes, Doctor. Whatever you say." Then she let me go.

"I'm glad to see you again, Paul. Truly. Especially here. Especially today. I'm glad to see you're on the right side."

She walked off to be interviewed. I hadn't corrected her, but I knew rightness had nothing to do with it; it was Laura's side.

I went back out with the rest of the crowd to listen to the speeches, but they couldn't hold my attention. I couldn't stop thinking about how different Laura seemed.

In spite of the vehemence and indignation that she displayed when she condemned the war and the United States' part in it, that anger didn't seem like the Laura anger of old. In the past, her fury had been without a source or an object, yet it was always there, smoldering, ready to burst into flame at any moment and burn anyone unlucky enough to be too close at the time. Back then, melancholy as well as anger seemed near her core, yet now she seemed cheerful and optimistic.

What had caused this change? Her social and political activism? That could give her a sense of purpose. But she had always had a cause to fight for. Her relationship with Roger Dale? But she had by now been with Dale for years. And, as I quickly reminded myself for my father's memory's sake, she had been in love before.

So what was it?

Through elimination I was left with this: She had stopped writing poems. Could that have changed her? Could anger and sorrow have left her when she sent the muse away? When she set down her pen, did she at the same time set aside her impatience and despair? I would have thought the opposite would be true, but the artistic temperament was so alien to me I couldn't be sure. I couldn't be sure of anything but the difference in Laura.

IT BEGAN WITH A SNOWBALL. . . .

At the back of the crowd a few of the demonstrators began to play in the snow, first building a snowman then starting a good-natured snowball fight. Then, either an errant snowball hit a policeman accidentally or someone couldn't resist aiming at one of those blue-capped targets. But a policeman *was* struck, and that set off something in the crowd.

And that gave the police the excuse they had been waiting for. Now they could disperse this crowd, send all these demonstrators packing for home, where anyone with any sense should be anyway.

Soon it was obvious why the police had arranged themselves in the parking lot as they had. They had formed their semicircle just for this moment, and as they moved in, they tightened the circle, the cops on foot cupping the demonstrators toward the center of the lot and the squad cars driving quickly up behind the stage to close off that area.

For a while it worked. The snowballs stopped flying; the demonstrators retreated at the police's approach and soon were clustered together like bees in a hive. I felt myself backing up too, yet I didn't have the sense that I was being forced in any direction. There was no alarm or panic on the crowd's part, at least not initially. The snow was still falling, the war was still being fought, and like the good middle-class citizens that we were, we were going where the police wanted us to go.

Then someone ran, then someone else, and soon people were scattering in every direction, trying to find some way to get out of the trap formed by the police line.

The police held their formation for a long time. Finally, however, someone broke through. And once a few people forced their way past the police line, the cops made the mistake of breaking ranks and going after them—which allowed more people to get away.

In spite of the fact that people were fleeing and the police were chasing them down, the scene still did not seem particularly frantic or violent. Perhaps that was because the snow, slippery underfoot, brought as many people down in comic pratfalls as the police did, and then it softened their falls. The police were also terrifyingly efficient. When a policeman grabbed a man, even if the man was much heavier, the cop was still able to push or pull him, whether through strength or leverage, in any direction the cop wanted him to go. Demonstrators moved so much at the police's will that it seemed as if it were a confrontation between children and grown-ups. For a while the kids were allowed to shout and play and run about in the snow but now the adults were rounding up the naughty children and sending them home. People who fought back against the police were comically ineffectual. They tried to dig their feet into the snow, but the cops dragged them skidding along anyway. And when protesters threw punches, they all looked like flailing schoolboys, striking out with looping, clumsy blows that cops merely turned away from, taking the punch on the arm or shoulder. The violence seemed cartoonlike—much shouting, pushing, and pulling, but no real damage being done.

But this soon changed—or I began to see things I hadn't noticed before. An older man in a tweed coat was led away by a cop who had the older man's arm bent behind him while the old man pleaded, "It doesn't go that way! I've got arthritis!" Two cops roughly dragged a girl across the lot, each of them holding a painfully widespread leg, and with every step her head bounced against the snow, and she cried, "Ouch! ouch! ouch! ouch!" I saw a cop bring down a young man running by with a deft, backhand blow to the head. He scrambled back to his feet and was off and running again so quickly that I didn't think he was hurt until I saw the bloody smear in the snow where he had landed.

All around me people were running, trying to get out of the parking lot, trying to find the friends they were separated from, trying to get away from the cops who were only a few steps behind. People were screaming—"Pig!" "Motherfuckers!" "Ronnie! Where's Ronnie?"—and the most chilling cry of all—"Don't! I'm pregnant!" The trampled snow was littered with the soggy debris of the battle: signs and placards dropped along with their sentiments—"Stop the War," "Impeach Johnson,"

"Bring Them Home"—a pair of broken glasses, a wool scarf, a ripped sneaker that probably wasn't doing much to keep the wearer's foot warm anyway, an army surplus gas mask, a dental plate still streaked with blood from the owner's mouth.

As strange as it may sound, I felt oddly safe throughout the riot. Somehow, in that totally unfamiliar situation, I discovered a way to survive. I found first of all that if I stayed near the center of the lot, near the point where the police seemed to be herding everyone, that I was okay. That is, the cops saw me as someone already taken care of, someone already under control. I stayed away from anyone who was shouting at or threatening the police, and I was careful not to let myself get trapped inside a group and so be carried off in a direction I didn't want to go.

While I was in my "safe" zone, I planned how I was going to get away. Most people were trying to escape by running north, toward the Field Museum and from there into Grant Park. A few others scattered south toward Burnham Park. No one ran east, where the harbor blocked the way, or west, where the wall of Soldier Field cut off escape. The police therefore concentrated on those fleeing north and south. I decided I would move toward Soldier Field, go all the way around and eventually work my way back to Laura's hotel.

Laura was my real concern. I knew she would not play it safe, and when I saw the police give the roughest treatment to those who antagonized them the most, I thought of her. Laura would certainly be one of the defiant ones, screaming obscenities, giving them the finger. I also knew, from what Phil and Alex had said, that the police would likely make an effort, when arrests were made, to bring in rally organizers, speechmakers, or "outside agitators."

Then I saw the Econoline van that Laura had been standing by earlier. It was heading south across the lot. A police car was speeding from another direction to intercept the van, and from the angle the squad car had, it was obviously going to broadside the van.

Perhaps because of the snow, the collision made a sound like an ice tray snapped open. The van, its side caved in, slid at least fifty feet before slowly, almost gently, tipping over on its side.

I was sure Laura was in the van, and I tried to run toward the accident.

Within a few feet I lost my footing and fell, a headlong slide through the slush that left me with soaked clothes and a jammed left wrist. I went down again as I scrambled to get my feet under me, and this time I landed hard on my ass, a fall that sent a shuddering vibration all the way up my spine.

By the time I got to the van, the police had already set up a cordon of officers around the overturned vehicle, and two cops were pulling occupants up and out through the passenger door. One of the people who came out had a cut across his forehead and blood covered his face like a veil. I didn't see Laura, so I tried to get closer to make sure she wasn't injured and still in the van.

"Hey!" A young skinny cop stopped me by putting a hand in my chest. "Where you going?" he said. "You ain't going anywhere."

I pointed to the man with the bleeding forehead. "I'm a doctor," I said. That was the first time I called myself that.

"Yeah? Think I give a fuck? Back." He pushed but not hard because he wanted to keep his hand in contact with my chest.

"Maybe I can help," I said.

"And maybe you can't. We'll never know."

I backed up but not far. I saw them pulling someone else out of the van.

It was not Laura but a woman in a pea coat who was screaming that she had whiplash. I walked slowly away.

By now the disturbance in the lot had quieted. Those people who wanted to run had gotten away or had had their minds changed by a policeman's baton. The cops had filled a police wagon and had carried still more demonstrators away in squad cars, so their arrest quota was filled. Ambulances were on the scene, and the injured were being treated, so the panic and outrage at the sight of blood had diminished. The television trucks had taken their footage back to the studios. A few people wandered about calling out the names of friends from whom they had been separated.

And where the police had only moments before been working to contain the crowd and keep it in the lot, now they were on bullhorns telling everyone to leave. At the same time, rally organizers were shouting to what was left of the crowd: "The march is canceled! There won't be a march tonight! No march! Burn your candles at home and remember what they symbolize!"

I was drifting out of the lot with a small group of demonstrators when I noticed a small circle of black cloth lying in the snow. A beret, a black beret. I remembered that Thanksgiving years before in Boston when my father brought Laura home. She had taken off her beret in a bar, and my father brought the beret home to Janie. I put the soggy cloth in my coat pocket.

I was cold, wet, tired, and I had to piss. I decided to go into the Field Museum.

On that Saturday afternoon the museum was practically deserted, and its warm, clean, white-stone quiet seemed as far removed from the violence outside as the great hall's stuffed elephants seemed from Chicago's streets. I used the rest room and then looked around for a place to rest. I sat downstairs on a bench in front of a display case filled with stuffed American songbirds, bird after mute bird perched with its bill open in the attitude of song.

I sat there for more than an hour, warming up and drying out. I told myself I was waiting, waiting until I could go to Laura's hotel. Yet as the minutes ticked by, I noticed I was not in any hurry to leave the museum, and the truth tucked inside that observation was this: Laura frightened me.

Laura could always seem intimidating or perhaps even dangerous in her hot-tempered unpredictability, in her willingness—or was it eagerness?—to step off the safe, straight paths of conventional behavior. From the time I had been a child, I had recognized that in her. Yet that aura of danger had been part of the reason I was attracted to her; it allowed me to get close to something that I couldn't come near in any other way.

The fear I felt now was different. Outside, the snow was soaked and stained with human blood. Men and women were in jails with steel bars. The wood of policemen's nightsticks was real enough, and when clubs would no longer do the job, they still had guns to draw. The pain I felt in my bruised coccyx or in my sprained wrist would fade long before the memory of the pressure of the cop's hand on my chest.

My thinking was not so tired and confused that I blamed Laura for
that violence, but neither could I separate thoughts of her from images
of students waving placards and cops waving truncheons. Though we
may never know well the history of the moment we live in, I knew that
something profound and fearful was happening in the United States in
1967 and that Laura was a part of it. And whether I would be or not was,
so far, a matter of my choice.

IT WAS DARK when I left the museum in late afternoon. The snow,
however, had almost stopped, and as I headed north toward Laura's
hotel, I saw for the first time that day the tall buildings of Chicago's sky-
line. It seemed strange to think that those buildings had been there all
day, obliterated by the lowered sky and the snow that wouldn't let you
see anything higher than the fourth floor. The sight of them now,
stretched out in all their cloudy reach and twinkling with random
squares of light, made me feel as though something had been restored.
The city's parks were once again snowy blank squares, and its buildings
were back where they belonged.

As soon as I arrived at Laura's hotel, I called her room from the lobby.
There was no answer, and I hung up, disappointed but not discouraged.
It was only six o'clock, and I knew she might not have yet returned to
the hotel after the afternoon's excitement. She might not have made
bail.

I went into the hotel coffee shop to have something to eat while I
waited. I sat at a table where I could watch the hotel's traffic and see her
if she walked by. After one hour exactly, I left the coffee shop and called
her room again. There was still no answer.

Finally, I decided just to go to Laura's room. I went to the elevator and
pushed the button for the eighth floor.

Standing outside Laura's door, I heard voices and what sounded like
music, so I knocked sharply. Through the peephole I saw the shadow of
someone coming to the door. The knob turned and the door came open
as far as its chain would let it.

"Who is it?"

"Paul Finley."

"Who?"

"Paul Finley. Laura—Miss Pettit—said I should stop by."

"Just a minute." He closed the door.

Soon I heard the rattle of the chain and the door opened. Standing right by the door but not looking at me was a young black man. He was short but his posture was militarily erect. He looked about my age, and he was dressed as I was in a crewneck sweater and chinos. He was clean-shaven and wore round, steel-rimmed dark glasses.

Then I heard Roger Dale's voice. "Is that the doc? Get him in here!" Bare-chested and barefoot, he came over to shake my hand.

The room was furnished like any hotel room—two double beds, desk, a television set on a stand, and a table in the corner with a couple chairs. The curtains were drawn and the television's picture was on but not the sound.

Besides Roger Dale and the man who let me in, there were nine other people in the room. Sitting at the table was a distinguished-looking older man. He wore a dark suit, smoked a pipe, and he had a pen poised over a yellow legal pad. Also at the table was another man in a suit, though he was much younger. His tie was loosened, and he had his glasses tipped up high on top of his balding head. He was also writing something on a legal pad. There were beer and Coke bottles, an ice bucket, and a bottle of J&B scotch on the table. Right behind the men at the table was a tall, beautiful black woman whose hair was cut so close you could see the shape of her perfect skull. She was wearing a plain, navy blue dress but had a bright orange, red, and yellow shawl around her shoulders.

A few feet from her stood two young men who looked like college students. One wore dress slacks, a white T-shirt, a red nylon ski jacket, and looked nervous and confused. He also had a Band-Aid above one eye, and a hinge of his horn-rims was held together with white adhesive tape. A rally casualty, I guessed. Next to him was a handsome man about the same age with a drooping mustache and dark hair that fell in perfect waves to his shoulders. He wore faded jeans, a well-worn corduroy sport coat, and beads.

Duane, the Vietnam vet, was there, still wearing his rain-and-shine coat, still looking blank. Lying on one bed were a man and woman dressed almost identically in blue workshirts and jeans. He had a scraggly beard and greasy dark hair that hung in his eyes. The woman looked much younger than he, in her early twenties perhaps, and she had curly dark red hair that circled her head like a halo. She lay with her head on the man's chest though he was drinking a beer and seemed to take no notice of her. Both of them were thin, but she looked close to emaciation.

On the other bed, sitting up against the headboard, was Laura. She was wearing a black cotton turtleneck and no pants, but a towel covered her from her waist to her knees. She had one foot propped up on a pillow.

"Hi, Paul," she said gaily. "You'll have to excuse me for not getting up." She lifted her beer can as if she were toasting me.

"What happened?" I asked.

"We were hauling ass out of the parking lot," Roger Dale answered. "Cops right behind us. Laurie went down. Wrecked her ankle real good."

"It was those fucking boots I was wearing," she said. "Those fucking high-heeled boots."

"But you got away," I said.

"Barely," Roger Dale said. "When she fell, these two guys with us turned around and went right at the cops. One guy growled—can you dig that? Growled like a fucking bear."

"My heroes," said Laura.

The younger man at the table said, "It was no accident, you know, that the police were after you. The government has put the word out: Make arrests and press charges. Inciting to riot, failure to disperse, public obscenity, counseling to resist the draft—anything."

"Oh, Christ, Howard," said Laura. "You and your government conspiracies."

"Wait and see," Howard replied. "A lot of people are going to do time in jail over this war."

"Howard," Laura told me, "is sort of our informal legal advisor." Laura went on to introduce the rest of the people in the room. The older man in the suit was Clifton Reese, and once I heard the name, I knew who he was. He had a career as a social and political activist going back to the 1920s. The black man and woman were David Cook and Mary Plank, both from a black student coalition. The two white students were from Students for a Democratic Society. The two on the bed Laura merely introduced as Edward and Rita. And, she said, "You know Duane and Roger."

"What do you say, Doc?" Roger Dale asked me. "Can you take a look at her ankle and see if it's broken?"

"I'm only a second-year student. I'm not sure I'll be able to tell anything."

"Leave him alone, Rog," said Laura. She patted the bed beside her. "Come and sit down, Paul. Have a drink. We're just plotting the overthrow of the government."

"Christ, Laura!" Howard threw his pencil down on the table.

"Oh, take it easy," she said. "Besides, this is just Paul. Paul's not going to tell on me. He wouldn't tell on any of us. Now come here."

I sat down on the edge of the bed.

"Take a look at the ankle, would you, Doc?" Roger Dale asked me again.

I looked at Laura. "Okay?"

Though it was not in the way of my examination, she pulled the towel up until it barely covered her crotch. As it was, I could see a tiny triangle of her underpants. I concentrated on her ankle.

"Go ahead," Laura said, the back of her hand raised melodramatically to her brow. "Do your worst! You'll never get me to talk!"

Her left ankle was badly swollen and discolored; a purplish blush crested at her ankle bone and tapered down toward the Achilles tendon.

I merely looked at first; then I asked her if she could lift her foot off the pillow so I could check the range of motion. She brought it up about six inches, and I quickly cradled it so she didn't have to hold it up without support. "Tell me if any of this hurts," I said.

I flexed her ankle slightly and tried to see if she could rotate it. She didn't complain but once gave a little involuntary gasp of pain when I pulled back on her foot a little too far. "Sorry," I said.

Her flesh was cold to the touch, as it had been that day in Vermont when I held her leg and tried to remove the beer can from her foot. If it weren't for the stubble of hair on her leg, I could have been holding a child's foot and leg, so small and delicate were her bones.

Roger Dale hovered over me. "What do you think, Doc? Great legs, huh?"

He startled me; I *had* been thinking of how beautiful her leg was and how lovely it felt to hold.

"What?" I said. "Oh. Oh, yeah. Right."

"That's what I'm always telling her. Great legs, great fucking legs. Even when she forgets to shave them."

Laura wiggled her leg in my hand. "All right. If you two are done discussing my attributes . . ."

"Yeah, Doc," said Roger Dale. "Is it broken?"

I lowered her foot gently back onto the pillow. "I don't think so, but I can't be sure. It would have to be x-rayed. You should go to a hospital."

Behind me, Howard muttered, "Not a good idea. Not today."

"Howard seems to think," Laura explained to me, "that I'm in danger of being arrested. That some people, people in authority, would like to blame me—me and others—for starting what happened out there today."

"That's not the way it happened," I said indignantly.

Howard laughed sardonically.

"Howard seems to think," Laura said again, "that the way it actually happened is of no concern to these people."

"Well," I said, "if it's only sprained, it'll get better eventually. But you have to stay off it. And you should put some ice on it to keep the swelling down. Keep it elevated too, just the way you're doing."

Roger Dale grabbed the plastic bucket and said he'd get some ice.

"But it could be broken," I said to Laura as sternly as I could. "X-rays are the only way to tell. You really should go in."

"We'll see." Laura smiled in a way that said she had no intention of following my advice. Then she raised her beer to me again and said, "Thanks, Dr. Finley. You've got a great touch and a great bedside manner." She gave "bedside" a special inflection so it sounded like the punch line of a dirty joke. I liked it.

The examination was over, but I wasn't in any hurry to move from Laura's bed. I pointed to a surgical scar's narrow track on her knee. "What's that from?"

"Cartilage," she said. "One walk too many, I guess. It finally went out on me last year when I was going down a flight of stairs. Very embarrassing."

"Does it still give you trouble?"

She smiled slyly. "Only when I'm running from the police."

Roger Dale returned with the ice, and after showing Laura how to use a towel to keep the ice on the ankle, I reluctantly left the bed and stood next to Duane.

Roger Dale picked up his guitar and sat down where I had been. With a delicacy and grace that seemed impossible in such a big, clumsy man, he began to pick out bits and pieces of songs, purposely muffling his strings. Though he wasn't doing much more than fooling around, his fingers flew up and down the frets and he filled the room with the beauty of his playing.

David Cook announced gravely, "We have to get to what we came here for."

"So talk," Laura said. "Start it off."

Cook looked deliberately at Roger Dale first and then at me. "The conditions," he said slowly, "are not right."

"Oh, for Christ's sake!" Laura said angrily. She flipped over toward Roger Dale, and as she did she exposed her white cotton underpants and their tight stretch over two small sassy mounds of flesh. She put her hand on the neck of his guitar, stopping his play. "Rog, would you take Paul out for a beer or something?"

Roger Dale bounced to his feet. "Sure thing, babe," he said cheerfully. He looked at the man and woman on the bed. "How about you, Ed? Want to blow some smoke?"

"I'll stay and keep an eye on the revolution," he said in a lazy low drawl.

Roger Dale pulled on a pair of cowboy boots and threw his parka on over his bare torso. He picked up two cans of beer and put one in each pocket. "Okay, Doc. Let's go."

As we were heading out the door, I heard Laura scolding the group. "I don't see the point of all this intrigue. . . ."

I hoped Roger Dale and I would leave the hotel and perhaps find our way to a crowded bar. I was flattered to be in the company of a celebrity and wanted us to go someplace where he would be recognized and I might be lit by his reflected fame.

Instead he led me to a back stairway of the hotel. We walked down two and a half flights, and then Roger Dale sat down on the step right above the landing.

"Park it here, Doc," he said, handing me a beer.

The staircase was narrow and I sat on the step above him. "Thanks."

"Man, I can't believe this. Last time I was in Chicago, I had a fucking suite at the Drake. But Laurie wants to keep quiet where she is. Be anonymous, that's what she wants. Shit, I'd just as soon everybody knew I was in town. You get more goodies that way."

He reached into the pocket of his coat and brought out a silver cigarette case. He popped it open and revealed a row of six or seven joints, all neatly rolled in wheatstraw paper. He took one out, lit it, took a long deep hit, and passed it to me.

What the hell, even if we weren't seen in public together, I could still tell people I smoked dope with Roger Dale. I inhaled until I felt the heat at the back of my throat.

"What are they talking about up there?" I asked, passing the joint back.

"Just what Laurie said. Revolution, man. Out with the old, in with the new."

"And those are the people who are going to make it happen?"

"A few of them. They all got connections. You know, they know somebody who knows somebody who knows somebody . . . Except maybe Ed. I don't know who the fuck Ed knows."

"Who's Ed?"

Roger Dale let out a lungful of smoke. "You don't know who Ed is? The famous fucking Edward? That, my friend, is Laurie's brother, and a stranger cat you're not likely to find."

"Edward . . . Yeah, I remember hearing about him. Wasn't he supposed to have been in prison or something?"

"Supposed to be? He was, man, and big time too. Armed robbery and assault. He just got out last summer, and Laurie's been paying for his ride ever since. I wish she'd cut him loose. He's a loser." Roger Dale threw his head back and in a falsetto sang a variation on a Beatles song. "He's a loo-oo-ser, and he's not what he appears to be. . . ."

"Is it true what I read," I asked tentatively, "that you were in prison?"

"That's just more bullshit from my publicist," he said, inhaling deeply. "I did a night in jail once." He exhaled hard and handed back the joint. "Sherry Bay, Florida. Sounds like a chick's name doesn't it? Sherry Bay. Drunk and disorderly. One night. Gotten a lot of mileage out of it though, haven't I? But Edward's the real thing. Iron bars and the whole trip."

I took the offered joint. "How's Edward going to help them make a revolution?"

"I don't know. Laurie's got some crazy fucking idea about ex-cons being a part of the Movement. You know, society's unfortunate or some shit like that. How the fuck do I know, man? I'm just a singer. Why do you think they kicked me out of there?"

I felt I knew Roger Dale well enough to say what I said next. "So you wouldn't be bored?"

"There you got it. Politics bores the shit out of me. I mean, I don't mind doing my part. Sing a few songs, say a few words. But then put it away. But Laurie can't do that. She gets set on something, she's set."

"And Edward gets to stay?"

"Edward gets to do whatever the hell he wants. Nobody tells Edward what to do." Roger Dale took another hit on the joint and followed that—without exhaling—with a long swallow of beer. "Ah, what do I care? It's just a matter of time until the miserable son of a bitch ends up in prison again. He can't miss."

"Are Edward and what's-her-name staying with you?"

"Rita. Yeah. Rita's nice, isn't she?" Roger Dale smiled broadly. "I like Rita. Nice ass. You notice that?" He handed the joint back to me. "What are you asking? All four of us in the room? Does that bother me? Nah. I'm used to performing for an audience." He laughed and playfully bumped his shoulder into my knee. "Besides, gives me a chance to show Rita my moves."

I held out what was left of the joint, nothing but a hot coal. "What do you want to do with this?"

He finished his beer and held the empty can out to me. I dropped the roach in and heard it spit and die. Roger Dale brought out his cigarette case again. "Ready for another?"

Somewhere flights below us someone opened the stairwell door and as the noise echoed up to us, I stood, ready to run. But no footsteps came our way, and I relaxed. "Why not?"

I knew that if I was arrested and convicted for possession of marijuana (in Illinois in 1967 one joint constituted possession, and that was a felony), my medical career would be over. There were stories circulating through medical school about unlucky students who had met just such a fate, but I was stoned enough not to care. Besides, Roger Dale was good company and instead of being jealous of him, as I thought I would be, I found myself liking him.

He lit the second joint and handed it to me. "Laurie and your old man, huh?"

I wasn't sure if I choked on the dusty, bitter smoke or Roger Dale's question.

"That's right," I answered once my coughing stopped.

"She told me all about him. Said they really had it going there for a while." He put his empty beer can down and stepped on it. "How about you?"

"I've still got some left," I said, holding up my beer.

Roger Dale laughed. "I mean Laurie, man. You and Laurie. You want to pick up where your old man left off?"

"What do you mean? Did she say something?"

"She didn't say shit, man. Just that you were your old man's kid. But I got eyes. You watch Laurie all the time, but sort of sneaky, like you're pretending not to."

I started to defend myself. "I was just—"

"Hey, no need, man. Doesn't bother me. You ain't the first guy got it up looking at Laurie."

All I could do was stammer. "She's beautiful."

"See, that's what I keep telling her," Roger Dale said thoughtfully, "but she won't believe me. She says I say everything's beautiful. And she's right. But Laurie is. Fucking. Beautiful." He jabbed his finger in the air to punctuate his remark.

"I'm not arguing."

"Okay. We got this far. You got a stiff prick for Laurie. All right. The question is, what are we going to do about the situation?"

I thought I knew then what Roger Dale had been working toward all along. All this fellowship, this dope-sharing goodwill, was an elaborate prelude to telling me to get the hell away from Laura and to stay away.

I started to stand, but Roger Dale grabbed my pant leg and pulled me back down. "Hey, man, down. Sit the fuck down. See, you're hung up on jealousy and possession and that whole trip, and you think everyone else is too. Not true, man, not fucking true. You want to get Laurie in the rack—I can dig that. I mean, why wouldn't you? Doesn't everyone?"

I was still wary. I knew that attitudes like Roger Dale's were in the air—it seemed every day the media made another leering reference to the era's "casual sex" and "free love philosophy"—but this was the first time I had bumped up against it. "Yeah," I said cautiously, "why wouldn't I?"

Roger Dale shrugged. "I know I got something good. I don't mind sharing." He began to rock rhythmically on the step. "So what do you say? You want me to put in a good word for you?"

"Doesn't she have anything to say about it?"

Roger Dale laughed. "Sure, man. That's why you got to win her heart! I can't do all the work." He dropped the second roach into the empty beer can. "Let's go back. If they're not through talking politics, fuck 'em. I want another beer. Dope always makes me thirsty."

By the time we got back, everyone but Edward and Rita had left, and they were still lying on the bed. The room's only light came from the television's bright gray flicker.

Roger Dale asked, "Where's Laurie?"

Edward answered. "She's in the head."

Roger Dale rapped hard on the bathroom door. "Hey, babe, we're back!"

"Is Paul still with you?" Laura called back.

"How about it?" Roger Dale asked me. "Are you here?"

Full of dope humor, I felt my arms and chest. "Most of me."

"Yeah, he's here."

"Come on in," said Laura. "I'm just soaking my ankle."

Laura was sitting on the bathtub's edge. As earlier, she was wearing her turtleneck but no jeans, and her bare legs were hanging in the tub. She was smoking and tapping her ashes into a glass ashtray on the tub beside her.

Laura smiled apologetically at me. "I ran out of ice. I thought I'd try cold water."

Roger Dale leaned over the tub and looked down into the water. "How's it doing, babe? Feel any better?"

"It's okay."

I came forward too and looked into the tub. Even through the water's distortion I could see that the swelling had gotten worse.

"You really should have that x-rayed," I advised again.

Laura put her finger to her lips and whispered, "Don't tell me what I should do anymore, okay, Paul?"

"Okay. It's your ankle."

"That's right. It's my ankle." She looked up at Roger Dale. "Could you give me a few minutes alone with Paul? I want to get his reaction on something."

"Sure thing, babe. I'm going out for pizza. Can't go to Chi town without scoring a slice."

"And then you're coming right back? You're not going anywhere else?"

He bent down and kissed her the way a boy might kiss his mother before he went out to play. "Whatever you say, babe. I'll make the Dockside scene next trip." The Dockside was a Chicago folk club.

Roger Dale closed the bathroom door behind him, but within a minute he was shouting through it, "Ed and Rita want me to bring one back for them. How about you?"

"Not for me," Laura answered. "How about you, Paul?"

I shook my head.

"No, nothing for us."

I loved hearing Laura say "for us," even if pizza provided the context.

Laura looked up at me. "Go ahead and sit down, Paul. I'm going to soak awhile longer."

I sat on the floor, my back against the wall. "He doesn't exactly seem your type," I said.

"Rog? Really? And what is my type?"

I wanted to say, *I am*, but I was not stoned enough. I wondered, in fact, if there were enough dope in the world to get me to say that. "I guess I don't know," I said.

"I guess you don't," Laura said. "Well, what can I tell you? He sings to me, he makes me laugh, and he's good in bed. And that's enough for me. For now, that's enough."

I changed the subject. "No more poems, huh? Were you serious about that?"

She smiled ruefully. "That wasn't as great a sacrifice as I made it out to be. I haven't been able to write a single goddamn poem for over a year. Since the last book, in fact."

"What's the matter?"

She stared down at the water and splashed her feet. "I'm not sure. Maybe it *is* the war. I know I can't stop thinking about it. Maybe I've used up my allotment of poems. Maybe I'm getting too old." She looked up, her expression brighter. "Or maybe it's Roger's dope."

Laura swung her uninjured leg out of the water and let it drip on the tile. She was facing me and straddling the tub and her legs were spread in my direction. A few strands of pubic hair curled out from her underpants' elastic. I bowed my head.

"What's the matter?" Laura asked.

Was it possible she didn't know what she could do to me? "Nothing," I replied. "You said you wanted to talk to me about something."

She lit another cigarette. "I wanted to ask you how involved you are in school."

"How involved? I go to classes or to the hospital during the day, and I study my ass off all night."

"I guess I want to know if you like it."

"What's not to like? I go to classes or to the hospital during the day, and I study my ass off all night. . . ."

"I'm serious, Paul. I need to know if you're finding yourself in your studies, if it's giving you what you need."

"To tell you the truth," I said, "I've been disappointed. I don't know exactly what I hoped for, but for the last year and a half I haven't done much more than memorize material from books or lectures."

"That's what I hoped you'd say! Okay. Let me tell you the plan. Roger and I and some other people are going to start traveling the country together. We're going to try to get a used bus and fix it up. We want to be able to carry plenty of supplies so we can eat in it, sleep in it—live in it. We're going to carry the protest movement all over America, concentrating on small towns. You know, the kinds of towns where no one has yet spoken out against the war. Except for college campuses, the Movement has been almost all urban."

"Antiwar sentiment isn't running real high in small towns, you know."

"We know that. We're not going out to preach to the converted. We expect this to be confrontational. We'll argue and debate this war in VFW clubs and in town squares, in bars and barbershops. One of the reasons people still support this miserable goddamn war is that they don't know the truth of it."

I wanted to share her enthusiasm, but I was skeptical. What's more, I was surprised at Laura's excitement. I had always thought she was too cynical to give herself uncritically and wholeheartedly to projects like this one.

"Whose idea was this?" I asked.

"Nobody's. Everybody's. We were sitting around talking one night. Someone had spent some time with Kesey and his Pranksters out in California and thought it would be terrific to do something like that, only political."

"What are you going to do for money?"

Laura laughed. "I love these questions, Paul. I knew you'd scowl just like you're doing now and look serious and worried and ask all these practical questions." She straightened up and stared straight ahead as if she were reciting for a teacher. "What are we going to do for money? That's a fair question. Well, I can give readings, especially when we go through a college town. Rog can give concerts. We both get royalty checks, though his are considerably larger than mine. We'll have enough to keep us in gas, food, and dope."

"Who's going to be on the bus? People who were here earlier?"

She shook her head. "I hoped so. I wanted us to have representatives from the major antiwar groups, but they're all into their own organizations and ideologies."

My legs were getting stiff, so I stood up and moved around. "Your bus idea sounds great," I said as convincingly as I could. "I'm not sure why you're telling me about it."

"Paul, Paul, you're always so slow on the uptake. Jesus. I'm asking you if you want to come with us.

"I'll understand if you say no," Laura added. "That's why I asked you about school. If you like it and want to stay with it, that's what you should do. But if not . . . I've been thinking about it all day. I thought, why not Paul? He'd be great to have with us."

Naturally I was flattered, yet at the same time I wanted to argue with her. I wanted to tell her how wrong I was for them, how I wouldn't be coming along out of political commitment but only so I could be near her.

"I'd lose my deferment," I said. "If I dropped out of school, the draft board would reclassify me like *that.*" I snapped my fingers.

"They'd have to find you. And we'd be moving all the time. You wouldn't have to use your real name."

"Are you sure you want me along?" I asked. "I couldn't give a speech to save my life."

Laura smiled. "We don't need more people to give speeches. We need someone practical, sensible. Someone who thinks right away to ask, how are you going to pay for that? Roger's no good at practical matters. He has the attention span of a four-year-old. Edward's temper always gets in his way. Mine too, for that matter. Besides, we could use someone with medical training. You know, someone who could do some bandaging. Maybe take a few stitches."

Ironies and paradoxes bounced around the room like echoes. She wanted me along because I was a practical man, yet I would have to throw away my career to go with them. She wanted someone with medical training, yet I would be dropping out of med school. She wanted a sane and sensible man, yet she was talking to someone mad with love for her—and someone who would do anything out of that madness.

"Christ, I've barely gotten out of the classroom."

Laura threw her hands in the air. "Okay, you're not perfect! If you could write a goddamn prescription, you'd be perfect. Now, what do you say? Yes or no. In or out."

"I have one more question," I said.

"What is it?" Laura asked.

"Why did you think you had to ask me? Why didn't you just call me up in the middle of the night and say, 'Paul, it's time. I'm coming to get you now.' Don't you know you can do that? Anytime, anyplace."

She looked at me curiously. At last, she said, "This is about politics though. Remember?"

"Sure, I know."

"I wasn't sure if you did. Now then," she said as she swung her other leg out of the bathtub, "help me out of here. My foot's beginning to freeze."

I hunched down and let Laura put her arm around my neck. Then, with me as a crutch, she hopped out into the other room and back onto the bed. I positioned the pillow again under her ankle.

Once she was settled, Laura said to Edward and Rita, "Good news. Paul's going to join us in our travels." Neither acknowledged her announcement.

"Just a minute," I said. "I should go back to Madison, shouldn't I? Pack some things, put things in order?"

Laura shook her head. "You can't go back. There isn't time. We're leaving tomorrow morning. You'll have to stay here. We'll buy you what you need."

It would probably be better that way, I reasoned. As long as I stayed close to Laura, I could believe that was where I belonged. If I went away for even a day, my faith might falter.

Rita left the room to take a shower, leaving Edward, Laura, and I to watch a western on television that only Edward cared about.

Edward finally spoke. "Is he bringing back pizza?"

"Roger? If he said he would, he will."

"He better shag his ass," Edward said and resumed watching the movie.

From the chair where I sat, I could see both Laura and Edward, and subtly as I could I studied them for any family resemblance. I didn't have to look long or hard. Though both of them were in repose, they still seemed to be in a state of readiness. They both had a sharpness to their profiles—chiseled beauty on her and menacing angularity on him.

No one spoke again during the movie, and when it ended, a late-night news program came on. It began with coverage of the demonstration, and Laura said, "I want to hear this."

I turned up the volume, and when I did, Rita came out of the bathroom. "Is that about us? Are we on?" She was towel-drying her hair, and she was completely naked. I looked away but not soon enough.

I had noticed before how thin Rita was, but now I saw how little there was to her beyond bone. Her elbows, wrists, knees, and ankles stuck out like knots in lengths of rope. With her arms upraised, her breasts shrunk almost to concavity, her nipples small leathery circles.

But what really struck me was her body hair. Her just-washed hair on top of her head—already drying back to frizz—was dark red, almost auburn, but the tufts of hair under her arms and the triangular patch at her pubis were bright red, the color of newly oxidized rust.

I thought I should say something. Perhaps a joking protest that since I wasn't a doctor yet, I wasn't accustomed to nudity. But whether I was going to speak or not soon didn't matter because when Edward noticed Rita, he sprang from the bed with a speed even more astonishing than her nakedness.

In an instant he grabbed a fistful of her hair and yanked her head back. She bent over backward, her face and tiny breasts pointed toward the ceiling

"What the fuck are you doing?" Edward screamed at her. "Parading around bare-assed in front of him!"

At first, all Rita could say was, "Ow! Ow! Eddie! Ow!"

Edward began to pull her across the room. Laura was sitting up in bed but looked too stunned to say or do anything.

I was right in his path, and Edward said, "Move, asshole!"

Reflexively, I obeyed.

Edward hauled Rita over to the window. "You want people to see your titties? Is that what you want? Go ahead." He pulled her closer to the glass. "Show the whole fucking city!"

With both hands Rita held on to Edward's arm—the one pulling her hair—and tried to relieve the pressure.

"Eddie!" she cried. "Eddie, you said we were going to be free! Like family! We wouldn't have to worry about clothes or any other hang-ups. Eddie! It's what *you* said!"

Edward said, "Free? You want to be free? I'll let you fucking fly—that's how free you can be!"

Then, still using only one hand, Eddie managed to unlatch the window and to open it. As soon as it came open, Rita began to shriek, "No! Eddie, Eddie! No, no, no! Please, please!"

The window wasn't open far enough for Rita to fit through, but Edward strained to lift it higher. His determination seemed so great I was afraid he might throw Rita through the glass.

I had no plan of action, but I knew I had to do something.

I hadn't taken more than two steps however when Edward whirled on me. I don't know how he saw me; perhaps there was a reflection in the window. "Come any closer, motherfucker," he shouted, "and you'll go out right after her!"

I stopped where I stood, but by then Laura was out of bed and hopping on one foot toward her brother. "Edward," she said in the soft, cooing voice a mother uses when she is trying to talk her baby to sleep. "Edward, Ed-ward, Ed-ward . . ."

Rita was trying to pull back from the window, reaching out with one leg, trying to hook it onto a chair. Now she was whimpering, pleading with him, "Please, Eddie. Please. I won't do it again. I didn't know, that's all. I thought it would be okay. I didn't understand what you meant. Please, Eddie. Please, please."

Then Laura got close enough to put a hand on Edward's shoulder, still murmuring his name, "Ed-ward, Ed-ward."

I had decided I would dive for Rita's legs and hold on as tightly as I could. That way, if he did try to lift her out, I would have a chance of keeping her in.

But somehow, the combination of Laura's touch and her soothing voice broke the spell of Edward's murderous rage. The window he had been working so hard to open he now slammed shut, and he spun Rita around by the hair and flung her toward the bed. "Fuck it," he said.

Rita scrambled up toward the head of the bed, grabbing a pillow and trying to cover herself with it.

"Shut the curtains, would you please, Paul?" Laura asked. She had her hand on Edward's shoulder again, and she used him to help her to balance on one leg.

Before I drew the curtains I glanced outside. Our window looked out at another building across the street, and as far as I could see, no one over there was looking in our direction. I latched the window again before I closed the curtains.

Edward walked over to the bed, Laura hopping alongside him. He pulled up the bedspread from the foot of the bed and flipped it at Rita. "Cover yourself," he said to her. He walked to the bathroom.

Rita wrapped herself in the brown satin bedspread and, sniffling, followed Edward. After she went in, I heard the door lock behind her.

Laura was back on the bed, leaning against the headboard and looking exhausted. "Come and sit down, Paul," she invited me in the same soft voice she used to tame her brother. I obeyed and sat down next to her. Laura picked up my hand and held it between hers. Predictably, her touch was cool.

"I'm sorry you had to see that," she said. Strange that she said she was sorry not that it happened but that I was a witness! "Your first day with us . . . This afternoon first . . . then tonight . . . What you must think!"

"Don't worry about me."

"But I do!" I noticed then that though she was talking to me and holding my hand, she was barely there. She was staring vacantly across the room and her voice was losing its inflection, fading like a radio signal you were moving farther and farther away from. "I do . . . And Edward. I want you to understand. He wasn't like this before prison. Prison made him like this. But he's getting better. We can make him bet-

ter. He's going to be okay. We'll all be okay soon." I wasn't about to con-
tradict Laura when she said Edward wasn't like this before prison, but I
remembered it was he who scarred Laura's face with a bottle cap.

Then Laura put her arms around me and pulled my head to her breast.
There seemed nothing loving or sexual about the embrace, however; she
put a hand over my ear, and I couldn't help but wonder if it was to keep
me from hearing something that was going on in the bathroom. Was
Edward beating Rita?

The Laura who held me close was not the Laura I thought I knew.
That Laura was uncompromising on matters of principle. This Laura was
willing to set her beliefs aside for the sake of family, to protect her black-
hearted, brutal brother, Edward.

She rocked me back and forth and continued to murmur in my ear.

"Tonight is already over," she said softly and into my ear. "You're with
us now. You're going to stay with us, and everything will be all right.
You're going to sleep right by our bed, and tomorrow we're all going to go
out and begin making a new world together. A beautiful, beautiful world."

Did Laura believe these things? I suppose she might have, but her
words didn't seem to have any conviction behind them. Instead, they
sounded like the words a parent coos to her child whom she believes is
not ready for the world's harsher realities.

Soon Edward and Rita came out of the bathroom. Rita was wearing a
bathrobe, and though she looked somber and red-eyed, I saw no signs of
her having been beaten. She and Edward lay down again on their bed. I
moved to a chair across the room, and the four of us remained that way,
in a silence as sad and thick as fog, until Roger Dale returned.

He was drunk, and he threw down on the dresser two grease-sodden
cardboard boxes of cold pizza. He said to Laura, "Bust my chops tomorrow, okay, babe? I've got to crash now." He dropped his coat on the floor
and fell facedown onto the bed.

Laura pushed at his motionless dead weight. "Goddamn it, at least let
me pull back the covers!"

Edward helped himself to pizza, complaining with every bite how cold
it was. After eating a few slices, he turned off the television and the
lights and retreated to his bed.

Roger Dale sat up unsteadily, his eyes closed and a blissful smile on his face. He was probably more stoned than drunk. He pulled off his boots, his shirt, and his jeans and then lay back on the sheets.

Laura gave me a pillow and the bedspread that Rita had wrapped around herself. "Is this going to be enough?" Laura whispered. "Do you want our blanket?"

"I'm fine," I said. After taking off my boots and sweater, I folded the bedspread on the floor next to Laura's and Roger Dale's bed. I lay on the blanket and covered myself with my coat.

The room then was dark and quiet, except for the mismatched rhythm of our five breaths and the metallic ticks and sighs of the radiator. The floor was hard, the carpet smelled of mildew, and when I closed my eyes, I saw policemen swinging billy clubs or Edward wrenching Rita's head around or Laura's pale bare legs. . . . Too much, too much . . . I gave up on sleep and tried to use the time to see into my future, my brand-new future.

Soon the day's hours that I had filled with medical studies would be empty, and I could put into them anything I wanted—long walks, bicycle rides, hundreds of sit-ups, or hours of Frisbee. I could read novels and the volumes of poetry that I had neglected in favor of textbooks. I could let my hair and beard grow. I could learn to throw pots, or I could spend the day writing letters to congressmen.

But my principal occupation would consist of nothing more than staying near Laura. I could bring her water when she was thirsty or a blanket when she was cold. When she needed flattery or encouragement, I could be there. If she fell into depression or despair, I could learn to juggle or do pratfalls to humor her out of her dark mood. If her shoulders were knotted with anxiety or overwork, I could massage her into relaxation.

This cartoon I was running in my mind snapped when a sound track that didn't match the picture intruded. I heard the springs of Edward and Rita's bed squeaking, and the rhythm could mean only one thing. They were fucking. And since I had to believe Edward was the instigator, I wondered what had turned him on. Beating Rita and threatening her life? Fucking in a room where others could watch? Whatever set him off, he was going hard—the bedsprings pounded violently, and Edward gave off chuffing little grunts. I didn't hear a sound from Rita, not even passion's rapid panting. Were Laura and Roger watching? I didn't dare lift my head to look at them, much less at the other bed.

Edward didn't last long. He gave out a self-satisfied, high-pitched snarl, as if something resisting him had finally given way, and then the bedsprings stopped bouncing as suddenly as they began.

The room was quiet again, but of course I could not return to the fantasy of the future I had been playing earlier. Edward had taken care of that, and perhaps he had done me a service.

I don't know how long I had been lying awake when Laura's hand swung down over the side of the bed. At first I thought she was reaching out to me, that she knew I was awake and was extending a comforting, calming hand for me to hold. But I stopped myself before I took her hand. Peering through the dark, I saw she had simply rolled to the side of the bed in sleep, and if she was reaching out with that hand, it was not to me but to someone in a dream. Nevertheless, I lifted my own hand until our two hands were a scant inch apart, and if she tossed again in sleep, our hands would surely touch. She didn't move, however, and I soon tired of holding up my hand in the vacant, loveless air.

As soon as I brought my arm back down, however, I was surprised by the thickness forming in my throat and the tears gathering in my eyes. Though I was in no danger of breaking down in sobs and though the tears hadn't sufficient volume to propel themselves down my face, they were real enough.

From where had they come? From fatigue certainly. It was the middle of the night, the previous hours had been harrowing, exhilarating, exhausting.

And they came from fear. I was afraid of Edward of course, but also of Duane and Rita and lawyers and revolutionaries and all those half-crazed and passionate types who found Laura and flocked to her. I was afraid of the age I lived in, of free love and free sex and free dope and politics by confrontation. I was afraid of the police and the draft board and what would happen if they found me and what would happen if they didn't.

But more than anything else, these tears sprang from self-pity. Never in my life had I felt sorrier for myself than I did at that moment. I had gotten what for so many years I had been yearning for, the chance to be near Laura every day of my life. In fact, if I would only doze off, I could be said to be sleeping with her! And the literal truth of that statement was the perfect punch line to the joke of what had happened when all my wishes for a life with Laura came true. Yes, here we were, lying less than an arm's reach apart, and I might as well have been back in Madison for all the good this closeness did me. And tomorrow we would set out to build a better world together—while I had to remember to be careful around Laura's brother so he wouldn't lose his temper and murder me.

Say this much for tears of self-pity: There is an embarrassing self-consciousness about them that dries them up quickly. Mine soon stopped. And finally I did fall asleep, though not comfortably or soundly. I woke a little after six so stiff and cold I knew I had to get up and move around.

I used the bathroom quietly, then decided that rather than lie back down on the floor and try to sleep for a few more miserable hours, I would go out for a Sunday paper. The *Chicago Tribune* would be full of news about the demonstration, and I wanted to see what it was like to be part of history.

The room and the morning were still dark, but enough light from the street oozed into the room for me to see the outlines of the sleepers.

Roger Dale lay on his side at the edge of the bed, a great mound of sheets, blankets, and body. Laura sprawled beside him on her stomach, one leg uncovered, her dreaming completely separate from his. Edward also lay on his side, facing Roger Dale. Edward slept with a hand over his face, palm side up. Rita, modest in sleep, lay flat on her back, blankets up to her chin.

I had put on my coat and was tiptoeing toward the door when Rita spoke, startling me.

"Good-bye," she simply said.

I glanced at Edward to make sure Rita's voice hadn't wakened him. He hadn't stirred.

I held a finger to my lips. "I'm going out for a paper," I whispered.

Rita smiled and got up on one elbow, in the process baring her shoulder. "I'll tell her you said good-bye," she said.

I shook my head. "I'm just going out for a paper," I repeated. "I'll be right back."

Rita's pale arm lifted from the blankets to wave good-bye.

I gave up trying to convince her and left.

Before the elevator reached the lobby, however, I knew what Rita knew: I was not going back.

The elevator doors lurched open, and I went directly to a telephone booth. I opened the directory and searched until I found Alex Hoover's number. I dialed the number and let it ring—six, seven times—until Alex's sleepy voice answered. I asked for Phil Reed.

Minutes passed before Phil came to the phone. "Yes?" he asked sleepily.

"Hi, roomie," I said. "Sorry to wake you."

"That's all right. Is something wrong? Are you okay?"

"I'm fine. But I need a ride."

"When? Now?"

"Now."

"Christ. Okay. Where are you?"

I told him.

"Okay. Give me a few minutes to get dressed. You're sure everything's all right?"

"Fine. Just one thing. Are you still going back to Madison today?"

"That's the plan," Phil said. "Why?"

"No reason. If you weren't, I'd catch a bus or a train or something."

"Whew!" said Phil. "You in some kind of hurry to get out of here?"

"Just come as soon as you can."

I hung up and went to the desk. I wrote a short note for Laura and asked the clerk to give it to her only if she asked if there were any messages. I wrote, "I decided to be a doctor after all. Sorry. Paul." Then I went outside to wait for Phil, though I knew it would be at least half an hour before he got to the hotel.

It had begun to snow again, but this time the flakes were fine and dry and so scattered that it would take a day of their falling to dust the sidewalks and the streets. The morning was cold, and I walked back and forth in front of the hotel to keep warm. But I did not return inside.

JUST AS IT is customary to conclude stories about the exploits of a family's wild child by telling what became of that child in adulthood, so it has become a requirement to end tales of the 1960s—our age's untamed offspring—with an afterword settling the fates of that decade's characters. This, then, is my summing up, the requisite coda to the preceding tale, my list of what became of whom. . . .

Do I need to repeat the story of how Roger Dale was found dead in a London hotel room, the needle still stuck in his arm? Surely not. Like Janis Joplin's or Jimi Hendrix's, his became one of those lives that everyone loved to cluck over—ah, the waste! the waste! He died in 1969, and he and Laura were no longer together. At the time of his death Roger Dale was married to Miriam Tepp, the lead singer with the British rock group Tempest. When I read about his marriage, I thought, and who now is singing to Laura? Who is making her laugh? And when he died, I was so disheartened by the news I could not even bring myself to tell anyone that he and I once smoked dope together in a hotel stairwell.

And the summer after that pathetic rally in a football stadium's parking lot, the whole world learned the same truth about the Chicago police that we learned that winter day. Witnesses at the 1968 Democratic National Convention not only saw the police brutally out of control gassing and clubbing demonstrators up and down Chicago's streets, but also saw them punching newsmen and pushing onlookers through the plate-glass window of a hotel. And this time there was no snow to cover the police's bloody tracks.

I don't know if Laura's plan for a peace bus ever came to pass. If it did, it was on so small a scale that the media didn't see fit to report on it and I never heard about it.

I learned later that Roger Dale's prediction came true and Edward ended up back in prison. For life. I don't know what became of Rita, though when I was in California for a convention in 1974 or 1975, I saw a television commercial for a local dry cleaners that featured a woman who looked remarkably like her.

Phil Reed remained true to his convictions and eventually moved to a small town in South Dakota where he could offer medical care to the nearby residents of a Sioux Indian reservation.

Laura finished the sixties teaching again at the small college in Vermont where she had taught earlier. The dust jacket bio on her 1970 collection of short stories, *Voices Coming from an Empty Room,* said she lived in rural Vermont with two cats and a dog. There was no photograph on the jacket. From this evidence, I concluded that she had once again retreated from the world.

In 1970 I was working a late shift at the university hospital on the summer night when the mathematics building on the University of Wisconsin campus was bombed, killing a graduate student. Afterward, I thought I had felt something—a vibration of the floor, a sound, a concussion of the air—at the exact moment of the explosion. I thought I did, but I couldn't be certain. You know what that's like. At some point you're no longer sure what you actually lived through and what you merely imagined.

Nine

$\mathscr{I}$n the years that followed I
made a sincere effort to transform myself. I tried to become a responsible
and, most of all, a reasonable man. I worked diligently at becoming a
good doctor, and if I can make this immodest claim, I believe I suc-
ceeded. In areas where I lacked skill or aptitude—I had particular difficulty, for example, in tying off sutures—I tried to overcome my shortcomings with extra study and practice. I once rode the bus from Madison
back to Fairmont, Minnesota, and throughout the trip I tied dozens of
knots in the length of triple-O black nylon I carried with me everywhere.

My approach to correcting the deficiencies in my personal life was
similarly disciplined and methodical. When my loneliness approached
the unacceptable stage, I settled on marriage as the answer, and I had by
that time begun dating a bright, attractive, companionable woman who
would make a fine wife. I came to this conclusion by a kind of deductive
reasoning. I could not have the woman I loved—Laura—so I would put
aside my obsession with her and love the woman I could have. The problem was that logic can neither remove love from nor lodge it in the
human heart. . . .

In the summer of 1973, a few weeks before I was scheduled to marry

Catherine Cameron, I toyed with the idea of writing or calling Laura to tell her of the upcoming event. I had her home address and telephone number (which I got from the department secretary at Laura's college with the aid of a lie: I said I was presenting Laura an award for her poetry), and every day I took them out and tried to think of what to write or say.

Dear Laura. I know I was supposed to stay with you in 1967, but I got frightened and ran away. Now I'm going to be married. . . .

Dear Laura. I'm a doctor now. I became a pediatrician because when I was a child, I fell ill with love for you and never recovered. Now I want to help children get better. . . .

Dear Laura. Catherine's a great gal, and I'm sure if you met her, you'd love her!

Plainly, none of these would do, yet neither would a wedding announcement with no accompanying explanation. The day of the wedding drew closer, and I still hadn't written. Perhaps I was afraid that if she knew of the wedding far enough in advance, she might come to the ceremony. How would I greet her? Ask her if she had come all that way just so I could see what I was missing by marrying another woman? How would I introduce her? "Catherine, I'd like you to meet the woman I wish I were marrying"?

Then it was too late. I didn't write, I was going to be married the next day, and no letter could reach Laura in time.

On the day before the wedding I went golfing with Catherine's father, her brothers, and Phil Reed and Bill Hazen from that years-earlier trip to Chicago. They had both driven to Hamilton, Wisconsin, Catherine's hometown, for the occasion. We started drinking beer before we teed off, and we continued to drink while we played. After nine holes we adjourned to the clubhouse for more beers before playing the second nine. The day was hot, I was already drunk, and I had played miserably, so I let them continue the round without me.

I was sitting in the clubhouse, looking out onto the course and trying to count its various shades of green when a drunken notion suddenly came over me—I would call Laura. Before I could ask myself what I intended to say to her, I had gathered a handful of change and was heading for the pay telephone. My finger shook as I dialed the number I had committed to memory.

After six rings Laura answered.

And at the sound of her "hello"—breathless, deep, and dry—I was struck dumb.

"Hello," she repeated.

I still couldn't speak.

"Come on, goddamnit," Laura said. "You brought me in from my garden, the least you can do is talk to me."

Two golfers walked past, and I wondered if Laura heard their spikes clattering on the tile.

"Is this long distance?" she asked. "This sounds like long distance."

I tried to imagine what she looked like. She had come in from the garden. Her hands were caked with dirt, and her hair, from hanging down toward the earth, kept falling across her face. When she brushed it back, she left a blush of dirt on her cheek.

"Goddamnit, I can hear you breathing. I know you're there."

I put my hand over the mouthpiece so she couldn't hear anything but the empty hiss of all the miles between us.

"Kenneth?" Laura asked. "Is that you?"

At that point I might have spoken up. No, it's Paul Finley. But it was too late. No matter what I said now, the subject of the call would be my initial silence. Let her believe it was Kenneth.

Something strange happened. Laura didn't say another word, but she didn't hang up either. A minute passed, and she met my silence with her own. I thought at first that she might have set the phone down and gone back to her garden, keeping the line open so that if this caller tried to phone again, he would be met by a busy signal. But then I heard her breathing, the steady quiet rhythm broken occasionally by a louder, longer exhale. I guessed she was smoking while she patiently waited for her secret caller to speak.

I remembered something Laura said on the night we first met, when she tried to hide in my bedroom. She complimented me that night on my ability to be silent, a quality she said too few people had. Maybe, I drunkenly hoped, she would recognize this silence as mine. Maybe she would divine my identity from the texture and duration of this silence—and she would find it as admirable as she once had. And as soon as she spoke my name—making a question of "Paul" as she had of the mysterious "Kenneth"—I could say, You see? I still have it; I can be as quiet as ever.

But silences can no more be read than blank pages, and when I came back around to that sober realization, I gave up and hung up the phone, replacing the receiver on the cradle so slowly and gently that Laura wouldn't be able to tell the exact instant that separated when I was there from when I was gone.

THE FOLLOWING DAY I married a woman nothing like Laura Coe Pettit. Catherine and I had met at Good Samaritan Hospital in Milwaukee, where Catherine was a pediatric nurse and I was a resident in peds. Shortly after our marriage I completed my residency, and we moved to Red Oak, Wisconsin, a small town between Madison and Milwaukee. I soon settled in as one of two pediatricians in the Red Oak Community Clinic. The twins, Nora and Doreen, named after Catherine's mother and mine, were born in July 1975.

Catherine is blond and blue-eyed, and if it were not for slightly crooked front teeth and a shyness so extreme it wants to cloud her radiance, she could be called beautiful—and only in that regard are she and Laura similar. She went from being an unselfish, devoted, loving girlfriend to being an unselfish, devoted, loving wife and mother.

Catherine grew up working on her parents' dairy farm. In high school she was an honor student, Hayride Festival Queen, and letter-winning athlete in volleyball and swimming. After high school she performed for one summer with the Tommy Bartlett Water-Skiing Show in the Wisconsin Dells. She attended the University of Wisconsin School of Nursing, and while she was there, her practical, single-minded nature allowed her to pass undisturbed through the turmoil of the sixties.

Before we met, she had had only two boyfriends of any duration, a boy she dated steadily during her junior and senior years of high school, and a young man she went with for three years in college. She slept with the second but not the first.

Catherine is a woman of moderation. She is careful about what she eats and that, along with regular exercise, enables her to maintain a lithe, slender figure. She is frugal, hardworking, and amazingly competent—she is able to unclog drains, sew clothing for our twin daughters, and coax beautiful flowers from the sandy soil our house sits on. She attends church every Sunday and is not disappointed in me because I do not. Indeed, anyone who knows her is taken with her good humor, her kindness, and her charity. The word that would probably come quickest to people's tongue if they were asked to characterize Catherine is "nice." And I recall that my father once said that Laura would have found death preferable to having that adjective attached to her name.

But I don't want to leave the impression that Catherine differs from Laura only in the fact that Catherine possesses virtues. Catherine, for example, though she is intelligent, is neither imaginative nor quick. Often the last to understand a joke, she will never light a room with the scintillation of her wit. But neither will she lacerate anyone—and mark that down to compassion. Her sensible, pragmatic bent inclines her away from the unpredictable or the adventurous. Finally, and this I believe is the chief point of difference, Catherine is not passionate. Steadfast, loyal, loving, affectionate—yes. But these are low and constant flames, and unlike the spontaneous, white-hot flash of passion. In bed, for instance, she has always been responsive and giving, yet I have always vaguely felt that she was *working,* not that she was unwilling but that she was momentarily hesitant, uncertain, consciously thinking of what to do and how to do it. Should I roll my hips in just this way? Does he want me to put my knees up or leave them down? Never during lovemaking has she cried out in ecstasy, praise, encouragement, or suggestion.

But now I am being unfair. I should not have contrasted Catherine with Laura when I have no way of knowing how Laura would behave. By any standard, Catherine was a good woman, the embodiment for many men of the Ideal Wife. Nothing in my description of her do I wish to mock or deride. As I said, that I did not love her I assign to my deficiencies, not to hers.

Nevertheless, questions of love aside, I found in marriage a kind of gratification I had never known before. Catherine provided companionship that was pleasant and without strain. The community where we settled had the attractions of small town living—the neighborliness, the security, the comfortable pace—yet it was close enough to Madison, Milwaukee, and Chicago that we could drive in to see a foreign film, a play, a ball game, to shop or visit a museum. We bought a large old house that, instead of breaking our spirits with the sanding, painting, varnishing, refurbishing, and remodeling that it required, gave us a knuckle-scraping pride and back-aching satisfaction. Through the clinic and the neighborhood we acquired a number of friends near us in age and interests. Every summer we rented a cottage in northern Wisconsin for two weeks of swimming, fishing, and boating. I played eighteen holes of golf every Saturday morning with three other doctors from the clinic. When jogging and fitness became national obsessions, I strapped on running shoes as well and slogged out my four miles daily.

And I discovered, perhaps to my own surprise, that I enjoyed my work. Many people—many doctors, in fact—don't understand what the practice of pediatrics is like. In medical school those who choose to be pediatricians are often assigned—by other students and physicians—one of the lower rungs on the ladder of medical status. I was often asked, "Wouldn't you rather treat *grown-ups?*" Worse was the question, posed always with the thumb and index finger held an inch apart, "So you're going to be a baby doctor?" People can see the rewards in treating the curable child, but they can't see how that can outweigh the heartbreak of confronting the incurable. The truth is, once outside the hospital wards of residencies and into the clinics, pediatricians seldom see a serious illness, and when they do suspect one, they send the case off to a specialist before the heartbreak stage. The special satisfaction in treating children is that they *do* get better. They seldom visit the doctor with anything more serious than upper-respiratory infections. They don't malinger, they don't read about exotic illnesses in magazines and concoct symptoms to match, they don't whine for new medications or increased dosages. Their lives are not so lonely that they visit the doctor for company. In fact, children sometimes have to be dragged or carried kicking and screaming to the clinic. They don't chatter during examinations or give you misleading responses. Simply put, almost none of them is gravely ill and almost all of them get better. Pediatrics even gives you an opportunity to conduct examinations that are rare in medicine, since they are almost always conducted on healthy patients—well-baby checkups and back-to-school physicals—and these were the office visits I most looked forward to.

And how could I go on this long about our life in Red Oak without mentioning my own children and the joy they brought me. From the moment the twins were born, I found myself in a condition of stunned bliss, so unaware was I—as first-time mothers and fathers usually are—of the enormous happiness that had simply been waiting for me, waiting for me to become a parent. To call me a doting father would be a gross understatement. The way some people are able to stare at a television for endless, undistracted hours, I was able to watch my daughters. And if there hadn't been two of them right from the start, I never would have believed that anyone could love both of his children so boundlessly, so without reservation, and yet equally.

Were there, then, any pieces missing that would complete the perfect puzzle-picture of me as a competent professional, devoted husband and father, contented suburbanite? Were there any hints at all that I was wedded to any life other than the one I walked through every day? Only a few. . . .

Freed at last from medical studies and the endless required reading of textbooks, case histories, and reports, I found time every day, usually late in the evening, after the twins went to bed, to do some reading of my own. And of all the books in the world, what did I pull from the shelves of the library or the bookstore? I began to read poetry. Not Laura's. Quite deliberately I did not go directly to Laura's work. I read her, but only as she fit among all the other American poets I was reading. I developed favorites, and truthfully, Laura was not among them. Her poems were still too clipped and cryptic for me to make much of them—perhaps my mother was right. I favored the plainspoken poets: Frost and Williams and the confessional Lowell especially. Soon I was subscribing to five or six little magazines, and eventually I felt I had some rudimentary understanding of the contemporary literary scene and Laura's place in it.

Of course, many people read poetry. It was nothing for me to hide. No symptom of discontent in that activity.

Neither could any outside observer have noticed the other change that came over me, for this had to do only with my mind and a trick it played on my vision. Starting the day I was married—the very day—I began to see Laura everywhere.

The first time this happened was at my wedding reception. We were all gathered at the American Legion Hall in Hamilton, the room Catherine's father had rented for the afternoon. I was standing up by the bandstand, where a terrible three-piece band—guitar, accordion, and drum set—played. I was looking out over the hall, trying to see if my mother, sister, or one of my friends or a relative was out there alone or bored and in need of rescue, when I saw her.

Laura.

Standing with my mother and Janie over by the bar.

Immediately I made my way across the crowded floor toward her. How had she heard of the wedding? Since she was with my mother, I could only think that it was my mother who notified Laura.

When I arrived at the trio, however, I saw it was not Laura but Becky Cameron, Catherine's fourteen-year-old cousin who was visiting with Janie and my mother. And Becky looked nothing like Laura. Her hair was the wrong color, she was not particularly pretty—she had the pushed-in nose that so many of the Camerons had and which Catherine fortunately escaped—and she was wearing a long, frilly pink dress that Laura would never have worn. The only thing right was the height; she stood not much more than five feet tall.

I stared disbelieving at Becky so long I made her nervous. My mother finally came to my rescue. "Did you want to take this pretty girl out onto the dance floor?"

I nodded dumbly and took Becky in my arms. As we waltzed away, my mother said, "Your sister and I are next!"

Out on the dance floor I continued to look at Becky, still trying to see if there was a gesture or expression—a way of touching her hair or pursing her lips—that could make me mistake her for Laura. I couldn't find anything, but since that was the first time it had happened, I marked it down to having drunk too much champagne.

But it happened a second time—at an outdoor band concert—and a third—at a University of Wisconsin football game—and a fourth—on a street corner—and each time I had to work my way across whatever distance was involved until I was close enough to know it wasn't Laura. By then I knew these mistakes had nothing to do with too much champagne or smoky dance halls.

Poetry and hallucinations, these were the remnants of those years of Laura blowing through my life. And I was stupid enough to cling to them like a shipwrecked sailor who holds on to a scrap of debris instead of climbing into the lifeboat. And I was stupid enough to believe I could go on living that way.

I TOLD CATHERINE about Laura, in a way. . . .

It was a summer night, unusually cool, shortly before the twins were born. We had been visiting friends and came home around midnight. When we got out of the car, we noticed that the northern lights were flashing their bars of light all the way up to the top of the sky's dome and waving back and forth in shadows of colors. Catherine and I set up lawn chairs in the backyard, got blankets from the house, and resolved to watch the lights as long as they continued.

We talked that night, as we often did, about our separate pasts, and gradually a theme emerged. We told each other about our Most Embarrassing Moments. Catherine told me about the summer days she spent walking up and down a country road in front of the farm where Gary Kliner, whom she had a crush on, lived, only to learn later that Gary spent the summer with cousins in Iowa. I told about rushing off to school in such a hurry one winter morning, that I wore my sweater inside out. Catherine got her period for the first time when she was sleeping over at Mary Anne Kaminsky's house, and Catherine tried to sneak the stained sheet off the bed and into the bathroom, where she could wash

out the blood. Mary Anne's mother caught Catherine in the hall and
told her not to worry—the stain would bleach out. And then Mrs.
Kaminsky said, "So our little Cathy is a woman now!" I was giving a
speech in eighth grade English class, and I couldn't figure out why I got
laughs when my topic was something as serious as ocean creatures. After
class, Mr. Strutz, the teacher, informed me that the correct word was
"tentacles." Catherine once asked in a Sunday school what a harlot was.
I tried to show off my knowledge of mythology in a grade school class but
pronounced "Hercules" as "Her-kewls."

It was in the spirit of this conversation, then, that I told Catherine
about Laura. I had wanted for a long time to talk to Catherine about
Laura—why, I'm not sure—but I could never find the opening. Now the
time seemed right. Though we were talking about these pathetic, humil-
iating moments, both of us were laughing about them. And perhaps the
time seemed right because that night under the northern lights nothing
human seemed of much significance.

We were lying back in our lawn chairs, our eyes not on each other but
on the flaring night sky, and I told Catherine the barest version possible
about Laura.

"As you know, my father was a real chaser," I said, "and once I met
one of his girlfriends. She came to the house, and I learned, through
eavesdropping, that they were, you know, involved. She was pretty well
known—you've probably heard of her—Laura Coe Pettit? No? Anyway,
she was a famous poet and she was great-looking and flirty, and I guess
the combination was too much for me. I developed a crush on her you
wouldn't believe. My father's mistress, and I was mooning over her like
a lovesick kid! Which is exactly what I was. I didn't know what I
wanted—for them to get married so I could be around her more often, or
for them to split up so I wouldn't have to compete with my father. Oh,
man, I really had it bad! I was a very sad case."

When I stopped talking, Catherine said, "And—?"

"And what? That's it. That's the story. My parents split up. My father
went out with her for a while, and then it fizzled out. He died. The end.
Your turn."

"No, I mean what happened with *you?*"

I reached over and took Catherine's hand. "What happened with me? I'm here."

She slid her hand away. "You know that's not what I mean."

"What happened? Nothing," I answered, content with that much truth. "I grew up. What happens with childhood infatuations? You get older, and they go away. Didn't you ever have a crush on one of your teachers? One of your brother's friends?"

"What I don't get," Catherine said, "is what's embarrassing about that story. Your father's the one who should have been embarrassed. Bringing one of his girlfriends home—my gosh!"

"I was a kid, and I had it bad for an adult. Not very realistic."

"But you said yourself—that happens. Little boys get crushes on their teachers, little girls fall in love with the boy across the street. It's common. Yours sounds sort of Oedipal though—I mean, your father's girlfriend? But it's nothing to be embarrassed about."

"What are you trying to do?" I asked testily. "Trying to argue me out of feeling what I feel? I said it's an embarrassing memory, all right? Can we let it go at that?"

"Okay," Catherine said softly. "Okay."

I stood up. "I'm going in. I'm cold and I'm getting a stiff neck. Are you coming?"

In the northern sky the lights still blazed, their brilliance so bright they should have given off heat.

Catherine struggled to sit up. "I guess I better. I won't be able to get out of this chair by myself."

I pulled her up out of the lawn chair and then walked ahead of her toward the house, my feet leaving dark tracks in the dew-wet grass.

Ten

$\mathcal{O}$ver the years I amassed a considerable collection of Laura Coe Pettit memorabilia: copies of her books; magazines and journals in which she had poems, stories, or essays; photocopies of reviews or analyses of her work; interviews with her; a bibliography of her work compiled by a Michigan State professor; and the letter I received from Laura on the occasion of my parents' divorce.

The year 1979 brought me the item that soon became my favorite. In September—twelve years after I last spoke to or saw her in person—a long article on Laura Coe Pettit appeared in *Esquire*. The piece was written by Maria Carr, a journalist with a reputation for writing celebrity profiles that, afterward, made her subjects wish they had never consented to be interviewed by her. Her piece in *The Atlantic Monthly* on Iowa senator George Hatcher, for example, was credited with removing his name from the list of potential Democratic presidential candidates. Carr portrayed Hatcher as he no doubt was, a man long on ambition but short on intellect and competence. She also got Hatcher to talk about his drinking habits, and though Americans might admire in their neighbor the ability to knock back bourbon with the boys, it is not a quality they want to see in someone wanting to be president. Nevertheless, politicians, movie and television personalities, writers, and public figures of all stripes still agreed to let Maria Carr into their lives, flattered perhaps that she would take an interest in them and believing that an article by her carried enough prestige to outweigh any possible deleterious consequences.

When the article on Laura appeared, her career was hardly in eclipse, yet she was not the literary sensation that she had once been. After that fallow period in the 1960s when she did not write or publish any poems, she began to produce again, and her work—poems mostly, but also an occasional essay or short story—appeared regularly in the leading literary journals and reviews. Critics still reviewed her kindly, and her collections sold modestly but steadily. Any listing of the country's major living poets was sure to include the name of Laura Coe Pettit, yet she was no longer as famous—as widely known, in that peculiarly American way, for being widely known—as she was in the first years of her career, when she was a literary enfant terrible, the sexy poet with the acid tongue.

Maria visited Laura at her home in Vermont and described, at disbelieving length, the house, grounds, and furnishings. Laura lived in the country in a tiny stone cottage that had at one time been the home of an estate's caretaker. The house on the estate had burned down fifty years earlier, and Laura's dwelling was now the only building left standing on the original grounds' twelve acres of grassy hills and groves of hardwoods. Laura lived five miles from the college where she taught, and her nearest neighbor was a half-mile away.

The cottage itself, wrote Maria Carr, was so austere that "had Thoreau had this for his domicile on Walden Pond, he would not have been able to stay the week." Laura had three small rooms: a living room with a stone fireplace, a straight-backed chair, a rocking chair, and a writing table; a bedroom with another chair, a dresser, and a narrow bed covered with an Amish quilt; a kitchen that "shouldn't really be counted as a room, since closets—which are rarely smaller—never are."

Maria Carr looked into Laura's closets and cupboards. Laura's wardrobe consisted of "the kinds of clothes a girl would wear to a private school where uniforms were required—a few dark gray skirts and white broadcloth blouses, and two sweaters, a sleeveless navy and a gray cardigan. One pair of black flats, one pair of torn tennis shoes. And for casual occasions, a flannel shirt and a pair of faded Levi's." In the cupboards were cans of tomato and chicken noodle soup, and the refrigerator was empty but for a few carrots, an apple, and a head of lettuce. There was a radio on the kitchen cupboard and an alarm clock on the bedroom dresser. On the writing table in the living room was a carton of cigarettes, an ashtray, a small stack of books, a portable typewriter, two notebooks, paper, pencils, a fountain pen, and a vase of flowers.

Those flowers were the house's only "decorations." Maria Carr devoted almost as much space to listing what was not in Laura's home: "No television, no stereo, no newspapers or magazines, no full-length mirror, no prints or paintings or posters or sculptures, no mementos, no objets d'art, no cosmetics or hair-care products . . ."

These spartan surroundings were the result, Laura said, of a "concerted effort to see what was essential and what was not. When I bought this place, I figured I was taking a large enough step into materialism so I'd better watch myself. I remembered Turgenev's novel about the man who killed himself because he could not simplify his life. So I decided to see how simply I could live. I kept throwing things out or giving them away until I was left with what you see here. The hardest things to get rid of were my books, but there's a library in town and at the college. I'm not sure, however, if I'm going to be able to hold out much longer. I passed a shop the other day that had a lovely antique brass knocker in the window. Now, what the hell do I need with a brass door knocker? But I can't stop thinking about the damn thing! What good is all this self-denial if your mind is occupied all the time with thoughts of brass door knockers?"

The Laura Pettit that Maria Carr described didn't look or sound much different from the thirty-five-year-old woman I had seen twelve years earlier. Her salt-and-pepper hair was still long, tied back in a thick braid that hung halfway down her back. She wore no makeup ("but her pale perfect skin and her wide green eyes gave her beauty all the help it needed"). She was thin, and on the day of the interview she wore faded jeans and a white shirt "with the sleeves rolled up to her elbows and buttons undone to the middle of her sternum." Maria Carr wrote, "a friend [of Carr's] insisted that only a few women could get away without wearing a bra. Laura Pettit was not one of them. She wasn't wearing one."

But Maria Carr didn't choose Laura as a subject in order to list the items in her wardrobe or to catalogue her home's furnishings. She chose Laura because of her reputation for being publicly short-tempered and opinionated. Indeed, it was that reputation that gave the piece its title—featured on the magazine's cover as well. The title was "America's Favorite Bitch." Writers had always known that Laura was good copy, and Maria Carr had the journalistic good sense to get out of the way and let most of the article be Laura's pronouncements on various topics.

ON POLITICS: "I admit it. They beat me. There was a time when I believed this society could change, that it could become more just, more humane, less masculinely belligerent and militaristic. I no longer believe that. Any way that our society changes for the better is only the result of political expediency and not out of a sense of compassion or justice or decency. So not only have I forsaken all political activism, I try not to even pay attention to politics. Powerlessness is simply too frustrating. Of course, I recognize that this is an absolutely horseshit attitude on my part, but what can I tell you? I've given up. Someone else can beat the drum, but I'm not going to march. I expect to live out the rest of my life writing a few poems, teaching a little, and fooling around in my garden."

ON POETRY: "That remark of Auden's, that poetry makes nothing happen, used to make me so angry. I believed poetry could save lives and make lives worth saving. Now I think that a life without poetry isn't any more impoverished than a life without opera or ballet. It would be nice if more people read poems—and bought books of them, so I could make a living writing the damn things—but that's the age we live in—too few people read poetry and too goddamn many write it."

ON NEVER MARRYING: "A successful marriage requires the partners to alter their lives so they fit the other. I could never do that. But I don't kid myself. I know the loss is mine."

ON HER REPUTATION AS A HARD DRINKER: "Shortly after Roger Dale died, I quit drinking and drugging. Rog died of an overdose, and I proceeded to go on a three-day drunk, ostensibly to drown my sorrows. When I sobered up, I saw the idiocy of what I had done. I mourned a man who killed himself with drugs by taking my own drug until I was in a stupor. I quit that day. And drugs were never the problem for me anyway. Oh, I popped my share of pills and smoked my share of weed, but drugs came on the scene a little late for me to really get into them. My addiction was booze, and the worst way I had it was that in my mind drinking and writing were connected. I never actually wrote under the influence, but I became convinced that booze was the only way I could come down after writing. Only booze could shut off the machine. I was wrong, but it took me a while before I was willing to find out. I still smoke too much, but tobacco is the only drug I'll touch."

ON THE DIFFERENCE BETWEEN MALE AND FEMALE WRIT-ERS: "Women don't use their writing to say fuck me, I'm wonderful. They might use it to say love me, I'm wonderful, but that's not the same thing."

ON TEACHING: "I only started teaching because I couldn't support myself writing. And for the first few years I despised it. I couldn't stand the students, their immaturity, their lack of seriousness. I hated their writing, their self-absorbed, puerile little poems. Most of all I resented the intrusions on my writing time that teaching caused. I kept thinking of Camus's remark, 'Whatever keeps you from your work is your work.' But somewhere I changed. And I know I was the one who changed, because the students sure as hell haven't—they're as muddle-headed as ever. But we get along now. I still tell them their poems are terrible if I believe they are. But I suppose I've mellowed. A student last year told me I wasn't the dragon lady I was supposed to be. I get along with my colleagues. They're even willing to have me in their homes and allow me near their children. And this year I volunteered to be on a committee! Volunteered!"

Accompanying the article was a full-page photograph of Laura that became my new favorite, supplanting the Thorpe photograph that appeared in *Life* so many years before. In the pages of *Esquire*, Laura sat in a high-backed rocker. She was sitting primly, stiffly upright, her knees and ankles pressed together, her white blouse buttoned modestly to her throat, her skirt pulled demurely over her knees. Her long hair was pulled back, and she was looking expressionlessly at the camera. In fact, there was only one thing in the photograph that kept it from being a perfect imitation of those sober-sided daguerreotypes of pioneer women who stared at the camera with a fierce blankness: while one of Laura's hands lay on her lap, the other was thrust upward, shoulder-high, middle finger defiantly raised. It was a literal expression of what she had been doing all her life long.

When I first saw the picture, I laughed out loud, and any time I have looked at it since, I have smiled. But since I keep that magazine, along with my entire collection in a locked drawer in my clinic office, that means that neither my wife nor my children have ever seen that particular smile or heard that laugh.

Eleven

One of the things that almost everyone remembers about my father is his fondness for spicy food. And when a meal wasn't seasoned to his liking, he would pour on the salt and pepper until his plate looked as though it were lined with rime and his food coated with ash. My mother, whose tastes favored the bland, would grimace in disgust.

As a child, I usually took my mother's side. I had a sensitive, timid palate, and I often wanted to ask my father, "What's the matter? Isn't it good enough for you just the way it is?" In my adult life, however, I developed a condition that enabled me to understand my father's need to ignite his tastebuds every time he sat down to eat. When I was in my midthirties, I began to lose my senses.

I know this phrase is more likely to be interpreted metaphorically—as of someone going mad—but I mean it literally: It seemed to me that my senses were gradually diminishing, and diminishing in a quite specific way. Certain tastes, sounds, sights, smells, and touches didn't offer up the pleasures that they once did. The sweetest candy needed more sugar. The volume of the twins' laughter needed to be turned up. Catherine's touch was too delicate. But the metaphor probably provided the more accurate explanation of my condition—I began to lose my senses.

I was about to say that this all started with a physical pain, but I'm sure that would not be accurate. The twinge in my chest simply alerted me to something that began—when? When a woman hid out in a boy's room? When that same boy saw that same woman in his father's arms? When the boy, trying to become a man but unsure of the example to follow, walked alongside that woman's train until its speed became too much for him?

MY EXERCISE REGIMEN normally included a long run on the weekends—longer than the weekday four or five miles—and on this early spring Sunday in 1980 I went even farther than usual because the day was warm and mild, one of the first after a winter that had seemed especially long and harsh.

After logging eleven miles, I still couldn't bring myself to leave the spring sunshine, so I stayed out on the back porch. I was in the middle of a quadriceps stretch when I felt a hot, pinching sensation in my chest just to the left of my sternum. The pain quickly passed, but from the kitchen window Catherine saw me wince and suddenly stop what I was doing.

She was out the door in an instant. "What's the matter?" she asked.

"Just a little stitch in my chest. It was nothing."

"Chest pains? You're having chest pains?"

"A chest pain. And not a pain. A twinge. And it's gone now."

Within the past year, my grandfather had died of a heart attack, and Catherine's father had had quadruple bypass surgery. Catherine knew as well that a coronary had killed my father before the age of fifty. In minutes she was on the phone with Ben Westwater, the cardiologist at the clinic. Ben and Catherine teamed formidably; the following afternoon I was in the local hospital, reluctantly greased and wired for an EKG and a stress test.

Neither of which showed the slightest irregularity or abnormality. The pain in my chest was likely caused, Ben concluded after questioning me, by my recent efforts to improve my upper body strength.

"Forget the weights," Ben advised me. "Unless you're trying to impress the girls at the beach, cardiovascular strength is all you'll need."

Ben didn't tell me anything I didn't already know. Reasonably fit thirty-six-year-olds don't drop dead of heart attacks, no matter who their fathers are.

Nevertheless, a few nights later when I talked to Janie in Lawrence, Kansas, where she taught entomology at the university and conducted research on a species of grain weevil, I mentioned both the chest pain and the hospital visit.

"For God's sake," Janie said, "don't tell Mom." Our mother was still grieving over her father.

"Don't worry," I said. "Anyway, I'm sure the cardiologist would never have bothered with the tests if it wasn't for the lousy genetic hand Dad dealt us."

Janie laughed at my suggestion. "You have nothing to worry about," she said. "*I* know what killed Dad, and you're immune. We both are."

I remembered the remark that one of my father's colleagues made at the funeral. According to him "young pussy" did my father in. I wasn't sure I wanted to hear my sister's theory, but I asked anyway. "Okay, I'll bite. What killed Dad?"

"His appetite. Or appetites, I should say. He said yes to everything. He would have loved the sixties. If it felt good, he did it. I'm always a little surprised that he wasn't fat, the way he took it all in. But I guess his vanity was stronger."

"All right, I'll go along with that. And we get our immunity from—?"

"Come on. You know the answer to that. Anyone who goes after a PhD or an MD has to know how to say no. If you're not able to discipline yourself, if you're not into self-denial, you're not going to make it in grad school. And I'm sure it's even more true of medical school."

There was no question but that Janie was describing herself. The relentless devotion to the life of the microscope and the mind that she had displayed early in life had continued unabated. She never married or had, as far as I knew, a relationship with a man or a woman. She paid little attention to her physical appearance. She had no hobbies, and until the twins were born, she showed little interest in anything or anyone outside her research. Being "Aunt Janie," however, pleased her, and she took the role seriously. Catherine and I frequently told Janie that her gifts to the twins were far too extravagant, but it was difficult to argue with her response: "What else am I going to spend my money on?"

Although Janie and I soon left the subject of our father behind in order to swap war stories about the pursuit of advanced degrees, her remark stayed with me. In the subsequent days and weeks, I began to notice how often I said no, and in situations when my father would have said yes.

Now, most of these occasions were not at all momentous—I turned down an offer to serve on a clinic planning committee, I told the twins I was too busy to take them to the playground, I declined a lunch invitation, I refused a young mother's request for antibiotics for her child, and I made up an excuse rather than play golf with an insurance agent whom I disliked. Indeed, to many of these I was right to say no. But right or wrong was not the issue.

I developed small tricks, dodges, "avoidance maneuvers" a psychiatrist would have called them, so I wouldn't have to say the word, as if the word itself was the problem. I shook my head. I waved my hands. I turned my back. I used phrases like "don't think so," "not right now," "maybe later," "none for me." But of course these were mere evasions, and in every one of these phrases and gestures, my nay-saying was as obvious to me as a sky rocket showering down a rain of black sparks.

Soon an all-encompassing hesitancy set in. It became more and more difficult to get out of bed in the morning, to enter the doors of the clinic, to leave the car and return to the house, to answer the telephone, all because I knew circumstances would arise to which I might want to say yes but likely would not, and my subsequent "no" would deepen my despair.

How simple to solve, you think. Why didn't I merely begin to say yes, yes to another cup of coffee, yes to greetings of "Beautiful morning, isn't it?", yes to every day's trivial invitations and requests. And perhaps it was that simple. But I could not.

I tried. I lay in bed one night, and after Catherine fell asleep, I began to mouth the word "yes" over and over, simply feeling the way my face formed itself around the word. Catherine stirred and groggily asked, "What?" "I was just yawning," I answered, because that was the shape my mouth took with the word. I waited until her breath resumed its sleeping rhythm, and then I tried again. I closed my eyes and whispered "yes" over and over, faster and faster and faster, until I wasn't doing much more than hissing.

Then, when I opened my eyes, the room's darkness startled me. Outside our window a streetlamp usually shone, but that night the light must have burned out, because when I opened my eyes the room's darkness was almost total. I believed—yet at the same time knew the belief was preposterous—that I had called this darkness down around us, that this was what I had said yes to.

I had, of late, become something of an expert on insomnia. My own bouts of sleeplessness had become so frequent and familiar that I knew, at the beginning of each one, the minimum hours of sleeplessness I could likely count on. This time, since my heart was beating so rapidly, I knew I would be awake for at least two hours.

Why didn't I avail myself of one of the remedies at hand—Jack Daniel's downstairs under the sink or Nembutal even closer in the nightstand? Well, why further numb myself when numbness was already part of the problem?

Besides, although it may have seemed as though I was simply lying in bed, watching the occasional sweep across our ceiling of a car's headlights as it made its way up our hill or listening for the air conditioner to kick in or shut down, in fact during these sleepless hours I was meditating on an image. You will not be surprised to hear—indeed, you may have wondered how much longer you would have to wait for her—that the apparition floating before my mind's eye was of Laura Coe Pettit. But of all the Lauras available to my imagination, why did the Laura of 1967, the Laura lying on the bed in a Chicago hotel room, so often make a nightly appearance?

Of course that was the Laura I had last seen in person, close to thirteen years ago. But with both a mind and a file drawer full of images—some much more up-to-date than Chicago—why not contemplate one of those? Why not return, for that matter, to a Laura unclothed in a Minnesota motel, as I so often had in my youth?

I still had some of the skills of my clinician's training. I had come up with a more specific diagnosis of my condition. I was not leading an increasingly anesthetized existence just because, unlike my father, I had too often said no to life. My plight could be traced back to a single negative.

The ruling passion, the obsession, that had pulled me through so many of the days of my life was love and desire for Laura Pettit, and in 1967 I sneaked out of her hotel room, in effect turning down her offer to join her on her peace tour of America's small towns. In Chicago in 1967 I had said no to her, thereby starting the affliction that had slowly metastasized over the years, inexorably impairing my ability to experience pleasure. I doubted the condition could be reversed, but somehow I had to stop its spread.

THE NEXT DAY, while I still had the will to do something, I called Lawrence Clausen, the psychiatrist at our clinic, and made an appointment to see him as soon as possible.

His office was in the basement of the clinic, and if you went down there and didn't turn to the left, toward the lab and X-ray, everyone knew you were going to see Dr. Clausen. Accordingly, Lawrence said he'd see me late in the afternoon, when most of the clinic staff had left for the day.

Lawrence Clausen had a delicate, slow-moving grace, surprising in a man as obese as he. He moved only when necessary, and his usual repose communicated an unflappable calm that his patients found comforting. He was a natty dresser, and on the day I visited him he wore a navy blue pinstriped suit, a red silk tie, and a white shirt, the collar of which was secured by a gold pin. He was pale and blond, although his skin had a pink sheen that glowed right through his thinning hair and closely cropped beard.

He motioned me to sit down in the chair across from his desk, and then he leaned back and clasped his hands across his chest. "Tell me," he said, "is this a matter that primarily involves the thinking or the feeling part of you?"

It was, I imagined, his usual opening gambit, but rather than dwell on the false distinction his question implied, I simply began to talk. I told the doctor a bit about my father, that he was a man who embraced life in all its richness and variety. I, on the other hand, had come to believe that the reason I was experiencing life in a diminished capacity was that, unlike my father, I said no more often than I said yes. I mentioned neither Laura nor my recent visit with Dr. Westwater.

When I finished, Dr. Clausen looked at me with exactly the same expression he wore while I spoke. Finally, he said, "Well?"

I turned up my palms. "That's it."

He continued to stare at me, then he leaned forward and picked up his pen. "Everything okay at home?" he asked.

"Fine."

"Your wife hasn't noticed a change in your behavior?"

"If she has, she hasn't said anything to me."

"Because you're a good actor?"

I shrugged. "I've been trying to deal with this myself."

He permitted himself a small smile. "Until today."

"So give me the pill," I joked, "and we'll see if it works."

His smile vanished, but his voice became warmer. "You're thirty-six years old?"

"That's right."

"Very near what may be the middle of your life. Or perceived as such."

I groaned slightly in anticipation of what was coming.

He held up his hand. "I know. I know. But just because it's a cliché doesn't mean it's not valid. Look, the clock is ticking for all of us—louder for you because of your father's age when he died—and since you're not sure how many more opportunities you'll have, you naturally think of what you've already passed on. You have regrets. We all do. Unless—"

"Unless what?"

"Is there more here than meets the eye?"

"No, that's everything."

He stared at me and tapped his pen on his blotter. He didn't believe me. The prolonged pause and the pen's persistent muffled thump were calculated, I thought, to cause me to blurt out the truth.

But accusing a patient of lying—especially a patient who was also a colleague—was not Lawrence Clausen's style. He was too fastidious for such a tactic. He clapped his hands on his thighs. "All right, then. Let's leave it there. Are you willing to try something?"

I nodded.

"For the next week—and I'd like you to come back in a week—I want you to try saying yes at least seven times. That's one 'yes' a day to something you might ordinarily say no to. This will require some effort on your part, but please try. Will you do that?"

I said I would.

Lawrence Clausen's pink complexion turned a darker rose, though whether he was flushing with the exertion of heaving his bulk out of his chair or blushing over the banality of his advice, I wasn't sure.

I KNEW WHAT Dr. Clausen was trying to do with that course of treatment. He was trying to change me from the outside in. Perform an act often enough and eventually it will become habit. Habitual behavior defines who we are. The theory was sound, but I wanted to hurry the process.

I had my first chance the night after my appointment with Dr. Clausen. A storm was approaching our community, and early in the evening, thunderheads hovered in the northwest. As the storm came closer, the thunderheads lost their looming definition. Now their bottoms were visible, and as they swirled and moved, their darkness spread across the sky like ink.

Since infancy Doreen had been terrified of thunderstorms, and that summer Nora caught the fear as well. Unable to calm each other, they would pass their terror back and forth until it gained so much power it brought them to the edge of hysteria. At the first far-off murmur of thunder they would head for the basement or their parents' bedroom.

It's difficult for me today to reproduce my thinking of that time, deluded as it was, but let me try: I wanted to spare my daughters the distress I had come to. My condition had started in my childhood. I didn't want it to start in theirs. They needed to confront their fear and to find affirmation in the storms that frightened them.

Therefore, while the television and radio stations droned their warnings about possible tornadoes, hail, and damaging winds, I told the twins to get into the station wagon, that we were going to find out the storm's secret.

Naturally, the girls were apprehensive, and while I was urging them to the car, Catherine came into the room.

"What's going on?" she asked.

"We're going for a little ride," I said. "We're going to watch the storm."

Catherine rubbed her forearms as though she had caught a sudden chill. She looked at the twins but asked me, "Where are you going?"

"Out in the country. Somewhere we can see the storm."

She turned her gaze to me and stared into my eyes for a long time. Was she looking for a sign that the man who used to live behind my eyes was still there? I realized at that moment that she would have given a very different answer to Dr. Clausen's question, *Has your wife noticed a change in your behavior?* Finally, she gave up on me and bent down to the twins. "This sounds like fun. Am I invited?"

Nora and Doreen nodded eagerly.

The sky was dark as we left town, although the lightning in the distance was so frequent the night seemed lit by a short-circuited lamp flickering on and off.

I drove into the country west of town and looked for a road that would lead us to the top of a hill. I finally found a bumpy gravel path and, following it, brought us to a spot that gave us a perfect view of the approaching storm.

With every flash of lightning we could see the towering anvil tops of the thunderheads and their heavy, low, sheared-off dark bottoms. Conditions looked right for a funnel cloud to dip down at any moment. The wind began to gust, rocking the car and ticking grit and chaff from the field around us against the fenders and doors. Doreen began to cry, a small mewing whimper that grew louder then softer with the thunder's crescendo and fall.

A bolt of lightning struck no less than two fields away, lighting the world for an instant like a photographer's flash and sending the ground's shock through us as if a twenty-ton weight had been dropped to the earth right behind the car.

Now Nora started crying.

Rain began to fall, huge drops splatting against the windshield with such force they seemed to have more substance than water.

I opened my car door. "Okay," I said. "Let's go. Everybody out! This is the last storm that's going to scare us! We're going to say yes to this storm—yes, yes, yes!"

"Paul, it's pouring," Catherine said softly.

"I know." I got out of the car, stepped back, and spread my arms wide. "You think I don't know? I'm standing in it!"

No one made a move to follow me out of the car. "Come on!" I shouted at them. "This is what we came out here for! We're going to stand out in a storm and see there's nothing to be afraid of!"

When I opened the back door, the twins immediately slid across the seat away from me.

I reached toward them. "Come on. It's okay."

"Paul," Catherine said too calmly. "It's really raining."

"But it's warm," I answered. "Like taking a shower."

I grabbed Nora's wrist and tugged gently. "If you come out, your sister will too."

Another bolt of lightning crashed nearby with a sound like a metal tree falling.

"Paul! I don't think this is a good idea. You get back in here too!"

I got in all right, just far enough to grab both girls' arms so I could haul them out of the car. I pulled, and Nora braced her legs against the front seat. She was no longer crying, though Doreen was wailing and clinging to the armrest on the door. Had I been sensitive to what was actually happening, I would have seen that Nora had taken on the role of her sister's protector. It was no longer important to Nora whether she stayed in the car or got out; taking care of her sister was all that mattered.

Catherine had turned around and was reaching over the front seat, grabbing my arm, trying to break my hold on the twins. "Don't, Paul! Leave them alone!"

But she could not break them loose. I was too far gone. I was intent on one thing only—hauling these two children out to stand under the crackling, howling night sky.

And I almost had them. By strength alone I slid them across the backseat until they were ready to fall out into the rain. Doreen was still shrieking, and Nora was flushed with the effort of trying to keep them both in.

It didn't happen.

Without my having noticed—so complete was my concentration on the twins—Catherine had gotten out of the car and come around behind me. Before I even knew she was there, she was raining her own blows down on me, her fists bouncing off me like hailstones.

When her punches had no effect, she grabbed me around the waist and tried to pull me away from the girls. She was so desperate to stop me she failed to notice that tugging at me from behind only helped me get the twins out of the car.

Nora popped out first and Doreen tumbled out right behind her. I let go of them and Catherine fell back into the mud.

I was the only one left standing. Catherine was lying on the ground on one side of me and the twins were sprawled on the other. If lightning had hit that hill, I would surely have been the one struck since nothing stood above me.

And perhaps it would have been better if that had happened. Something had to stop me. My girls were weeping in fear of me. My wife had been reduced to striking me in order to defend her children. This was the scene I had created. This was what I said yes to.

Lightning did not strike me dead, but something flashed brightly enough to allow me to see—if only for an instant—what I had come to.

"Let's go home," I said, and bless them, every member of my family was willing to get back into the car with me.

CATHERINE WALKED INTO the house ahead of me, and as she did I noticed her foot was bleeding and leaving bright red tracks across the kitchen floor. The seat of her once-white shorts was muddy, and her wet sweatshirt hung shapelessly on her.

"Your foot's bleeding," I said to her back. Catherine said nothing but walked into the living room, paying no attention to the bloody trail she left on the carpet. "You better let me take a look at it."

She still said nothing but climbed the stairs, following the children.

"You might need stitches!" I called after her.

But she was already gone, off to comfort her babies.

THE NEXT MORNING, Sunday, I waited until Catherine and the twins went to church. Then I took a suitcase down from the hall closet.

I had already made my calculations. From Red Oak, Wisconsin, to New Hampshire was approximately twelve hundred miles, and if I was on the road by noon and drove straight through, I could be there by Monday afternoon.

And where was "there?"

"There" was Warren, New Hampshire, site of the annual Warren Writers Conference, held this year from July 17 to 31. I had read about the conference and its participants in a literary journal. A roster of distinguished writers and editors would be there, conducting workshops, giving readings and lectures, and consulting on manuscripts. Laura Coe Pettit would be among this year's guest writers.

After the thunderstorm debacle, I had realized that it didn't matter how often I said yes in my daily life, whether seven times a week, according to Dr. Clausen's prescription, or seven times an hour. I could stand out under a blazing sun or a driving rain. I could cover my food with spices, take my children to the park every day, or pinch the ass of every woman who caught my eye. I could accept every invitation or indulge every appetite, and it would have no effect. I had only one chance to be restored—to stem the loss of my senses—and that was to stand before Laura and say yes. And what if she, in turn, said no to me? What if she spurned me, cursed me, or refused to speak to me altogether? My only answer to those possibilities took the form of another question: What if I went on living this way? I didn't see that I had a choice.

I left a note for Catherine, brief, general, and trite:

Dear Catherine,

I have to get away for a while to see if I can't straighten some things out for myself. I'm okay. Don't worry. Please call Charlie and see if he can cover for me at the clinic. My love to you and the girls.

Paul

At eleven-thirty A.M. I threw my suitcase into the backseat of our rusting 1975 Volkswagen Rabbit and backed out of the driveway. When I looked back at our house, I wondered if it was for the last time.

DRIVING HAS ALWAYS been for me—as assembling ships in a bottle or doing crossword puzzles is for others—one of those activities that commands my entire attention yet relaxes me. When I am behind the wheel, my thoughts are on little but my driving, yet in spite of this concentration the hours pass easily, and I often arrive at my destination more refreshed than when I began.

I mention this so you may understand how I was able to spend all that time alone in the car without once giving myself over to the kind of introspection that would inevitably have me asking myself—outside Chicago or Gary or Cleveland—what the hell am I doing?—and having no reasonable answer available, turning immediately around. I drove in a high, a condition of euphoric resolve; my teeth were clenched but in a smile. I had help in achieving this state: I left the house with a supply of amphetamines; these and the cups of coffee and the Cokes that I dosed myself with kept me plugged in and humming with current.

I slept once. Somewhere in Ohio I felt suddenly, breathlessly tired, as if I had sprinted up a flight of stairs. I pulled into a rest area and fell immediately into a shallow sleep. I dreamed I was in my car and behind the wheel and again speeding down the highway. But I was unable to control the car. I couldn't move my arms to steer or my legs to stop, and though the car was staying on the road, I had no way of knowing how long it would. When it suddenly veered toward a ravine, I jolted awake before I went over the edge.

I started the car and drove quickly away.

Only once did I waver. Shortly after I crossed into New York State, a thunderstorm that had been gaining for hours finally caught me, and in the slowed miles I drove in its downpour I thought of my daughters and their fears. One more had been added to the list. Spiders, snakes, Rudy Kubiac (the bully of our neighborhood), thunderstorms, and now, Daddy. If I didn't see them again, their memory of me might always make them shudder and cower. The rain let up, and I pushed the gas pedal to the floor, as determined to outrun my own doubts as the storm.

WARREN, NEW HAMPSHIRE, was a small New England village that lay half in a valley and half up the slopes of a green mountain that hovered protectively over the town on its eastern side. I thought at first that I would simply drive to the conference site, relying on my internal Laura-compass to lead me to her. But good sense prevailed, and I stopped at a gas station to ask directions. The Warren Writers Conference was held at a summer resort about five miles south of town.

The camp—a collection of hardly new, mismatched cabins—was strung out along a stream in a deeply wooded glade. I parked on a small square of asphalt in front of the main lodge. The early afternoon warmth, the sunlight dipping and flaring through the leaves, the odor of rushing water and damp earth—these combined with the knowledge that I had arrived at my destination made me feel safe, the way a child feels about his home when he has outrun a bully to get there.

I walked toward the lodge and immediately saw Laura.

She was on the lodge's wide, rough-timbered porch, with five other people. Laura and an old man with wispy white hair were sitting on aluminum lawn chairs, while the others, three men and a woman, sat on the porch's wooden floor or on the concrete steps. The old man was reading out loud from a sheaf of manuscript pages, and everyone was listening so intently they didn't see me approach.

Laura's hair was long and full, and she wore it straight, letting it fall of its own weight to her shoulders. It had gone completely gray. Actually, it was too light to be gray; it was a kind of metallic silver, closer to the brightness of chrome than the dullness of gunmetal. Despite the gray hair, she looked as beautiful as ever. I quickly computed her age. She was twelve years older than I was—she was forty-seven. If the years had been hard on her, they must have confined their damage to her hair and her spirit; her face still contained those contradictions of delicate high cheekbones, full lush lips, large green eyes, and slightly bumpy nose that together shouldn't quite have worked but in Laura combined in a perfect, stunning, lovely mystery. She was deeply tan, thin, and dressed in a gray University of Massachusetts T-shirt and cutoffs.

When I saw her, my concern—one I didn't even know I had until I felt it lift—vanished. I had worried that Laura would have changed, that I would no longer find her attractive, that I had been cherishing an ideal that no longer existed. The relief I felt doubled my already crazed elation. I didn't know whether to leap ecstatically in the air or fall gratefully to my knees. Instead, I stood silently until Laura looked up and saw a man dressed in wrinkled chinos and a white shirt with its tails hanging out, a man who hadn't shaved in days, a man with an inexplicably giddy grin gashing his face.

Laura stared hard at me, then said, half in recognition, half in uncertainty, "Paul?" She cocked her head. "Paul? Is that you? Paul Finley?"

I threw my arms jubilantly in the air. "Yes," I said, "it's me."

Laura got out of her chair and came cautiously forward. When she reached the porch steps, I threw my arms around her.

I might have been content to stay like that forever, but Laura finally said, "Come on, Paul. Jesus. Let me go."

I withdrew my arms.

"What the hell are you doing here?"

"I had to see you," I said. The triteness, the ordinariness of my statement pained me. It did so little justice to all I had come through to arrive at this point. Should I say nothing more? Should I let my silent presence be all the explanation?

"Are you here alone?" Laura asked.

"Yes."

The people on the porch were all standing now. The white-haired old man came to the steps. "Miss Pettit," he said in an elegant drawl, "if this time is inconvenient for you . . ." I recognized him now; he was Harley Garrett, a poet from Texas who had made a fortune in oil but in his sixties had given away most of his money and started writing poetry and plays. I had read some of his work, largely to see if I could find some insight into a man who gave away millions. I couldn't then, but I thought I knew now. He met Laura, she asked him to give his money away, and he couldn't get rid of it fast enough.

Laura turned to Garrett and the others on the porch. "We'll have to continue later. What time is it now? How about five? Can we meet here again at five?"

Everyone drifted away but a plump young woman with frizzy black hair and a complexion so sallow she looked jaundiced. She said to Laura, "I can't then. I'm supposed to meet with Gregory."

Laura shook her head wearily. "Okay, Elizabeth. How about if you and I meet privately later? Can you come to my cabin before the reading?"

Elizabeth looked right at me. "Are you sure you're going to be free?"

"I'll have time for you, Elizabeth. I promise." Elizabeth followed after the others.

Laura turned back toward me. "Where's your family, Paul? Where's your wife?"

"You know I have a wife?"

She nodded.

"And twins?"

"Your mother sends me a Christmas card. And she always includes a bit of news about you and Jane."

I threw my hands up. "So you know. They're in Wisconsin. I left them all in Wisconsin."

"Do they know you're here?"

"They know I'm out there. Somewhere."

Laura returned to the porch and picked up a pack of Marlboros. "Chicago, right?" She lit a cigarette. "December '67?"

I nodded.

She came forward to the porch railing. "I thought my trail had gone cold by now."

I tapped the side of my nose. "Good tracker."

"Jesus, I guess."

I approached Laura and gripped the porch railing on either side of where her body leaned. "You recognized me? You knew me right away?"

"I didn't recognize *you*, Paul. I recognized your father. I looked up and there stood Robert Finley—I almost had a heart attack. It took me a minute to get it together."

"I don't look that much like him."

"No, I suppose you don't. You're leaner. Paler. Your lines are drawn with a finer point. But there's something there. No question whose son you are."

"I'm thirty-six years old. I don't think I'm anybody's son anymore."

Laura threw her head back and laughed. "Paul. Baby. You're *always* somebody's kid."

I rested my chin on the porch railing. "You haven't changed," I said. "You're as beautiful as ever."

She laughed again. "We'd better get you out of the heat. Come on. Let's go to my cabin."

I followed Laura along a stone-bordered walkway that wound around behind the lodge to a scattered string of small cabins. As we walked along the pine-needled path, Laura said, "Most of the writers and students stay in town during the conference. But since I don't need to be near a bar, I stay out here. And it's free."

Laura's cabin had a porch with an old refrigerator and a vinyl-and-chrome kitchen chair taking up most of the space. Inside was a tiny kitchen, an even tinier bathroom, and another room furnished with an old green couch that presumably folded out into a bed, and a small desk and chair. The walls were covered with knotty pine paneling and the floor with a worn and matted gold shag carpet. A large window looked down a steep, wooded hill to a small dock and a lake.

"What do you think?" Laura asked. "It's not much, is it?" She walked to the window. "But I do like the view."

I looked around again, this time for clues about Laura's life. There weren't many. A carton of cigarettes on the desk. On the floor a large canvas book bag overflowing with books and manila envelopes. Visible under the closet curtain, Laura's small suitcase.

"Sit down, Paul. You look tired."

I sat on the couch and felt its springs sag.

"I can't believe you're here," Laura said, shaking her head. Laura pulled up the desk chair, spun it around, and straddled it, resting her arms along the chair back. The pose was familiar, but I couldn't quite place it.

"I saw your name in a magazine," I said. "That you were here, I mean." Then it came to me—that was precisely the way she sat for the famous Thorpe photograph. How many years ago had that been? Twenty?

"It's not as though I'm hiding out," Laura said. "I'm not that difficult to find. And that's not what I'm talking about. This isn't about me being here. It's about you. You still haven't told me why you came. I know you didn't just drop in because you happened to be in the neighborhood."

The miles were catching up to me. All the energy that had carried me across the country to Laura began to bleed away now that I was actually in her presence. Why hadn't I planned something—anything—to say? Perhaps if I backed up and gave her the history of my coming to New Hampshire, I would stumble on something in the narrative that would finally present me to Laura in the light in which I wanted to be cast.

"Not long ago, I had a little medical situation. Chest pains, and I—" Laura suddenly went pale as if she herself had been stricken.

"No, no," I added hastily. "I'm fine. Fine."

I raised my arms and flexed my biceps, exactly the pose my father struck so many years before when he and my mother assured me he did not have cancer.

"I'm the picture of health, in fact." Now however there was no possibility of storytelling: I had to jump to the lesson. "But it started me thinking. How I'm like my father. Or *unlike* him, I guess would be closer to the truth."

"No," Laura said. "You're very different." She looked away from me as she said this.

"But you—you and he were alike. At least in one important way."

"And what's that, Paul?" Her color had returned, but she still looked unsettled. I had the feeling that although she had asked the question, she didn't want to hear the answer.

"Saying yes." I spread my arms wide in a gesture meant to take in everything in this room and beyond. "Saying yes to it all. Embracing it all."

Laura laughed caustically. "Well, you have me there. I've said yes to an awful lot over the years. Robert did too."

"Exactly! And now I'm trying to learn to do it too—to stop turning away. To stop saying no. I don't ever want to sneak out before dawn again."

If Laura caught the allusion to that event thirteen years in the past, she did not acknowledge it. "And yet your father died a relatively young man. Only a few years older than I am now, if I recall correctly. Not a pattern you'd want to emulate, I wouldn't think."

"At least what he had was full, intense. At least he didn't have to watch while his life steadily dwindled."

"Ah, yes." Laura nodded sagely. " 'What to make of a diminished thing.' " She took the time to light a cigarette, inhale deeply, and then blow out a great cloud of smoke before going on. "So your coming here—it's in the nature of a pilgrimage? You've come here to learn from me how to embrace life in all its richness and variety?"

Although there was something faintly mocking in her tone, I felt I had no choice but to assent. "Isn't that who you are? Don't you say yes to every experience, every possibility, every challenge? What have you ever turned your back on? What have you ever regretted?"

She shook her head sadly. "Is that what you think, Paul? Is that who I am for you?"

Laura walked to the window again. She stared out for a long time, but just at the moment when I thought she had forgotten about me altogether, she turned back to me. It was not, however, to answer any of the questions I had put to her.

"I'm not being a very good hostess, am I?" she said, smiling genially. "And after your long drive. . . . Can I get you something? Are you hungry? A drink maybe?"

I didn't want to talk about such mundane matters. "I'm okay," I answered.

Laura ignored my response. "I don't have anything here," she said, "except some cans of iced tea in the fridge. I'm addicted to the goddamn stuff—Lipton's iced tea. In a can, for Christ's sake. What's become of me?" She stopped chattering and pointed a finger at me. "You wait right here. I'll go over to the lodge and find something for you. If no one's in the kitchen, I'll fix you something myself. If you want to lie down and rest for a while, go ahead."

She was out the door before I could stop her.

I walked over to the window to see if I could find what Laura was looking at. I saw nothing exceptional. Trees, elm and birch, with a few dots of wildflowers around their trunks. Sparse, uncut grass. Stones. The planks of the dock and the far reach of calm water beyond.

But remember, I reminded myself, not to reject this sight and the natural world it represents. I spread my arms wide before the glass and whispered, "Yes. I'm here."

I was tired to the bone but not, I believed, from the long drive. Frustration exhausted me. Here I was, transformed, neither the child nor man Laura knew before, yet I could not convey to her why I had come or what I hoped for our reunion. I returned to the couch, lay down, and within minutes I was asleep.

When I woke, it was from one of those paralyzed, dreamless sleeps that may have lasted for seconds or hours. Elizabeth, the frizzy-haired young woman who had been on the porch with Laura, stood over me. "Where is she?" Elizabeth asked. "Is she here?"

I sat up, rubbing my eyes. It felt as though bits of grit were under the lids. "She said she was going to the lodge. I don't know when . . ."

"Are you taking her away?" Elizabeth asked belligerently.

"What?"

"The last two conferences she's left early. Two years ago it was one of the students, one of the goddamn *students!* Last year she took off with some agent. He was just here for a morning session, but when he left, she went with him."

"I'm not—"

"I paid good money to come here to work with Laura Pettit, and goddamnit, she better be here."

I stood up and tried to look around Elizabeth. "'I'm sure she'll be back."

Elizabeth turned to leave but paused at the door. "Tell her she missed our goddamn appointment. Again."

I had a moment of panic then. Laura had left, not to avoid Elizabeth but to get away from *me*. Since I had tracked her down, she had no choice but to run from her own cabin, to take nothing with her, to run, run . . . . Then I noticed my suitcase beside the desk. Laura must have put it there while I slept. My panic turned to elation. She wanted me to stay! She *planned* on it!

Laura's voice called softly from outside the door. "Are you awake? Can you get the door?"

I ran to let her in. She was carrying a tray with a bottle of Gordon's gin, Schweppes tonic, a tall glass filled with ice and a slice of lime, a club sandwich, and a small bag of potato chips. "The owner of the resort is the cook too, and he's always hanging around during the conference. He thinks one of the writers might write a review of his resort or his food, so he's always willing to do favors."

Laura set the tray down on the desk. "Go ahead."

"How about you?" I sat down at the desk while she brought another chair from the porch and sat by my side.

"I'm not hungry. And I don't drink anymore." She uncapped the gin. "But I love to watch other people." She poured the glass half full with gin, then topped it off with tonic.

I took a long drink, the mingled smell of gin and quinine reminding me, as it always does, of some ridiculous combination of pine trees and gasoline.

Laura said wistfully, "God, I loved gin and tonics in the summertime. With lots of lime. Damn." She lit a cigarette and watched me eat and drink.

"Did you bring my suitcase up here?"

"I had someone carry it."

Earlier, my attempt to use the historical approach to explain my presence in New Hampshire hadn't worked very well, so I decided to try something much more direct and of the moment. Between mouthfuls I asked, "Can I stay here? With you?"

Laura looked steadily and seriously at me before she answered, and the two simple words she uttered were weighted with what seemed to me the gravity of both her years and mine and the intervening heavy snows and heavier nightfalls, of arrivals and departures, of long waits and longer disappointments, of deaths and births . . . "All right," she said.

I put my sandwich down and returned her gaze. Her eyes were sunken and dark-rimmed, but there—there, almost hidden in the widening cir- cle of creases and wrinkles—was the old scar, the bottle-cap scar that Laura had once let me touch. I thought of it now as mine, as everything of Laura now was mine.

"Just one thing, Paul. I'm going to have to ask you not to make so much of my being able to say yes. From your point of view it might seem like a desirable quality, but the fact of the matter is I do have regrets and almost all of them come from saying yes, yes to something I should have said no to."

I wanted to argue with Laura—to defend my definition of her—but before I could say anything, she held up her hand to stop me.

"Yes, yes, I know. This ability, this willingness to open wide and let it all in might seem appealing. As a literary motif, it can be impressive. The truth is, it plays better on the page than it does in life. And as a per- sonal philosophy, it's much overrated. And very troublesome. I wish you could see how I live, Paul. You'd see how I've tried to simplify my life, how I've tried to say no to what so many others say yes to." She smiled and looked down at the cigarette burning between her fingers. "Now, if I could find a way to say no to Marlboros and Lipton's iced tea, I could probably qualify for the monastic life."

" 'Yes' or 'no,' " I said. "It doesn't matter. It's you. I had to see *you*. I couldn't stay away any longer."

Laura crushed out her cigarette and stood. "I suppose I should be flat- tered. Nobody else has driven halfway across the goddamn country lately to see me. And you wouldn't be the first stray I've taken in. But look, I'd better track down Elizabeth and read her wretched poems before she finds a way to sue me. And there's going to be a reading tonight and probably something after. I'll be tied up for a while. I've got obligations here. You're welcome to come along. It'll be boring as ice melting, but come if you like. Or stay here. Sleep some more. You still look tired."

"I'll think I'll stay."

Laura stood in the cabin's doorway and looked at me for a long time before leaving. "Well," she finally said, "I wonder what I'm saying yes to this time."

AFTER LAURA LEFT, I went for a walk to stretch out my legs after the long cramped hours in the car.

A few miles from the camp I came to a junction on a busy highway. Across from me was one of those peculiar resort area combinations—a gas station, tackle shop, ice cream counter, grocery store, miniature golf course. This one was Vic's Gas and Recreation, and I crossed the highway to its parking lot.

Two teenagers, a boy and a girl, leaned against the hood of a bronze Trans-Am. The girl was holding her long hair up on top of her head. The boy had his nose pressed to her neck. Was she wearing a new perfume? Did he like it? Did it please him? They were in love, dripping its juice and breathing its air. I wanted to approach them, to tell them, yes, I know what you're feeling. My woman is nearby, and later we'll be together. I will take in all her body's perfumes, from her mouth, her armpit, her hair . . . Laura would have no inch of flesh, no sigh or smell I would say no to.

Another girl came out of the store and joined the young lovers. She had to be the girl's sister. They had the same shade of oaky-blond hair, and they were dressed identically in khaki shorts and white polo shirts. They were both thin and had the same wobbly posture, as if none of their joints were tightly secured.

Twins.

And as long as I was here—where following Laura had led me—I would not see my daughters. I would never see them squinting in the July sun, laughing at their secret, private jokes. I would never see the boys, sniffing around as if a girl's identity were in her scent.

Next to the gate of the miniature golf course a pay phone hung on the wall. I could call the twins. I wouldn't have to say anything, not now. Just tell them I was all right, that I loved them, that I would see them again someday, just keep their hearts open, just keep the line open. . . .

No.

Now I was here. I couldn't live in two places at once. Not anymore.

The traffic thinned, and I sprinted back across the highway. I didn't stop running until I was deep in the woods along the road leading back to Laura's cabin.

LAURA DIDN'T RETURN until after ten o'clock, and when she arrived, I was teetering on the brink of drunkenness, sipping warm gin because I had run out of tonic and ice. The tiny cabin was dark, close, and humid. A thin but persistent rain was falling.

"Paul?" Laura said to the dark room.

"Yes."

"Where are you?" I could see her form's darker shadow as she groped her way toward the desk to turn on the light.

"I'm here."

The ember of her cigarette glowed. "Did you want to keep it dark?"

"I'm just thinking. . . ."

"Deep, dark thoughts no doubt." She switched on the light, and I squinted at its brightness.

"Eyes accustomed to the dark," she said. "I've always loved that phrase. 'His eyes had grown accustomed to the dark.' I was going to use that as a title for a collection of poems."

"Where were you?"

"Gee, Dad. I didn't know you were waiting up."

"I was just wondering."

"Don't. I was working. Remember? I'm not on vacation; you followed me to my fucking job."

As if I were swallowing a pill, I tossed off the last of the gin in my glass. "Sorry."

Laura sat down on the other end of the couch. "I was going over Elizabeth's poems with her. Elizabeth's obvious and overfed poems. And then we gathered in the lodge and a couple people read their work, and we followed that with a question-and-answer session. What can I tell you? It's a drag, but that's what we do here. I've been to other conferences where it's nothing more than, how little can I do and how much can I drink and who can I fuck? But this one is fairly serious. Does this meet with your approval?"

"I said I was sorry."

"So you did." Laura kicked off her sandals. "I'm going for a swim. Want to come?"

"I didn't bring a suit."

"Oh, come on. It's just going to be the two of us. Wear your underwear if you're going to go modest on me. It's dark out there and darker in the water. No one will see you."

"All right."

Laura went into the bathroom, closed the door, and came out in a few minutes dressed in a black one-piece bathing suit and carrying two towels. The suit fit her poorly, as if it had belonged to an older, larger sister or Laura fifteen pounds ago. The material gapped at the legs and arm-holes, and her breasts didn't quite fill the cups.

She saw I was staring at her and flung one of the towels at me. "Let's go. Swimming is the only goddamn exercise I get lately and I don't like to miss a day."

I took off my shoes, socks, and shirt, but I decided to leave my pants on until I got down to the water.

Laura brought a flashlight, and I tried to follow its wavering light down the damp, cool, sandy path. The gin, the darkness, the feel and sound of rain dripping from the trees, the steepness of the trail—I felt as if I were now inside a new reality, one in which you walked in the rain, put your foot down in darkness, and loved the woman your father loved.

When we got down to the dock, Laura said, "The bottom's rocky right here, but once you get out about twenty feet it's smooth."

"How deep?"

"It's over my head soon. You could probably walk out a ways." And then she was gone—one long, low racer's dive, a watery splat, and she was out of sight.

I stripped down to my briefs—the only thing whiter than my pale flesh—and quickly lowered myself off the end of the dock.

The water was not terribly cold, yet when it hit my scrotum, I gasped. Then it was up to my chest and there was no turning back, so I dropped

down and let the water close over my head. I opened my eyes, but it
didn't matter. The underwater darkness was complete, although there
was something to it that made it seem green-tinged, as if my eyes were
bound by a dark green, almost black, blindfold, just the way the night
sky even at its blackest still carries the idea of blue. I brought my hand
up before my face and wiggled my fingers, but I could only feel their
nearness.

In the seconds before I had to come up for air, I spun myself around in
a slow underwater float so that when I came up, I wouldn't know which
direction I was facing.

It worked. Then, before I caught my bearings from a light on shore or
the slant of the rain, I pushed off hard and swam furiously toward . . .
Toward what? Whom? This was just motion, and if no one stopped me,
if I didn't beach myself somewhere, I'd keep swimming until I lost my
breath and strength and drowned.

I stopped and began to tread water in a slow circle. I let myself sink a
ways and groped with my toes for the bottom. It wasn't there, and I
kicked furiously upward.

"Laura!" I shouted. "Laura!"

I knew she was gone, that she had gotten me out here for just this reason, to escape me, to swim away under the cover of the black night.

I called her name again, then waited and listened. The sounds that
came back to me were a chorus of watery trills from the frogs onshore,
the soft splashing of waves rolling gently over each other, and the tiny
tapping of the rain, a miniature sound that crept in and out of the
rhythm of my breath.

Frantically, I began to thrash my way back toward the dock. When I
got close enough, I stopped swimming and waded in across the rocks. I
kept calling Laura's name, but there was still no response. Her towel was
on the dock.

I looked back out to the lake, hoping I would see a flash of Laura's pale
arm rising out of the water. Nothing.

I turned back toward the dock, and just as I did, a figure burst out of
the water and at me! I stepped back, losing my footing and falling back
underwater.

Coughing, I came up right away, and as soon as I did, Laura wrapped one arm around my neck and clasped a hand over my mouth. *"Ssshh,"* she whispered. "Not so loud."

I regained my footing. The water where I stood was chest deep. If Laura were not clinging to me, she would have been in over her head.

"Keep me off the rocks," she said, tightening her grip around my neck. Her face was so close to mine I felt her breath cooling my cheek.

I took a few backward steps until I felt sand underfoot. Laura moved easily with me. She was light anyway, and with the water releasing us from gravity's usual requirements, I could hold her up effortlessly. I remembered something I used to tell Nora and Doreen when they were learning to swim. "Don't forget," I used to say, "the water wants to hold you up."

"I thought I lost you," I said.

"I was over in the shallows. Watching you. Once I was so close I could have whispered your name and you would have heard me."

"Why didn't you say something?"

I felt her shrug. "I wanted to see what you'd do."

Laura let go of my neck, but just as she did she brought her legs up and wrapped them around my waist. Then she let herself fall back, floating, her silver hair fanning out on the water's surface like a reflection of moonlight. I put my hands under her waist and held her up.

For a long time we remained that way, Laura gazing sightlessly up toward the source of the rain and I watching her, adoring her.

Then, when I couldn't stand it any longer, I pulled her up toward me. She rose easily out of the water, put her arms around me again, and when our bodies were pressed so tightly together no water could flow between us, she asked, "Are you sure? Goddamnit, you better be sure."

"Yes."

She pressed even harder against me, grabbed the hair at the back of my head and pulled so hard I was afraid we would both topple over. The moisture of our mouths, of our tongues slipping back and forth on each other, made the water of the lake—the water we stood in—seem somehow insubstantial, thin, not wet enough compared to the slippery oil of our bodies. And the night sky was not dark enough compared to our bodies' interiors, its height nothing next to our depth.

Our mouths separated, and with the help of my hands on her buttocks, Laura rose higher out of the water. As she did, she shrugged the straps of her swimming suit off her shoulders and wriggled it down to her waist. With my mouth I felt how her nipples had shriveled and shrunk in the water and the night air, but as I tongued and sucked, I felt the slack flesh harden further inside my lips. I took my mouth away and lowered her slightly, letting the lake have its turn lapping her breasts.

She let go of me again, and just before she slid underwater she said, "Don't go away," her voice as soft and throaty as if it had been out all night in the rain.

Laura disappeared, but then I felt her tugging at my shorts, pulling them out from my stiff cock that tried to hold them up, then pushing them down my thighs. I helped, lifting my legs and awkwardly stepping out of them. I felt them float away.

Laura surfaced and swam a slow circle around me, only her head above water. I turned to follow and face her, and as I did, my foot touched a small mushy pocket of sand that was softer than the rest of the lake's bottom. Instantly a rush of cold water exploded upward, and when its chill brushed my genitals, it only intensified the ache of desire.

"Come here," I said and reached for Laura.

"It's over my head," she answered. "You can't let me down."

She climbed onto me and again wrapped her legs around me. She had removed her bathing suit as well.

"This is it," Laura whispered to me. "There's no going back."

We kissed again, long and deep, and while Laura clung to me, I let my hands swim over every part of her I could reach, tracing the knobs of her spine, caressing her buttocks, following the muscles of her thighs up to the wet tangle of pubic hair, counting the spokes of her ribs—she let her body come and go to ease access for my hands—up to her breasts, where their softness said stay.

Laura lowered herself, slowly, the boat coming to dock, until there, there, I was in her, she coming down lower on me, I rising in her, there, there . . .

I am here, in Laura, *here, here,* I kept thinking, a thought full of wonder and awe and relief, as if I had finished a journey so long and dangerous any hope of completing it had long ago ceased to seem possible.

Into my ear, Laura said, "Oh, God. Oh, Jesus, you don't know how long it's been!"

With as much force as the water allowed, I thrust deeper into her.

"No," she said. "Not yet. Be still. Let's not move. Not yet."

So I stood as motionless as I could. For how long? Thirty seconds? A minute? Twenty-five years? Then I felt the slightest movement at Laura's hips, but I couldn't tell if she was breaking our stillness or if it was merely some waver in the lake, some underwater current, some small wave only now reaching us from a branch falling in the water a mile away.

Then I felt it again, and again and again, not strong enough to be thrust or draw or contraction but a motion too concentrated, too muscular to be water's, and then Laura was climbing higher on me, staying, whispering, "God, you don't. Know. How long," and letting herself down again and climbing again and lowering herself, climbing and lowering faster and faster, and then falling back on the water again—my hands, her legs, my cock, the lake, holding her up—and then we gave our motion to water, and the hard rhythm of our hips together sent waves all the way to the shore, where they climbed as high as they could and died.

When I could hold back no longer, Laura somehow got her legs behind my knees, pushed and pulled simultaneously, and brought us both down, tumbling backward into the water, and when I came, it was into Laura, the lake, the night, and I held my breath just in time, my lungs filled while my seed emptied. We were both rolling underwater, locked and coming in wave after wave. And in that orgasmic release we let go of each other and let the water carry us apart.

I stayed down as long as I could, stayed in that blind underwater world where only Laura and I existed. And when I couldn't stand it any longer, when I was close to passing out, when the simple need of oxygen became more important than living with Laura, I burst out of the water into the dear, lush air.

Laura was already there, treading water and laughing. "You didn't happen to see my suit down there, did you?"

"You . . . almost . . ." I gasped, "drowned . . . me."

She laughed harder. "It was fantastic, wasn't it? Haven't you heard about men who have died because they've hanged themselves while they're masturbating? Trying to intensify their orgasm?"

I reached for Laura, but she flipped herself back and floated away.

"Don't," I said. "I want to hold you. I need to."

"You already held me. Now you have to let me go. I want to swim some more."

I dove for her, but she slipped to the side. I came up, and she rolled over and began a fast crawl in the direction of the dock. Even if I had had my breath and strength, I couldn't have kept up with her.

"I'm going to wait!" I called to her. "Over by the dock!"

I was tired and cold, but I was not about to climb naked from the water until Laura returned. I waited, hanging on to a steel support under the dock.

Perhaps Catherine and Dr. Westwater had been right in urging me into the hospital after I had chest pains. Something had been wrong with my heart, although medicine had no instruments that could identify or measure its trouble. My heart had been dying, kept from what it needed to live. In my case, however, it was not veins or arteries that were blocked; it was not lack of oxygen that was shriveling that fist-sized muscle. It was lack of Laura, but now my heart was flooding again, beating with so much love it felt as though it could send wave after wave out across the lake.

Then I heard waves coming toward me—the sound of Laura's rapid strokes carrying back to me.

She reached up and grabbed the same bar beneath the dock where I held on. She was barely able to catch her breath.

"Where were you this time?" I asked.

"You can't see it from here," she finally said, "but there's a Boy Scout camp across the lake. That's my nightly swim, over there and back."

"You swam to a Boy Scout camp—naked?"

Laura leaned over and kissed me lightly. "That's my Paul. The voice of sweet reason."

She hoisted herself out of the water and onto the dock. As she did, her bare ass flashed by my face.

"Besides," she said down to me, "they're not going to be interested in this old woman's body."

I looked up at her. She was toweling dry her hair. Through the darkness I saw the darker shadows of her nipples and pubic hair. "You look terrific to me."

"And that's my Paul too. As blind as ever. I love it." She wrapped her towel around her torso. "I've got to get to the cabin before I freeze. Are you coming?" She picked up the flashlight, turned it on, and pointed its beam straight up into the sky. In the light's shaft tiny droplets of rain hung in the air like a swarm of tiny insects. Laura turned off the light and ran blindly up the path.

I swam around to the ladder and climbed out of the water. I didn't take time to towel off—pointless in the rain—but covered myself quickly, grabbed my pants, and then carefully walked up the slope.

Laura had turned all the lights on. I liked it. It signified not only illumination but also reality. See, this incandescence said, this woman is here too. She is as real in this brightness as she was in the darkness.

"I'm going to take a shower," said Laura. "I hate that smell of the lake on me."

While Laura was in the bathroom, I dried off quickly, took some clothes out of my suitcase, and put on underwear, a clean pair of chinos, and a sweatshirt. When Laura came out, she was wearing a white terrycloth robe and had a pale blue towel wrapped around her hair.

"Going out?" she asked, gesturing at my clothing.

"No . . . I was just . . ."

"I need some sleep. You don't have to work tomorrow, but I do. Those goddamn conferences start at nine."

I wasn't sure what she wanted me to do.

Laura clapped her hands. "Well, come on. Help me. That couch folds out, but I almost broke my fucking back the first time I tried."

I took the cushions off and pulled out the heavy mattress. A fitted sheet and a tangled top sheet were already on the bed. A pillow was stuffed into the space between the mattress and the back of the couch.

Laura lowered the blinds on the window and shut them, though not tightly. Then she sat down on the edge of the bed. "I get this side. I like the sunlight coming in in the morning."

I stood at the foot of the bed.

"Are you wearing that to bed?" she asked.

"Just a minute." I got my travel kit out of the suitcase and took it into the bathroom.

I decided not to shower but to let the lake be my bath. Besides, the smell that Laura wanted to wash off I wanted to remain on me forever, since it had become for me the smell of our lovemaking. I took off the clothes I had just put on, brushed my teeth, sprayed on some deodorant, then crept out to get into bed with Laura.

She was at her desk, smoking and writing furiously in a spiral notebook. Without looking up, she waved a hand at me. "I'll be right with you. I've got some night thoughts here I want to take care of."

I got into bed and covered myself with the sheet.

When she finished writing, she closed the notebook and dropped it into the book bag on the floor. Without turning around, she said, "If I ever caught you looking in that notebook, Paul, I would cut off your nuts and feed them to the fish."

"I wouldn't."

"I know you wouldn't."

Laura rose, turned out the desk lamp, and turned to the bed. "Are you cold? I've got extra blankets."

"I'm fine."

"I'm sorry there's not another pillow. Tomorrow I'll get one at the lodge."

"That's okay."

Laura shrugged out of her robe and lay it across the foot of the bed. She was wearing nothing but a pair of white cotton panties.

Before she got into bed, I said, "Wait. Stand there a minute."

She put her hands on her hips. "What are you looking at?"

"Your hair. I can't believe the color. It's so silver it almost sparkles."

She ran her hand through her hair just the way she used to when it was short as a boy's. "I keep saying I'm going to color it. I mean, eighty-year-old women don't have this much gray hair. But then I think, fuck it, I earned these gray hairs." She reached down to pull back the sheet.

"Not yet," I said. "Let me look a little more."

Laura looked down at herself, directing her attention where she thought mine was. She cupped her breasts and lifted them slightly. "I know," she said. "Pathetic. I used to have great tits. I wish you could have seen me then."

I could have said, I did. I saw you astride my father in a motel room. But I didn't. Instead I sat up in bed, swung my legs to the floor, and reached for her. She stepped forward into my embrace.

"You look wonderful to me. Magnificent. All of you."

I came off the bed so that I was kneeling before Laura. I let my kisses trail down and, with my hands, pulled her panties down until I could press my lips, my tongue into the bristle of her pubic hair and deeper still into that wet warmth that still smelled like the lake, the lake and the rain and the black night, and deeper yet, to a smell-taste as briny as an ocean waiting to be discovered.

Laura leaned her pelvis forward and simultaneously pushed at the back of my head. "Did I tell you I've been celibate, Paul?" Her voice was as breathy as a whisper, but it rose from deep in her throat. "For almost a year. No one. I simply couldn't stand the . . . the . . . the complication. And now. Now." She laughed, a sound like a dry leaf folded into your fist. "Now. What could be more—complicated—than *this?*"

She pressed my face so hard into her my teeth rubbed against her. She shuddered, pulled away slightly, came back hard, and pulled away again.

Laura pulled me up, pushed me back onto the bed, and lay down on top of me. She wiped my mouth with the heel of her hand, then kissed me until our breathing seemed to be in rhythm.

Then she straddled me, and when I easily entered her, I experienced once again an instant of purest ecstasy. Orgasm may have been more intense, but it could not match this moment's quiet, complete joy. I closed my eyes and softly whispered, "Yes," but it was the loudest affirmation of my life.

Laura had her own message to murmur. "Keep your eyes open, Paul. I want you to know who you're with."

I opened my eyes to the sight of her rocking above me.

Laura did not have to obey her own command. She closed her eyes and leaned back against my legs. When she came, she tossed her head from side to side as if she wanted to twist away from thought and only feel.

Afterward, Laura lay by my side and asked, "Well, which is better— with weight or without? Water or dry land?"

"I'm willing to try the other two—air or fire, as long as it's you."

"Why, Dr. Finley," Laura laughed, "it sounds as though you're working on a poem!"

"You inspire me."

She laughed again. "Now, your father—he refused to make love in the water."

I tried to kiss her to keep her from saying any more, but she turned her head aside.

"I tried to get him to do it in a lake once, but he wouldn't. See— there's something he wouldn't say yes to."

"Don't."

"He said we'd get infections from the water."

"Don't, please."

"Why? What's the matter? Don't tell me you're one of those men who won't let a woman talk about her past lovers?"

I sat up on the edge of the bed, the foldout bed's iron bar pressing into the back of my legs.

Laura shook my shoulder. "Paul?"

"Can't this just be you and me? Can't we . . ."

"No." Laura's voice was emphatic. "That's the one way it can never be. Never. You hear these goddamn pop psychologists and part-time Buddhists telling us we have to learn to let go. But we can't! We must not. You're married; you have a wife, kids. I've had a carload of lovers, among them your father. These are facts. Not open to interpretation. That's what we have to carry. If we go on from this moment, it will be with that baggage. Or we won't go on."

She was right. I knew that. If I didn't understand anything else— about my own heart, mind, or motive—I knew that. I was relearning the old lesson: the cost of loving Laura. "This is all a little confusing," I said.

Laura said sympathetically, "Come here. Lie down."

I lay stiffly along the edge of the bed.

Laura stroked my neck and shoulder with one finger. "Was this too much? All at once?"

"It's okay."

"I wanted to make sure you understood. I wanted to establish some ground rules."

"I understand."

"Do you? Are you sure? Maybe you should repeat it back to me."

"You want me to face facts."

"That's close enough. Now then . . ." Laura let her finger trail from my neck down to my chest. She lightly circled my nipple, then continued her slow descent, down to my cock. "Would you like to try for one more?"

"I don't think I have it in me. . . ."

"Are you sure?" asked Laura. Her fingers went down to my scrotum. "I have these magical powers . . ."

She might have been right. If I could have closed my eyes and let the current carry me, I could soon have been hard. "No," I said, and squirmed away from her touch. I rolled back toward her. "Let's just talk awhile. Can we?"

"Isn't that a woman's line?" She settled in comfortably by my side. "Sure. What about?"

"Do you remember the first time we met?"

"Oh, God!" Laura laughed. "Do I remember? I wish I could forget. What did I say? Did I *tell* you that your father and I were having an affair?"

I laughed too. "Almost. I think you wanted my help."

Laura put her hands in front of her face. "I don't believe it. Jesus, I had brass. That, and booze. It's a fucking miracle I survived."

"What else do you remember?"

"Let's see. A bike ride? We went for a bike ride together. I felt so terrible about what I had said I wanted to make it up to you. And to keep your mouth shut."

"What was the weather like? Do you remember that?"

"It was hot, wasn't it? I remember sitting in the kitchen of that big old house and sweating so much my blouse stuck to me like paste. And the air didn't move. I had to get outside or get to a window. I think that's how I ended up in your room; I had to get some air."

"That's right," I said. "That's exactly right. That was the hottest summer we ever had. What else? Do you remember the other times we met?"

"Oh, Paul. You don't ask much, do you? You know, I used to have a wonderful memory. Now it's shot to hell. I don't know if there's so much I *want* to forget or if it's just a case of too many burned brain cells. But, okay. I'll try. You have to help."

Together we started over.

Laura lay in my arms and remembered. The night before Thanksgiving when Janie and I went to dinner with Laura and my father. The trip to Minneapolis when my father and I met Laura at the hotel—dinner with Stanley Fowler . . . the drive through the blizzard. . . . My father's funeral—the schoolhouse . . . Laura's poetry reading that I attended with Martha. Chicago . . .

As she remembered each of our meetings, she wove together her memories and mine, and the results were new tapestries—richer, brighter, more orderly than my chaotic, emotional memory alone could ever make. And before long I could see what Laura was doing: she was giving my own life back to me but giving it back with a beauty and meaning that was beyond any power I had to bestow.

I don't know when I fell asleep. It was still dark, but birds had begun to sing at some suggestion of dawn I couldn't see. And Laura was still awake. She had stopped talking, but she still lightly stroked my forehead. I fell asleep feeling her touch.

THE MORNING WAS bright and clear—the air full of that just-washed summer freshness that follows a night of rain. Distances reappear with startling clarity. Birds' songs carry farther. From the sofa bed I could not see the lake, yet I sensed its sunlit sparkle, almost as if it were reflected in the sky the way sky is mirrored in water.

Laura was already awake, standing in front of the window, smoking, and staring out. She was wearing one of my T-shirts, and the sunlight coming through the window outlined her body through the white fabric.

I drank in the sight of her as if she were a potion especially concocted to make even the brightest morning seem brighter.

Softly, so I would not startle her, I said, "Good morning."

She did not turn around right away. I saw her hesitate, pull her hand back through her hair, and when she did face me, her expression was so grave I wanted to turn away immediately, to close my eyes again, to go back to sleep, to see if I could wake again, this time to another truth. I knew what she was going to say.

"You can't stay," Laura said.

The pain of her remark struck me instantly, yet I also felt it find a home in me, the way a child feels when he hears there is no Santa Claus. The news is sad, yet it makes so much sense, there is such a rightness about it, it eliminates so many uncertainties and inconsistencies, that he cannot help but feel relieved to hear it.

But I had to argue; I *had to* or be untrue to my entire life.

"I can . . . It will work. At first it will be awkward, but before long we'll adjust and—"

Laura shook her head.

I pushed on. "I can practice in Vermont. Or we can move someplace. Someplace that would be ours—"

"No."

"You wouldn't have to teach. I'd work, and you could write—"

"No, Paul."

"Please. . . . Let's try it for a while and—"

"No. Now stop."

"If . . ."

Laura held up her hands. "Stop it! Don't you get it? I'm not telling you this so you can change my mind. I'm not telling you this because it's what I want. Goddamnit! This is what's *right*. We don't belong together. As much as you might like the idea or as much as I might. It's *wrong*. I thought about this all night. I'd fuck up your life so bad you'd never get it untangled. And you'd get in the way of mine. No. It's wrong. It's simply wrong."

"But it's all I've wanted." I could hear how close I was to begging, but I didn't care. "Ever. All my life."

Laura walked over to the desk and stabbed out her cigarette. "Then you've wanted the wrong thing."

She went into the bathroom. Suddenly I felt embarrassed to be lying in bed naked and alone. I rose quickly and dressed.

When Laura came out—no longer wearing my T-shirt but wearing a navy blue one of her own and white jeans—I tried again, though a part of me had long since been convinced it was futile.

"I'm willing to try other arrangements," I said calmly. I had nothing specific in mind; the phrase simply sounded reasonable and workable. "If you'll let me stay."

Laura went to the desk and began to stack up books and notebooks that didn't need stacking. Her back to me, she answered, "Don't, Paul. Please. No more. If you keep pushing, I'll have to say something cruel to drive you away. Neither of us wants that."

"I can't go back."

Laura finally turned around, allowing me to see what she had been keeping from me. She had been crying. The tears had dried, but her eyes were still red-rimmed and glistening. "That's not really the issue, is it? Besides, what makes you so sure you can't?"

I shook my head. "I've ruined that."

She shrugged. "What do you want me to say? Do you want me to allow you to stay out of pity? Because I feel sorry for you? I don't think you want that."

"If that's the only way . . ." I put on my best I'll-be-any-kind-of-fool-for-love smile.

And for a moment it looked as if it might work. Laura stared at me for a long time, trembling between a smile and more tears. Then, with no warning, she ran at me, and before I could get my arms up to embrace her or to defend myself—and I wouldn't have known anyway which I should do—she hit me squarely in the chest with the heels of both hands. The force of her charge moved me back.

"Go!" she shouted, and pushed me back again. "Just go, goddamnit! You don't *belong* here!"

She kept pushing me back, but by now she was crying again, and each sob seemed to weaken her, so there was no force behind her shoving. I still made no move to stop her.

"No matter what you think," she said. "You don't belong. Not here. Not with me."

Finally she stopped pushing and collapsed against me, her arms crossed on my chest. I let her remain there and gently put my arms around her. If I could hold her there long enough, a few minutes more, until her tears stopped, until her breathing slowed, until her heart rate matched mine . . .

But when she spoke again, her voice was wrapped tight with reason and resolve. "This sounds so familiar. Haven't I told you this before? Haven't I told you over and over what's right for you? Why won't you listen? Why don't you do what's right? Instead of what you want—which is exactly what got your father into so goddamn much trouble."

I started to say something, to argue, to plead, but before I could get out more than, "It's not that way—" Laura interrupted me. "Please, Paul. If I mean anything to you. No more. Can't we please stop this? Now I'm the one begging."

"All right," I said. Yet I still held her. Loosely, but I held her.

She remained for another moment, and then she pushed away. "I have to go. And so do you."

I HAD JUST put my suitcase in the trunk when Laura crossed the parking lot toward me. I didn't stop but slammed the hatch and walked around to the driver's door. I felt it was best that I keep moving.

"All packed?" Laura asked. "That was quick."

"The advantages of traveling light. You can get out in a hurry."

Laura crossed her arms and smiled. "That's always been my motto."

"I know."

She had stopped about six feet from me, a distance that seemed deliberate. If I made a grab for her, she could easily skip away. I opened the car door and got in; when I did, Laura stepped forward. I slammed the door, and she came closer still.

"Good-bye," she said. "It's been fun."

"Is that it? Anything else?"

"What do you want to hear?"

"I'm not sure. I guess I won't know until I hear it."

She looked away, but I knew there was nothing in that treetop that was commanding her attention. "Nothing will make any difference."

"That's probably true."

"Let's keep in touch," she said. "There. How's that?"

"That's not bad." I turned the key in the ignition, and the engine fired right away. Over its throaty hum, I said, "That's not bad at all." Then I smiled at Laura one more time before I drove away.

DOES IT SEEM surprising that I left so quickly, that I made so little fuss? After all, considering that I had been in love with, obsessed with, Laura for most of my life, shouldn't it have taken a whip and a chair to drive me off, and a court order to keep me away? Mark my lack of fight down to Laura's character. In her life she may have made wrong turns and bad decisions, but she did not waver and she did not turn back. It made as much sense to argue with a force of nature as to argue with Laura. If you do not like the climate where you live, you may as well move. The weather will not change to accommodate you.

So as I put miles and New Hampshire behind me, I tried to turn my despair to something I could live with. Laura and I could still be friends. We'd exchange Christmas cards. Maybe Catherine would take me back. Laura could visit us. I wasn't wrong to love her. She and Catherine would become friends. Laura would call me late at night, worried and complaining about the pain in her left shoulder. I would assure her that it was only bursitis. How could loving Laura be wrong? She would take the twins for walks and show them how to see the world with her poet's eye.

Then, idly, I lifted my hand to my face, perhaps to scratch my nose or to brush an eyelash from my cheek. And I smelled my hand. It still held that hint of brackish odor from the lake.

That was all it took.

I had to pull over to the side of the road, not only because my sudden, hot tears flooded my vision and made driving dangerous, but because I could not breathe. The crying had come on as abruptly as a blow to the chest, and I felt as if I were having an attack of tachycardia. I hung my head on the steering wheel and sobbed uncontrollably, gasping for breath and letting the tears fall and stain dark circles on my trousers.

When my crying began to subside, I lifted my hand to my nostrils and breathed in its odor once more. And my sobbing immediately surged again. I kept up this process until I was certain I had no tears left or the smell was gone. I couldn't be sure which.

Then I drove on.

IT WAS NOT until I was past Chicago and speeding toward Wisconsin on the Illinois Tollway that I began to think about what I was moving toward.

Could I expect to have the family I left behind? Would Catherine and I separate? Would I become one of those fathers who only saw his children on weekends? There were likely answers to those questions, but I tried not to speculate. Wait, I told myself; wait until you see the look in their eyes.

As I got closer to home, I remembered an incident from my childhood. I must have been seven or eight, and we still lived in Boston. My mother, sister, and I were all waiting for my father to return from a business trip to California. My father traveled often, but his trips were usually brief—into New York or Philadelphia for a day or two. This time, however, he had been gone for over a week, and we were all anxious for his return.

The hour came when my father was supposed to arrive, yet he still was not there. It was late fall, and as the afternoon made its rapid descent into evening, the house dimmed just as a midsummer day gives up its light to an approaching storm. For some reason, no one turned on any lamps, and Janie, my mother, and I sat in the gloom waiting for my father.

Suddenly my mother, who had been staring into thin air, cried out, "Robert!"

My first chilling thought was that she had seen a ghost, an apparition of my father in the shadowy gloom. Then a second thought—and to a seven-year-old more frightening than the first—was that my mother was hallucinating.

Before I could verify either fear, my father, who had come in the back way, said, in his voice that always seemed too loud for our ears, "Jesus, can we shed a little light on the subject." And threw the switch that made us all blink at the sudden explosion of light.

Long after I learned that fathers could not be counted on to return, this memory still carried a mythic power for me, representing as it did that ancient promise kept of a father coming back from his journey and banishing darkness upon his return.

THERE WERE NO lights on and Catherine's car was not in the garage when I pulled into the driveway. I knew no one was waiting inside for me in the dark, though at that moment I wanted nothing more fervently than to see my daughters and to hold them in my arms.

The house was empty, but Catherine obviously expected my return. She left a note on the kitchen table.

Dear Paul,

Laura Pettit called to say where you were and that you are fine. I wish you had been the one to call, but I guess the important thing is that you're all right.

The twins and I are at Mom's. I thought it would be better if we weren't home when you got back, at least until we get some things straightened out.

Please call when you get back and let us know how you are.

Catherine

Oh, the injustice of it! Here I was; I had the house to myself—just as my father had his to himself after his wife and children returned to her childhood home. But it wasn't fair! I *left* Laura! I came back. I broke the cycle! I *came back!*

Then the real significance of what I had just read sunk in. Laura had called Catherine. Laura and my wife spoke. My wife knew about Laura and me. I wasn't sure what I felt. Fear? I had no secrets now. Anger? How dare Laura reveal what I wanted hidden. Gratitude? Yes, gratitude. Laura explained to my wife what I could never explain. Laura was trying to right my toppled life, to set it on the course I had such difficulty navigating. And now Catherine knew. If she heard Laura's voice, Catherine knew.

Catherine's mother's number was printed—in Catherine's tiny, precise handwriting, which I now found inexpressibly dear—on a hand-painted wood-framed index of "Numbers to Know" hanging by the phone. I dialed the number, closed my eyes, and waited for an answer.

After four rings, Catherine's mother answered.

"Hello, Nora. Is Catherine there?"

Did she hesitate? Was she wondering whether she should allow her daughter to speak to me?

Or did I imagine it? "Just a minute," said Nora.

In the interval before Catherine came to the phone, I thought I heard the twins in the background, and the sounds of their mingled laughter, screams, and squeals seemed as if they were coming to me not across distance but over time, as if I were listening to a tape. *There, there are the voices of your children as they once were, and though you can hear them over and over again, you can never touch again the moment in which they live. Distances can be crossed, but time passed is time lost. . . .*

Then Catherine came on the line. "Hello, Paul. Where are you?"

"I'm home."

"You got my note?"

"I'm looking at it now. I called right away. I haven't even unpacked." I cringed at my presumption. Unpack. Maybe she didn't want me to stay.

"You're in the kitchen," said Catherine, as if she were trying to understand something through geography.

"How are the girls? I heard them. . . ."

"They're fine. Do you want me to put them on?"

"No. I mean, Jesus, what they must think of me. . . ."

"You're their father, Paul. They love you."

"But I mean, the way I left. The way I was acting . . ."

"I explained to them. I said you were feeling a lot of pressure. You lost your temper. They understand. Really, Paul, they've forgotten that night already. Things aren't as important to kids."

I had no doubt Catherine believed those things. And I had no doubt she was absolutely wrong. You might *think* they have forgotten. They may never mention it again. But somewhere it would remain. In some fold of the brain there it was. And someday, perhaps twenty years from now, perhaps Doreen—perhaps on her wedding day—would look at me, and her eyes would be full of it: *You brought me out in a storm; you wrenched my arm and brought me out in the wind and the rain; and you went away.*

"What about you?" I asked Catherine.

She sighed, and in that little exhalation of air was Catherine's very spirit. Words, angry words, would be tumbling from another woman's mouth by now, but Catherine had still not decided: should she speak her mind or should she let this go?

"You've lied to me, Paul." I could also tell now from the tone of her voice that she was more tired than angry. That worried me; I would have had a better chance against rage than exhaustion. "From the very start. You've lied to me for years."

I should have agreed, if not for the good of our marriage then for my own mental health. Instead, I tried to get by on a technicality. "I haven't lied," I said. "I told you about Laura."

"Oh, please. You told me nothing. *Nothing.* Withholding the truth can be the same thing as lying. I got more of the truth from five minutes of conversation with Laura Pettit than from you in all the years of our marriage."

"What did she say?"

"Not yet," Catherine said. "I think I'll hold on to that for a while. But don't worry"—she sniffed—"it's nothing you haven't always known about yourself."

"All right."

"Just promise me one thing, Paul."

"Anything."

"No, not anything. Just this. Don't explain anything to me. Don't try to make me understand. I can't, so don't try. And even if you feel you have to tell me, even if you're dying from not telling, don't. I don't want to know. At least right now. Do you understand?"

"I understand."

"And you can keep it in?"

"I can."

Catherine inhaled sharply. "Of course you can. Why did I even bother to ask?" She cleared her throat. "We'll be home day after tomorrow. Mom wants to take the girls to the zoo in Milwaukee tomorrow. They're all looking forward to it."

"I understand."

"You don't understand a goddamn thing," Catherine said and hung up.

THE NEXT MORNING I was up early. I called the clinic, made my apologies, and assured them I would be there Monday morning. Then I went outside and began to work.

At the edge of our backyard, right before a stand of jack pine and pin oak, was a five-foot-wide strip of weeds and tall grass that I had always meant to cut down, dig up, and reseed, thereby enlarging our yard. Why I was intent on doing this, I wasn't sure; all I would accomplish would be to give myself more grass to mow. That morning, I started on the project.

The day was overcast but hot. The dust that rose up with every shovelful stuck to my sweaty body. My back ached from its unaccustomed labor. Dirt, sweat, pain, and thirst—these suited my purposes. I was trying to do penance.

Then, in early afternoon, suddenly breaking into my reverie and rhythm of shovel, hoe, and rake, came the shouts of the twins. I turned, and there they were—dressed in identical pink sunsuits and tumbling across the grass as freely as if they were windblown. Doreen's voice carried the high registers, and Nora's hit the low notes, but they sang the same song—"Daddy! Daddy Daddy! Daddy!"

And they ran into my arms without any regard for my dirt, sweat, or foolishness. They ran into my arms without any thought that I might muff the catch. They ran into my arms with the abandon of forgiveness.

I held them both tightly and stood and saw Catherine come around the corner of the house. She was dressed in white, and as she moved through the heavy summer air, her clothing, her presence, seemed like a substitute for the light the day was supposed to provide. She came to the spot on the lawn where the turf softens and dips, and I thought—but couldn't be sure—that her gait quickened. I was sure, however, of her smile; it was sudden, complete, and unwilled, like that of a chaste young girl who is determined to be solemn but hears something—a dirty joke's punch line, a bawdy remark—and can't help herself; she is betrayed by her own pleasure. "We decided to skip the zoo," Catherine said. I turned my head and buried my face in Nora's midriff so none of them would see my tears.

DESPITE THIS HAPPY REUNION, eleven weeks passed before Catherine and I made love. I didn't feel I had the right to ask; furthermore, it seemed fitting that some time elapse since Laura and I made love.

One night in October I was awakened at two A.M. by Catherine pressing the length of her naked body against my back. The pressure was so insistent it was almost enough to move me across the bed. She reached her hand inside the elastic of my pajamas and grabbed my cock. I was hard already—after this long I was so ripe with need I was about to burst. She didn't caress, stroke, or tickle me; she simply held my cock tightly and used it to lever me onto my back.

Without a word or a kiss, she climbed on top of me, exactly the position I had been in the last time I made love. Catherine straddled my hips, and I slid into her. She ground down on me with such pressure I could have been a length of wood. She leaned back and caressed her own breasts, something she had never done before in our lovemaking. When she came—in a fraction of the time it usually took—it was with a force that astonished both of us. She gasped and exploded into spasms so violent it seemed as if her muscles would tear loose from her bones. My own orgasm, seconds later, was a feeble coda compared to her crescendo.

Just as our bodies had come together, they fell wordlessly apart. Catherine got up to go to the bathroom. Humbled and emptied, I lay quietly in bed. Soon I fell back to sleep, the sleep of the chastened child who has finally learned his lesson.

* * *

FIVE MONTHS PASSED before Catherine told me what Laura had said when she called the previous summer.

I came home late from the hospital after admitting a two-year-old with pneumonia. The twins were in bed, but Catherine was still up, sitting in the kitchen and drinking wine. She also had a glass waiting for me.

"She called again," said Catherine.

Though I knew immediately of whom she was speaking, I asked anyway. "Who?"

"Her. Laura Pettit." Catherine laughed nervously.

This was in March. The day had been warm, melting some of the snow, but that evening the air turned cold, and the wind was blowing hard, whistling around the windows and turning the day's puddles back to ice. Catherine said Laura's name, and I wanted to check the doors to make sure they were shut tight.

I took off my coat and hung it on the back of the chair. Instead of sitting down, I picked up my wineglass and stepped back, leaning against the sink. "What did she want?"

Catherine drew her robe tight at her throat and stared evenly at me. "She wanted to talk to me."

I raised my glass in salute but said nothing.

"She wanted to know how you were. She wanted to know if you're all right."

"And what did you tell her?"

"What *should* I have told her?"

"That I'm fine. I'm fine."

Catherine nodded and looked down at the tabletop. With her finger she traced a pattern on the wood. She seemed to be drawing an asterisk. "I was thinking tonight, when I was waiting for you, that I've never known any woman I can talk to. Not my mom. Not any friends I can think of. Then this woman who my husband . . . my husband . . . *knows*, calls, and suddenly I'm saying things to her that I've never said to anybody. That I scarcely knew I thought."

"Like what? What kinds of things?"

Catherine shrugged. "Nothing very important. About you. About me. How we're different."

"How?"

She shook her head. "I don't want to start anything. That's not why I brought it up."

"No, go ahead. I want to hear. It's okay."

"I'm sure this is nothing new. And it's certainly nothing very profound. It's just that I am . . . satisfied. Grateful. Usually. And you're not. You never seem to be."

I walked to the table and sat down across from Catherine. "What else?"

"She said people like you, it's hard to give them what they want because wanting is who they are."

I reached my hand toward Catherine. "That's not who I am. Not now. Not anymore."

She did not take my hand but picked up the wine bottle. "Would you like some more?"

I withdrew my hand and covered my glass. "What about last summer?" I asked. "What did you talk about then?"

"I'm thinking about going back to work," Catherine said. "Did I mention that? When the twins start school, I think I'll go back to the hospital. I was talking to Mrs. Hopkins, and she said they're so desperate for nurses I could practically name my hours."

"That would be fine."

Catherine's eyes flared. "I'm not asking permission."

"I know you're not."

"It wouldn't be for the money."

"I know."

"It's just something I might decide to do."

"Last summer. What did you talk about *last summer?*"

Catherine paused for a long time, and when she looked up again, her eyes were wet with tears. "I wasn't going to say anything. Tonight, I mean. I wasn't going to tell you she called. I know what it means. She's thinking about you. No matter what else, it means that. I thought, oh, God, if I tell him, it's going to start up again." She wiped her eyes. "But maybe it never stopped, so why not?"

I went back to the table, stepped behind Catherine, and began to massage her shoulders. "What did Laura say when you talked to her last summer?"

I felt Catherine's body relax, as if she had just immersed herself in a hot bath.

"She said she was going to try to cure you, once and for all. No matter what she had to do. And she said she had to find out something for herself. I wasn't sure exactly what she meant, but I had a pretty good idea. She said she'd tell me everything if I wanted to know, but she didn't think I did. She was right. I didn't want to know. Not then."

I didn't want to know either, but it was too late for me. I knew what Laura's cure entailed. She made love to me and then sent me packing, believing that sex would allow me to leave with at least that longing finally satisfied. Laura's theory was sound, but because she lacked my training—going back not to medical school but to childhood—she could not see the flaw in her reasoning. There was no cure.

Catherine tilted her head back and looked up at me. "I still don't want to know."

"Okay."

She stood up and took our glasses to the sink. "She said she'd like to come for a visit sometime. See our house, where we live. Meet me. See the girls. 'See Paul's girls,' she said." Catherine thrust her hands into the pockets of her robe and smiled. "I'm sure she was just being polite. But do you think she might really come?"

"She might. I doubt it, but she might."

Catherine went back to her chair, sat down, and bent over to put on her slippers. As she did, her robe came open and exposed one of her breasts. The room's only light came from the stove light, and Catherine's breast coming free, out of fabric, out of shadow, looked as pale and lovely as moonlight. Outside, the branches of a tree or shrub I had neglected to trim rattled and scraped against the house.

"Let's go to bed," I said.

Twelve

I was sitting in the waiting room of the dentist's office thumbing through a copy of *People* magazine. It was the morning following the season's first hard freeze, and outside the window, frost still glistened on the matted-down grass, while the leaves from a nearby maple were falling by the score, as if the tree were trying to unload completely within an hour. Looking for a way to avoid thinking about the unpleasantness of having my teeth cleaned—the process always left my teeth and gums buzzing and aching for a week—I lighted on an article written by Benjamin McCall, the son of the former New York congressman, Martin McCall.

The senior McCall had once been one of the nation's best-known legislators, a leader in fighting for civil rights legislation. Now he was living in a rest home, a victim of Alzheimer's disease, unable to recognize family or friends, estranged from his own life. The son's article was about his father's disintegration, about how what began as mild forgetfulness eventually became an oblivion where no one owned a name, address, or past.

As sad as the congressman's plight was, it was not what claimed my attention most urgently. Following the article was an interview with a neurologist who commented on Alzheimer's, how it struck not only the elderly, how it was not an inevitable consequence of aging. Medicine was working hard to find new treatments, he said, and though it was tragic when such well-known people as former-congressman McCall or Rita Hayworth or poet Laura Coe Pettit fell victim to Alzheimer's, their fame—as well as their misfortune—helped bring the public's attention to this disease.

I did not drop the magazine. I closed it quite deliberately, put it back with the other magazines, rose, and went to the receptionist's desk.

"Yes?" she said, smiling politely up at me.

"I have to leave," I said. "I have to cancel my appointment."

Her smile did not waver. "Is something wrong?" Surely she was accustomed to calming panicky patients who decided they could not, after all, lie back in the dentist's chair.

"No, nothing. It's just . . . I remembered. I have another appointment. Someplace I have to be."

For the first time she released me from her kindly gaze and glanced down at her appointment book. "I see. Would you like to reschedule?"

My legs asked me if we couldn't please move, couldn't we please run from this room with its faint odor of ground bone and hot silver and fear, its far-off sound of drills, its cheerful receptionist, its view of falling leaves, its magazines that pretended that the worst news in the world could be borne if accompanied by enough photographs?

I granted my shaking legs their request and backed quickly from the waiting room, telling the woman, "I'll call you. . . ."

BEFORE I KNEW how or why I decided to go there, I was home, parked in my own driveway and staring into the black slot of the garage, the one place sheltered from the day's sunlight and its tumbling leaves.

I waited a long time before I got out of the car, trying to think, trying to make sense of time, as if that was where sense lay.

Seven years had passed since I last saw Laura, since I found her in New Hampshire, and she sent me home. In those years I had not stopped thinking of her, yet something had changed. I had almost lost my wife and daughters, and in regaining them they became ineffably precious to me. I did not want Laura any less, but Catherine, Nora, and Doreen I wanted more than ever. I thought I had finally become rational about something I had been irrational about all my life. Or perhaps I had simply run out of stamina. I was forty-three years old, and I had begun pursuing Laura, in my fashion, when I was eleven. That was a long chase, enough to tire any hunter. And the last time I found her, she had dismissed me away with a finality that, on some days, had me feeling like the quarry rather than the hunter, like a fish too puny to keep, and on other, better days, like a wanderer finally pointed toward home.

So I had given up the quest, and in doing so, a part of me that had always been in turmoil calmed down. But like a dog that no longer hunts, sometimes I felt dull and fat in retirement. In a way I missed heartbreak. Pain can prove our pleasure, and our love.

I saw Laura once, though not in person. A few years earlier she appeared in a CBS *Sunday Morning* segment on the American Academy of Arts and Letters. Catherine and I were drinking coffee and watching television in bed when the feature came on, and Catherine immediately called the twins into the room.

"Do you see that lady?" Catherine asked the girls of Laura's image. Laura was dressed in pearls and a black evening gown and looked imperially beautiful—those sculpted cheekbones, full lips, and her silver hair in a French roll. She was being interviewed in a Washington arts center on the occasion of her induction into the academy.

"She's a friend of Daddy's," Catherine explained to the twins.

"Is she famous?" asked Nora.

Had Catherine asked me, I would have told her not to call the twins into the room.

"She's a very famous writer," Catherine said.

Laura was telling the interviewer that clubs and awards for writers generally made her uneasy, but this was truly an honor.

"Are you famous, Daddy?" asked Doreen.

"No, I'm not," I replied. And the interview with Laura was over.

On that auspicious occasion, had it already begun? Had that crease in the brain where memories live already begun to fold over on itself? Had all the usual familiarities of life started to become strange to her?

I got out of the car, and Catherine opened the front door to greet me. She had also taken up jogging, and she had just returned from running. She was wearing sweatpants and a T-shirt. Her hair was matted to her forehead and along the sides of her face, and her cheeks were reddened and chapped from the morning's chill. I loved this glistening, unself-conscious look of hers. I felt I was seeing into her past, the way she looked as a girl.

"That was a quick trip," she said. "Let's see that smile."

I pushed past her into the house without saying anything.

Whether it was out of fear or respect for what might lie in my silences, there was once a time when Catherine let my brooding be. In recent years, however, she made a point of chasing down every mood of mine until she came to its source. And both of us were better for this new persistence.

I walked directly to the kitchen, Catherine close behind. "What is it?" she asked. "Paul? Did you see Dr. Keene? Did he say something?"

"I didn't see him. I canceled the appointment."

"Why? Is something . . . Do you feel okay?"

I turned on the tap and drank two full glasses of cold water.

Catherine put her hand on my shoulder. "Paul. What is it?"

I stared out into the backyard. The hoses. I would have to put the hoses into the garage for the winter.

"Paul." Her voice was sharper, her hand heavier.

Without turning to face her, I said it, the quickest, plainest version I could conjure. "Laura Pettit has Alzheimer's."

"What? Are you . . . How did you find out?" Catherine's hand fell from my shoulder, and I sensed her take a step back.

"In the waiting room. I was reading a magazine."

"Are you sure? How bad?"

I turned around to face her. "I don't know. The article didn't say. Bad enough."

Catherine pulled out a chair and sat down. "Do you think there could be a mistake?"

"Could be. I doubt it."

"God. It's awful. It's worse than . . . How old is she?"

It took me a moment. "I'm not sure. I don't think she's sixty."

"When she's that young . . . ? Is that possible?"

I shrugged. "It's rare. But it happens."

Neither of us moved or spoke. Minutes passed. The emptiness of the entire house entered the kitchen. I still had not taken off my jacket.

Finally I said, "I have to do something."

Catherine started to say something, then suddenly stopped herself, and the only sound that came out was a half-strangled sigh. In her eyes I saw the competition of fear and worry. "What are you going to do? What can you do?"

"I don't know. I'm trying to think."

"What do you want to do?"

"I told you. I don't know."

My confusion, my uncertainty, must have softened her heart. She walked over to me and looped her arms around my neck. "Honey," she said, "I don't think there's anything you can do. What can anybody do?"

LATER THAT DAY as I rode with Catherine to pick up the twins at school, I told her my decision.

"I'm going to see her," I said.

Catherine pretended that concentrating on her driving prevented her from answering. But she drove this route every day, morning and afternoon, and her tight grip on the wheel had nothing to do with right and left turns.

Only when she was parked in front of the school did she speak. "Do you know where she is?"

"Not for certain. No."

"That she wants to see anybody? To be seen?"

"No."

"How far the disease has progressed?"

"No."

"That she'll know you?"

"No."

Her hands gently tapped their way around the circumference of the steering wheel, as if, like dough, it could be reshaped by touch.

"But you're just going to take off." Catherine shook her head and stared straight ahead at the trunk of the car in front of us. "Again."

"I'll call first. Or write. I'm not sure."

"Do you think—" She stopped herself and turned away again, this time to the street and the slow crawl of cars going by.

I knew I should say something, but I kept quiet. At some point I had decided I was not going to say or do anything that would allow Catherine— or anyone—to dissuade me from going to see Laura one more time.

Nora and Doreen were among the last to emerge from school. They ambled down the sidewalk to the car, and as soon as they got in and slammed the door behind them, Catherine looked back at them and asked cheerfully, "How would you like to miss a few days of school so all of us can take a trip with Daddy?"

The twins exchanged high-fives. "A vacation! All right! Where are we going?"

Catherine didn't say anything, but she turned to me. Her jaw was set, and her eyes were blazing, their fire fueled by defiance and resolution. She was not going to let go; I had to see that. No matter what winds might blow, she would not let go.

What could I do before that power? I could not meet her gaze or match her strength.

"I don't know," I told the twins.

SIX WEEKS LATER, in November, Catherine, the twins, and I were on an Eastern Air Lines flight to Burlington, Vermont. From there we would drive a rental car to a place called The Pines, right outside the town of Garrett, Vermont—all of these locations near Laura's home and, by eerie coincidence, none of them far from the house my parents used to rent every summer, the house where I first met Laura. As I understood it, The Pines was a private nursing home, according to the brochure "a full-care facility in a serene rural setting."

My understanding of The Pines—as well as the directions on how to get there and the information that Laura was a patient—came, though not without considerable difficulty, from a mysterious, strangely powerful man named Joel Shumate.

Right after it was decided—right after Catherine decided—that visiting Laura would be a family venture, I set about trying to find out Laura's condition and her location.

I phoned first, and met my first obstacle: a recorded message that said her number had been disconnected.

I wrote next, a carefully worded letter addressed to Laura that said I had heard she wasn't "feeling well" and asking if there was anything I could do. Weeks passed, and I heard nothing. Then, one day a photocopied letter came in the mail. It said:

> *Laura Coe Pettit is in seclusion and for the present would prefer not to be in communication with the outside world. If you wish to be excepted from this decision, please return this letter briefly stating your reasons for wanting to see Ms. Pettit and your previous relationship with her.*

It was signed by Joel Shumate, who was, according to the title below the signature, "Secretary to Laura Coe Pettit."

The letter offended but did not deter me. The same day I received it I sent it back with the following simply worded reply:

> *Laura Pettit is an old family friend. I have heard that she is ill, and I would like to see her once more. My wife and daughters have never met Laura, and I would like them to.*

I signed the letter "Paul Finley, MD," the only time outside of official correspondence when I used those initials behind my name.

Within a week I received a response both heartening and discouraging.

Dr. Finley:

> *You would be able to briefly see Ms. Pettit by visiting The Pines facility any Saturday or Sunday afternoon between the hours of two and four. Ms. Pettit does not have a telephone. This is the only way you can communicate with her. Should you wish to visit her according to this schedule, please stop at The Pines front desk and ask for me. I will be*

able to take you to Ms. Pettit. I have enclosed a brochure with
instructions on how to find The Pines.

Yours truly,
Joel Shumate

Once again, I resented Mr. Shumate's proprietary tone, but I set that
feeling aside and concentrated on the fact that I was going to see Laura.
That we were going to see Laura. I could not help but feel uplifted by that.
Yet I also knew what it meant that Laura was now in a place like The Pines.

If Laura was in a nursing home, she was no longer able to care for herself. Though she might live for years, it would not be much of a life. We
had to see her soon.

So that the twins would miss as little school as possible, we left the
Friday after Thanksgiving and planned to return the following Monday.
This would be the first time, since moving to Red Oak, that we would
not spend Thanksgiving with Catherine's family. I said nothing to Jane
or my mother about the trip or the reason behind it. My report to them
would wait until I returned. Until I had seen Laura.

WE STAYED OVERNIGHT in Burlington, and the next morning, with
Catherine mapping the way, we drove secondary and county roads to
Garrett, taking our time and giving the twins a chance to see something
of Vermont's countryside, its villages and winding roads, its switchback-
ing hills that gave off to sudden views of distant mountains with their
lee-side scant patches of snow and their bare but hopeful tree-cleared ski
slopes.

The day we drove through was cold and iron gray, light notable for its
absence, the sky so cloudy no clouds were visible. The girls knew I sum-
mered in Vermont as a boy, and they peppered me with questions as I
drove: What did I do? Did I swim? Canoe? Water-ski? Hike? Who was a
better swimmer—Aunt Jane or me? Did Grandma swim? Where was our
place? Was it a cabin? Had I been to where we were going before?

I found it hard to concentrate on their questions. Driving through
this landscape, I was visited by ghost after ghost, each finding a different
house in me to haunt.

The region *did* remind me of my childhood—something in the car's lean and sway, strain and dip as we negotiated the curves and hills brought back those annual summer excursions. My father driving, Mother pouring coffee from the Thermos. Janie and I watching for land-marks—the Mobil station with its flying horse, the house with the stone fence, the farmers' market in Newbury. Those had always been summer trips; now the season's bare trees and sere fields were the perfect emblem for the losses of the years.

The last time I had been in New England was the last time I saw Laura, and now I was back in that territory with a similar mission—but this time with my family in tow. I couldn't shake the feeling that I was going to be found out, that something in a native tree or bird or bush was going to declare my guilt. At home I could keep my secrets, but not here.

And Laura, Laura. I thought I had put her away, shoved to the back of the shelf. But now that I was going to see her again, everything was tum-bling down. I was feeling again what I felt as a child, a teenager, a young man, an adult losing his senses. . . . And add to this anticipation, fear of what she had become.

Alzheimer's is a disease that does not always run a predictable course Some of its victims remain relatively unchanged for years after diagno-sis, still working, still functioning in the day-to-day world by finding ways to compensate for the disease's earliest, mildest effects. Other vic-tims are not so fortunate. Deteriorating rapidly, they can be dead within two years of onset and lost to their families, friends, and self long before that. I feared that Laura's symptoms would put her in this group.

WITH ITS STRETCHES of redwood walls and timbers, its great expanses of plate glass, its angles of concrete and chrome, The Pines resembled a conference center more than a nursing home. I parked in the visitor's lot, took a deep breath, and turned off the ignition.

"Leave the keys," Catherine said. "We'll wait here for a while. You can come for us when you're ready."

"Are you sure?"

"Get going." She put her hand on my shoulder and pushed me out the door, both affection and encouragement in her shove.

The building I entered felt so new I thought I smelled the faint odors of carpet glue and fresh paint. Nothing in the immediate surroundings made it seem like a nursing home, and I wondered if I had gotten the directions wrong. No one was in sight, and the building's sound system was softly playing what sounded to me like Bach.

Then I caught another faint odor, lurking under all the sterility, and I knew I was in the right place.

My mother used to say, and I never came across evidence to refute her, that all nursing homes smelled of urine. She was endlessly grateful that neither of her parents had to be put in a home. My grandfather's fatal heart attack occurred when he was shoveling snow; he was dead within an hour of being admitted to the hospital. My grandmother was dead four months after having been diagnosed with non-Hodgkin's lymphoma. Hospice arranged for her to die at home, her daughter at her bedside. My mother's health was still excellent, but she had extracted vows from both Janie and me that we would never put her in a nursing home. "You can leave me out on the heath to die, like Lear," my mother said, "or you can set me out on an ice floe like an old Eskimo; I don't care. Just don't let me end up in one of those places."

"May I help you?" A woman's voice startled me.

Off to my left, a woman in a nurse's uniform stood behind a desk, and I walked over to her. She had a long, thin, sharp face, plain and kindly looking, yet with something hard and disappointed in her expression, as if this day, like all the others, had not quite met her expectations. I wished I were wearing my white coat and had my stethoscope around my shoulders. I am not one who much cares about rank, but I wanted something to declare mine, and to declare it above hers.

"I was supposed to meet someone," I said.

She smiled. "If you'll give me the name of the person you're meeting."

"Joel Shumate. He's supposed to—"

She was way ahead of me. At the mention of his name she picked up the telephone. "I'll page him for you. Who's here to see him?"

My opening! "Dr. Finley. Tell him Dr. Finley is here according to our arrangement."

Momentarily she announced, "Mr. Shumate will be right down."

Within five minutes a short young man was striding across the lobby toward me.

"Dr. Finley?"

I extended my hand, and he shook it, his grip cool and uncommitted. He was dressed in tennis shoes, sharply creased khakis, a button-down blue oxford, and a navy blue knit tie. His glasses were wire rims, 1960s vintage, and his hair was 1950s short. I guessed he was in his late twenties.

"Dr. Finley, I apologize in advance for what I'm going to ask, but it's necessary." He had a soft, deep voice and a faint southern accent. "Would you have some identification that will prove you are who you say you are?"

It was another disagreeable step in the increasingly complicated process of getting to see Laura, but long before, I had decided none of these things would deter or distract me. Obediently, I took out my driver's license and handed it to Joel Shumate.

As he studied it, he said, "I hate doing this. I know you don't believe it, but I simply don't have any choice. Someone might pretend to be someone else just to get close to Miss Pettit. A journalist, a photographer, somebody." He handed my license back to me and nodded curtly.

I put my billfold away. "How is she?"

"Not good." He glanced around the lobby as if he were looking for spies. "What can I tell you? She has deteriorated rapidly. Rapidly. One doctor said he can't remember an Alzheimer's patient who went downhill so quickly. And the initial diagnosis she took very hard. Very hard." He made a diving motion with his hand.

I nodded unenthusiastically. I felt he was telling me too much too soon.

"The disease's onset was classic. She began to call things by the wrong name. 'Ball' for 'bug.' 'Cap' for 'sky.' Can you imagine? A writer . . . she lives her life for the right word, the *precisely* right word, and she loses the ability to do this. God."

"That sounds like a stroke."

Joel Shumate nodded knowingly. "The doctors said there may have been one. Or some. I don't remember anymore. I heard so many things."

"When may I see her?"

He stared at me for a long time. "Are you sure?" he finally asked.

"I've come a long way. . . ."

"But I must warn you: You're not going to see the Laura Pettit you once knew."

I gave Joel Shumate a long, steady stare, trying both to intimidate him and to convince him of my readiness. "I know what I'm doing."

He smiled, the sudden, sly grin of someone who knows a secret but isn't telling. He thrust his hands into his pockets. "Okay. Let's go."

I followed him to the elevator. Inside he pushed a button, and we rode up in silence. With every breath I took, I could feel the acid of fear burning my stomach. When the elevator stopped, Joel Shumate stepped out and, walking briskly, led me down a long, dark, silent corridor that reminded me of a hotel's. Every door was numbered and every door was closed. At the end of the hall he stopped in front of room 2232. "Ready?"

Before he could reach the doorknob, I put out my arm and stopped him. "Just a minute."

"Second thoughts?"

"Who *are* you?"

"I have Ms. Pettit's power of attorney—"

"That's not what I mean."

"—and I serve as her personal secretary. . . ."

"Where did you come from?"

Joel Shumate stepped back from the door, removed his glasses, and rubbed the bridge of his nose. Without his glasses he looked older. He took a long time putting them back on, carefully hooking and adjusting his glasses behind his ears before he said, "I understand what you're asking me, Dr. Finley. You want to know what I am to Laura. You want to know how I came to be the one in this . . . 'position.' Well, no one else is going to do it, Dr. Finley. Laura needs someone to take care of her. All the time. And there's no one else. She has no family. Her friends are not the sort to assume this kind of responsibility."

"She has a brother," I said.

"She *had* a brother. He died of cancer a few years ago."

Edward was dead. Well. Was there anyone who mourned his passing? Laura, Laura would.

"I'm not questioning what you do, Mr. Shumate. That you're looking after Laura is admirable. I'm glad someone is willing to do what you're doing. I was curious. How you met Laura. How long you've known her."

With the compliment, Joel Shumate's defensiveness ceased. He looked shyly down. "I was a student of hers. An undergraduate. Trying to write poetry. Failing miserably. Fortunately, Laura recognized that I had other talents. Her telephone call placed me in a good graduate program in English. Her letter of recommendation helped me get a teaching position. I've done some critical studies of her poetry, exploring especially the light imagery in her work. Have you noticed that, Dr. Finley? What a student of sunlight Laura has been? I know painters who don't pay attention to light and shadow the way she does."

"I haven't read her quite as systematically as you have."

He blinked and nodded eagerly in understanding. "You should. Everyone should. She's a great writer. A major, *major* poet. Someday that will be understood. Her work will be reappraised, and she will be recognized as one of our greatest. Emily Dickinson. That is the company she'll be placed in. Whitman. In fact, I was working on a book-length study of Laura's poetry when she became ill. I dropped it and took a leave of absence. Without pay. I dropped everything to take care of her. Which might very well cost me my chance at tenure. But nothing I've ever done—nothing I could ever do—could matter as much as being here with her now."

"As I said, I have nothing but admiration for what you're doing. But I can't help wondering. . . . How old are you?"

His tight little smile returned. "You mean, have I been her lover? Isn't that what you want to know, Dr. Finley?"

"That's not what I was asking—"

"I'm twenty-nine. Laura's old enough to be my mother. And I'm gay, Dr. Finley. Which is the reason, I believe, Laura and I have been so close. Because I'm one of the few males who hasn't been trying to get into bed with her. She trusts me. I trust her. Now. Is there anything else you want to know?"

"Twenty-nine," I said. "That's a good age. Now let's go in."

As soon as Joel Shumate opened the door, I heard the television, the sound of the crowd and commentary of a college football game. Next came the smell of perfume, as strong and lushly charged as when the woman in the department store thrusts the open bottle under your nose.

The room was a facsimile of the hotel room where Catherine, the twins, and I had stayed the night before—two double beds, a desk and dresser, a table and two upholstered chairs, one door leading to a closet, one to a bathroom, the television mounted high on the wall hospital-style. I had expected a small apartment, not this Holiday Inn room. In front of the window was a wide, high-backed rocking chair, the kind that John Kennedy popularized.

In the chair, hands lightly gripping the arms, rocking so slightly it seemed as though some unevenness in the floor caused her movement, sat Laura. *In front of the window. The first time I saw her, she was standing in front of my window. Staring out at the Vermont night.*

Her hair had lost its chrome-silver glint and was now pure white. It was long and wiry, and its loose strands made her look as if she were encircled by a halo of white fire.

She was wearing a simple navy blue dress with a little lace collar—the kind of dress a schoolgirl would wear to the Christmas pageant. She was wearing slippers that looked like a ballerina's toe shoes.

I stepped closer until I could see her face straight on.

Since I last saw her, she seemed not to have aged. Her face had lost little of its beauty—oh, she was lined, and deeply around her mouth and eyes, but the structure, the ideal of form, was untouched. Little of the gauntness of age and none of the puffiness. It was one more cosmically cruel joke—to keep her looks and lose her mind.

Nevertheless, in spite of all the ways Laura was unchanged, I had the distressing feeling that I could have passed her on the street and not recognized her. And this had nothing to do with white hair or wrinkles or the uncharacteristic doll's dress she wore.

Laura's eyes were blank, as clouded over as the gray November sky. Joel Shumate and I had entered the room, but her distant gaze had not flickered from the window and whatever lay beyond. Instead of speaking to her, I felt as though I should wave my hand in front of her face to test her vision. Through much of my life I couldn't be sure what fueled the fire that burned in Laura's eyes—anger, passion, love, hate, or some combination beyond my understanding—but I knew now that that fire was who she was. Now it was out and she was gone.

Before I greeted Laura, I turned once more to Joel Shumate. He must have thought I was questioning him about the room, because he quickly said, "I've tried to block out any of . . . of the unpleasantness of the environment. That's why I keep the TV on; so she doesn't hear anything from the halls. And the perfume covers up the smell of the place. It's not on her, by the way. I put it on the bedspreads and on the drapes and chair cushions and on the lightbulbs. It's . . . it was her favorite perfume."

I couldn't remember Laura ever smelling of perfume, but I didn't say anything. There was so much I didn't know.

I stepped over into Laura's line of vision, but she did nothing to acknowledge my presence. I waited a moment; still nothing.

I wanted to take a deep breath, but two sensations prevented me: first, a weight pressing in on my chest that wouldn't allow my lungs to expand, and second, what felt like a wad of cotton halfway down my windpipe that wouldn't let me do any more than sip at the air.

I squatted beside Laura's rocker and said, "Hello, Laura. How are you feeling? It's Paul, Paul Finley. Do you remember me?" As soon as I spoke, the knot loosened, and I felt better.

From Laura, nothing.

"How long has it been this time? Six years? Seven? I lose track. . . ."

There was not even a variation in her rocking chair's rhythm.

"I was so sorry to hear you weren't feeling well."

The darkness of her eyes was like something that absorbed light but gave nothing back.

I glanced to Joel Shumate. "She hears," he explained. "Or she hears sometimes anyway. Occasionally you can tell her to do something, usually having to do with food—time for breakfast, time for dinner—and she'll respond. She almost never speaks. A word or two every few days. Never a complete sentence. This all happened suddenly, not gradually like some of the other problems. It was as if one day she simply willed

herself into silence. Her last act as herself. The last thing she could control. I don't understand. No one does."

I turned back to Laura. We could have been talking about the furniture. . . . I put my hand over hers; even in the room's warmth, her flesh
was cool, like the stone on the forest floor that can never be heated, no
matter how hot the sun shines. What had she once said about how cool
she was to the touch? That it came from pretending she was dead when
she was a child? I wished she were pretending now, that she could stand
and walk out of this tomb.

I asked Joel Shumate, "Would it be all right if I had some time alone
with her?"

His head swiveled back and forth in a curious owl-like way. "Sorry. No
one is allowed to visit her unless I'm present. And that, Dr. Finley, is
Laura's rule. Before her condition worsened, back when she still had her
good days, she made me promise that I would be with her at all times.
She made me *promise*."

"Good rule," I said more to Laura than to Shumate.

"My room is across the hall, Dr. Finley. I'm always here. I live here."

I stood and faced the window. Laura's view, if her gaze was ever
directed outward, was the back grounds of The Pines, a steep rocky hill
thick with the white shadows of birch trees and a few stunted firs.

"I was hoping you could see the parking lot from here." I spoke to Laura,
though I knew she couldn't hear me. "I brought my family, and I was thinking you might be able to see them from here. You should see the twins. . . .
They're going to be beauties. Taking after their mother. I don't know what
they got from me. Big feet, I guess. Nora, now Nora might have some talent for writing. She's already writing poems and stories. And Doreen draws.
And they're good kids. Such good kids. Christmas coming up and they
haven't asked for a thing yet. Oh, they will. I know that. But they'll try to
hold it down. And Doreen will say, just like she did last year, that if she can
have a horse we don't have to get her anything else. Not ever. But what
would we do with a horse? Catherine checked into it last year. There's a sta-
ble about five miles out of town where we could board it, but then you've
got to pay for the feed on top of that. One of us would have to drive her out
there. . . . I don't know. I'll probably break down one of these years. . . ."

Joel Shumate tried to interrupt me. "Dr. Finley."

". . . Of course it's Catherine who holds it all together. And you don't even notice her doing it. She's a marvel—"

"Dr. Finley."

"—Hardly a day goes by when I'm not astonished at her resources, her strength. I know I'm not the easiest—"

Joel Shumate put his hand on my shoulder and shook me.

That stopped me.

"She's sleeping, Doctor. She can't hear you."

Against a dark outcropping of rock on the hill I thought I saw a few snowflakes, white, mica-light shadows drifting weightlessly down. I blinked, looked again, then couldn't be sure. . . .

"Laura's sleeping," repeated Joel Shumate. "She does that, falls asleep in her chair."

Her rocking had stopped, and her eyes were closed, the lids dropped down so smooth and untroubled they reminded me of those ancient Greek and Roman statues in which the eyes were always sightless blanks of stone. What did she dream of? Did her past return in her dreams? Or do dreamers always live in the moment? I tried to think of my own dreams but gave up when I realized I was staring at the object of so many of my dreams.

I knew I was looking at Laura for the last time, so I wanted to gaze long and hard, a drink deep enough to last me until the end of my own days.

I couldn't. The pain of looking at her body when her spirit was absent was too much. It reminded me of staring at the house where someone you once loved used to live . . . of revisiting an old neighborhood and finding everything changed. . . . There was no point in saying anything, but I said it anyway. "Good-bye, Laura. This is Paul. Saying good-bye." I bent down and kissed her cheek. At the touch of my lips she seemed to flinch slightly, but her eyes never opened, so it must have been nothing more than a muscle twitch.

My eyes stinging with tears, I stood and shouldered my way past Joel Shumate. "I have to go. . . . Thanks. . . ."

Behind me Joel Shumate called out, "Wait! Dr. Finley!" but I didn't stop. I was waiting by the elevator when he finally caught up to me.

"Dr. Finley, wait. I have to speak to you."

By then I had had time to get my handkerchief out and blow my nose and wipe my eyes.

"Are you all right?" he asked.

"I'm fine."

He craned his head around to peer up into my eyes. "Yes?" he said.

"I'll be fine."

"It's hard. I know it's hard. I saw it come on in stages, so it wasn't as, as shocking."

"I don't know what I expected. . . ."

Joel Shumate reached up and patted me on the shoulder, three little taps that seemed more as if he were trying to get my attention than to comfort me. But he was trying. I knew he was trying.

"But as you well know, Doctor, her condition is harder on us than it is on her. She doesn't have any—"

"I know. Look, you have to promise me. If there's anything I can do— if I can help make any medical arrangements, if she needs any money, bills, expenses—you'll let me know. And when, when—" I couldn't say it! "When it happens, call me. Collect."

Joel Shumate stepped back. "There is something. Not now. I'm going to write Laura's biography. Actually I've started already. I'm dividing her life into decades, and I have a separate notebook and file for each decade."

I put my handkerchief away. "Laura once told me she wanted to make her own life."

He seemed not to have heard me. "Yet you must agree that it's an interesting life. That it needs to be told."

The elevators clattered open. The air that exited was so chilly it felt as if an outer door opened on us. I stepped in then turned back to Shumate. "Yes, I suppose you're right."

He held the doors open. "Laura's told me a lot. Almost everything, I believe. But it occurs to me that in certain critical areas you might be the best . . . the only informant."

My name in a biography of Laura's life? For some reason, that seemed wrong, a mistake of proportion. Now, her name in my life's story—yes, yes, on every page!

Shumate's voice softened to a conspiratorial whisper. "I would acknowledge your help. I mean, your name would be listed. . . ."

"I'll have to think about this."

"I understand," Joel Shumate said, perhaps having already gone further than he wanted in asking for my help.

I punched the button for the first floor. "Remember. Call me."

I WAS RIGHT. It had begun to snow, large, light, random flakes that fluttered down like shreds of cloth. The twins were out of the car and running around the parking lot. They had their heads thrown back and their tongues stuck out, trying to catch snowflakes.

I called to them. "Okay, I'm ready to go."

Nora answered for both of them. "Just a second. Just a few more!" And she staggered off in pursuit of a particularly large flake.

Catherine had the car running and its heater on. The car's interior was as warm as Laura's room.

"I'm done," I said. "We can leave."

"Did you see her?"

"She's sleeping."

"We can stay," Catherine said kindly. "Or wait. Or we can come back later."

I shook my head. "She wouldn't know me. There's no point."

Catherine lightly touched my knee. "I don't mind staying."

"No, I'm ready."

Nora and Doreen piled into the backseat, loudly arguing about whether Vermont snow tasted any different from Wisconsin snow.

Catherine stared at me intently. Finally she said, "And what about later?"

"This is it. I'm ready to go."

"We came so far. . . ."

Fat snowflakes made small silent explosions when they hit the windshield. Darkness was coming on fast. Even the car's idling engine seemed impatient for me to make a decision.

"Let's go to Boston," I said. I am not a man of imagination or inspiration, but that suggestion seemed to have the surprising rightness of a poem's end. "It's less than three hours drive. We can show the girls the city. Do some Christmas shopping."

The twins liked the idea right away and shouted their assent. In the face of their enthusiasm Catherine could do nothing but smile and shrug helplessly.

I put the car into gear, then turned to the twins. "Maybe we can find the house where I used to live."